PENGUIN BOOKS

HER
HIDDEN
FIRE

CONTENT NOTE: This book includes references to coercive behaviour and sexual and physical assault. Some of the interactions in this book may be distressing for some readers. There are organizations in every country that offer support on these issues, so if you have been affected please do reach out to them.

HER HIDDEN FIRE

CLÍODHNA O'SULLIVAN

PENGUIN BOOKS

PENGUIN BOOKS

UK | USA | Canada | Ireland | Australia
India | New Zealand | South Africa

Penguin Books is part of the Penguin Random House group of companies
whose addresses can be found at global.penguinrandomhouse.com

www.penguin.co.uk   www.puffin.co.uk   www.ladybird.co.uk

First published in Great Britain as *Her Hidden Fire* by Penguin Books 2026.
This book is based on material originally published in Great Britain
as *The Stone Keep* by Heroic Books 2021.

001

Text copyright © Clíodhna O'Sullivan, 2026
Map illustration copyright © Sally Taylor, 2026

The moral right of the author and illustrator has been asserted

No part of this book may be used or reproduced in any manner for the
purpose of training artificial intelligence technologies or systems. In accordance
with Article 4(3) of the DSM Directive 2019/790, Penguin Random House
expressly reserves this work from the text and data mining exception.

Set in 11.5/15.5pt Bembo Book MT Pro
Typeset by Jouve (UK), Milton Keynes
Printed and bound in Great Britain by Clays Ltd, Elcograf S.p.A.

The authorized representative in the EEA is Penguin Random House Ireland,
Morrison Chambers, 32 Nassau Street, Dublin D02 YH68

A CIP catalogue record for this book is available from the British Library

ISBN: 978–0–241–71481–2

All correspondence to:
Penguin Books
Penguin Random House Children's
One Embassy Gardens, 8 Viaduct Gardens, London SW11 7BW

Penguin Random House is committed to a
sustainable future for our business, our readers
and our planet. This book is made from Forest
Stewardship Council® certified paper.

For Conor, Maya-Rose, Éanna & Aodhán

Most of the names in *Her Hidden Fire* are variations on Irish names. Some are derived from an ancient Irish tree-based alphabet known as Ogham. The symbol at the start of each chapter represents the first two letters, 'Éa', of Éadha's name in Ogham script. Below is a rough guide to the Irish pronunciation.

DOMHAIN
Dow-in ('world' in English)

AILM'S KEEP
Ailm – *Al-im*

Family castle north of the Blackstairs: the large mountain range in northeast Domhain

Éadha – *Eh-ya*
Ionáin – *Yun-aw-in*
Aedan – *Ay-dan*
Úra – *Oora*
Béithe – *Bey-he*
Huath – *Huw-ath*
Ferne – *Fearn*
Jarlath – *Jarlath*
Treasa – *Tra-sa*
Magret – *Magrette*

LAMBAY
Lambay islands: a group of three islands off the east coast of Domhain, named First Island, Second Island and Domhain's Eye

APPRENTICES – CHANNELLER
Senan – *Senan*
Linn – *Linn*

Coll – *Coll*
Cormac – *Cormack*
Eoghan – *Owe-an*

APPRENTICES – KEEPER
Gry – *Gry*
Ailbhe – *Ale-va*
Síofra – *Shee-fra*
Cara – *Car-ah*
Muir – *Mwir*
Béibhín – *Bey-veen*
Nuala – *Noola*
Sibéal – *Shib-ale*
Síle – *Shee-leh*

MASTERS
Dathin – *Daw-hin*
Irial – *Ir-ee-al*
Cathal – *Coh-hul*
Joen – *Joe-en*
Ruadh – *Roo-a*
Odhran – *O-ran*

HEAD KEEPERS
Fiachna – *Fee-ach-na*
Maebh – *Mayve*

FODDER
Seoda (also known as Donn) – *Show-da*

PART I

Ailm's Keep

I

BEHIND THE GREAT CASTLE known as Ailm's Keep, there was no more than a suggestion of daylight when a black-clad figure appeared, racing towards its East Tower.

She halted at a massive oak tree near the tower and pulled herself up on to its thick branches; they were still bare and would be for weeks yet. The spring thaw had only just begun. Around her the air was filled with the roar of meltwater pounding down the mountain stream behind the Keep, into the small lake just past the oak tree. The thick ice that'd gripped the lake all winter long had shattered overnight, leaving small white islands bobbing and turning in the water. Éadha was glad of the water's roar, masking any sounds she might make. With her cloak tied back over her shoulders to avoid snagging, and her cloud of dark hair tucked inside her hood, she climbed swiftly up through the branches.

Soon she was level with the high wall along the Keep's central courtyard. Even though it wasn't quite dawn, already she could see figures moving about below. Stable lads lighting fires in big iron braziers to burn off the chill in the air for the crowds arriving later. The courtyard wall was narrow, only just wide enough for one person to balance on top of. Spreading her arms out wide like a dancer and with a small prayer no one would look up, Éadha began inching along over the weeds that'd seeded themselves in cracks. Her foot slipped on a dandelion root and she fell into a wobbly crouch, grabbing the top of the wall with her hands to stop herself falling, while one leg dangled over the long drop.

'Bugger,' she muttered, her heart skittering as she eased her leg oh-so carefully back up on to the wall until she could stand again. The wall ended at the side of the East Tower, and she reached it just as the sun broke free of the horizon. It was going to be a clear day.

Above her was a stone window ledge. She could just reach it if she leaned out and didn't think too much about what'd happen if she missed. She caught at it, first with her left hand, then, swinging her legs out into space, with her right, offering up her thanks there hadn't been a Channeller in Ailm's Keep for the past quarter century to keep its walls whole. It meant there were cracks in the tower wall deep enough to wedge her toes into and push up; she got one elbow over the ledge, then levered the rest of her body up until she was crouching on the narrow stone lip.

The window in front of her was made of dragonglass, the thick, wavy glass formed when a dragon burns the far sands of Westport, where the Channellers fight their endless battle to hold them back from Domhain's mainland. Through the glass was a large bedroom with stone walls hung with tapestries of the great Channeller battles. To the right, the embers of a fire glowed in a slate fireplace, casting a golden-red glow over the room. Directly in front of her stood a large four-poster bed with a worn velvet cover, perfectly smooth and clearly not slept in. At the end of the bed sat a young man of about seventeen or so. He was already dressed in a cambric shirt of fine, white linen and dark pants. His elbows rested on his knees as he stared into the dying fire, while his tawny, tangled hair stood on end, as if not too long ago he'd been pushing his hands through it. Éadha stared in at him for a moment, her expression unreadable, then rapped once on the glass.

Ionáin turned his head at the sound, looking wholly unsurprised to find a tall, hooded girl dressed in black crouched at his bedroom window. Standing with a small stretch, as if he'd been sitting still a long time, he crossed the room to swing open the latch.

'Hey,' he said, turning away again.

'Hey,' said Éadha, easily swinging herself in through the window and sitting down on the ledge, as if she didn't feel entitled to come any further in. The window was high off the ground, so that at full stretch, her long legs in their battered leather boots only just grazed the floor. Lowering her hood, she gripped the window ledge, tense now as she watched Ionáin. He'd gone to stand in front of the fire. To his left, on a rosewood stand, hung a set of long, heavy robes embroidered with gold thread and embellished with precious stones. His Reckoning robes.

'D'you sleep?' said Éadha quietly.

'Nah. No point even trying. You?'

Éadha shook her head while Ionáin cleared his throat before going on. 'I've had an idea though.'

'Oh yes?' said Éadha.

'How about if I just tell them – my Family, and all those Masters and Channellers downstairs right now – that it's a bit unfair, really, to reduce my entire existence to whether I have this one mystical ability, here in my head.' He tapped his temple before looking across at Éadha with a small smile. 'Then they might reconsider all this?'

He gestured towards the ornate robes and past them to his bedroom door. Beyond it, they could already hear the sounds of the Keep coming to life.

Éadha gave a small snort of unwilling laughter. 'Do I think that if you point out to those old men downstairs that their precious, centuries-old Reckoning ritual is, in fact, "quite mean", Master Dathin will slap his forehead and say, "You're so right, let's just cancel the whole thing"?'

'Well, yes,' said Ionáin, a grin breaking across his face as he looked at her. 'I mean, I do have other good qualities.'

'Such as?' said Éadha, her voice teasing now.

'Have you seen me with kittens? Not to brag, but I'm fairly sure I'm the world's best kitten wrangler.'

At this Éadha laughed out loud before leaning back against the window and folding her arms. 'Ah, well then, absolutely. They'll probably thank you for pointing out the cruelty of their system, tell your Family they can hang on to the Keep regardless, maybe channel some repairs and be gone by lunchtime.'

They both chuckled, though it only lasted a few seconds before trailing away, their hearts not really in it. After all, the stakes were too high, on this, Ionáin's Reckoning day. The day he turned seventeen, and the day he'd finally find out if he had the ability to channel magic or if instead he — and his Family — would lose everything. His father Aedan had failed his Reckoning a quarter century earlier, and the rule was ironclad. If two successive generations of a Family failed their Reckonings, the gift was deemed to have died out in their bloodline and the Family was disavowed.

Silence descended between the two of them, broken only by the soft *whump* of ash collapsing in the grate and throwing out sparks. Éadha felt all the tension return to her body. Ionáin meanwhile stuck his hands out in front of him and said,

'I can't seem to stop them from shaking. I've been trying, you know, all last night.' He looked up at her, and this time the simple anguish in his eyes twisted her heart — the shared knowledge that in the next few hours he'd either be the saviour or the damnation of his Family, and he had absolutely no control over which it'd be.

'It's funny,' he went on. 'I'm almost as worried I'm just going to embarrass myself when I walk out there in front of everyone. I'll stutter or, I dunno, trip over those stupid robes.'

'You won't though,' said Éadha. Ionáin turned to look directly at her, his eyes a midnight blue in the firelight.

'I missed you, you know, last night. I wish you still slept there.' He nodded towards the fireplace and the rug, where she'd slept on a makeshift bed for years. An orphan since early childhood and raised by her uncle, a Keep herder who spent long weeks on the mountains, she'd become Ionáin's scáth, his shadow. Stationed in his room at night since they were both eight years old so his mother, Lady Úra, could focus on nursing his older brother, Dara, through one illness after another. Until he'd died two years ago, aged sixteen, not long before his own Reckoning, when a bout of influenza swept through the Keep, leaving Ionáin as the Ailm Family's last surviving heir, their last hope of keeping their title and their home. 'It would've made it easier to get through,' he said.

Éadha slid down from the window ledge, crossing the room to stand beside him in front of the fire. So close together, they were a study in contrasts. Ionáin with the mop of tawny-gold hair he'd inherited from his mother's side, his face drawn and pale from lack of sleep, the shadow of stubble on his jaw. Éadha's heart-shaped face meanwhile was framed by her cloud of black hair, while her honey-brown skin was still flushed from her climb earlier. Growing up, she'd always been the taller one, though he'd caught her in just the last few weeks – a thing she still wasn't used to. It meant their eyes were level now as she fixed him with a fierce stare and said, 'You know you don't have to do this. Play their stupid game. You, me, out this window. We'd be into the forest and across the Steps before anyone knew you were gone.'

'Again with this?' said Ionáin.

'It's a good idea. And I'm persistent,' said Éadha.

'Yes, but you also know why I can't do it,' said Ionáin. She did. If he ran, his parents would be condemned as the family of a cowardly traitor who couldn't even face his own Reckoning. At least if he stayed, even if he failed, he'd have proven his Family's loyalty. He and his father would still be sent to Westport to face the dragons, the fate of a failed bloodline; but it left open the chance his mother's powerful brother, Lord Huath, might take pity on her and let her live out her days in some corner of his lands.

The two of them were standing so close together now their shadows on the wall behind them seemed to merge, waving and flickering in the firelight.

Staring at Éadha, Ionáin's voice deepened as he went on. 'But, Éadha, if I fail today and Huath takes over, you'll need to run. Promise me —'

He never got to the end of that sentence because as he spoke, his bedroom door swung open. The two of them sprang apart. In the doorway was Béithe, the white-haired housekeeper and Ionáin's old nurse, balancing a tray filled with food. She marched past the pair of them to set the tray down on a low table by the window.

'At least you're half-dressed, young sir,' she said, her voice tart. 'But you might want to get the rest of the way there before your mother arrives in with the multitudes, looking to get those robes on you.' She turned to look at Éadha. 'As for you, young one, you'll have to get yourself out the way you came in before Lady Úra gets here. On with you now, and mind you come back in through the kitchen like a normal person. Magret's looking for you.'

Éadha knew Béithe was right. That, unbelievably, after a lifetime waiting for this day, their last moment had passed and there was no choice now but to face what had to be faced.

Still, though, she hesitated, turning back towards Ionáin. He was bending to pick up his tunic from the floor and didn't see the look that came into her eyes as she said, in a voice far more urgent than before, 'Ionáin, listen; there's something I need to . . .'

But whatever it was she wanted to tell him went unsaid as Béithe caught Éadha by the arm and hustled her back to the window.

'No. No more chat, young one. The time for that is gone. He's to get ready now, and you've to go get yourself in position. On with you now.' Éadha had no option but to go out of Ionáin's window and climb back down the way she'd come.

Her last sight of Ionáin, as she lowered herself from the ledge, was of him approaching the heavy robes with his shoulders straight and squared, like someone getting ready to march to their own execution.

By the time she reached the courtyard, it was already overflowing with people from the local village. As was the way for Family Reckonings, the whole village had been invited by Ionáin's father, Lord Aedan, to bear witness to his son's trial. They milled about, men and women stiff in their best clothes, shushing their children as they dashed across the cobblestones, squealing excitedly. The older men had clustered around the bonfires burning brightly now in the deep braziers, murmuring quietly as they warmed their hands on the flames.

Just as Éadha reached the kitchen door, a head poked out. It was Magret, the choirmaster. 'Éadha!' she said, her voice exasperated. 'Where've you been? I swear you'd be late for your own funeral. Come on.'

Éadha said nothing, only following Magret in. The kitchen was in an uproar, the wooden tables piled high with food, servants running in and out to reload silver platters with force-grown fruit and refill carafes with channelled wine. Because the Ailm Family hadn't had a Channeller since Ionáin's grandfather's time, it'd all been brought in specially for the Reckoning on carts from the white marble city of Erisen, across the Cooley Plains and over the Blackstairs mountains that separated Ailm's Keep from the rest of Domhain. The journey took weeks, but as the Family had no way to channel crops or force-grow fruit of their own, they'd had no choice.

In spite of everything, Éadha had room for a flash of wonder at the sight of all this plenty laid out in the normally bare kitchen. Mounds of luscious red strawberries, heaps of shining nectarines and grapes, all channelled by Master Growers, so the air was filled with the tang of fruit and the warm smell of freshly baked loaves and pastries. It was more food than she'd ever seen; despite herself, her mouth began to water at the scents and sights around her.

Not, she thought, that any of this plenty was for her or the villagers outside. It was too rare a thing for that. Rather, it was for today's real guests, the Masters and the Families gathered in the Great Hall at the centre of the Keep. All come to see if the Ailm Family would still be one of them by the end of the day.

Magret was steering her through the chaos, on towards the tunnel of dragonglass that connected the kitchen to the main Keep. It was lit now by flickering candles set in dips in the marble floor along each side of the tunnel, their flames reflecting in the thick, wavy glass above. About halfway down Magret paused, looking first up and down the tunnel, before leaning in to Éadha and whispering, 'Have you your thought-wall in place?'

Éadha frowned then nodded. 'Yes.'

'Master Dathin will only be inches away when he reckons Ionáin. You need to be sure.'

'I'm sure, all right?' Éadha interrupted. 'Anyway, he'll be focused on reckoning Ionáin –'

'Yes, but he's so powerful . . .'

Éadha's expression was stony as she replied, biting out every word, 'My. Wall. Will. Hold.'

Magret stepped back a little, her eyes widening at Éadha's sudden ferocity. After a brief moment, she nodded once, abruptly. 'Very well. We should get into position.'

They continued on down the tunnel without another word.

Everything feels wrong today, Éadha thought as they reached the end of the tunnel, where it opened out into the Great Hall beyond. Leaving Ionáin up in his room being forced into those awful robes. Those ghouls out in the courtyard waiting to see if he'd fail. All that food in the kitchen and none of it for the underfed people who actually lived in the Keep. And now the Great Hall. For as long as she'd known it, it'd been a dimly lit, empty space with maybe just a single fire smouldering in one of the slate fireplaces that lined the wall, the wolfhounds asleep in a pile in front of it. Today, though, it was bright with the light of hundreds of candles and overflowing with people and noise.

Directly in front of her rose one of the great yew trunks that held up the ceiling of the Great Hall, garlanded for the ceremony in fresh pine branches. An iron-bound spiral staircase wound round the trunk up towards the walkways that crossed the higher levels of the hall, lit candles set into each step. Meanwhile the flickering light from the bonfires outside shone in through the row of windows at the end of the Great Hall, bringing to life their stained-glass images: scenes of long-ago battles between dragons and Channellers, golden sunflowers being coaxed from the soil by a Channeller's power, porcelain-white buildings towering above the tiny figures of the Channellers raising them.

In the centre of the hall stood a wooden stage, a dais built specially for the Reckoning ceremony. The other members of the choir were already beginning to climb its steps, and Magret hurried on ahead to join them.

Directly in front of the platform Éadha could see small groups of the most important guests: the Channellers were marked out by the silver brooches on their tunics or cloaks, their Keepers by a wide silver wristband. All the Channellers present were men, forbidding in the absolute security of their power. Their Keepers, the holders of their power, almost all of them women, stood a little behind. Some of the Channellers were heads of Great Families, dressed in rich cloaks and furs, while others wore the simple grey marking them out as a Lambay Master. They were men who spent their lives on the islands of Lambay training the next generations of gifted youngsters, securing the Channellers' rule over Domhain as they'd done for four centuries now. Dotted among them were a few who wore the black of dragon-slayers. If Ionáin passed his Reckoning, the grey-clad men would be his tutors for the next two years, each one a master of his art, the most powerful Architects, Growers, Illusionists and dragon-slayers in all of Domhain. If he failed, they'd be the ones deciding who got Ailm's Keep after his Family were cast out.

Among them moved Lord Aedan, Ionáin's father, tall and dark-haired, with the slim build Ionáin had inherited from him, dressed for the ceremony in the Ailm Family colours of silver and blue. He quietly greeted each person, bowing deferentially to the Masters and the Channellers. Éadha saw, though, how they reacted to him: glancing at him and then away as if the very sight of him embarrassed them. That'd been his life, she thought, ever since the day he failed his Reckoning almost twenty-five years ago, setting his Family on the path that led to today and his son's own Reckoning. Their Family's final chance to prove the gift hadn't died out in their bloodline.

As she watched Ionáin's father move among the crowd, it dawned on her the hall's unfamiliar brightness was coming not just from the hundreds of candles below, but from golden were-lights circling far above them, just beneath the dome of the hall. Tilting her head back to stare up at them, she let out a small gasp of wonder and fear. Wonder at the impossibility of those small yellow flames flying through the high air. Fear in remembrance of the only other time she'd seen lights like these in this hall, just two days before. Éadha looked down again to see it was indeed the same man channelling these were-lights. Lord Huath. Ionáin's uncle, and the most powerful, most cruel Channeller on all of Domhain. His white-blonde hair unmistakable as he stood a little to one side of the dais, his pale eyes scanning the crowd while his right hand moved almost idly, keeping the were-lights flying above them all. Beside him stood his Keeper, Treasa, a distant look in her eyes as she funnelled Huath's power, her fingers moving like someone working the threads of a loom. She knew Huath didn't need Treasa to be able to use power, but since the early days of channelling, Channellers had used Keepers to marshal their strength for them.

As she fought down her nausea at the sight of Huath, a murmur ran through the crowd. Lady Úra had appeared at the top of the spiral staircase nearest Ionáin's room. He was ready. It was time.

Éadha slipped around the back of the stage, clambering up and pushing through the choir to her spot in the middle of the front row. She'd made sure of it during rehearsal, once she'd worked out it'd be the one closest to Ionáin during his Reckoning. Magret gave her a sharp look, but there was no time for anything else. Lady Úra had reached her place, and now Master Dathin, Ionáin's Reckoner, was climbing the steps to stand on the stage just in front of Éadha. The senior Master on Lambay, he'd travelled all the way from the islands specially for Ionáin's Reckoning. It was not every day, after all, that the fate of a Family hung in the balance.

As Dathin took up his position just in front of Éadha, silence spread across the Great Hall, stilling conversations and rippling outwards into the courtyard where the villagers waited, wordless now too. Ionáin appeared at the top of the stairwell, and, with a sweep of her arm, Magret gestured to the choir to begin. Their voices rose into the still air as he began his slow descent of the spiral staircase, his steps matching the beat of the first canto. Éadha watched as he reached the last step and walked through the crowd, his pace unwavering and his head erect, the gold of his hair catching the candlelight as he made his way up on to the dais until, with perfect timing, long rehearsed, he turned to face the Master in the moment the choir fell silent.

Master Dathin was a bear of a man, bearded and massive in his heavy cloak pinned by a clasp in the shape of a silver dragon, marking him as a dragon-slayer. Even in his Reckoning robes, Ionáin looked heartbreakingly slender beside him, his face gone paper-white with the strain. Without a word, the Master placed his hands on either side of Ionáin's head, preparing to step into his mind. To Éadha, invisible in the choir but just inches away from where they both stood facing each other in front of her, it felt as though all the air had been sucked out of the hall. She watched as Dathin's huge hands gripped each side of Ionáin's face with a hold that couldn't be broken until the Reckoning was over. This was it.

As the ritual demanded, the entire congregation bent their heads; the one concession to privacy for the young man on the dais before them. Every one of them except Éadha, who kept her eyes fixed on Ionáin, standing there in Dathin's grip. She saw his eyes widen and knew he was feeling the shock of the Master entering his mind. Involuntarily he stepped back a little before steadying himself, closing his eyes and holding himself still as he'd been trained to do.

Still watching, Éadha saw it – a small frown beginning to appear on Dathin's face. His brows furrowed, as if searching further for something he thought he'd sense right away. The silence in the Great Hall began to stretch thin. Éadha's heart started to hammer in her chest. She knew Ionáin must have power, but she knew him so well – in times of stress his instinct would be to go still, to go deep. His gift could be hidden deep within him. If he'd the true Reckoner's skill, Master Dathin would surely eventually find it, but what if he mistook it? What if he took it for a weak gift, not worth cultivating, or for the lesser power of a Keeper? Anything less than a hallelujah in this moment would surely break Ionáin's heart. But still Master Dathin frowned. He wasn't finding it, this gift he'd come expecting to find.

And Éadha realized it was happening, right there in front of her. The worst thing. The thing she'd never allowed herself to think might really happen. Any moment now, Dathin was going to drop his hands and step back, shaking his head, and that'd be it. The end. Of Ionáin's dream of saving them all, of his Family, of Ailm's Keep, of the only life she'd ever known.

And she understood that she couldn't – she *could not* let this happen. She couldn't abandon Ionáin, the person she loved most in all the world, to this fate. And so instead, in that moment she opened her heart and made the most fateful decision of her life. One that was to change her life, Ionáin's life, and the life of every person in the Great Hall that day; one that would in the end change the very fate of Domhain itself.

2

One week earlier

BEHIND AILM'S KEEP, OAK forest rises in an almost unbroken line up into the foothills of the Blackstairs, known as the Steps. But, just where the forest starts to thin and the bones of the earth shoulder their way to the surface, there's a small, grassy plateau. It sits sheltered in the lee of the Steps so that even in late winter the grass still has growth on it, and the frost doesn't linger long, even on the coldest mornings.

So it was that early one morning, a week before Ionáin's Reckoning, with freezing mist still clinging to the trees, Éadha was to be found guiding the Keep's small flock down the avenue from the Keep, before diverting off on to a forest trail and on up to graze on the plateau. Cú, a half-grown wolfhound, loped alongside her, puffs of breath billowing out ahead of the two of them. The sheep were skittish in the fog, but she and Cú were canny herders, and soon enough they'd cajoled them up on to the grass.

Éadha was dressed for the cold in an old grey tunic, worn trews, her battered leather boots and fingerless gloves, with a leather satchel slung across her body under her cloak. All hand-me-downs from her uncle; it was one advantage of being tall for her age, even if it did mean people always thought her older than she was. Seventeen now, just. Old enough to be expected to be of use, she chose herding like her uncle rather than work in the Keep like her aunt. She chose the sky, with Cú and the sheep for company.

On their scramble up on to the plateau, Cú sniffed out some wolf droppings, but they were old, and Éadha wasn't worried; the ground up here was open enough to spot any predator from a good distance out. At the eastern end there was a steep drop down into a disused quarry. Centuries ago men had quarried granite there, but stone-working by hand was forbidden after the Channellers came to power, with their ability to raise whole buildings from the earth. The quarry had lain empty since then. Éadha made sure none of the animals were grazing too close to the drop – there was no accounting for how stupid sheep could be – then clambered up on to a rocky outcrop so's to have a good view over them all.

As she climbed, a falcon broke with a screech from a hidden perch on the overhang above, swooping directly above their heads. Éadha gripped her staff, ready to swing, while Cú let out a deep growl of warning; in lambing season the creatures could be a menace. This time, though, it flew straight on, out over the forest in the direction of the Keep.

Something in the swoop of the falcon's flight reminded Éadha of the dragons she saw from time to time when she was out here herding on the Steps. Flying so far above her they seemed to be little more than bright sparks blown on the wind, their wings reflecting the sunlight as they flew. In her lifetime they'd done no more than that, for all the Channeller tales of fiery monsters liable to burn everyone out of their beds. Flying on over her head, past Ailm's Keep, mostly headed for the high peaks of the Blackstairs.

Sometimes, after she'd seen one, etched against the blue sky and the black hills, it'd follow her into her dreams that night. Dreams where she flew up alongside it, into the bright air of morning to arrow across the icy peaks of the Blackstairs, and away. Away from the herding, and the sheep, and her uncle's cottage, and the *smallness* of the life that lay ahead of her already, at just seventeen. Dreams so real that when she awoke, they ached like memories.

She told no one of these dreams, not even Ionáin.

She sat down cross-legged on the ledge and dug into her satchel to see what Béithe had given her. She could feel two – no, three – apples, small, wrinkly and tasting of summer; and, underneath – oh joy – a small bannock of bread still warm from the Keep's oven. With no Channeller to channel grain crops like wheat, bread was a scarce, precious thing in the Keep. *Béithe must've been in a good mood this morning*, she thought.

Leaving her hands wrapped round the little loaf for the last of its warmth, Éadha kept watch until, just as the sun climbed to its highest point and the mists below finally cleared, a familiar tousle-haired figure appeared at the edge of the plateau. Even from a distance Éadha could see Ionáin was grinning widely. Which meant that someone somewhere was annoyed with him.

She rolled her eyes even as Cú loped over to greet him, leaping up on two legs to lick his face. Ionáin grabbed the huge dog in a bear hug so the two of them staggered and almost fell over, Cú yipping in excitement as if he were still a puppy. Éadha, on the other hand, didn't move, only calling down to him from her rocky perch when he was close enough to hear – 'Ionáin!' – putting as much exasperation as she could into that one word. Béithe would be proud of her.

'What?' he said innocently, shielding his eyes from the sun overhead and grinning up at her.

'So who've you pissed off now?'

'Only cousin Jarlath.'

'You know this is the bit where I'm supposed to chase you back down the mountain. Before Béithe realizes you've mitched off your lessons *again*.'

Ionáin laughed out loud. 'With what? Will you flap your cloak at me, like you're shooing a goose? Shoo, Ionáin, go learn the history of the Channeller wars even though you already know it off by heart. Shooo.'

Éadha snorted at the ridiculous image but sobered almost at once. 'Come on, Ionáin, they just want to see you taking things seriously now . . .' She paused as she realized, too late, where that sentence was going. Ionáin finished it for her.

'Now Dara's dead and I'm my Family's last hope, you mean.'

Éadha didn't say anything. There wasn't anything to say to that, unless she was prepared to lie.

Strictly speaking, of course, he wasn't the only one facing a Reckoning in a few days' time. Everyone else who'd turned seventeen in the Keep or the village, including Éadha, had to be reckoned too, while the Masters were there for Ionáin's big Reckoning ceremony. But almost no one outside the Families was gifted these days. Or, as Béithe liked to say, 'That's what centuries of Families only marrying each other gets you. A shrinking pool of gifted ones and every one of them afraid to stick a toe outside it.'

Ionáin, meanwhile, was clambering up beside her, his long fingers finding handholds and pulling himself up with ease, until he reached the stony ledge where she sat. 'Anyway, Mother's so busy getting ready for the Reckoning she won't even notice I'm gone, while Father's too busy having flashbacks to his own failure to say anything.'

He scrunched down, nudging her over with his hip to make room for him to squeeze in alongside her. They were, Éadha realized with a small start, finally the same height. His head was level with her own, which, after a lifetime of her being the taller one, felt unsettling.

Beside her, Ionáin finished on a quieter note. 'I just needed to get out for a bit. To breathe.'

Éadha glanced sideways at him, her heart softening. She'd get in trouble for this later, she knew. Béithe would come to the cottage tonight and lecture her about 'letting' the young master waste his time out herding with her again. But that was tonight, and this was now and he was here, and this was, after all, how it'd always been, all their lives until now. The two of them together, and how could she give up on having just one more day like this?

So instead she butted Ionáin's shoulder and held out her

satchel towards him. 'Be honest: this is what you came for, isn't it?'

Immediately Ionáin began rummaging about inside until he pulled out the little loaf and brandished it in the air.

'Aha! So this is why you were so keen to get rid of me. Hmmm. I always knew you were Béithe's favourite.'

Éadha's eyes flew open. 'You must be joking,' she sputtered. He only laughed and tore off a small piece of bread before lying down with one hand over his eyes. Beside him, she drew up her legs, wrapped her arms round them and rested her chin on her knees.

'They haven't been the same anyway,' he said.

'What?'

'The stupid lessons. They haven't been the same since you stopped coming. They were better then.' Éadha gave him a small nudge. In truth, most things were better then, back when Dara was still alive and his mother more inclined to indulge Ionáin, including when he insisted Éadha be allowed to start lessons with him when they were both nine.

'You make her sleep in my room,' he'd said to Úra, his small face determined, 'so you can look after Dara when he's sick at night and not have to worry about me. So it's only fair she can do the lessons too.'

It meant she'd a basic grasp of reading, writing and map-making, unlike most of the other Keep servants. Map-making had been her favourite lesson, her nose almost on the page as she painstakingly traced the delicate blue of the Anála Sea, stippled with the black of the dragon archipelago off Westport. But Ionáin's tutor Jarlath (a pompous, ungifted cousin from Úra's Debruin Family) had shaken his head in disapproval when he saw she'd sketched in a tiny dragon, all claws and wings, to mark their island domain.

'Art is the preserve of the Channellers, and rightly so, for nothing we ungifted could ever draw could match the wonders of a Channeller's illusions. Your place is to support their gift. It is most certainly not to be drawing –' he pulled the sheet away from her, crumpling it up – 'those awful creatures.'

She'd stopped going to the lessons at the same time she'd moved out of the Keep and into her uncle's cottage – after Dara died, his father powerless to help him and no Channeller near enough to be able to save him, and everything changed.

There was a short silence between them while Éadha watched Cú doing a lap of the plateau, going back again to sniff the wolf spoor. Beside her she felt Ionáin digging into his pockets as if he were looking for something. Then he poked her hip and, when she turned towards him, waggled his closed fist at her. 'Put out your hand and close your eyes.'

As she did, he dropped something hard and smooth into her palm. As soon as she held it, before she even saw it, she knew it for what it was. In the sunlight it glowed with veins of red and gold, too-bright colours for a winter-bleached hillside. It was an amber shard, no bigger than her cupped palm, a model of the White Tower of Erisen. Tiny windows and arches all picked out on the smooth amber, as immaculate as it'd been the moment it was channelled by Ionáin's great-grandfather a century ago. He'd been a Master Architect, one of the greatest of his age, and had channelled this model as a toy for his grandchildren.

She stared at it for a moment then looked down at Ionáin. 'Won't your parents mind?'

He shrugged. 'You know Father – he won't care. And I doubt Mother would notice if I took an actual building as long as it wasn't needed for the ceremony.'

'I don't need a birthday present, you know. Truly.'

'We've been over this. I know you don't need a present. I want to give you a present.' He poked her in the hip again. 'You really are the worst person to try and be nice to, you know. Just so we're clear: your proud independence is in no way compromised by this spontaneous giving of a gift that will not incur a debt of any kind towards me. So go on, like we practised. Just say thank you.'

'But you'll get into trouble.'

'Try it, go on, just for fun. Thank you, Ionáin. Thaaaaank you.'

She looked across at him, his tawny tangled hair full of burrs, his blue eyes laughing up at her from under his hand. Accepted the sudden clench of happiness that pushed her up on to her feet, where she gave an exaggerated bow from the waist with a broad smile and said, 'Thaaaank you, kind sir.'

Ionáin scrambled to his feet, too, laughing. Now he was standing in front of her on the ledge. He swirled his hand as Éadha began straightening up to face him, then said in his most pompous voice, 'You're most welcome, my lady. And happy birthday,' before leaning in to kiss her on the cheek; but in the same instant Éadha lifted her head, so that instead his lips dragged softly down the skin of her cheek and brushed her mouth. And on that frozen rocky outcrop high above the Keep, everything stopped as the two friends pulled back and stared at each other.

He hadn't planned to do it; Éadha could tell by the shock on his face. He'd just been caught up in the joke. But when his lips touched hers it hadn't felt like a joke. It felt as though he'd just swung open her heart, and now the space inside her was five times greater than it'd been before. And he felt it too; she could see it in his eyes as the shock in them faded, replaced by a question. A question her heart already knew the answer to. For it was truth, that kiss. It made no sense, and she knew there was no room for it in his world. But it was truth, and her heart wouldn't let her deny it, not now he'd set it alight. So she looked him in the eye and kissed him back, another soft brush across his lips. And they were so warm and alive that she wanted only to be kissing him still. But Ionáin flushed bright red and stepped back a little.

'Happy birthday,' he said again, for there not to be a silence.

'Yes,' she said, and it was her turn for her cheeks to burn red, as her mind caught up with what her heart had just done.

They both sat down again, though closer now, their hips almost touching, facing outwards as the heat on their faces slowly cooled, and never in her life had Éadha been more aware of another person than she was of Ionáin in that moment. And though she knew him better than she knew anyone else, it felt like she was seeing him for the first time. The line of his hip, inches away from her own. The warm flush on his cheeks. His slender fingers resting on his knees, drawn up against the chill. A shiver went through her suddenly at the thought of those same fingers touching her.

But even though reaching across that tiny space between them would've been the most normal thing in the world just seconds ago, now it felt like an impossibility. Because he'd kissed her but he'd also stepped back and she didn't know what to do.

Between them, the silence began to stretch until, in the middle distance, a solitary rider appeared on the avenue leading towards the Keep. Behind him a cart followed.

Beside her, Éadha sensed Ionáin stiffen. Glancing sideways, she saw he was glaring down at the rider. Quietly she said, 'Red doublet, packages tied on the back. Spices for the feast?'

'Silk. More of the finest Erisen silk. Can't have enough silk for a Reckoning,' said Ionáin, hunching his shoulders. 'It's from the De Lane Family. Their son Senan passed two months ago and they've been crowing about it ever since. He'll be one of the strongest apprentices this year, though one of the First Families have a son turning seventeen too. Gry. Their Channellers are always really powerful.'

Beside him, Éadha took a deep breath, willing the new, unfamiliar tension out of her body, before going on. 'How about the cart with the two big bundles getting stuck halfway up the lane?'

Ionáin rolled his eyes. 'Featherbeds for the Debruin cousins. We'd be shamed for all eternity if Lady Ferne sleeps on a lumpy mattress.'

'Blue with a yellow stripe, single rider on a fast horse?'

Ionáin sat forward abruptly when Éadha said that, staring down at the new rider who'd just appeared on the lane. 'Those are the Manon Family colours. His twins, Coll and Linn, passed their Reckonings when they turned seventeen last month. Linn's the first girl in five years to pass as a Channeller. That must be Lord Manon accepting Father's invite. As if any of them would miss the show of the year. Come all, see the young lord bring glory or ruin to the once noble Ailms. If he fails, you can say you were there for the fall of a Family.'

Turning towards him, Éadha held out the amber tower on the flat of her palm. 'But if you pass, you'll be able to do this. And go there,' she said, gesturing towards the Blackstairs and all that lay beyond: the white city of Erisen with its marble towers and the islands of Lambay where the Masters had trained generations of young Channellers for four hundred years.

Ionáin said nothing. It was the one thing he wouldn't talk about, even with her. What'd happen if he passed. Éadha understood. He couldn't let himself think it. It meant too much.

As the Manon rider disappeared into the Keep, the silence between them turned heavier and Éadha could feel Ionáin slipping away from her, further away from that one shining moment they'd shared.

'I'd better go down,' he said, not meeting her eyes as he climbed to his feet. 'They'll be looking for me, to tell me about the Manon letter.'

As he stood, she wanted to put out her hand to him, as if she could somehow reach past all these things pulling him back into his world. But it was too new, too wordless, the feeling that'd swung open in her heart when their lips met. She didn't have the words yet to try to hold him, only the longing he wouldn't go. So she said nothing, just nodding as Ionáin jumped lightly to the ground.

Raising a hand behind him in farewell, he disappeared down the slope, Cú loping devotedly alongside him. Éadha hadn't the heart to call the wolfhound back. She'd get the sheep down on her own.

Instead of making a start on it, though, she sat on, staring at the spot where Ionáin and Cú had disappeared, as the sun faded behind the hills and the mist reclaimed its old ground. It felt colder with them gone, the chill needling through her layers, but still she didn't move, her hand cupping her chin so her fingertips were touching the spot where Ionáin had kissed her. It'd only been a few seconds, but she could remember every curve and dip of his lips where they'd brushed against hers. The heat of it and the sense of something new coming alive.

It was almost dark when she finally roused herself to begin rounding up the flock for the long trudge back down the fell. But as she started a headcount, she heard a panicked bleat from the far side of the hill, by the drop down to the quarry. Breaking into a run, she raced towards the sound.

As she sprinted, ahead of her she heard the rushing sound of stones giving way, followed by the flat thump of a body hitting rock. She skidded to a stop, only just keeping her own balance on the loose stones, and peered down. The yearling must've wandered too close to the edge and slid right off the shale, over the drop. It'd been saved only by a narrow outcrop that jutted out about six feet down. Now it was lying on the ledge, unmoving but still breathing, winded by its fall. Directly beneath it were the steep pits of the quarry. As soon as it tried to move, it'd surely topple over the edge and fall to its death.

Throwing herself down flat on her stomach, Éadha strained downwards, towards the trapped animal, stretching her staff out as far as it went, trying to hook the creature's neck. But it was just out of reach. She needed to get closer. Cautiously she inched forward, over the loose shale, but as soon as she did the stones began to gather speed beneath her. She only just managed to push herself out of the rush as a hail of pebbles went tumbling down, clattering off the ledge below.

Her heart thudding with the terror of almost going over the edge, she dropped her head. 'Stupid, stupid, how could I be so stupid?'

Sitting there mooning over one impossible kiss while the animals she was supposed to be minding went wandering off. How could she lose one so cheaply with food always short? They'd all be so disappointed in her – her uncle, Ionáin's father, even Ionáin. No. She couldn't bear it. She wouldn't bear it.

Even as she thought that, she seemed to feel an echo of the sensation she'd felt earlier when she'd kissed Ionáin, of something within her coming to life. It was almost completely dark, winter's night coming on quickly as she lay there on the gravel, the first lights shining up from the village below. Jamming one hand under a tiny outcrop for a grip, her arm shaking with the effort of clinging on, she swung out over empty air, trying again to reach the yearling. The rush of the air beneath her brought her back to the silent swoop of the morning's falcon. Hanging there, half-suspended in darkness, the world about her seemed to narrow to a falcon's flight. In that moment she became the hunter. A creature of instinct, hunting for the power she so desperately needed, and there, from one heartbeat to the next, there it was. A living, silver thread, shining out in the darkness.

Even as she saw it, beyond thought she knew the way of it, reaching out with her awareness for that silver thread and pulling it hard into her. As she did, the world went white around her, then snapped back to black as inside her head a star exploded. Life filled her, shining, pulsating life pouring into every cell of her until she must surely burst with the effort of holding it in.

She let go of her handhold, dropping fast and hard through the winter night to land on the narrow ledge where the sheep lay. It was just starting to come around. She caught it up with one hand. Panic-stricken, it kicked every part of her, fighting to get free. But she gripped it easily, impossibly, and climbed with it back up the vertical cliff. Not until she'd reached the fell-top once more did her knees buckle, the shining energy that'd poured into her suddenly spent. She collapsed on to the shale at the cliff edge, the sheep writhing out of her arms and scrambling, bleating, back to the herd.

For a moment she lay there, panting, staring up at the dark sky where the constellation of the Sídhe, the Old Ones, had appeared low on the horizon. Her mind was strangely calm, as if what she'd done had happened on a level below conscious thought, and she hadn't caught up yet with its simple impossibility. But the sheep were milling about anxiously. There was nothing for it but to haul herself carefully back up on to the grass and shepherd the flock on down the fell-side, the dark path between the starlight and the firelight.

3

AS SOON AS THE sheep were safely back in their pens for the night, Éadha was away, heading down the tree-shadowed avenue towards the Keep. The moon had risen enough to light her way, reflecting on puddles already freezing over in the mud churned up by the day's traffic. She'd started shivering uncontrollably, her body aching as if she was running a fever. All she wanted to do was get to her cot bed and pull the covers over her head until this pain left her. But as she forced her shaking legs on down the lane, she heard feet coming up behind her, moving far more surely and swiftly than her own. Turning, half fearful of what else this strange night might have in store, she made out the features of the singer Magret.

Béithe's cousin Magret was a short, vigorous woman with a weathered face framed by cropped white hair. A renowned singer and musician, she could easily have found a permanent berth with any Family. Instead, though, she chose a nomadic existence, travelling from Family to Family throughout Domhain, there to mark their Reckonings and betrothals, births and deaths. She'd sung at Dara's funeral when he'd died two years ago, and now she was on her way to Ailm's Keep to take charge of the music for Ionáin's Reckoning ceremony.

As she drew closer, Éadha saw Magret was bleeding from a deep cut on her temple and her face looked drawn.

Peering at Éadha in the moonlight, Magret asked, 'Child, what has you out at this hour?'

'I was herding on the fell but I'd a bit of trouble with a yearling,' Éadha replied, her heart sinking as Magret fell into step beside her. The calm she'd felt after rescuing the yearling was wearing off, replaced by a growing bewilderment. She just wanted to get away to her room.

Magret, though, gave her a sharp glance. 'What d'you mean?'

'It slid down the shale side and on to a ledge over the quarry.' As she said this, the two of them had almost reached the main Keep courtyard. It was lit with torches for Magret's arrival. She tugged her hood down as if to hide her temple, where the blood from her cut showed black in the moonlight.

'Are you all right?' said Éadha. 'That looks deep.'

'I'll be fine. Do I look a sight though?' said Magret, then, without waiting for Éadha to answer, she sat down on a stone bench in the shadow of the courtyard wall, facing out towards the Keep gardens. Taking up the corner of her cloak, she spat on it and rubbed at the dried blood until all that was left was the cut itself, just under the hairline. 'Now?'

Éadha nodded. 'You'd hardly see it. Did you fall?'

'Such a stupid thing. I stopped off at the quarry to look for some quartz and I must've tripped. One minute, I'm climbing over some rocks, and the next I'm face down with this cut on my temple.'

Magret paused and stared directly at Éadha, an intent look coming into her eyes. 'You must've been right up above me when I fell. Rescuing that yearling. How did that happen, did you say?'

Éadha shrugged, at the same time feeling a twinge of unease. There was something in the way Magret was staring at her, almost like a hunger.

'I don't know,' she said slowly, fumbling for words to describe something she didn't understand herself. 'The sheep was stuck. I felt bad; I didn't want to let everybody down. I jumped down and then – all of a sudden – I could lift it . . .' Her voice trailed away as she realized how bizarre that sounded.

'Can you come sit here?' said Magret. Éadha didn't want to, but neither could she see how to say no, and so she came and perched uneasily on the edge of the bench. As she did, Magret swivelled and caught Éadha's head between her hands, holding it in an unbreakable grip. 'This may hurt a little, but it'll only last a moment.'

The next second Éadha felt icy hands reach inside her skull. She gasped with the shock of it. A presence had entered her mind as if it were just another room to be walked into. Squirming and pulling as hard as she could, she tried to break free, but Magret's hands were like bands of iron clamped on either side of her head, immovable.

Desperate, she turned inwards, instinctively trying to push out the invader inside her mind, but nothing happened.

She could still feel the calm presence moving about in her head. It wasn't painful after the initial shock, but it was utterly alien, the fundamental wall between her mind and the world outside ripped down, her every thought naked and exposed.

An iron sense of refusal rose up inside her then. Closing her eyes, she reached out with her awareness as she'd done up on the fell, and immediately she could sense it. A silver thread of power shining out *there*, much closer this time. Without needing to think, she pulled on the thread, as hard as she could, and felt the shining strength pour into her again. With a flick, she sent that strength powering up from the depths of her, shooting through into the surface of her mind to drive out the invader, a giant wave exploding out from the silvery heart of her.

Magret had no chance against this tsunami of Éadha's violated rage; she was driven out of Éadha's mind on the thump of a heartbeat, her grip broken and her body flung backwards, off the bench and on to the ground. Éadha's only thought, meanwhile, was to get away. She staggered up from the bench and stumbled out of the courtyard, on to the grassy mounds of the Keep gardens beyond.

From behind, Magret's voice called after her. 'Éadha, Éadha, don't go. I'm sorry, Éadha, that was a Reckoning, that's all. Just let me explain.'

Éadha stopped short. She was due her Reckoning right after Ionáin's Reckoning day. Was Magret a Reckoner then, sent from Lambay? It made no sense. Looking back from where she stood in the shadows, she saw Magret pull herself back up on to the bench and hunch over, resting her forearms on her thighs and bowing her head.

'Éadha, I know you're out there. I need you to listen. You have the Channeller's gift. From what I can tell, a rare gift, strong and sure. I guessed when you told me about the yearling. How else do you think you were able to climb up, carrying such a weight? I just needed to be sure.'

Éadha reeled where she stood. Not since she'd been a very young girl playing games of make-believe with Ionáin had she ever imagined she might be a Channeller. Even in those games Ionáin would always argue she couldn't play the Channeller, because girls hardly ever were. No more than one or two in a generation and always Family daughters. Not girls like Éadha with no name, no history of the gift.

The realizations began to multiply, bursting silently one by one in her mind like a shower of stars shooting across a winter sky. This changed everything. She could be the Keep's Channeller. Grow the crops, guard the animals, heal the Keep itself, protect against dragon raids. And Ionáin. His Reckoning didn't matter any more. He didn't need to be a Channeller to save the Keep any more. She could do it for him.

She covered her face with her hands, breathing hard; it was too much to take in. As she did, Magret reached her and stretched an arm gingerly across her shoulders.

'There now, it's a lot to hear, I know.'

But when Éadha lifted her head to look at Magret, her eyes were blazing with the intensity of her realization of what all this could mean for her, for Ionáin, for the whole Keep.

'Are you a Reckoner? Were you sent by the Masters? How can you be sure?'

Magret gave a short laugh. 'The Masters aren't the only ones with the ability to search for the gift. But no, this wasn't your official Reckoning. I'd wager my life though that you're a Channeller born. The way you channelled power just now to throw me out of your mind is the purest proof there is.'

At this, Éadha pulled herself out of Magret's grasp. She had to get to the Keep, find Ionáin, say the words to break the curse that'd held him for so long. In her mind she was already there. He was already hugging her so hard she could hardly breathe and – her throat tightened in sudden longing – then he'd lean in and he'd kiss her, only this time he wouldn't stop. Because what this gift meant was she was going to *be* someone. To actually belong in Ionáin's world of Families and Masters, power and magic.

'Éadha, I need you to listen to me now.'

Magret's sober tone jolted Éadha back to the frost and the starlight, the bare branches of the oak tree along the Keep wall and the ice-covered lake in front of them.

'A gift like this isn't something to be taken lightly, a toy. There's so much you don't know because there's been no channelling here in the Keep in your lifetime. You've no idea – how could you – what it's like everywhere else. What this power means.' She paused and stared at Éadha. 'I'm sorry. This is a lot to take in. I want to stay, but there isn't time. I'm already late, and they'll be out looking for me any minute. But I need you to promise me one thing. Until we speak again, swear to me you'll tell nobody what happened this evening, and you won't use this power again.'

Éadha stared at Magret in disbelief. How could she ask her not to tell anyone? Not to tell Ionáin? But Magret gripped Éadha by the shoulders, her hard fingers digging into the bone.

'I mean it. Surely you at least know the Masters control all channelling on Domhain?'

Éadha nodded.

'Channelling without first winning your staff on Lambay is utterly forbidden. It's the Masters' strictest rule. So you absolutely can't tell anyone what you did this evening. Lord Huath arrives any day now for his nephew's Reckoning, and he's the most brutal Channeller on all of Domhain, with every reason to want the gift to die out completely in Ailm's Keep. You've no Family, no name, no one to protect you from him. You cannot give him an excuse to hurt you; do you understand?'

Éadha stared at the slight singer, unblinking, as her heart rate slowed and she took in what Magret was saying. Finally, she nodded again.

'Good,' said Magret, looking relieved. Behind her there was the sound of the Keep's massive oak doors opening. A shaft of light arced across the courtyard. 'I have to go,' she said. 'But we'll talk very soon, I promise.' And with that she hurried into the courtyard, where voices called out in welcome. Éadha was left standing alone in the shadowed gardens, trying to take in the fact that after this night, nothing in her life would ever be the same again.

4

ÉADHA STAYED STANDING FOR a little while. She was on one of the grassy mounds that ringed the ice-bound lake. Above her the Sídhe still shone bright in the full-starred sky of winter. In that cold and starry stillness everything seemed hyper-real, etched in silver and filled with meaning. The branches of the oak tree dipped in black, the white glimmering of the lake, the Keep's ancient towers rising behind her. She was gifted. She was going to be a Channeller.

She stared down at her hands. Her body felt strange, fizzing and restless, but it took her a beat to understand why: the remains of the power she'd drawn earlier to throw Magret out of her mind. Churning now still, inside her, unused. Was this how Channellers felt, she thought, rising up on the balls of her feet and spreading her fingers out wide, filled with this sense of *possibility*. And underneath it, too, something else. Something new stirring deep inside her, a silver fish that darted out of sight as soon as she tried to look at it.

How was she going to keep this a secret, she thought, when she could barely hold still, barely hold it in? Her eyes went automatically to the East Tower and Ionáin's window, but it was dark. No doubt he was downstairs in the Great Hall, welcoming Magret. Restlessness surged inside her; she needed to *do* something. She'd promised not to draw power again, but what was she to do with this power she already had? Behind the East Tower, stark against the moonlight, she glimpsed the outline of the Lady's Well.

There, she thought. Smoothly, effortlessly, she broke into a run across the grassy mounds, barely noticing how fast she was moving, and moments later she was slipping in through the stone archway into the Lady's Well, a marble cloister open to the sky.

In years gone by, it was where the ladies of the Keep sat while the old Lord Ailm, Ionáin's grandfather, wove them illusions from the great dragon battles. Its tiled floor was covered with mosaics while a stream sang down its centre before beginning its quick fall towards the lake. And its marble walls rose high above Éadha as she stood there now, hiding her from any curious eyes.

Standing in the centre of the Well, she tried to remember the stories Ionáin used to tell her about Channellers and their gifts back when they were smaller, before Dara died and everything got too serious for stories. How they could create were-lights and fireballs, draw crops and buildings from the earth, fight back the dragons in aerial combat over the sea beyond Westport. How they could fly.

Taking a deep breath, she concentrated on the power she could still sense inside her. On an out-breath she pushed it down, and down again, right through her, until it was pushing against the ground beneath her feet. For a moment nothing happened, and then slowly, impossibly, her body began to rise up into the air. It was as if she was suddenly weightless, the power pushing her off the ground and holding her, cushioning her on the air. Seeing the ground dropping away beneath her, a sudden panic gripped her: what was she doing? She wobbled, her arms starting to flail. But she could still feel it, the power, pulsing through her, and after a moment she steadied herself, concentrating on keeping it flowing smoothly, like breathing. As she did, her body went still, and then she was just . . . there. Floating in the air, about six feet off the ground. She let out a small cry – of disbelief, of wonder. She could fly.

Focusing again, very gingerly she pushed herself higher, gradually getting the feel of it, how to turn, how to move, like a swimmer diving through the air. Soon she was circling the Well, round and round, first slowly, then, as her confidence grew, faster and faster, until she was racing. With a sudden flick, she lifted her hand above her head and shot upward, up and up, right until she was level with the top of the Well, almost back out into the moonlight again, the ground fifty feet below her. She knew she couldn't risk flying out into the open air. Instead, with her hand still raised above her head, she began to spin, her hair flying, her cloak whipping, until she was going so fast the stars above became white streaks and she the centre of a vortex of power and of life that was going to set the world on fire.

The power went out almost as suddenly as it'd filled her, spent. She began to fall from the air. Human again and tumbling down past the marble walls towards the mosaic floor. She only just managed, with the last dregs of power inside her, to slow her fall enough that it didn't kill her, though she still landed with a bone-crunching thud on the stone floor, every last bit of breath knocked out of her.

She lay there for a little while, her cloak crumpled around her, her head on the ground inches away from the stream, listening to its quiet babble as her breath eventually returned and her heart slowed to normal. Everything hurt. Inside and out. The best she could do was to drag herself over to a corner of the cloister, where there was a small pile of broken tiles. Resting her aching head on the tiles, she pulled her cloak over her for warmth and slipped into the relief of unconsciousness.

'Éadha!' Someone was calling her.

She tried to ignore them, but they wouldn't stop. Couldn't they see she needed not to be awake right now? When awake meant bruises and every bone in her body stiff and aching?

'Éadha, wake up.'

Ionáin. It was Ionáin. How was it Ionáin? Finally her brain started into life and it was like the flickering of lightning, the scattered racing of images across her mind. Rescuing the yearling. Magret's hands gripping her head. Drawing on the silver thread. Flying in the Lady's Well. Falling. And Ionáin. Kissing Ionáin.

Her eyes flew open.

Ionáin's face was only inches away as he crouched down towards her, his eyes a midnight blue in the morning-shadowed cloister.

'What're you doing here?' he said.

She pushed herself up, suddenly desperately conscious of what an odd, bedraggled sight she must make. Her curls limp and beaded with dew, all of her coated in dust and damp from lying on the cloister floor all night.

'I . . . I was restless last night,' she stammered, scrabbling to get her thoughts straight, to remember what she could and couldn't say. 'After I got the sheep back, the moon was so bright – I went for a walk. I must've fallen asleep.'

She sat up further, only taking in now how different Ionáin looked.

His eyes were looking straight into hers, with no trace of his normal grin. Almost as if they were two strangers meeting for the first time. Instead of his normal worn tunic, he was dressed in a fine navy jacket and wool trews. It made him look older, more intent, and the unfamiliarity only heightened that sense of meeting a stranger. Someone, she realized, she was almost painfully conscious of now. His tanned skin against the dark collar, the fall of his hair, the way his eyes seemed almost blue-black. The fullness of his lips. A shiver went through her at the memory of how they'd felt, brushing against hers high on the fell yesterday, and she realized she wasn't ready for him to be this close to her when she still didn't fully understand what'd happened between them.

As the silence began to stretch, she saw Ionáin was studying her face too. It reminded her of the look he'd get when they were younger and Jarlath would let them pore over the maps of the dragon archipelago where his grandfather had fought. Now he was studying her with that same intensity, as if she'd become some kind of new terrain, a land unknown. His expression was unreadable while he took in the dust on her cheeks and coating her lashes, the upturned tilt of her lips. She'd never been stared at so intently before, and a flush began stealing across her cheeks. As it did she could've sworn his eyes darkened, until finally his questing gaze dropped to her hands, still on the floor, catching sight of the little pile of broken tiles next to them. And it was like a spell breaking when he cleared his throat and said, with a hint of his normal smile, 'D'you remember those, the last time we were here?'

The familiar memory steadied her, reminded her that this intent, handsome almost-stranger was still the tousle-haired boy she'd grown up with, the one who walked with her through almost every memory.

'They were our drums,' she said with a small, rueful smile. 'That's how Béithe caught us that day. I was battering them with a stick when you decided to sing along at the top of your voice. Stealth was never your strong point.'

Ionáin laughed, his face lighting up. How had she never seen that before, she thought. The way he lit up a room when he smiled like this, with his whole self. How much of her joy was already in this boy.

'That's how the Dragon Song is meant to be sung.' He grinned. 'At the top of your voice as you ride west across the stony barrens to Westport to fight dragons, because you're terrified you're going to be burned to death by some angry dragon mother and singing is the only thing you've got to keep you going.'

Straightening up, Ionáin threw his head back.

> *'Westward the dragon flies and so must I*
> *Naught but a yew staff by my side*
> *My one heart's wish that you are there to keep for me*
> *When I ride to Westport's shore, but it cannot be'*

As he sang, Éadha saw the two of them riding west together as Lambay apprentices to join the Channellers' never-ending battle against the dragons. Fighting together, shoulder to shoulder. And the longing to tell Ionáin about her new gift was so strong that before she could even remember her promise to Magret, she'd climbed to her feet, her mouth open to tell him everything, just as she always had her whole life.

The look of strain that came over his face as he finished singing stopped her.

'I only came in because Béithe sent me. She wanted me to make sure it's clean, in case Lady Ferne wants to sit here. But I'm glad I found you. I need to talk to you about yesterday.'

Éadha stared, the words she was about to say dying on her lips. Why wasn't he meeting her eyes any more? Why had one hand gone to his head, twisting into his tangled mop, his old familiar tell of worry?

'I shouldn't have done that. Kiss you.'

A chasm seemed to open up inside her. How could he think that moment they'd shared had been something wrong?

Glancing up and seeing the expression in her eyes, Ionáin hurried on. 'I mean, not that I didn't want to.' He flushed and his voice trailed away. They were so close they were almost touching, and the longing that surged inside her was as sharp and strong as the twist of her power last night – to reach up and cup his cheek, to turn his mouth to hers. To see if the same shock would go through them, if his lips were as firm and as warm as she remembered. She could see, too, the same question in his eyes. In the way they were locked on her lips now, as if they held the only answer to that question. Her hand was already beginning to lift towards him when he finished more quietly, 'But I've no right to do anything like that. Not until after my Reckoning.'

Éadha dropped her hand, frowning in confusion. 'But it doesn't make any difference to me what happens at your Reckoning. It never has, not ever.'

Ionáin half smiled, the look of strain on his face fading as he said, 'You know you're the only person on all of Domhain I'd believe when they said that?'

'Well then?' said Éadha.

'You know if I fail I'll be sent to Westport and I probably won't come back. I can't tie you to me while that still might happen. It wouldn't be right.' At his words, Éadha's new power surged furiously. *Let them try*, she thought.

Ionáin was still talking. 'And it matters to me too, whether I pass or not. I need to know who I am before . . . before I start anything else. Even that.'

'Why?' she said stubbornly. 'You'll still be you; I'll still be me. We'll still be us regardless. Power won't change who you are.'

Ionáin looked at her directly then and, just for that moment, of the two of them he seemed for the first time ever to be the older one. 'You know that's not true, Éadha. Not on Domhain.'

And Éadha remembered the power flooding into her last night. How it'd changed her whole sense of the world, made it seem limitless, and she knew even though she'd told the truth, Ionáin was right too. In the same moment she also realized it wouldn't be right to blurt out the news of her own gift to him. Not while he was still trapped like this, in an agony of waiting to find out whether he'd a gift of his own. It wasn't, she thought, that Ionáin wanted just anyone to be the Keep's Channeller; *he* wanted to be the one to save his Family.

Even as she thought this, Ionáin leaned in to her again, this time resting his forehead against hers. She could feel his warm breath soft on her cheek and an involuntary shudder went through her at the heat of it. Reaching down, he caught her hand, stroking his thumb along the inside of her palm, and it felt like she was being marked, that if she looked down she'd see a line drawn across her skin.

'This'd be a lot easier if you weren't right here though.' He lifted his other hand to tuck a stray curl behind her ear. Éadha swallowed, her throat going dry at the absorption in those blue eyes now. As if he couldn't help himself, his finger slid down to the sensitive skin behind her earlobe, then traced slowly along the line of her jaw, coming to rest against her mouth. Without thinking, her lips parted at his touch, so his index finger slipped down to rest on the top of her lower lip. Ionáin's eyes widened and for a second she thought his self-control would break, but then he let out a frustrated growl and stepped back, raising his hands in the air like someone pleading for a truce.

'This is only going to work if I don't touch you. Possibly also don't look at you. So maybe you go over there –' he pointed to the other side of the stream – 'while I stay here. Push me in the stream if I look like I'm cracking.'

Éadha grinned suddenly at how ridiculous this was: two old friends suddenly not able to stand beside each other. 'I think we'll manage,' she scoffed.

'Speak for yourself,' was all Ionáin said as he bent to begin gathering up shards of broken tiles, and after a minute, she crouched down to help him.

By noon they'd tidied the Lady's Well to Béithe's grudging satisfaction. But there was to be no let-up from Reckoning preparations, as she immediately sent Éadha up to the East Tower to help her aunt and the other seamstresses with Ionáin's formal Reckoning robes, while Ionáin was told to go and entertain the newly arrived guests. Éadha's heart sank; she was well aware of how clumsy her fingers and how precious the robes were, handed down through generations of Ailm lords.

Her aunt greeted her with a matter-of-fact, 'You can hem the undergarments. That way if you prick your finger and get blood on them, no one will see it.'

Relieved, she settled down in a corner of the high, bright sewing room. The hemming was mechanical work, and her mind was free to wander into daydreams of her aunt's face, and the faces of the other women in the room, when they found out she was gifted in just a few days' time. After an hour or so, though, the peace in the room was broken as Lady Úra, Lady Ferne and her attendants swept in, pulling Ionáin along in their wake. The new guests, it seemed, wanted to see Ionáin dressed in his ceremonial robes.

Watching from her corner, Éadha groaned inwardly, knowing how much Ionáin despised all this. The fuss, the women cooing and laughing around him.

Lady Ferne was talking to her sister-in-law as they both sat down. 'You know my view, Úra. You need to be thinking about pairings already. Lambay is too late. Have you thought about the Manon girl? If her father would consider Ionáin, she'll be this year's prize, no doubt.'

Úra smiled politely but didn't respond directly, instead saying, 'Indeed, Ferne. I think, though, we're ready now for the fitting.'

Éadha's aunt stepped forward with the heavy robe. The room fell quiet as Ionáin began to strip, and though Éadha knew he loathed being put on display like this, she still felt proud of the way he held himself, there in the centre of the room. As he tugged his tunic off, her heart twisted in sudden longing to see his lithe frame appear, tanned a golden brown. The narrow hips framed by slim-fitting pants, his long, finely muscled legs. But, like everyone else in Ailm's Keep, he was also especially lean after a lifetime of tight rations, and as soon as the robe was draped across him, it was obvious it'd need to be taken in.

'Well, if even the robe doesn't fit . . .'

It was Lady Ferne again, her voice loud in the silence, while her attendants turned their faces away, tittering. Éadha felt her new gift stir into restless, furious life. How dare they? She had to fight down a sudden urge to lash out.

'Remove it, please,' said Lady Úra, her voice tight. But the robe's gold ties had become knotted. For a few horribly long moments Ionáin was stuck, surrounded by a huddle of women nervously unpicking the knots. Finally they released him, and he strode out of the room without a word. Éadha tried to catch his eyes, but they were fixed on the door, and in a moment he was gone.

Later she went looking for him, clambering up on to the Keep roof, even hiking out into the forest, but no one could hide like Ionáin when he didn't want to be found.

The next morning she woke before dawn. Her sleep had been broken by a nightmare in which she'd taken Ionáin's place in the sewing room, trapped, immobile beneath the jewelled carapace of heavy robes. She'd stood surrounded by a throng of noblewomen pressing in on her, watching her in scornful silence as she tried again and again to find and hold a thread of power and channel it through a needle held by Lady Ferne.

When she woke with a start, in her mind's eye she sensed at once two silver threads shimmering in the air in front of her. Just like the ones she'd seen before, on the fell and in the courtyard. Still not fully awake, her heart pounding from the nightmare, she reached out towards one of them without thinking. Catching it with her awareness and unspooling it very gently towards her. As she did, a shock ran through her. Where before she'd drawn power from the threads only to fling it out immediately once more, this time she just lay there for a moment, letting it pour softly into her.

Wide awake now, she sat up in her bed and concentrated on the energy fizzing gently inside her. Holding one hand out in front of her, she imagined a tiny were-light and sent the energy flowing into her hand. Immediately, a scalding flame burst into life above her hand, burning her palm. Startled, she flung the light away from her. It flew off around the room, whizzing in a circle above her head while she sucked at her burnt hand. Terrified something would catch fire or the little light would go shooting off downstairs, she closed her eyes and concentrated on the feeling of power being snuffed out. After a moment the were-light wavered, came to a halt, then vanished.

Heart pounding, Éadha lay back. She could still feel the power churning inside her. It was like having a fire set burning in her core, and the urge to keep using it, to send it out of herself and see what she could do with it, was irresistible. She forced herself to remember Magret's words in the Keep gardens two nights before. *Until we speak again, swear to me you won't use this power again.*

But as she lay on her bed feeling the power inside, insisting on itself, her promise to Magret suddenly felt very far away and hard to understand. Because, after all, what was this power for, but to be used?

Without giving herself any more time to think, she swung her legs off the bed, stood in the middle of her little loft and called up another were-light in her outstretched palm. This time, by concentrating fiercely she managed to control it so it floated safely into the air just above her hand. Then with a flick of her wrist, she sent it dancing about the room, a grin spreading across her face as she realized she really could do this. Soon she'd called up three separate were-lights and set them all flying in interweaving patterns above her head, concentrating so hard she didn't hear her aunt climbing the steep wooden stairs to her room, only realizing she was there when she called from outside her door.

'Éadha. Éadha, are you awake? Don't forget you've choir this morning.'

Éadha froze, while above her the little lights all blinked out of existence.

Choir. She'd completely forgotten. Magret had chosen a ragtag mix of Keep servants and herders to make up her choir for the Reckoning ceremony, and this morning was their first rehearsal in the Great Hall.

Dressing quickly, she hurried out of the cottage, running across the lake-bridge to the Keep. She reached the Great Hall just as Magret clapped her hands for everyone to assemble on the new wooden stage in its centre. As she climbed the steps, she felt the last traces of the power she'd drawn earlier ebbing away from her. Around her the other singers were humming and coughing, getting ready to sing, while up above them, Ionáin's head appeared over the cross-walk leading from his tower.

This time he was in a rich, dark-red velvet jacket that brought out his golden colouring, while his tangled mop of hair had been trimmed. Standing in the crowd below, Éadha swallowed as she took in how handsome he looked. The way the aristocratic clothing and the neat hair made him seem, suddenly, so far beyond her reach even as he stood right there, just above her. In that moment, the touch of his hand in the Lady's Well yesterday seemed more inconceivable than the little were-lights she'd channelled earlier. In front of her, meanwhile, Magret gestured with a sweep of her arm for them to begin.

The first song was the familiar 'Welcome Canto', the song to greet Ionáin at the start of his Reckoning. It began with a single deep voice, a subterranean thrumming that seemed to rise through the floor, then gradually each layer of voices added its own melody, filling the great space with a multitude of harmonies until every voice stopped together on a heartbeat. This was the moment when Ionáin would reach the stage and face his Reckoner.

Éadha and the other sopranos were to lead off the second verse, starting high and cascading down before lifting again to the highest note of all. As she began to sing, she could see Ionáin watching from the cross-walk above, his chin resting on his forearms. He looked preoccupied, as if his mind was far away, thinking about his Reckoning and his Family's fears, all the things pulling him away from her. And in that moment Éadha was gripped by the need to make him *see* her too.

Focusing, she reached out with her awareness, looking once more for threads of power. It was the first time she'd tried to do it consciously and now, rather than just two threads like earlier, she could sense many. More than she could count, all shining around her. With the gentlest of touches she reached to first one, then another and another, pulling tiny sips from each towards her, feeling power build within her as she watched Magret lift her hands into the air as the song reached its climax. Then with a sweep of her own, Éadha shot that power from the centre of her, sending it pouring into her voice so that it flew up and up, and as the song reached its highest note, she sang it out with such purity and power, a thing of such outrageous freedom it forced the breath out of every listener in the room. She saw Magret's eyes widen and Ionáin's head lift to stare at her, but she didn't care any more, completely absorbed now in the flow of her power.

But even as she held that last, impossible note, the Great Hall filled with a crashing sound, as if someone outside was trying to smash the hall's doors apart. The singing stuttered to a halt as servants peeled away from the choir and ran to open the doors before they were broken down. Lord Huath appeared, outlined in the doorway, and shoved past them without a word, followed by guardsmen who swiftly took up positions at every doorway and stairwell.

Huath's expression was livid, his jaw rigid with fury as he stalked to the podium, his pale eyes scanning the choir. As he did, every head in the room bowed; every breath went shallow with fear. Behind him, his Keeper Treasa readied herself to hold his power. With a flick of his wrist, he snapped multiple were-lights into existence. They swarmed down from the dome to hover above the heads of the singers, illuminating every bowed head and clenched fist.

In the centre of the choir, Éadha was close to collapsing in sudden terror. Magret's warning came screaming back to her as she felt something stir in front of her, as if a much larger creature were unfolding itself where Huath stood, his power radiating out from him. The heat of that power began building against her skin, a prickling, crawling sensation. She remembered how easily Magret entered her mind two nights ago and knew it'd only take him seconds to rip into her consciousness and lay bare her every pathetic attempt at channelling.

Four singers down from her, at the edge of the front row, one of the stable lads let out a muffled shriek as, with a gesture, Huath lifted him up into the air, enveloping him with his power. Forcing the boy's arms out cruciform and his head up, Huath stepped in for a closer look. His face was millimetres away from the boy's, like some sinister predator sniffing out his prey before, with another flick, he released him so he crumpled on to the floor, unconscious.

Within her Éadha could feel her own telltale power, still pulsing gently with the energy she'd drawn moments before. Now in her mind's eye she grew a sheet of ice above it, dull, thick ice, a blank surface to reflect the glare of the winter sun and blind the eye. She sent her silver fish diving, deep beneath the ice into the depths of her, to hold perfectly still. But the heat of Huath's power was relentless, even from where he stood, and he was moving closer and closer, stepping from one singer to the next. He'd reached the girl beside her, his face implacable as he scoured out her mind, and she whimpered in bewildered agony.

Now Éadha was next. In only a few heartbeats more, her ice sheet would shatter and she'd be exposed. Huath stood in front of her, his pale eyes taking her in: the raised chin and the clenched fists as she waited for his strength to overwhelm her. She could feel the heat of his power against her skin, building and building; but in the very last second, before he could rip into her mind, Magret spoke out. Her voice was quiet and deferential, but it rang clear in the silvery acoustics of the Great Hall.

'Lord Huath, pray forgiveness for my intrusion. I thought you'd want to know your nephew Ionáin stands above you. If you've sensed the first flickerings of power even before his Reckoning, this would be the most wonderful news.'

The hot breath on Éadha's skin snapped out as Lord Huath's head shot up to see Ionáin, still standing on the crosswalk above, watching on in shock. It was enough to end the Inquisition. Released, Éadha saw how Lord Huath visibly damped down the power flowing through him. Saw too how forced his smile was as he straightened to address Ionáin. 'Why, nephew. I didn't see you there. This is remarkable. If the flare I sensed as I rode in is any guide, you've a great gift indeed.'

From where she stood watching, Éadha saw disbelief then hope chase a dawning joy across Ionáin's face as he took in what his uncle was saying.

'Oh, Uncle. Truly? You sensed something? Some power? I never . . .' Ionáin stopped then, looking down and drawing a deep breath before looking up again, his eyes blazing now with happiness.

'We have to go tell my parents.' He raced down the steps to embrace his uncle before pulling him away with him.

Left to itself meanwhile, the choir broke apart, too scared and bewildered by Huath's brutal Inquisition to sing again that day. Head down, Éadha began shuffling out with the rest, still shaking from the fright of almost being caught. But then Magret called after her, 'Éadha, can you come here, please? I need another pair of hands to carry these music sheets.'

For a moment Éadha thought about pretending she hadn't heard, but the people around her were already looking at her. There was nothing for it but to turn back. Magret handed her a bundle of music sheets and nodded for her to follow. She crossed the Great Hall, making for a low archway set into the wall underneath the spiral staircase and half hidden in the shadows behind a bust of Ionáin's grandfather. Éadha's steps faltered. Magret was headed into the old tunnel connecting the Great Hall to the West Wing.

Its black mouth had always frightened Éadha, like something lying in wait beneath the stairs, a pit waiting to swallow any who came too close. She'd never been down that tunnel; it'd been closed off since Ionáin's grandfather died. Now she tried to force herself to follow Magret but her feet wouldn't move, as a nameless horror gripped her like the cold air that coiled out from its black, lightless mouth. Magret, though, was unyielding, her face grim as she stepped out, caught Éadha by the arm and dragged her the last few steps into the tunnel.

As they ducked through the opening Éadha saw there were signs of recent passage. The gate was open, dust was stirred up in places and, further in, torches cast an uncertain light. Even in the midst of her fear, she felt a twinge of surprise.

As soon as they were out of sight of the Great Hall Magret turned to Éadha with a furious whisper.

'You stupid child, have you any idea of the danger you were in just now? I warned you not to channel before your Reckoning and not only do you ignore that, but you stand there in the Great Hall, brazen as you like, drawing power from all around you and roaring it to the heavens with the most brutal Channeller in the entire Domhain outside the door. Oh, you little idiot, you're playing with something you've no conception of. Being surrounded by the blind doesn't make you invisible. To those that have eyes for power, everything you do with your gift might as well be written in lines of fire across the sky.'

Éadha's eyes filled with tears, Magret's words reigniting her terror at Huath's Inquisition and the narrowness of her escape. But there was no hint of compassion in Magret's face. 'Come. There's something you must see.'

Taking a torch from its brazier, Magret pulled her the rest of the way down the tunnel and into a room just beyond it. As they stepped in, Éadha realized there were signs of occupation. A lighted candle on a righted table, a water jug, some husks of stale bread, and, along the far wall, people. Four of them in a row, in tattered clothes and bare feet, on stone seats that jutted out from the walls. Two men, two women, all of them slumped as if too exhausted to hold themselves up. Peering in from the doorway, as her eyes adjusted to the dim light, she realized with horror that iron chains bound them to their seats.

'So, child, what do you make of this?' asked Magret, moving to hold her torch over one of the men. His face had caved in, worn to the bone. As the light cast its feeble shadow across him, he stirred weakly, too tired to rouse himself to look back at the woman and the girl staring at him. The other three paid them no heed at all. One of the women was resting her head on the shoulder of the other woman, their eyes closed as if they were asleep, or unconscious, but Éadha saw they were still holding hands, tightly, as if they'd braced together against some violent impact.

'I don't understand,' she replied. 'Who are they?'

'These, my dear, are Fodder. The inevitable end of a path that leads from you sipping power from the threads that link you to your fellow singers and whoever else you've been thieving life from, all the way to this foul place, to these poor husks of what once were men and women. Huath drained them just now for the power to do his Inquisition, after he sensed your little stunt in the choir.'

Éadha was crying now in earnest, but Magret continued in a harsh, angry voice.

'This is your gift, child. Look upon it. To reach out along the silver threads that bind us all and drain the life from the people around you to play lords and ladies. To take their life force to make dancing lights and fine singing. Is the journey from Erisen to Ailm's Keep too long, too tedious? Well then, drain a herder or two, so much more civilized, don't you think, to arrive in time for dinner? Perhaps you grow bored of your castle; why, summon the Fodder, and a Master

Architect will draw from them the towers of your dreams in no time at all.'

Éadha tried to turn and run, but Magret held her in an unyielding grip, fingertips tightening down her arm.

'No, you will see this. You won't just run away to join those pampered idiots on Lambay, all trace of the reality of their power carefully hidden away from them so they drain and play away with no idea, no thought of the consequences of what they do until they're too far gone to ever care.'

'You're hurting me; please, let me go,' begged Éadha.

Magret only turned to face her and said, 'Two nights ago, the cut on my temple, you remember? It wasn't because I stumbled. It was because you drew on my life force for the power to save that animal, and I collapsed. My thread. That was what you drew on.'

This brought Éadha up short. She sagged and would've fallen but for Magret's hold on her, as the full force of her words hit her. 'But I didn't mean . . .'

'Oh, you learn fast. The perfect Channeller answer. They never *mean* to hurt people. All they want is to build a beautiful house, or draw out the crops or create some wonderful illusion. The harm they do is merely an unpleasant by-product, not to be talked of in polite society.' Magret spoke with a controlled rage, eyes blazing as she gestured towards the pathetic heaps before them.

'We have to help these people,' stammered Éadha, desperate to somehow make things right. 'I'll bring food and clothes from the storerooms . . .'

'You'll do no such thing. We'll leave this room now and it'll be as if we were never here.'

'What d'you mean? We can't leave them here in this cold – they might die.'

'You really have no clue of the system you're part of now, do you? You'd be condemning yourself and everyone working in the Keep to suffering far worse than theirs if you lifted a finger to interfere with Lord Huath's Fodder. There's nothing you can do here that wouldn't make things much worse for many more people, people you love. Don't worry; they won't die. Lord Huath needs them to draw power for the Reckoning. They'll be fed and kept alive until then at least and quite possibly afterwards. Huath is well aware of his sister's squeamishness about the realities of channelling.'

Magret drew her out of the room and, stepping carefully, led them both outside, through the rear of the West Wing. The first frost had thawed, uncovering a clear day. Éadha's face was ashen and tear-stained, and she was shivering uncontrollably with a mix of horror and shock. It was almost too much to take in, how this upended everything she thought she knew. About channelling, about Masters, about Families.

They walked unspeaking back to Éadha's cottage, empty at this time of day. The embers of the fire were still warm. Magret stoked it up with logs from the woodpile outside while Éadha went to the rainwater barrel at the side of the house, plunging her head into the icy water. The cold helped to steady her a little. She folded her aunt's cloak round her and sat on the stone fireseat.

Magret's normal calm demeanour had returned, the livid rage revealed in the Fodder Wing hidden once more. Speaking more gently than before, she addressed the silent girl. 'This knowledge is painful, and it's not your fault you didn't know. You grew up with Ionáin here in the Keep without any Channellers, so all you heard was the fairy tale the Families tell their children. Only about the power, its might and its beauty. Not its source.'

'But Béithe and the other older servants, they must've known from before. Why didn't they tell me the truth?' said Éadha.

'Why bring in the darkness?' said Magret simply. 'Old Lord Ailm, Ionáin's grandfather, was a cruel man, and every person in the Keep suffered terribly under him. These last years, while Ionáin's father had no gift, have been a blessed respite. Can you blame them for choosing to forget for a little while and letting you have a childhood unshadowed by dread?'

Éadha tilted her head back against the chimney wall and looked across at the woman opposite. 'And now it's too late. It's only a few days until my Reckoning. My Reckoner will see my gift and I'll be sent to Lambay to train. I'll become a Channeller. I've no choice in this. Why show me those poor people now, when it's too late, when there's nothing I can do?'

'Because you can refuse. Because you've the chance to be something extraordinary, something almost unheard of: a gifted child who escapes the poisonous grasp of the Masters and the seductive enchantment of Lambay.' Magret rose, unable to sit still, eagerness in every line of her stance, holding herself back as if fearful of scaring the girl away, but willing her to heed her words.

'I don't understand. My Reckoning is set. I can't refuse to appear.'

'Yes, but knowing you're gifted, there's a way for you to hide it from your Reckoner. You got part of the way there this morning yourself. I saw how you damped down your power just as Huath reached out to search the choir. It'd be a deeper, stronger concealment than that, but there's just enough time to prepare for it. I can teach you.'

Éadha stared into the fire, at the flames leaping hungrily up along the line of the wood where she and her uncle had split it in the autumn. She wished she could set a fire inside herself, burn away this revulsion. All the joy she'd felt in her gift, the excitement and pride that she'd be Ionáin's saviour, the Keep's protector, ripped down to reveal the dull horror of those dark rooms.

How could something so beautiful, so joyous, be the cause of such pain? The threads that'd filled her with such power – was she to cut them all, for always?

Magret had subsided back into her seat, knowing that to push now was to drive her away. There was a long silence, filled only by the quiet crackle of the flames. Éadha looked up at Magret across the firelight.

'All I've thought since you told me I was gifted was that I could save Ailm's Keep. If Ionáin fails his Reckoning, I could be the Keep Channeller, save his Family, stop Lord Huath from taking over.'

But Magret was already shaking her head. 'It doesn't work like that. If Ionáin fails his Reckoning, then he loses the Keep and he and his father are condemned. You passing your Reckoning wouldn't change that. You don't come from a Family; you've no name. It'd take you years to become a full Channeller, years more before you could earn yourself a Family title and land. Ailm's Keep would be long gone by then, taken over by Huath.'

Looking down at her hands, Éadha fought back tears as her disappointment hardened inside her, like a stone right in her centre. She wouldn't cry again in front of Magret. After another long pause she lifted her head and said, 'Even if I can't save the Keep, you've still no idea what you're asking of me. Sitting there saying I should give up my gift and go back to being a helpless nobody.'

'You're right. I don't have your gift and I don't know what it'd be like to give it up. But it doesn't make me wrong. Stop thinking about what you want, and think about what you know in your heart to be right,' said Magret quietly.

'You said almost. That I'd be something *almost* unheard of. So there've been others? Others like me?'

'Child, you must understand I can't talk to you about this now. If you make it through your Reckoning undetected, then we can talk. But I can say you're not the first to trigger their gift before the Masters reckon them, and so earn themselves this chance to choose the path they take. You wouldn't be alone.'

Éadha stood up, arms wrapped about her, eyes still staring into the fire. Her voice was very small, almost inaudible as she said, 'I will refuse.'

Magret bowed her head then, in thanks, in pity for the straight figure before her, rigid with misery. 'Tomorrow I will teach you concealment. There's just enough time before the Reckonings begin.'

Éadha stayed standing until Magret left. Then with unsteady feet she climbed the stairs to her nest, crept beneath the covers, and cried and cried.

5

SHE SLEPT BADLY THAT night, her head filled with nightmares about the people in the Fodder Wing. Dreams where she knelt pouring energy into the first man to try to revive him, only for a woman lying beside him to begin screaming in pain. She'd turn then to pour power into her until the man began to scream. On and on it went, endlessly round and round as she kept draining one to try to save the other, her ears filled with the sound of their screams.

The next morning, at choir, all the talk was of Huath sensing power in Ionáin. Éadha stood silent in the middle of the chatter, her arms wrapped tightly round her, earning a scolding from Béithe.

'Have you nothing to say? To be gifted is all that boy's wanted since the day he was born. Put out he'll be leaving you behind once he passes his Reckoning, are you? But that was always the way of it.'

Éadha said nothing but felt a warning twinge of worry. It'd been *her* power that Huath sensed yesterday. Magret only said it was Ionáin to deflect Huath before he caught her. But now that lie seemed to be taking on a life of its own.

After rehearsal, Éadha followed Magret once more, and together they headed deep into the forest beyond the Keep, far from any prying eyes. It was a long, chilly walk up to where the trees began to thin at the start of the Steps. They stopped at an open space at the very edge of the treeline, Éadha eyeing Magret warily, half expecting more anger.

Instead, to her surprise, Magret took her hand. 'I'm sorry for yesterday. It's a hard thing to hear and I delayed longer than I should have.'

Éadha thought of the beauty of the little were-lights darting about her room, of flying in the Lady's Well, and knew in her heart she wasn't sorry she'd had that brief chance to know her gift. She said nothing though, and after a short pause Magret went on: 'Tell me how you created your barrier yesterday.' When Éadha explained about the ice sheet, Magret was impressed. 'You did well. A Channeller as strong as Huath would expect to identify anyone using the gift in a heartbeat. You must've shut yourself down very fast.'

'The ice was about to crack when you spoke up.'

'Back in the Channeller wars, it was a prized skill to be able to slip close to an enemy Channeller without being detected. Less so now, with all the Channellers supposedly united through Lambay. It's why these skills aren't taught on Lambay, because to the Masters, any kind of concealment goes against the whole idea of a united Channeller elite. But not all Families approve of the Masters' version of channelling, with its Fodder Holds and its Inquisitions, its brutality and control. And given the Masters' absolute intolerance of dissent, they have a need to be able to conceal their true opinions from Inquisitors. So this knowledge has been preserved in a few places.'

Magret produced a yellowed book from beneath her cloak. 'This text has survived from the time of the Channeller wars. It has some skills in it I daresay even Lord Huath is not familiar with. Things like face-shifts, using illusions to disguise your features and thought-walls to hide your true gift.'

Éadha opened pages stiff with age and dried ink. Images glowed up from the paper, pictures of tiny figures swimming across the page, of wolves poised to spring and, on one page, a fish leaping from the water as it swam upstream.

'These notes were written by Channellers over generations. Power is a difficult thing to convey because every Channeller experiences it differently; some will talk of colours or lights, of swimming through water, while others talk of animals, birds, fish.'

Looking closer, Éadha saw how even the words contained pictures, lovingly drawn in fantastical detail: an eagle whose wings formed the shape of an 'm', a fox peeping between the legs of an 'n'. And everywhere the silver threads, radiating out from figure to figure, hands raised towards each other. There was so much joy, so much love and pride in the gift, that even in her sadness it made her smile.

'In hiding your gift, the trick is to create an illusion of transparency. If you simply build a wall in your mind, your Reckoner will see you're hiding something and use his strength to break it down. You must give the impression he's seeing all of you, while hiding your power as deep inside yourself as there are depths.'

Magret pointed her towards an illustration in the book of a man standing above another man, gripping his head. Inside the seated man was drawn a tapestry, itself woven from even smaller images: hands, faces, trees. From behind the weave a light glowed.

'He's created a wall made of thoughts. Think of the things that fill your mind on a normal day. Family, or chores, then use them to weave a thought-wall, a set of images woven together and placed across the space where your power resides. It needs to be smooth so the Reckoner can't see the join between your actual thoughts and those you're using to hide your power. You use your power to fire the thought-wall into life, so they move and change the way true thoughts flit through our minds.'

'All right,' said Éadha, closing her eyes. 'Here goes nothing.'

In her mind's eye she wove together images of herself out herding, Béithe catching her swiping apples from the pantry. But every time she felt she'd created a reasonable imitation of her mind's normal flow, Magret stepped into her head and shattered it.

As she groaned out loud after yet another failed attempt, Magret said calmly, 'This is a deeply demanding art. The Masters teach us power can only be taken from another because it suits their purposes. But go back a few hundred years when channelling was new in the world, and it was well understood a Channeller could draw small amounts of power from their own life source. Only a spark, for sure, but enough for minor acts like firing a thought-wall. Then again, it's always easier to reach out and snatch fruit growing in another's orchard than it is to grow it in your own.'

She pointed again at the illustration. 'Nothing in these images is without meaning. See how the thoughts in his wall reflect the images around him. He's taken thoughts that are meaningful to him. This opens his heart so the power can flow from it. This is where you must find the power. In your heart; in your belly.'

Bowing her head, Éadha tried again, this time using memories closer to her heart. Drawing the map of Domhain in lessons; Ionáin climbing up the fell on her birthday. Now it was stronger. Magret was right. These thoughts sparked something deep inside her, a pulse of electricity that shot up into her mind to fire her wall. But still Magret was able to break it.

'That's better,' she said, stepping back.

Éadha, though, wanted to scream in frustration. 'How are you able to break it then?'

This time the look in Magret's eyes was sympathetic. 'The thoughts you've chosen, they're precious but they're stained with worry. All I have to do is press it. If you're going to use them you need to find a way to keep the insecurity out.'

The sun was setting when Éadha returned to the cottage, her head aching from a long afternoon of failed thought-walls and the knowledge she'd have to do it all again tomorrow. But when she stepped into the cottage, Ionáin was sitting at the table with her uncle. Grinning widely, he sprang to his feet and hustled her on upstairs to her loft, where he flung himself on to her bed.

She sat in beside him gingerly and Ionáin shifted round so he was looking at her. 'My parents haven't stopped talking since Uncle arrived. He told them if the flare of power he felt was anything to go by, I could be a really gifted Channeller like him, and my Reckoning should just be a formality now.'

He stood again, unable to hold himself still, his eyes shining in the dim light that came up into the loft from below. 'All this time I've been so worried about failing, I've never let myself think what it'd be like to actually pass.'

'How does your uncle think it happened yesterday, the flare?' asked Éadha, and though her voice was steady, inside she was fighting down a growing sense of panic.

'Nobody knows really. I was just watching the choir, worrying about my Reckoning. Huath said sometimes power comes to the surface in moments of stress.'

Listening to Ionáin talk, Éadha felt sick, as it sank in just how much she'd accidentally raised the stakes for him. Magret had only pointed Huath towards Ionáin to cover for her reckless channelling from the other singers in the choir. Now his hopes had been raised, his devastation would be even worse if it turned out he'd no gift. And if he did fail he was on his own, because with her promise to Magret she'd abandoned him. Because she'd promised to do . . . nothing. Even if he failed. Her fantasy of saving the day, of using her power to fight off the Masters if they tried to take Ionáin away to Westport – all nothing now.

Ionáin was still talking. 'They're inviting even more guests now they think it'll go well; they want to make a bigger show of it all.'

Éadha wrapped her arms round her legs, overwhelmed with guilt, but even as she did, Ionáin sat back down beside her.

'I know I said wait until my Reckoning.' He paused, his eyes going to her face, to her mouth, the expression in them darkening as he stared at the curve of her lips, their fullness. Éadha's heart thudded to see the open hunger in those blue eyes now, and an answering longing surged up inside her. Any moment now, he was going to reach out towards her, and it was all she wanted, had wanted since that moment on the fell. For him to come to her, for it to be real. But then she froze, as it hit her that she couldn't. She couldn't let their first real kiss be based on a lie, and so she leaned back out of his reach, her shoulders digging into the wall behind her. Ionáin stiffened.

'Hey, what is it? What's wrong?' He slid off the bed and crouched in front of her, trying to make her look at him. Still she avoided his eyes. 'Is it your own Reckoning? I'm sorry, I've been so focused on mine I keep forgetting you're worrying too.' He rubbed her arm. 'Honestly, though, all we need is for my Reckoning to go as we all hope now. I'll be Lord of the Keep, and I'll be more free to choose who . . .' He flushed bright red.

A sob rose in Éadha's throat. She couldn't let him start making promises to her, not when it was her fault his hopes had been raised like this. When he'd only ever been completely honest with her. Leaning forward, she flung her arms round his neck, forcing him back on to his heels so he'd to grab for the bed frame to stop them both toppling backwards on to the floor. Just so she wouldn't have to keep looking into those trusting eyes, while all the time the words she couldn't say pounded through her mind.

I picked Magret and her secrets over you. I picked hiding my power, over you. And if you fail your Reckoning now, I can't use my power to fight for you, because I've sworn not to channel any more.

Even as she thought this, her mind felt as though her promise to Magret didn't make sense any more. How could it be wrong to want to use her power to fight to protect Ionáin? How could hiding and helplessness be the right answer?

Standing up, she pulled him over to the stairs and back down to where her uncle sat at the kitchen table. There she launched into empty, half-hysterical small talk with the two of them while Ionáin stared, baffled by the change in her. All just to stop him saying something else kind. Something only he'd ever think of saying to her. Because if he did, her fragile promise to Magret would shatter into a million pieces like her failed thought-walls in the woods, and she knew she wouldn't be able to make another one.

6

SPRING RAIN FELL SOFTLY overnight, warming the frozen earth, filling the Keep gardens with the rush of meltwater. The ice on the lake cracked, and inside the Keep, the final preparations began before the sun had even risen above the horizon. Ionáin's Reckoning day had arrived.

Éadha spent the night sleepless, staring up at the ceiling of her loft. After another chilly afternoon in the forest with Magret, she'd finally come by the trick of creating a strong thought-wall. How to fire a small spark from within herself, drawn from belly to heart, using it to power a mental barrier woven of thoughts and memories. Now as she lay in her bed, unable to sleep, she methodically bricked in her power behind a thought-wall, though she could still feel it, her silver fish flickering in the depths of her.

Above her the rain had stopped, and the stars visible through her loft window were beginning to fade. It wasn't long now until sunrise. She pushed herself upright and thought of Ionáin looking out at the same sky. Of all the times she'd woken at this hour in his room over the years, back when she'd been his scáth: his shadow. It started because of the nightmares, the ones that began after a visit from Huath when he was eight years old and his uncle had gleefully explained to his small, worried nephew exactly what was going to happen if he and Dara failed their Reckonings. How the Family's entire fate rested on them passing.

For years after that, barely a night went by without Ionáin waking soaked in sweat and screaming from some nightmare of a failed Reckoning. Of the Masters turning away from him, shaking their heads sternly, of soldiers hammering on the doors of the Keep, come to remove him and his family from their home. Úra, though, had been more focused on caring for Dara, driven by the unspoken belief their firstborn son was the Family's better chance. That they needed him more. So Béithe had made up a small bed for Éadha on the rug in front of Ionáin's fire so at least he wouldn't be alone when he woke screaming in terror. He'd listen for her soft breathing as she lay there by the fireplace and, reassured, drift off to sleep again. On the very worst nights, when sleep deserted him completely, she'd climb in behind him, resting a hand on his back, and together they'd watch the stars fade outside and the sun climb above the horizon. Two small souls, finding a home in each other the rest of the world wasn't inclined to give them.

Éadha's throat caught as she sat there, thinking of him alone in that room now. How lonely, she thought, to know in his bones at the moment of his Reckoning that his Family had never seen him as anything other than a means to an end. Not a person, never even really a boy, only ever their last hope. She knew then she had to go to him. To let him know there was at least one person he mattered to, no matter what happened today.

So she pulled on her cloak, hoisted herself out through the loft window and ran to the oak tree, and climbed up to Ionáin's window where he let her in, to sit on the window ledge and listen to him try to find some bleak humour in it all, while deep inside her power twisted. In rage, in frustration at this self-imposed helplessness, at the impossible price of her vow to Magret. How could she leave this boy she loved more than anyone else on this earth and not *fight* for him with everything she had? And then it was too late. Béithe was there hustling her back out, and then everything seemed to happen in a blur of short, unstoppable moments, each one following the next until there was nothing left for Éadha to do but to take her place in the front row of the choir, her heart already hammering, the blood pounding in her ears as their voices rose in song to begin the ceremony.

To watch as Ionáin, his face drawn but determined and so heartbreakingly beautiful, came down the spiral staircase to stand in front of Master Dathin. To see the hope mixed with terror etched on his face as Dathin gripped either side of his head and he closed his eyes, accepting his fate – and feel in that moment how all the air seemed to go out of the hall, as if every person in the room was holding their breath in desperate anticipation. To be the only one still watching when the frown appeared on Master Dathin's face, as he searched Ionáin's mind and realized he wasn't finding the gift he'd come expecting to see.

To understand, as her heart began hammering in her chest, this was it. That it was happening – the worst thing. Any second now, Dathin was going to drop his hands, shaking his head, and it'd be the end of everything.

And in the end, it wasn't really a choice because, after all, she couldn't, she *couldn't* leave Ionáin there to fail, alone before the world. She could see the thread leading to him, shining in her mind's eye, right in front of her. So, quietly, instinctively, she opened her palm to touch Ionáin's robe in front of her, and she focused on the power buried deep inside her, the molten core of her gift, so that from belly to heart her power surged. But this time, instead of earthing it in a thought-wall as Magret had taught her, she threw open the doors of her heart, urging it on out of her towards Ionáin. Released from behind her wall, her gift flew, rocketing out of her along the link from her palm into Ionáin. She felt it steady him, fill him. She poured all of her love, all of their shared life into him and saw Master Dathin's head shoot up then in astonishment before he dropped his hands to his sides and turned, beaming, to the assembled crowd to shout the formal words of finding.

'Rejoice, all of you! For the gift is with this young man. May all his days be filled with power, and may all who hear this give of their strength freely that his power might be great, to the glory of his days and of Domhain!'

An enormous cheer rose through the Great Hall, resounding to the domed ceiling above while Magret swept the choir into the Song of Rejoicing.

Éadha meanwhile had dropped her link to Ionáin as soon as the Master's head went up. And if anyone had been watching her, they'd have seen her eyes widen in shock as she stared down at her empty palm. They'd have seen her voice fail so she could only mouth along the words as her mind caught up with what her heart had chosen. As it hit her what she'd just done, what she could never now undo.

But no one was watching, and no one saw Éadha's shock, because every eye in the place was on the golden-haired boy radiant with relief. As Éadha watched, Ionáin's parents stepped forward, kissing him on each cheek, followed by members of the wider Family.

Then Master Dathin formally summoned Ionáin to Lambay. 'Ionáin, of the Family Ailm. You have been reckoned and found gifted. In the name of the Masters of Lambay, upon whose authority I speak, I hereby requisition you as one gifted in the ways of channelling, to report to Lambay soonest, there to be trained in its arts.'

As she watched with growing horror, while Master Dathin told the world Ionáin was gifted, all Éadha could think was that it'd been such a small thing, what she'd done. A reaching-out to her friend. But now even as she watched, it was growing huge. Bigger than her, bigger than Ionáin, her little lie becoming fact, the foundation stone for a new reality where everyone believed Ionáin was gifted and the Keep was saved. It was all going too fast, and she wanted to scream to them all, 'Stop!' but in the same moment she couldn't. The word wouldn't come. She couldn't do it, not in front of them all like this, exposing Ionáin, exposing herself. It was all going too fast; she needed to think; she couldn't think, there in the heart of it all as the choir sang and the crowd cheered.

The formal words spoken, the festivities could finally begin. In front of her Éadha saw Ionáin's mother directing him towards the long line of guests pressing forward to congratulate him, each one to be greeted and thanked. Meanwhile she stood invisible in the choir as it sang on, songs of praise and thanksgiving. Nothing about ending or regret, she thought, no gesture towards the innocence soon to be lost in the brutality hidden at the heart of the Channellers' art. It was only and all about the power, the getting and the glory of it.

At the entrance to the West Wing Master Dathin's Keeper took up position beside Treasa, the two women nodding coolly to each other before concentrating on their Channeller's calls. So began a display of the Channeller's art as hadn't been seen in the Keep in a generation, as Dathin and Huath each sought, genially and with impeccable manners, to outdo the other. Children were lifted and swept up to the ceiling, shrieking in terrified delight. Rainbows arced from one end of the Great Hall to the other, only to dissolve into multicoloured raindrops that evaporated before they could touch the elegant outfits of the guests below. Images of dragons were chased by hunters across the ceiling; fragile snowdrops opened their petals at the guests' feet.

At last, the songs were done and Éadha released. Seeing this, Ionáin came rushing over, catching her up in an enormous bear hug and twirling her round. In all their life together she'd never seen Ionáin as he was in that moment: blazing with such relief and happiness he seemed to shine. Setting her down, his arms tightened round her, one hand flattening into the small of her back so she was pressed against him as he whispered in her ear, 'I want to kiss you so much right now,' and Éadha felt a shiver go through her body at the hunger in his voice, the brush of his lips against her ear. He pulled back and looked her in the eyes, his own so endlessly blue in the golden were-light. 'You'll wait for me? When I'm away in Lambay? Everyone says the time goes quickly; two years and a few dragons, then I'll be home again . . .'

This was her chance, there in the still centre of the Great Hall. She could see it almost as if it were happening, as if she'd split in two, and one part of her was taking him by the arm and leading him out into the courtyard. Out there it'd be chilly and quiet, just the two of them alone together. She'd look into his eyes and tell him what really happened in those flashing moments up there on the dais. How her power had flowed into him so just for that moment, her gift became his gift and then Master Dathin declared him a Channeller. But there the vision stopped, and her heart failed her. Even in her mind's eye she couldn't do it. Couldn't make herself picture the joy on his face dying as she told him that in the very crisis of his life she'd made a lie of him, of who he was.

So, after all, she didn't speak, there in the still centre of the crowd, only hugging him back instead. The next instant Ionáin was gone, swept away on a wave of well-wishers cheering his gift and his name.

7

AFTER IONÁIN WAS PULLED away from her, Éadha stood for a moment, then turned and began pushing her way through the tightly packed crowd. It was all too much: the relentless noise, the swirling lights, the ceaseless cheering from the hundred or so noble guests in the Great Hall. She couldn't think; she needed to think. Pushing and straining, she managed to reach the dragonglass tunnel, stumbling and almost falling as she finally broke free of the crowd. On down the tunnel and into the kitchen she fled.

'Hush now, we always knew this time'd come to an end,' Béithe was saying to one of the maidservants. The girl's eyes were red, as if she'd been weeping. 'At least it's not Lord Huath. And we'll endure as we always have, Sister save us.'

'Sister save us,' came the quiet reply, and something in the way they spoke caught at Éadha even as she hurried past, almost like they were praying. But there was no time to wonder what it might mean, and she kept going, on out into the night air.

It was as cold and quiet as she'd imagined when she'd stood in Ionáin's arms, the shock of the night's chill enveloping her, but she was alone beneath the silent sky. Inside, her mind was filling with panicky images: of Ionáin travelling to Lambay, being surrounded by grey-robed Masters asking him to use the gift they all thought he had. Of the look on Ionáin's face when he failed. Stumbling a little, she forced herself into a run, as if she could outrun her thoughts. On out of the courtyard, into the gardens, past the silvered yews and the moon-shadowed lake until she reached the oak tree. Now she could no longer hear the sound of the party; it was only herself beneath the oak branches. Sitting with her back against the trunk, she forced herself to breathe. In, out, while her heart rate gradually slowed and her mind went back to the flashing moment on the dais when she'd unleashed all that pent-up power and sent it pouring into Ionáin. And even in the heart of her shame she still felt the subterranean joy of it, the sense of release when she'd reached inside herself as Magret had taught her. But what she'd found hadn't been the weak, fragile spark Magret had spoken of. It'd been something far greater, as if, in her desperation, she'd uncovered instead a great hidden well of power fathoms deep inside her.

Staring down at her hands, she tried to focus, reaching inside herself to try to find again that secret well of power. But her gift made a liar of her as her hand remained stubbornly empty while she tried and she failed, and failed again, to come by the trick of it, to find again the door to power she'd opened in her heart.

Forcing down a mounting sense of panic and frustration, she tilted her head back and stared up through the still-bare oak branches, at the Sídhe burning brightly far above her. She remembered how, when they were little, she and Ionáin used to plan their great adventures across the Steps and into the Blackstairs. How they'd navigate their way by those same stars that shone above her now. He was her heart, she thought. He'd always been her heart, and it was his need that'd let her find that well of power inside her. Closing her eyes, she focused once more, this time though on the sense of absolute need she'd felt in that moment on the stage. And then there – there it was. In front of her, on her outstretched palm, a tiny were-light flaring into life. A light drawn not from any thread but from inside herself. She'd found it, the way back down to draw on her own heart's strength.

She opened her eyes and stared for a long time at the little light, bobbing and dancing on her palm, bowing to its sister stars above. And she knew, now, what she had to do.

'Let all those who have passed the age of seventeen come forward for their Reckoning.'

It was almost noon of the following day. Lord Huath sat in a red velvet cloak and leather gloves in the centre of the muddy village square, the cloak's gold lining gleaming in watery sunshine just breaking through after early-morning rain.

In front of him stood a group of ten seventeen-year-olds, Éadha among them. They were mostly from the village, with a couple like her, from the Keep. She was the youngest. She knew them all to see, though she wasn't close to any of them. Ionáin and her own company had been all she'd ever looked for.

She hadn't slept all night and was glassy-eyed with exhaustion, but as she stood there waiting for her turn she felt no fear, only calm certainty. It was, she thought, like preparing a house before visitors arrive. Hiding away all your private things, arranging it carefully to give the right impression. Inside her mind, just as Magret had taught her, she'd packed away all thoughts of her full channelling gift, behind a thought-wall woven of her memories and fired by her own heart's will.

Glancing across the square she saw Magret standing with Lord Huath's party. Treasa, Huath's Keeper, stood beside her. But there was no sign of Ionáin. A chill wormed its way into Éadha's thoughts. This wasn't like him, not to come and support her. Surely he'd come riding up at the last moment. But he didn't come, and now it was too late, as Huath began the Reckonings.

He kept his gloves on, raising his hands with a bored expression as each young person was presented to him. Each of them flinched with shock when he stepped into their minds, some starting to cry and others trying to squirm free. Each time, after a moment's focus, he waved them away. The square was so still, the nervous coughing and shuffling of those still waiting could be clearly heard, while from outside the square, birdsong flowed into the silence. It was almost Éadha's turn. She saw Magret push her way to the front of the group for a clear line of sight.

Now it was her turn. She stepped forward and saw recognition in Huath's eyes. 'You live with my sister's seamstress, yes? Ionáin's little playmate?'

'Yes, Lord Huath, may it please you,' came her dutiful reply, keeping her eyes low and her voice monotonous. Even so she sensed a flicker of something, some straightening as if Huath was bringing his energies into full focus. Éadha braced herself, and there he was, stepping fast and hard into her head. This was no cursory examination. Huath was far, far stronger than Magret, the scale of his power almost enough to unbalance her. But she steadied herself, and there it was, so carefully laid out right in the centre of her mind for Huath to find. Just enough of her gift and not too much. She could feel Huath weighing it, then for just a moment she felt him pull back and sweep all through her mind, but she'd prepared for this and held steady. He flickered across the careful domesticity of her thought-wall, with its images of milking goats and (*nice touch*, she thought) her humble awe at his power on Reckoning Day. As quickly he was gone, out of her mind, dropping his hands. She allowed herself the tiniest release of breath as he called across to his party.

'Treasa, it seems we've not entirely wasted our morning here. We've one of your kind here, a Keeper. Not bad strength either.' Huath glanced down at Éadha. 'Well, girl, it seems you'll remain at my nephew's side a while longer. Congratulations. In the name of the Masters of Lambay, I hereby requisition you as one gifted in Keeping, to report to Lambay to be trained as a Keeper and assigned to a Channeller, fate willing. Report to Lord Ailm's quartermaster at the Keep; he'll provide you with a mount. We depart for Lambay in the morning.'

She turned to face the crowd. She'd been the last to be tested, and people had already begun to disperse. She saw them standing in knots on the edge of the square and looking back from up the lanes as word spread outwards that Lord Huath had declared her a Keeper. She didn't know what reaction she'd expected, but it hadn't been this. Muted, serious men and women she'd known all her life looking at her and then looking away. As Huath rejoined his party, Éadha was left standing alone in the centre of the square until at last Magret came over and embraced her carefully, like some fragile thing that might break if she was roughly handled.

'You did your best, child. Don't blame yourself. Huath was just too powerful. At least he didn't find your full gift. He believes you're only a Keeper,' Magret whispered quickly in her ear before turning to Lord Huath.

'My lord, if I might. I'll bring her home and ensure she's readied for the journey.'

Huath nodded in Magret's direction, already losing interest. 'See that you do.'

PART II

Lambay, First Island

8

SHORTLY AFTER DAWN THE next morning, Éadha made her way over the lake-bridge to the Keep courtyard. Her satchel was slung across her chest, with Magret's book and Ionáin's amber tower inside, along with a change of clothes.

When she'd come down from her loft, her aunt and uncle had been standing in the middle of the kitchen, their faces full of wordless grief, and as she embraced them, her aunt had whispered in her ear,

'Just . . . try to stay yourself. In that place.'

Éadha's heart had caught at her then, at the courage it took to say those few words. Catching her aunt's hand, she'd replied, 'It won't change me, I promise you. And when I'm back everything will be better, because Ionáin will be Lord and I'll be his Keeper.'

For this was her great plan, conceived as she sat beneath the oak tree and called up a were-light with her own heart's power. To make a kind of truth of her accidental lie, by following Ionáin to Lambay and supplying him with her heart's strength. To be his Keeper, and in the process lend him her ability and with it her own life force so he wouldn't have to draw on Fodder. To have everyone, even Ionáin, go on believing he was gifted. He'd save Ailm's Keep by becoming its Channeller, and stop Huath from taking over. And she'd never have to tell him how, in his moment of Reckoning, she'd made a lie of his life. She'd never have to face that.

As she reached the courtyard, she saw it was already full of horses and people. Their party were fifteen in all – Ionáin, Huath, his guardsmen, Treasa and several Keep men. Magret was to ride with them as far as Erisen. The Keep men would stay with them through the Blackstairs then turn back. Although the winter snows had melted, the way was still difficult this early in the spring. Packs of wolves and solitary bears roamed the foothills, hungry after the long winter, while dragons sometimes flew through the high passes.

In the middle of all the hubbub was Ionáin. His parents were embracing him, his father stern-faced, his mother in tears. He was in high spirits, laughing and joking, coaxing a smile out of his mother, reassuring his father before swinging up on to his horse and urging it into a canter. Slipping into the crowd unnoticed, Éadha was gripped by a sudden terror. It was one thing to make tiny were-lights that sat in her palm, another thing entirely to send her power into Ionáin every day under the eyes of the Masters. What if Ionáin was exposed, or she was caught? But even as she thought this, Ionáin's horse came around and he saw her standing there.

His face lit up. 'Hey, sleepy-head. Good of you to join us,' he called, grinning.

And it was his old grin, the one that threw open every door in her heart. It was as if he'd heard her question and sent his answer flashing back to her across the courtyard. She wouldn't fail. Their bond was too strong. It was why she'd been able to send her power into him at his Reckoning. That hadn't changed. It'd never change.

With a whoop Ionáin urged his horse into a gallop, on out of the yard. Huath nodded to the rest of the party to follow, calling back over his shoulder, 'Don't worry, sister, I'll make sure he arrives safely.'

That first day they made good time, climbing steadily. Luck was with them as the Steps were little damaged by the winter storms. They paused below the crest of the first peak for one last look back at Ailm's Keep. Only the North Tower could be seen, spearing above the surrounding forests. To the east the sea glittered in fleeting sunlight, choppy with white tops racing wave after wave to the shore before the hard spring winds. They turned and descended into the stony valley below.

Ionáin rode with his uncle at the head of the party, while Éadha and Magret were near the back. Bringing up the rear was a windowless, iron-bound wagon, its wooden wheels juddering along the steep paths.

'Huath's Fodder wagon,' said Magret quietly, seeing Éadha glance back at it. 'Bringing those people you saw back to Erisen. They won't take those wretches out while young Ionáin is here. Too much of a shock. You'll see when you get to First House. For the Masters it's all about the Stages. Corrupt them first, before they ever see the people they drain.'

Magret had been gentle with her, as they had walked together back to the Keep after her Reckoning. 'You did your best. Huath was just too strong. You did well to have him think you're only a Keeper. Take comfort in that, and if you work at your craft, you may be able to shield the Fodder a little from the really savage Channellers.'

Now Éadha was marked for the Masters, though, Magret spoke little to her. As they rode through the mountains side by side, Éadha ached to question her. Maybe she'd understand this new strength, how she'd been able to send it into Ionáin. But that'd mean telling her Ionáin was powerless, and that secret couldn't be spoken out loud to any living soul, not if she was to keep him safe. So she stayed silent.

That night they camped under a rocky out-hang deep in the mountains. It was bitterly cold. Éadha lay beside Magret, and under cover of her blanket tried to return the little book of drawings Magret had given her in the forest. But Magret wouldn't take it.

Propping herself up on her wiry forearms, her short white hair just catching the firelight, she whispered, 'Your need is far greater than mine, child. Don't underestimate the danger you face bringing your gift to that place, the very heart of their power. Their whole system rests on controlling every Channeller and every Keeper. If they ever find out you're hiding a Channeller gift from them, there's no saying what they'll do to you.' She paused, her expression darkening as she gripped Éadha's forearm with one hard hand. 'And even if they don't, it'll still take every bit of your strength to resist the lure of their seduction. Keep the book with you, and when next we ride together, give it to me then.'

★

The next morning, cloud blanketed the mountains as they set off, the only sounds the occasional clink of sword against sheath and the rumbling of wagon wheels over stony ground. At about mid-morning they reached the highest point of the Steps and Lord Huath called a brief halt. Magret sent Éadha to refill their water bottles, pointing her towards a ridge.

The clouds had lifted off the Blackstairs as they rode, and retreated to the sky. Now Éadha scrambled up over the ridge to where a lake lay utterly still, a shard of sky fallen into the mountain. She crouched down by the water's edge, unwilling to disturb its perfect smoothness.

With a quick glance to make sure no one was watching, she closed her eyes and pulled gently on the thread she could feel all the time now, running from belly to heart, using it to call up a miniature were-light in her hand and feeling a start of joy at seeing her power respond. It was quicker than when she'd channelled strength from others, because now she was drawing only on her own strength. Staring at the dancing flame, she itched to try it out properly. Could she make a fireball, or lift off the ground and fly, like a Channeller? But she knew it was far too risky with Huath so close by, and so instead, turning her hand palm down, she held the little light out over the water to see its reflection, smiling as the mirrored flames bowed to each other.

The next moment her were-light flickered and was almost snuffed out by a down draught of air.

A shadow passed above her head. Long and sinuous, the dragon spread its wings to their fullest extent as it glided low across the lake, bending its neck to drink from the icy waters as it flew, then raising its head again, drops glittering on its scales. Its wings beat the water once as it climbed from the surface, sending waves racing to Éadha's feet where she crouched at the water's edge, watching its flight in disbelief.

She'd never seen a dragon this close. When they crossed the sky above Ailm's Keep they always flew far above them all, so high they seemed no bigger than eagles. But the dragon gliding away from her above the surface of the lake was fifty feet or more in length, more again from wing tip to wing tip, and as it flew the reflected sunlight seemed to ripple across its scales like a silver flame.

She rose to her feet, the tiny were-light still dancing on the palm of her hand. She knew from all the stories she should feel petrified but all she could think, with a kind of savage joy, was she'd never seen anything more glorious. And deep inside her power surged, as if it was urging her to fly up after it, alongside it, like she used to in her dreams.

As she watched, the dragon reached the far end of the lake. But instead of flying on out across the mountains, with a single tilt of its wings it curved about and came flying swift as thought to where Éadha stood. With impossible grace it reared up to its full length, holding itself steady in the air to stare down at the tiny figure below it, the were-light still cupped in her hand.

For a long, stretched moment there was silence as the dragon stared at the girl and the girl stared up at the dragon.

'*Mahera*,' the dragon hissed then, as its wings beat down, once, twice, flashing, almost transparent in the sunlight.

From inside Éadha there came a galvanic kick, as her own power lit up inside her in recognition, and she would've bowed to the great beast, but already from behind her there were guards' voices shouting, 'Get down! Get down!'

With a sweep of its wings the dragon immediately shot upward, wheeling about as it rose. Clenching her fist, Éadha killed her were-light with a thought.

As it flew up, Lord Huath's guards came racing over the top of the ridge and scrambled down to the water's edge, readying their bows. Lord Huath appeared at a run behind them and laid his hands on their arrows, power flowing from him until they glowed red and shot high into the blue sky, bulleting after the disappearing shape of the dragon. But the dragon was already away, shooting up and over the next peak, lost from sight. Lord Huath cursed, grabbing a bow and loosing one last arrow straight up into the sky so it plummeted into the lake, the waters bubbling and hissing with the heat of its passage.

'Did you see? The bitch was heavy; she must be due soon. We'll have to send a hunting party,' he shouted.

There was a new urgency now as they began their descent. Huath had to stay with the party while they were still in the mountains, but as soon as they reached the relative safety of the foothills, he and Treasa galloped on ahead to Erisen to assemble a full hunting party to try to kill the she-dragon before she could hatch her brood. He was in his element, a fierce joy in him now the hunt was on for the she-dragon. All Channellers spent at least a year on the western borders after they'd won their staff on Lambay, patrolling for dragons, raiding out on to the islands to keep their numbers down. It was difficult, dangerous work, for the dragons were cunning and ferocious, savage fighters when defending their colonies. Huath had stayed on in Westport for years and tales of his skill and ruthlessness as a hunter were legion.

With Huath gone, the mood in the group relaxed. They made good time, striking camp in the early evening, and as they were preparing to turn in, Ionáin picked up his bedroll and crossed over to Éadha and Magret's side of the campfire.

'Do you mind?' he said to Magret with a smile, nodding back to where the guardsmen were already settled into their bedrolls. 'Everyone's getting a little ripe on that side after a few days' riding.'

'Of course, my lord,' said Magret, her tone polite if a little wary. Ionáin dropped his bedroll to the right of Éadha. It was the first time he'd been this close to her since the party in the Great Hall after his Reckoning. But even though he hadn't been near her, she'd still felt connected to him ever since that moment on the dais when she'd given him her power. Now, as he sat down beside her, she had the sense of everything being doubled: a kind of shadow bond beyond sight, mirroring the real, physical awareness of him. He was still dressed in his riding leathers, the narrow-fitting pants tucked into his riding boots and his cloak pulled round him as he stretched his hands out towards the campfire.

Glancing across at her as he sat down, he said with a grin, 'You look very calm for someone who was only just saved from being incinerated by a dragon earlier.'

Éadha gave a small laugh before saying with a shake of her head, 'She wasn't going to hurt me.'

'What was it like?' Ionáin said, and then more quietly, 'Truly?'

She looked across at him, and in the same quiet voice said, 'She was beautiful. They leave that part out of all the stories. How beautiful they are.'

In her mind she saw once more the sunlight glittering on the dragon's scales as it dipped its head into the lake, and heard the single word it had called her as it reared up. *Mahera*. No one had ever told her dragons could speak.

'I'm sorry I missed your Reckoning,' said Ionáin then. 'I was all set to go, but Mother said I shouldn't be hanging about down in the village now I'm going to be a Channeller. I didn't want to fight with her when I was leaving so soon.'

Éadha looked at him. 'It's fine – don't worry.'

'What was it like being reckoned by Huath?'

'Very strong,' said Éadha, 'but, after all, it's only a keeping gift. It didn't take him long to see it.'

Ionáin frowned. 'Don't say "only". I know it isn't as strong as a Channeller's – as my – gift, but you know how rare it is to have power at all outside the Families. And it means we might even be paired together with you as my Keeper. Like Erisen and Bríd.'

Éadha's heart thudded but she kept her voice light as she

replied, 'If I remember rightly, Bríd sacrificed her life for Erisen in the final battle with the dragon, Kaanesien. I wasn't planning on dying for you.'

Ionáin laughed. 'Hmm. I'll have to tell the Head Keeper. "Keeper has attitude problem: lacks willingness to die for me."'

Éadha tilted her head back and laughed up at the star-filled sky, loud enough that one of the sleeping guards opposite stirred drowsily before turning over. She hadn't realized how much she'd needed this, the normality of Ionáin teasing her. He grinned before going on.

'Seriously though, Éadha, it's going to be so much fun from everything Huath's told me. Giant halls just for creating illusions, combat yards and handball alleys for training, these huge studios where we'll channel buildings out of stone, greenhouses where we'll learn to channel every kind of fruit and plant there's ever been. I'll be flying within the year, actually flying, can you believe that? Huath said Second Island's wilder than anything I can imagine, though Mother shushed him, saying we have to respect the Stages.'

As he finished, Magret, who'd been sitting quietly listening to their chat, climbed to her feet. 'I'll fetch our bedrolls,' she said to Éadha. 'We should turn in soon.' And she headed over to where their horses were tethered for the night, on the other side of the rocks their party was sheltering against. Across the campfire, the guardsmen were all asleep already.

Left to themselves, the silence between Éadha and Ionáin deepened, becoming charged, as they both stared into the flames. At the same time, Éadha sensed the silver thread binding her to Ionáin grow taut, glimmering with the reflected intensity between them now. After a little Ionáin said quietly,

'I've always wanted this. More than anything. To be of use. Save my Family.'

Éadha nodded, staring straight ahead.

Ionáin shifted round to look directly at her, lifting his hand to catch her cheek and turn her face to look at him. In the firelight, his eyes were dark and his cheekbones shadowed as he studied her. 'What I'm trying to say is I've always known I have to serve my Family. But you are mine.'

Éadha felt her breathing grow shallow as his eyes roved over her face. There was a fierceness and a clarity to him she'd never seen before. She could feel it in the roughness of his fingertips where they pressed into the hollow of her cheek, holding her there even though there was nowhere else she wanted to be.

'Everything else of me they get. Everything but this. You. You are my one thing.'

With soft but irresistible pressure, his hand pulled her even closer, tilting her face up towards his so she felt his breath on her lips before his mouth descended on hers. It was their first real kiss, and it had all the pent-up urgency of all the days since the fell, of the longing that'd built inside them since then. Ionáin's mouth on hers now was hard, demanding, full of an urgent desire as his lips crushed hers, claiming her in the few moments they had before Magret returned. Her lips parted beneath his, kissing him back fiercely, and there was between them the same jolt as when their lips first touched on the fell, only this time they were ready for it: hungry for it. At the same time, in her mind's eye, Éadha could feel the silver thread between them thrumming with the intensity of their connection, filling her head until she almost couldn't think, couldn't feel anything but this moment.

And the sweetness of it, of finally letting go, letting themselves just feel, and touch each other, quickly deepened, became something more intense. As if the release of all that longing had only triggered another, deeper hunger inside them. Ionáin leaned closer, his hand sliding behind her head to hold the nape of her neck, burrowing his fingers into her heavy curls, gripping them softly and pressing her closer. Éadha's hands came up in turn to hold his face, glorying in finally being able to touch him. Feeling the angular planes of his cheekbones under her fingers, her thumb stroking the softness around his mouth as he kissed her deeper and deeper still. Desire roared up inside her, fierce and bright, like the sun flashing on the dragon's wings earlier.

But from behind them came the sound of Magret's footsteps, crunching across the stony soil. Immediately they released each other, turning back to sit facing the fire as Magret reached them, though Ionáin left his hand by his side so he was just touching her fingers where they rested on the ground, out of Magret's sight.

Crouching, Magret began unrolling her bedding on the other side of Éadha. Taking the hint, Ionáin climbed to his feet to move a polite distance away from the two women. Éadha could still see him in the glow of the embers as he lay down, his forearm resting across his forehead as he stared up at the sky.

She lay back herself, unable to sleep, her body still flushed and restless as she stared up at the stars too, and listened out for the sound of Ionáin's soft breathing, so close by and yet just out of reach.

She was riding into the heart of the great lie that channelling was built on. A lie of power without price. And into that big lie she was bringing her own smaller lie: that the beautiful boy she'd loved her whole life was powerful too.

But in return for that lie, she was sleeping alongside Ionáin beneath the stars, she'd crossed the Blackstairs' icy peaks, and a dragon had spoken to her beside a shining lake. That was enough and more than enough for now.

9

THE EAST WIND WHIPPED the waves into white tops that curled and collapsed at their feet as Éadha and Ionáin stood, staring out to Lambay First Island. Magret had left their party earlier that morning as they passed the gates of Erisen, while Huath's guards sat on their mounts behind them on the sand, waiting until they crossed to First Island before they departed.

The island's shoreline was densely wooded, the only sign of human habitation a narrow stone dock directly opposite where they stood. As they watched, a grey figure appeared. He walked up to the water's edge holding a yew staff out in front of him, and after a few moments, there came the massive, grinding sound of tonnes of rocks lifting themselves from the seabed to form a slender stone walkway running from shore to dock. Water poured off the rocks as they settled inches above the waves.

From behind them a deep voice spoke. 'Come along. The way won't stay raised long.'

It was a second man, also wrapped in Master's grey, riding up to them on a silver cob, followed by three other riders.

All three looked about seventeen, but there was no time for introductions as the Master was urging them to keep going, on to the land-bridge. Ionáin and Éadha swung up on to their horses to follow them, picking their way gingerly across the stones, which were slick and slippery. Éadha's mount was nervous, whinnying as waves splashed across the path and hit her legs, and it was a relief when they reached the dock, where Ionáin leaned in and whispered, nodding towards the man who'd raised the land-bridge, 'That's Master Irial. Uncle Huath told me he always meets the new apprentices. He used to be in charge of Westport postings until he got badly burned saving a Keeper from a dragon.'

'Welcome, apprentices,' said the Master in a clear, ringing voice. 'I'm Irial, and this is Master Odhran. You're the last of the new class to arrive. Now, come.'

With that, he swung up on to his own mount, and led them on to a curving path that climbed steeply away from the jetty, up under the trees with Master Odhran following them. Éadha thought she glimpsed a wagon similar to Huath's Fodder wagon behind some bushes, but it didn't follow them. As they rode, the roar of wind and waves faded. It was so quiet she could hear birdsong and the muffled clop of hooves on the matted forest floor. Here and there they saw the remains of fantastical buildings half fallen in, branches threaded through what once were windows, roots snaking down crumbling stairs.

After a short climb they reached the end of the treeline, where the ground fell away beneath them into a deep half-valley that flowed out into a sandy bay. On either side, forest stretched down to the sea, while before them a carpet of grass unrolled down the hillside to fetch up against the walls of First House, cupped in the valley and facing away from them out to sea.

On their ride across Cooley Plains, Ionáin had told her how First House was channelled originally by Erisen the First Channeller, before being made over to the Masters as a training school in the shattered years after the Channeller wars. A hulking grey building raised to withstand winter storms, it formed a long rectangle with narrow outstretched wings at either end, creating a sheltered space between the House and the valley side. Nestled there Éadha could see south-facing greenhouses, while at the northern end, still deep in shadow, were handball alleys and battle-yards for combat training.

Staring down at its great grey walls, Éadha felt her stomach clench in fear. This wasn't a place to be bargained with or withheld from. In its terrible strength it demanded her soul. She wanted to turn and run, back through the forest, across the land-bridge and not stop running until she was back in her aunt and uncle's cottage, sitting by the fire, listening to them weaving a day from small deeds and unwavering love.

Then Ionáin's voice broke into her thoughts and with it her reason for being there, on a windy hillside, with the might of Domhain's Channellers assembled below her.

'Come on,' he called over his shoulder, as he urged his horse into a canter. 'Time enough for daydreaming of epic victories when we've settled in.'

With a nudge Éadha sent her horse down the hill after him. A little later they arrived through a stone archway into a stable yard where groomsmen took their mounts, and the two Masters led them on into First House. Inside it was unexpectedly bright and warm. Circular light wells pierced the ceilings to make alternating pools of light and dark; candles flickered in bell jars set in recesses along the walls. A long corridor opened out into a round central hall, panelled in oak and topped by a dragonglass dome. It was already almost full of people, a mix of grey-robed Masters and new apprentices.

Log fires burned in enormous slate fireplaces set at intervals along the walls, while above them were-lights circled just below the dome. Food was set out on rosewood tables in the centre. Piles of freshly channelled strawberries and soft purple plums, warm bread with mounds of butter, hot chocolate drinks steaming in silver cups. Éadha had to resist the urge to gawp. Apart from Ionáin's Reckoning, she'd never seen so much food. Beside her, she saw Ionáin's eyes widen too before he checked himself to say only, 'Not bad,' before stepping into the room. Following more slowly, Éadha picked up a cup of fragrant hot chocolate. As she did, someone called Ionáin's name. It was a lanky, dark-haired young man dressed in navy pants and a sheepskin cloak. His long hair was tightly tied back, which only made his narrow face appear more angular, all sharp edges. Alongside him stood a girl, strikingly similar in looks and almost as tall, dressed in hunting gear.

'Hey there, we heard about your Reckoning; it's all anyone is talking about. Is it true you almost knocked Master Dathin over, your power flare was so strong?' said the young man, grinning at Ionáin.

'Éadha, this is Coll and his sister, Linn, of the Manon Family. Our grandparents were apprentices here together,' said Ionáin, who'd gone bright red. 'And they should know better than to listen to gossip. Of course I didn't knock Master Dathin over. I was just glad to pass.'

Another voice broke in. 'Well now, if it isn't the most exotic and wonderful twins. I bow before your mighty power, my lord and lady.'

The speaker was large, florid and fair-haired. Even at seventeen the big man he'd become was evident in his thick neck and broad shoulders. He was dressed in furs and sweating already in the warm room. 'Good to see you too.' He nodded to Ionáin. 'Family back from the brink, eh?'

His eyes flickered restlessly about the room to the other new arrivals, already beginning to coalesce into small groups of twos and threes, before coming back to rest on Éadha.

'Well, well, could it be we've another girl Channeller, Ionáin?'

'Don't be daft, Senan. This is Éadha; she's a Keeper and we're all very proud of her,' said Ionáin. Éadha said nothing.

'Strange,' said Senan. 'I thought I sensed something.'

Éadha tensed, suddenly petrified she'd let her thought-wall slip. But Senan had already lost interest. 'Never mind. It must've been someone else. There's so much power sloshing around this place, it's hard to read it.'

'... thirty-seven, thirty-eight,' Coll was counting quietly under his breath. 'I'd say forty all in as there are bound to be stragglers,' he said, before turning to Ionáin and smiling.

'The Masters must've been mightily relieved when Ailm's Keep came good at the last moment with a Channeller and a Keeper. Makes the numbers a little less dire this year.'

Ionáin grinned. 'As if it was ever in doubt. Good hearty stock, us northerners.'

'My, and don't you bounce back quickly too,' drawled Senan. 'It's as if you were never away. But my cousin's class ten years ago had twenty-five Channellers. What do we have – fifteen, and the rest just Keepers?'

At that moment Coll caught Ionáin's arm to point him towards another apprentice, and as he turned away, Senan stepped in a little closer to Éadha, murmuring, 'We might need to start thinking about allocating more than one Keeper girl to a Channeller to get the birth rate up, eh, little Miss Not-Channeller?'

Éadha stared at him in confusion. Senan, though, just raised an eyebrow at her before drifting off across the room, helping himself to fruit and nonchalantly greeting other students. She was left standing unnoticed while Ionáin chatted and laughed with Coll and some other apprentices. Watching him, all Éadha could think was how this place *fitted* him, like he'd pulled on a coat made specially for him.

Seeing her standing alone, Linn stepped a little to one side of the Channeller group and said quietly, in a kind voice, 'Don't mind Senan. He can be a little direct. I know it's all very hierarchical here, but I still think you're lucky to be a Keeper. I doubt I'll be so much as allowed outside on a wet day; you'll have much more freedom.'

'Why wouldn't you be allowed outside?' asked Éadha.

'Linn's a Channeller,' said her brother Coll, seeing the two of them talking. 'The first girl Channeller for five years. She's worried she's going to be wrapped up in cotton wool until the Masters have married her off to some nice Channeller boy to make lovely Channeller babies. Isn't that right?'

Linn rolled her eyes at her brother. 'Once I can use my power, I'd like to see them try.'

'Hey, Ionáin, looks like Ailbhe's on her way. Seems we're not the only ones to hear about your oh-so strong Reckoning,' Coll muttered. Looking around, Éadha saw an exceptionally pretty girl heading for them from the other end of the Round Hall, a bright smile on her face. She was richly dressed in a travelling habit, her brown hair caught up in a filigree net that reflected the were-lights above them.

'But I thought she and Gry . . .' said Ionáin, looking suddenly disconcerted.

'Didn't you hear? Mr First Family only managed to pass as a Keeper. I'd almost prefer to have failed completely. The Family are trying to put a brave face on it, but there's something humiliating about being quite so mediocre.'

Senan had wandered back to their group, and his tone was gleeful as he watched Ailbhe push her way through the crowd, nodding hellos to other apprentices as she passed. 'Of course, that means any match between Gry and Ailbhe is off now. There's no way her father would let her marry a Keeper. Serves her right. Remember how she wouldn't even look at any of the rest of us when we were younger, she was so sure of her First Family match? About time she learned a little humility. I'm going to enjoy this.' He chuckled, waving cheerfully towards Ailbhe as he spoke out of the side of his mouth: 'I'd make her work for it, Ionáin. Doesn't do to make it too easy for those Keeper girls. Let the mating season begin.'

Ionáin had gone red again at Senan's words and Éadha felt a sting of unease. Not so much at Senan's glee as at Ionáin's reaction, how thrown he was to see Ailbhe. She reached them just as Senan finished speaking, but at the same moment a gong sounded, summoning them into the next room.

Éadha fell in behind Ionáin as they filed in. He was talking to Linn now, their heads bent together, already completely at home with all these people whose names she only knew from his tutor's stories. Manons, De Paors, De Lanes. To her these were the names of legendary dragon-slayers, Master Architects, Growers and Illusionists. But to him they were friends, the children or grandchildren of people who'd trained on Lambay with his uncle or grandfather. And though she'd known this, not until this moment had she understood it – just how much Ionáin was already a part of this whole other world she neither knew nor understood.

But as they stepped through into the next room, those thoughts were driven out of her mind by the heady smell of a space filled with books, shelf after shelf of varnished oak stretching away as far as she could see. This was the Library, a long, high chamber with a barrel-vaulted ceiling, its dark wooden floor burnished by the passage of generations of apprentices. Here, Ionáin had told her as they rode together, stood all the records of Channeller lore and history – the *Annals of the Three Brothers*, the first Channellers; the witness accounts of the Channeller wars, collected by Lady Huris when peace finally returned to Domhain; the vast body of dragon lore added to each year by Channellers returning from the western borders.

The shelves stretched far beyond the reach of human hands, yet there were no ladders. Éadha saw instead that dotted about the shelves were cushioned nests where Channellers could fly up to sit and study. Breathing in the dry air, watching dust motes spin in the slanting sunlight, just for a moment she let herself imagine using her power to fly up to sit in one of them and read about the dragon wars. But Master Dathin was standing there waiting. From behind them Master Irial called, 'Channellers to the centre; Keepers to the side.'

Rows of chairs cushioned in red velvet stood in front of Dathin, while plain benches were lined up sideways on. As Ionáin took his seat on a red velvet chair, Éadha, who'd been quietly shadowing him, had no choice but to go and perch uneasily on the edge of a Keeper bench.

It was her first chance to get a look at the wider group. All the Keeper novices on the benches with her were girls. Most of them were elegantly turned out for the journey to First House in riding habits with soft leather boots, clearly Family daughters, though there were a couple in plainer tunics and thinner cloaks. Commoners like Éadha, looking as uncertain as she felt. As the Family girls sat down, they broke into small groups, whispering to each other under their hands as their eyes darted about the Channeller apprentices in front of them. At the centre of one Keeper group was Ailbhe, the girl

Senan had talked about. Up close she was just as pretty, but now Éadha could see how tense she and the other girls looked. It felt, she thought, like she'd walked in on a game already under way, one being played with deadly seriousness by the people around her; one where she didn't know the rules.

As she thought this, she was joined on the narrow bench by a young man who grimaced as he sat down and whispered, 'Doesn't take them long to separate the wheat from the chaff, hmm?'

She glanced sideways. There'd been no bitterness in his tone, only a kind of detached amusement as he sat back on the bench beside her. He'd the dark skin of a westerner, with deep brown hair cut ruthlessly short and startling grey-green eyes that gave his face a bright intensity. His beautiful soft leathers marked him out as another Family son, the only one so far to take a seat on the Keeper benches, and he was, she realized, looking directly at her with those bright eyes. This wasn't part of the plan; she'd far too much to hide to draw anyone's attention. So she nodded but didn't respond, focusing instead on the Channeller apprentices in front of them.

Ionáin was on a plush wide-armed chair a little in front of her, waving hello to this and that person. Beside him sat Coll and Linn, and in front lounged Senan, one leg crossed above the other knee and an arm draped over his chair as he candidly assessed the group. Linn was the only girl on a red velvet chair. All the rest, she counted fifteen, were richly dressed Family sons nodding familiarly to each other and staring about confidently.

Following her gaze, the apprentice beside her said quietly, 'Better get used to it. All the rooms are the same: red velvet in the centre for the Channellers, wooden benches sideways on for us Keepers. After all, how're you to know you're special, unless someone else is being treated as less than you?'

Éadha turned back towards him as she realized what she hadn't been able to put her finger on at first. He was the only apprentice she'd seen so far who didn't seem excited. Everyone else radiated a barely suppressed delight; even Senan, for all his snark, was clearly thrilled to be there among the chosen ones. Instead, something in the young man's stance reminded her of the wolfhounds at home when they picked up a predator's trail. For all the easy cynicism of his words there was an intensity to him, a sense of controlled focus. But there was no time for Éadha to make sense of any of this, as a hush fell over the group. Master Dathin had started to speak.

10

'WELCOME, NEWLY AWAKENED CHANNELLERS, to this, the four-hundred-and-fifteenth year of the House at Lambay. Only the most gifted in all Domhain are invited to our islands, where generations of Channellers have walked before you. Each of you is here because you have a rare and priceless gift.'

From where Éadha sat, she could see Ionáin's profile. The relaxed look had disappeared. He was completely focused, his jaw set as he listened.

'Look about you, to the left, to the right. You are the elite. You're the future of Domhain, its salvation and its glory. Here on Lambay you'll receive the training and the knowledge to unlock the power within you. I won't deceive you. The way of the Channeller is hard. We expect the very best from you. Complete dedication to the realization of your power, fealty to the Masters, and devotion to the Channeller way. Those who win through to bear the yew staff are the leaders of our land, heads of our Families. Defenders of our realm, Master Architects, Growers and Illusionists. Succeed here and you will be set upon a life of power, honour, prestige and wealth beyond measure, first among men and women. May the power newly awakened within you flow all your days in channels true.'

Dathin paused as a young man dressed all in white handed him a large, beautifully bound book.

'These are the *Annals of the Three Brothers*, the first record of the birth of the Channeller gift. Every Channeller apprentice swears their fealty on this, the wellspring of our history.'

Master Dathin rose into the air, to where the spring sunshine shone aslant through the dragonglass dome, then one by one lifted the Channeller apprentices up into the air to swear their oath.

'I swear fealty to the Masters in my thoughts, words and deeds. For channelling is the power and the glory of Domhain and I its vessel now and always.'

Ionáin was the last to be raised up, his voice ringing clear and vibrant in the hushed room. As he was returned to the ground, Master Irial stepped forward and gestured to the Channeller apprentices to follow him from the hall. While they filed out, a severe-looking woman in black took Master Dathin's place at the podium. Her voice flat and toneless, she addressed Éadha and the other Keeper novices, still perched awkwardly on their narrow benches.

'I am Fiachna, Head Keeper. Here on First Island you will learn that as Keepers, our vocation is one of service to our Lords Channeller, our gift one that only gains meaning from theirs, as we carry their power upon which Domhain depends.'

As she spoke, Éadha saw how Fiachna's pale face had become flushed. 'Only in submission are we truly blessed.

You'll have the privilege of studying alongside the Channeller apprentices initially, as the skills taught are common to both classes. Never forget, however, this privilege is subject to strict compliance with the Keeper's Code. A copy is nailed above each bed in your dormitories. Read it; memorize it. We begin with the ritual of Matins in temple at daybreak tomorrow.'

Éadha, though, didn't hear a word of this. She was too busy watching Ionáin leave the Library with the other Channellers. She hadn't expected this. Her whole plan relied on being close enough to send her powers into him without anyone seeing. As she watched, Ionáin disappeared through the doorway at the far end of the Library. Éadha bowed her head, trying to hold in her mind a sense of the thread linking the two of them, but as he moved deeper into the House it winked out, and she couldn't find it again. Losing it unbalanced her, like being asked to stand steady on one foot.

She was being gently nudged by her dark-haired neighbour to stand up. As they shuffled together out of the Library he whispered, 'I'm Gry, from House Flemin. You?'

'Éadha, of the Ailm household,' she said, and even through her distracted focus on Ionáin, Gry's name set up a chime of recognition. It made him the 'Mr First Family' Senan had gloated about earlier. The other Family names around them, Manon, De Paor, Ailm, were all ancient Families. But in Channeller lore, Gry's name was *the* oldest, marking him as a direct descendant of one of the Three Brothers, the original Channellers.

'You came with Ionáin then?' Gry was asking her.

Éadha nodded, still only half listening, more focused on trying to pick up Ionáin's thread and trying not to panic.

Gry's face was sympathetic. 'You won't see him again today. He's off to the Channellers' quad where they all have their own apartments.'

Éadha flushed as she realized how pathetic she must look. He could have no idea of the real reason she couldn't afford to lose sight of Ionáin.

Head Keeper Fiachna, meanwhile, was shepherding them out through an oak door set in the immensely thick walls and on into a shadowed cloister. Along one wall, figures were carved into the stone in bas-relief, scenes from the wars and their aftermath. On the right a colonnade overlooked a smooth lawn. It glowed in the late-afternoon sunshine like a jewel set within the walls, water singing as it flowed up and out from a marble basin in its centre.

Fiachna pointed them to it. 'The Fountain of Beginning, where the First Channeller drew fresh water from the earth. The earliest known use of channelling, and the reason why Erisen chose to build First House on this spot.'

She looked at Gry, gesturing towards three figures carved around the base. 'Here by this Fountain was also one of the last times your ancestor Shem was seen on Lambay with his older brothers,' she said. 'I believe, Lord Flemin, you may be the first male descendant of Shem to ever grace the Keepers' quad.'

'Indeed, Head Keeper,' replied Gry, his voice deep and seemingly unperturbed while the other Keeper apprentices turned to stare at him, several of the girls nudging each other. 'And am I not fortunate to serve our Lords Channeller, as you do?'

Fiachna frowned, but Gry's response had been too smooth to pick holes in, and after a moment she moved on through a narrow tunnel, then out into the sunshine, into the Keepers' quad, their home on Lambay.

At its centre stood a thicket of oak trees, still bare of leaves. Above their heads, high cross-walks linking each side of the quad intersected in the middle of the thicket. The buildings were of plain sandstone, each one divided into dorms with five beds each, although as the sole male Gry had been given a room to himself. The dorms themselves had dark wooden floors with white walls, white beds and marble busts of past Keepers set into recesses.

Éadha was in a dorm at the eastern end of the quad with four other girls, including Ailbhe. Her bed was in the far corner of the room, opposite a bright window.

As the Head Keeper had said, a copy of the Keeper's Code was nailed above each bed.

The Code of Keeping

1. *A Keeper's role is to serve their Channeller with all of their strength, to the greater glory of their Channeller.*
2. *Channellers must at all times be treated with the deference owed to their gift.*
3. *Keepers must give way to Channellers.*

4. *Keepers may not sit in the presence of a Channeller unbidden.*
5. *No Keeper may speak to a Channeller until so bidden.*
6. *No Keeper may visit a Channeller uninvited.*

As soon as Fiachna left, a babble of talk broke out. The other four girls all embraced, asking after each other's Families and gossiping about Reckonings. Left to herself, Éadha quickly unpacked her one change of clothes into the locker by her bed, hiding Magret's book and the amber tower underneath.

After a few minutes Ailbhe stepped forward, her hand outstretched. 'I'm Ailbhe, of House De Paor.'

'Éadha.'

'I saw you talking to my dear friend Ionáin earlier. How d'you know him?'

'My family are of his household,' said Éadha, flushing awkwardly.

'Ah. Isn't that good of him, looking out for the staff?' said Ailbhe. Behind her the other girls tittered. 'Perhaps you waited on me then, when I visited dear old Ailm's Keep?'

Éadha stared. Ionáin may well have visited the De Paor Family's home on trips with his mother, but this girl had never been to Ailm's Keep. If she had, she'd have seen her. Looking into Ailbhe's eyes, she realized it was a test, to see if Éadha would challenge her. There was a brief silence as Éadha took this in and understood she couldn't. She couldn't afford to make enemies here on Lambay. Neither, though, would she outright lie, so in the end she just said nothing and hoped that was enough. It seemed to be, as after a moment Ailbhe turned away, saying to the other girls, 'Of course,

Ionáin was always terribly sweet on me. He used to follow me around everywhere like a little puppy when he and his mother came to stay with us. It'll be lovely to see more of him here on Lambay. Now, ladies. Hauls out, let's see what you've got!'

The four girls upended their cases. Heaps of clothes, silks and fine brocades, embroidered dresses and hunting gear cascaded on to the beds, the girls shrieking as they caught sight of each other's stash. Just for a second, Éadha pictured the looks on their faces if she were to use her power to call up a small fireball on each of those piles of costly clothes. She pushed the thought away though, and after a few moments slipped out unremarked.

Retracing her steps, she made her way down the long corridor, with tall windows set in stone arches on one side, and bedroom doors on the other. As she passed the dorm assigned to Gry, she saw his door was ajar. Inside, he was sitting on a single bed, his bag beside him still untouched. He looked far too big for the narrow white bed, his dark colouring stark against the whiteness of the room. He was staring down at his hands and didn't see Éadha pause, peering in through the gap in the door, caught by something in the slope of his shoulders. All the cool authority from earlier was gone, and now he just looked weary. Éadha was caught for a moment by a feeling of recognition. Something in the way he seemed to be bracing himself, as if facing into something he wasn't sure he could do. But then she gave herself a shake. She'd nothing in common with some pampered First Family heir just because he hadn't managed to pass as a Channeller and now he was facing a bit of snobbish embarrassment. She needed to focus on what she'd come here to do. She had to find Ionáin. As she moved on, out of the dormitory building, she pushed down the thought of the Keeper Code nailed above her bed – *No Keeper may visit a Channeller uninvited*. Ionáin wouldn't care about any of that, not with her.

Outside all was quiet. Through an archway opposite she glimpsed an open space encircled by trees sloping down to the sea. Out on the water lights twinkled as sailboats made for Second Island, where the second-term apprentices lived and trained. Its high cliffs were outlined black against the fading light while, to the south, she could just see the smaller shape of Domhain's Eye. But even in the quiet twilight she could find no trace of Ionáin's thread.

Trying not to panic she hurried back into the main building. She peeped into empty classrooms with their rows of cushioned Channeller seats and plain Keeper pews sideways on, slipped past high-ceilinged studios filled with blocks of marble ready to be channelled into fantastical shapes. On and on she walked the polished, silent halls until, at the very furthest end, she reached another archway.

Stepping through, the towers of the Channellers' quad soared above her, carved and turreted with stained-glass windows and balconies bound in metal spirals. Chains of were-lights dangled from the walkways that criss-crossed the upper levels above the lawn. Voices called from room to room through open windows, white curtains dipping in the sea-breeze, bursts of laughter echoing around the green.

With a surge of relief Éadha picked up Ionáin's thread in a building on the other side of the lawn. Slipping across the grass she peered into a firelit sitting room, the dancing flames reflected in the polished wooden floorboards covered with thick rugs. Along the walls stood rosewood sideboards bearing silver trays and delicate crystal decanters, while jewel-coloured cushions were scattered in front of the fire. To Éadha, used to the shabby austerity of Ailm's Keep, the room's opulence was overwhelming: a barrage of colour, texture and light.

As she stared, Ionáin walked in chatting with Coll and Senan, his face bright. They were followed by a man dressed in servant's clothes, carrying Ionáin's pack, and instead of the relief she'd expected to feel, she felt a sudden anger. He clearly wasn't missing her in the slightest. She wondered if he'd even thought of her since that moment he'd taken his seat earlier on a red velvet chair. She'd taken this enormous gamble so he could have his dream, yet he seemed to have forgotten her the minute he'd arrived here, like some young prince coming into his throne.

The next moment a heavy hand caught her by the shoulder. 'Keeper, what are you doing here?'

It was Fiachna, looming over her, her tall frame belying the soundlessness with which she'd come up behind Éadha.

'I . . . I was looking for Ionáin,' she stammered.

With grim satisfaction Fiachna said, 'When you arrived on this island today, you entered the service of your Lords Channeller. You are forbidden access to the Channellers' quad unless by their invitation. Be thankful this is your first day, otherwise your punishment for breach of the Keeper Code would be severe. Return to your quarters at once.'

As they spoke, heads began appearing at windows, peering out to see where the noise was coming from. As quickly as she could, Éadha escaped, away back through the stone tunnel. Her heart was still racing – with humiliation, with hurt, but more than any of that, with fear.

She hadn't planned for this, had crossed the mountains and the sea to Lambay with a naive certainty she and Ionáin would be together – if not in the same room, at least nearby. From Ionáin's talk of a Masters' House, she'd pictured it as another Ailm's Keep. But First House was something far greater, far heavier than that. Not just the scale of it – huge though it was, many times the size of the Keep – or the thickness of the walls. It was the power she could sense all around her, weighing her down. Confusing her mind as she tried to find the link to Ionáin. And if he was to be hidden so far away in the Channellers' quad, if she'd no way of getting close to him when the time came and she needed to give him her powers, then her great gamble in coming here to this place was lost before a single die was thrown.

II

THE NEXT MORNING SHE was hauled awake an hour before dawn by the tolling of the temple bells, summoning all to the Matins ceremony, as it would every day during their time on Lambay. Groggily she pulled on the red Keeper robe laid out at the end of her bed. About her the other girls did the same.

As her head cleared, the dead thud of yesterday's panic kicked in her stomach, but the night's sleep had calmed her a little. Fiachna had said yesterday the Keeper and Channeller apprentices would study together. This surely meant she'd be near Ionáin during lessons at least, and after all, on the Steps Ionáin had talked about her being assigned as his Keeper. She just had to be patient.

The other girls were filing out of the room. As she followed them, she bowed her head under her hood and built her thought-wall, swiftly creating a new display, her silver fish flickering restlessly in the depths as the last blocks slid into place. She couldn't stop her worry colouring her thought-wall though, staining it with her anxiety. With a final tug she pulled power up the thread, setting the thoughts circling in random patterns through the day.

When she reached the courtyard the other girls were already forming a line, but when she tried to join them, they moved closer so there was no room. From her place at the front, Ailbhe glanced back, her face expressionless and said, 'Commoners go last.'

Her face burning, Éadha began making her way to the end, where the other commoner girls, Béibhín and Nuala, were already standing. When she got there she saw Gry had arrived, and he stepped back to make a space for her. As she took it, Ailbhe glanced over her shoulder then rolled her eyes at him. Gry though just grinned back at her cheerfully until she turned away.

In silence they followed the Head Keeper's swinging lantern through the cloisters, feet echoing on the bare stone. In the predawn darkness, the temple was lit by torches set in braziers along the walls. Bundles of fragrant pinewood burned in fire-wells at intervals up the centre aisle, creating circles of heat in the frosty air. Ahead, the Channeller apprentices filed into their plush red-cushioned seats in the centre while the Keepers slipped into the high-fronted Keeper pews, set sideways on. Éadha could see Ionáin's tawny head in the middle of his class, flanked by Senan and Coll.

The senior Keepers stood behind the pews, hoods raised so their faces couldn't be seen, hands crossed and tucked into their sleeves, like living statues lining the temple wall.

As the bells stilled, four Masters paced slowly up the centre aisle, swinging incense-laden thuribles on long silver chains until the smoke filled the temple, drifting over the Keeper pews. Éadha's head began to swim as a potent blend of incense and some other, unfamiliar smell surrounded them, the smoke filling her lungs and dimming her eyes. At the same time, a single drumbeat began thumping in rhythm with her heart. Gradually, it was joined by other deeper, more complex rhythms that built and echoed with fierce intent.

The incense and the pounding of the drums were making her dizzy, forcing her to grip the pew in front to steady herself. As she did, the Masters stood as one and began to chant. In their song Éadha heard the ferocity and joy of power, coursing through the heart, the body, the mind. From nowhere a sudden wildness gripped her. Urged her to rip down her thought-wall, to reach out and drain the life force from everyone around her until they collapsed in a pyre at her feet, and she rose like an arrow, blazing out with all the power she was capable of, shattering through the dome above.

Her power surged up inside her, demanding to be unleashed. She fought to hold it down, but as she did the drums kept up their relentless beat, faster, and faster still until they merged, collapsing to a single racing beat that arrowed into her mind and slammed into her worry-stained thought-wall. For one frozen instant it held against the impact, and then it shattered into unbeing, her true thoughts fleeing all through her mind.

Out of the corner of her eye she saw a hooded Keeper's head shoot up, whipping this way and that, like a blind creature trying to locate the source of a sound. And beside her, she sensed Gry's head inching about, his eyes sliding sideways towards her.

Éadha knew the power holding her thought-wall together had shone out in the moment it shattered. That the Keepers' grasping, spidery senses must be spooling outwards now, searching for the source of that power flare. The part of her that could still think through the drug haze and the drumbeats was screaming in terror, scrabbling to rebuild her thought-wall from the scattered images ricocheting through her mind.

But each time she managed to cobble her thoughts together, the drums pounded them apart once more. And mutely, sullenly, deep inside her something else was resisting too. A part of her that'd stayed standing in the Channellers' quad last night staring in at Ionáin's rich apartment and whispered to her now that it was all too hard. That maybe it was better like this. Better to be caught now and recognized for what she was, a Channeller born, and take her place like Linn, in a turret with stained-glass windows, and sit on a red velvet seat, and be kept in out of the rain.

But as she struggled, the drumming finally stopped, and the congregation rose and began to sing. It was the refrain of thanks, the same song she'd sung with the choir at Ionáin's Reckoning, and as the melody rose around her, from note to well-loved note she climbed, pulling herself away from the seductive drumbeat of despair and desire. She remembered the promise she'd made to protect Ionáin, and built back a shining thought-wall of music and memory that deflected the searching Keepers' creeping threads so they withdrew, thwarted.

A little later, as the apprentices shuffled out through the temple doors, a voice behind her said, 'Are you all right?'

It was Gry. 'You seemed a bit . . . wobbly back there.'

'The smoke and the singing, I dunno, it affected me,' she replied, her head clearing quickly in the morning air. He fell into step alongside her. Éadha felt a twinge of surprise and, underneath that, fear.

'I wouldn't worry, that's normal. They burn molash potions with the incense to heighten the rush from channelling. You'll get the hang of it. You should see how it affects the new Channeller apprentices. Of course they're far more sensitive than us lowly Keepers. Some have even been known to lose it and start trying to channel right there on the spot.'

She looked at him sharply, but Gry's eyes were wide, full of nothing but a seemingly innocent concern. Still, though, this was far too dangerous a subject, and so she said abruptly, 'How do you know so much about this place?'

Gry's eyebrows twitched as if to say he'd registered the topic swerve before he said, 'My cousin graduated a few months ago; he told me about what to expect, and then my Family goes back a bit. So plenty of nurse's tales for me and my sister, since we could first sit on her knee. I used to long for a story that didn't involve battling dragons or raising palaces – possibly something involving cows,' he finished, with a slight grimace.

'So what happens now?'

'Well, breakfast in the ref now. After that the real work begins.'

Éadha's anxiety began to churn once more. Her thought-wall was back up but she wasn't any closer to reaching Ionáin unseen in time for his lessons.

The refectory was in the main House, its east-facing windows lit by the rising sun as the apprentices trickled in, some as dazed-looking as Éadha. The same buffet was laid out as yesterday – mounds of fresh fruit, warm bread and steaming hot chocolate. In front of her, two Keeper girls were chatting as they inspected a glistening pile of strawberries in a porcelain bowl, carefully selecting the ripest, roundest berries.

'They're very good – much better than our crops this winter,' said one.

'Mother always says Master Cathal could channel pomegranates from a teaspoon of soil in a snowstorm,' the other replied.

'But look out for the tomatoes; they're the hardest to get right. Best avoided for the first term, at least until the new Channellers get the hang of them.'

Standing behind the two girls, Éadha wondered if she was the only person on Lambay who didn't already know everything there was to know about First House, from the hazards of tomatoes and drugged incense to the Masters and their talents. She felt like someone playing a high-stakes game of blind man's buff, flailing as she tried to feel out the obstacles and pitfalls ahead while all around her the smugly sighted looked on, sniggering. How had she thought she could outwit the Masters when she didn't know the first thing about this place?

A group of black-robed Channeller students burst in, talking loudly, pushing and shoving each other in high spirits. Ionáin was in the middle, laughing and ducking to avoid a cuff from Senan. They were followed more slowly by Ailbhe and the other girls from Éadha's dorm. All sat down at a long table, though not before the Keeper girls bowed to the Channeller apprentices.

Seeing Éadha, Ionáin jumped back to his feet, waving to her to come over. Awkwardly she did so, Gry strolling alongside her, for all the world as if they were old friends rather than two people who'd barely met. And Éadha had the sense of a decision having been reached by the tall, dark-haired young man beside her. One she'd no say in at all.

'Éadha, there you are,' said Ionáin. 'You know Coll and Linn and Senan from yesterday. Everyone, this is Éadha, from home. She's the one I told you about, who faced the dragon in the Blackstairs on our way here.'

Éadha smiled self-consciously.

'Yes,' snorted Senan. 'The word "faced" is doing a lot of work there. Anyway, I heard Huath chased off the bitch but not before its spawn had hatched, so they're hunting for them now.'

'It was so lucky your uncle Huath was there,' said Ailbhe, leaning in to the conversation, gazing wide-eyed at Ionáin. 'Though I'm sure you'll be as strong a slayer as he is.'

The talk turned to the different Channellers, with Ionáin loyally backing his uncle against younger Channellers recently returned from the western front with tales of new techniques, new slayings. But when Gry made some small remark about his cousin, Senan's head whipped about like a snake. 'Ah, the boy Keeper. How are you doing in your Keeper dorm? I heard your aunt Hera cancelled the midwinter festival at House Críoch rather than face the pitying looks from her sisters. I think I'd prefer no power at all than to be a Keeper. So very mediocre, don't you think? At least being powerless has that whiff of notoriety, eh, Ionáin? What girl in their right mind would have you now?'

Gry had flushed at Senan's onslaught but his voice was calm as he replied, 'At least my parents didn't have to ask the Reckoner to keep going for – what was it? – a whole ten minutes before you finally managed to pass, because we already have a Channeller in the Family.'

'That's a lie and you know it!' Senan sprang from his chair and had to be held back by Ionáin. 'You're lucky there's a power ban or I'd show you what a real Channeller looks like.'

Gry sat unmoving, other than to pop a strawberry in his mouth, and after a moment Senan subsided into his chair once more. There was a short pause, then the chatter rose around them again. Éadha, though, was more interested in what Senan had said.

'What did he mean, ban?' she said to Coll beside her.

In between mouthfuls of food, he explained, 'Well, as Master Irial will no doubt lecture us about later, it's all about the Stages. "Purifying" our bodies and minds into worthy vessels. So, basically, no flying, fighting or anything else fun for the first while.'

It was a reprieve, she thought. An unexpected gift of time. Time to find the way to reach Ionáin with her power unseen, to keep her promise after all. And the relief of this realization was so strong Éadha swayed slightly in her seat.

She straightened up then, looking around the sunlit ref with a new sense of possibility. Ionáin glanced her way, and she grinned impulsively across at him. He smiled widely in response, blue eyes shining with their old shared laughter, before turning towards a knowing kick from Coll.

From the darting looks of Ailbhe and the other Keeper girls around her, Éadha knew that in that one moment, with that one shared smile with Ionáin, she'd managed to make an enemy of Ailbhe after all, but just then, just there, she didn't care.

12

IT WAS LATER THAT morning. Éadha and the other novices stood shivering in the stone handball alley at the northern end of First House. Though the high walls sheltered them from the sea winds, it was still bitterly cold in the thin spring sunshine. Master Irial stood before them holding a net of handballs – small balls made from twine and covered in leather. He was a tall, slim man, well muscled, with keen eyes and an amused expression. His long hair was tied back, and his cloak off, though Éadha could see no trace of the dragon-burns that'd ended his posting in Westport.

'Today begins your first Stage: preparing yourselves in mind and body to be worthy vessels of power,' Irial began. 'You'll need immense physical strength, agility and flexibility to contain and use your power, whether in dragon combat, in the peaceful arts of building and growing, or in the weaving of illusions. We begin with handball. A sport that requires speed, agility and coordination of the hand and eye, all essential when wielding the yew staff. So – any volunteers?'

Ionáin's hand went up to cheers and backslaps from Senan and Coll, as he stepped out from the Channeller apprentices in front of Irial. The Keeper novices were in a separate group a little to one side, watched over by Fiachna. Quickly he stripped down to his tunic, the wind tearing at his hair. Éadha felt a twist of longing when she saw how lean and strong he looked in the Channeller uniform, with its slim-fitting pants and narrow top, his skin golden-brown in the sunlight. Beside her, Muir, one of the girls from her dorm, gave Ailbhe a meaningful nudge while stifling a giggle.

Irial meanwhile threw the ball in the air and smashed it with his hand against the far wall. It rebounded towards Ionáin, hitting him hard in the chest and he doubled over, the breath knocked out of him.

'As I said, speed and agility. Also, quick reflexes.'

Laughing good-naturedly, Ionáin picked up the ball, and Master Irial walked him through the serve, showing him how to place his feet to react swiftly to the flying return, how to twist his body to avoid being hit, how to throw himself across the court in a diving catch and hit the ground in a roll. Ionáin quickly took to it, and soon all of the apprentices were playing with varying degrees of success, the air filled with the sounds of balls hitting walls and various tender body parts as they ricocheted back.

Standing there in the spring sunshine, watching Ionáin race around the alley, for all Muir's stupid giggles Éadha was still fizzing with the relief of knowing she didn't have to find a way to supply him with power just yet, and with another, deeper feeling she wouldn't admit to herself but that filled her until she almost had to rise up on to the balls of her feet to hold it in. The feeling of being, for just a little while, free.

She'd come here to protect Ionáin, but for now he didn't need her. She was free to just be. In this place of power and wonders, she'd nothing to do but train like all the Family apprentices around her.

When her turn came to step into the alley, she threw herself into the game. Her hands were calloused from herding, making it easier for her to strike the hard ball. She adapted quickly to the game's rhythm, anticipating the flight of the ball and positioning herself instinctively to send it flying back against the wall and beyond reach.

As the morning wore on, Master Irial set up a tournament that quickly turned competitive. Ionáin was knocked out early on, Linn defeating him with a practised smash that bounced off three walls before whizzing past his outstretched hand.

The next game was between Gry and Ailbhe. As the two names were called, Éadha sensed a collective in-breath from the other apprentices. Gry stepped forward, shrugging off his cloak. Underneath the uniform, his arms were taut and muscular, his smooth, dark skin gleaming in the afternoon light. Beside her, Muir gave a small sigh and whispered to another apprentice, Síofra, 'Such a waste.'

'I know,' Síofra replied. 'I mean, why even bother when he's only a Keeper.'

'Still though,' said Muir. 'Maybe he's hoping Linn will take a chance on him? That name still means something.'

Meanwhile, Gry had taken up position in the stone alleyway. Watching him, with his cropped hair and his lean fitness, once again Éadha had the disconcerting sense he'd arrived somehow more ready for Lambay than the rest of them. As if, long before he'd got here, he'd been preparing himself, almost like a warrior preparing for battle. But still, as Ailbhe stepped forward, there was no aggression to him, only a kind of pained embarrassment as he nodded to her politely. Her expression was considerably more chilly, barely acknowledging him as she drew on a pair of soft leather gloves.

The match was over in minutes, Ailbhe sending the ball slamming around the alley at a speed Gry, for all his apparent strength, was seemingly unable to match. Though Éadha couldn't help noticing how perfectly timed his misses were, every time his hand falling just millimetres short of where the ball landed. And as he returned to his spot, while Éadha's dorm-mates loudly cheered Ailbhe's win, she could've sworn she saw something very like relief on his face.

She, meanwhile, had come through the first few rounds, Ionáin loudly cheering, 'Victory to House Ailm!' when she beat Síofra in a close game.

And even though it was the most normal thing in the world for Ionáin to cheer for his oldest friend, Éadha still felt relieved to hear it. Because, she realized, after less than a day on this island she was no longer sure what was normal any more.

Next up was Ailbhe. She stepped into the alley with smooth confidence, her shining hair tied into a neat bun. They were well matched: Ailbhe with the superior skill and experience, Éadha relying on her longer reach and natural agility to stay in points. Almost everyone else had been knocked out by now, the Keepers returning to stand behind Fiachna. The Channellers sat high above them on the alley walls, feet dangling as they looked down at the two girls racing about the alley, diving and twisting. Ionáin was still noisily cheering Éadha on, while Ailbhe's dorm-mates cheered for her. Ailbhe was perfectly composed, her skin only lightly flushed as she served ball after ball. Éadha suspected it was almost as important to her to make it look easy as it was to win. But she could also see that after several hard matches Ailbhe was beginning to tire. Saw, too, her quick, irritated glance upward when Ionáin gave a particularly loud cheer. 'Come on, Éadha! Show them what us northerners are made of!'

Here it comes, she thought, and there indeed it was. A deceptively quick serve, sent deliberately high against the wall so it'd shoot back directly into Éadha's face. Ailbhe, it seemed, was sending her a warning. She wouldn't be beaten, in anything.

As the ball rocketed towards her face, Éadha felt her power start to uncoil in response. In her mind's eye she saw her silver strength so easily channelling power to her legs to somersault back and out of the flight of Ailbhe's vicious serve. Saw herself coming round to whip the ball back and into the composed, utterly entitled face of the girl beside her. But in the same moment she knew it wasn't a choice she had. Not if she was to protect Ionáin. So, with an effort she pushed her power back down and braced instead to take the blow. As the ball slammed into her temple her neck snapped back and she went flying backwards on to the ground.

Irial hurried over to where she lay dazed, blood trickling down the side of her forehead and into her hair. Above her Ailbhe said, 'Oh, dear, how unfortunate,' her pretty face twisted into a blatantly insincere expression of concern. Ionáin jumped down, but the Master waved him back before calmly asking, 'How's your head?'

'It's fine, just a cut.'

'Still, we wouldn't want to leave a scar now, would we?' and there was enough of a smile in his eyes to show he guessed Éadha had been wondering about his own scars.

He closed his eyes and Éadha sensed him draw power. Instinctively she tried to follow it, a thread running across the alley and out into the quad behind, but there she lost its path, unable to trace where the Fodder were hidden. Even as she did this, she realized she hadn't seen any trace of Fodder since they'd arrived on First Island the day before. Wherever they were keeping the people they were using, they were well hidden. Irial stretched his hand out just above her cut, there was a tingling and the pain disappeared, snuffed out.

Reaching up, she felt the skin on her forehead. It was whole, the cut healed. Master Irial handed her a cloth to clean away the dried blood and then looked up at the rest of the class.

'For those of you from the Families this may come as a surprise, but you're not loved, out there, in the world beyond your Houses, beyond Lambay. There are many people – the ungifted, the poor, your own servants and bondsmen – who chafe under the Channellers' yoke. They depend upon us to grow their crops, raise their buildings, protect them from the dragon menace; yet they hate us for it. For our power and for the price it exacts. So know this. It's natural for you to see each other as rivals, just like these two young women. But never for a moment lose sight of the fact you're all on the same side, facing a common enemy. You're the elite, you're not loved, and all you have is each other to maintain the Channellers' rule.'

He paused, then smiled. 'Now. I've some power left over from that healing. Who'd like to see how this game can be played?' Sending the ball against the end of the alley above, he raced to the side wall, running vertically up it. With a flick he pushed off to reach the ball in mid-air as it came flying back, before somersaulting to land lightly on the ground. Taking off again he whipped the ball improbably high into the sky, then went shooting up into the air to meet it as it descended, volleying it with his foot against the end wall in mid-air. He dived head first towards the ground, rolling at the last second to come up and catch the ball calmly in one hand as it flew back once more.

When at last he floated to the ground, calm and unruffled, excited apprentices clustered about him, teeming with questions. Éadha could see reflected in them the hunger she'd had in those few days in Ailm's Keep when she'd drawn on the silver threads. The hunger she still had churning inside her. The beguiling, seductive appeal of being able to pass beyond normal human boundaries and become something more, effortlessly soaring above the rest. But Irial was well used to managing new apprentices, and soon they were on their way back to First House in their separate groups. As they walked, Gry caught up with Éadha again, his grey-green eyes amused as he looked down at her.

'Unintentional, my foot. Ailbhe De Paor was the junior Erisen handball champion when we were younger. She knew exactly what she was doing when she smashed that ball at your face. I thought I was the only person she detested that much. So, Ailm, what did you do to annoy her?'

'Smiled at the wrong person, I think,' said Éadha ruefully.

'Well, try not to make a habit of it. With those Family girls, it's a hazardous undertaking.'

'Why?' demanded Éadha, suddenly exasperated. There were too many games in this place, and she was getting tired of not understanding the rules. She turned to look at Gry, her hands on her hips. She was still deeply wary of him, but he was the only person on Lambay who seemed willing to talk, and right now she'd take that.

'One word,' he replied with a wry grin. 'Power.'

His grin widened as he took in her look of incomprehension. 'You really have wandered into the dragon's den without a staff, haven't you?' He gestured towards the high walls of First House ahead of them. 'This place, it's all about power. Having it, keeping it.'

Stung, Éadha replied, 'I know that.'

'But not just in the way you think. How do you become powerful?'

'By being gifted.'

'True. But how do you stay powerful? By marrying someone gifted. This place, it's not just a school. It's a Family mating zoo, where all of us offspring try to pair up with each other so we can be sure our children will be gifted and our Families can stay powerful. We're all terrified of ending up like Ionáin's Family – having the gift die out and trying to survive on scraps while you spend years praying the next generation will be born gifted.'

He shrugged. 'Ailbhe's from one of the most powerful Families and only the top Channeller apprentice will do for her. She thought I was a good bet because of my bloodline, before I went and let everyone down by only being a Keeper. I'll just have to cope with the devastation.'

Éadha glanced at him. It was hard to imagine anyone less devastated-looking. His grin faded a little, though, as he went on.

'I do feel bad it's turned out like this for her – suddenly under pressure to find a Channeller to pair up with because of me. She's the kind of person who should really be running a small city, or at the very least head of a Family. Instead, she's stuck as a Keeper novice where the only measure of success is finding a powerful husband. With the added bonus if you marry early, you'll probably duck out of a Westport posting because there's always more Keeper apprentices than Channeller apprentices every year. Us Keepers are a bit more likely to get fried by a dragon than a Channeller.'

'But no one's even used their power yet. Why focus on Ionáin now?'

Gry shrugged again, his voice matter-of-fact. 'My guess is she thinks he's her best bet. He's from two ancient families and everyone's heard about the huge power flare at his Reckoning. All the gossip is Master Dathin said he couldn't remember the last time he'd felt one that strong. And it's a match both Families would support – they've been allies forever. At the very least, she'll be making sure she's assigned his Keeper when training starts.'

They'd reached the Keepers' quad, where she followed Gry up the stairs towards their dorms; she was glad he couldn't see her face while she took in not just what he'd said, but the casual way he'd said it. As if Ionáin being traded away to some Family girl was just what was to be expected, when to her it felt as though her heart had just been pulled out through her chest. At the top of the stairs, he glanced back at her, all traces of humour gone as he said, 'Good. Now you get it. This isn't some game to these girls. This is their lives, and they'll do whatever it takes. Clear any threat out of the way. I know Ionáin's your friend, but he's away in the Channellers' quad and he can't protect you here. So you need to watch yourself, do you understand?'

Éadha could only nod mutely. Gry's stark expression softened a little, and he said more kindly, 'Go on, you'd better get changed, we've history of channelling in a few minutes. Want to bet we'll get the Three Brothers for our first lesson?'

As he walked down the whitewashed hallway towards his room, he began reciting the opening words of the Annals in a sing-song voice.

> '*There was once a primitive land whose people dwelt in ignorance, huddled in hovels, their fields barren and their buildings ramshackle, scourged by the dragon menace.*
>
> *Unto this land three brothers were born, the first of their kind, Channellers born, and their gift was to be the salvation and the glory of the land . . .*'

13

SO BEGAN PURIFICATION, PHYSICALLY the toughest of all the Stages they'd face on First Island.

From the first their routine was relentless, with every moment of every day scheduled, from the clanging instant the temple bells hauled them out of bed before daybreak for Matins, until they collapsed exhausted after the Vespers ceremony in temple each evening.

Each morning after Matins they stood for an hour in silent meditation. Fiachna and her Keepers patrolled the ranks of sleepy novices with bamboo switches, swishing them smartly across the back of anyone found dozing. From there they marched to the shore below First House and straight out into the freezing waters of the bay, swimming a half-mile out and back. Soaked and shivering, they then staggered up the beach and on to a ten-mile circuit of the island. Up into the hills and through the forests behind First House they ran, along narrow animal tracks and over fallen trunks.

They trained in handball and staff combat, the stone yards at the House's northern end filled with the thump and clack of yew staffs as they learned to whirl, feint and strike, in readiness for the power that'd one day pulse through the long staves.

The training came more easily to Éadha than most, hardened as she was from years of herding. Even so, her back was often raw from the swoosh of Fiachna's switch, quick as a snake to catch her nodding off. She knew it had to be harder for Ionáin but he gave no sign of it, throwing himself into the training with a determination she'd never seen in him before.

But though they all quickly became fitter and faster, the Masters were relentless. Upping the intensity every few days so no matter how much stronger they became, the exhaustion never lessened. Yet they all persevered, through the stiffness and the pain, drawn on by the siren song of power for those who made it through.

Despite the exhaustion, Éadha never lost sight of her real mission: to supply Ionáin with her powers once their lessons in channelling started. From the first day's training she was studying the routine, trying to work out when she could get closest. She'd need to stand right beside him – like she had at his Reckoning – so no one would see the strength flowing down the silver thread between them.

She realized immediately Matins was no use. He was too far away on his red velvet seat with Masters all around him. Meditation was too heavily supervised. The daily run, she thought, was her best bet. Fiachna ran with them, but the apprentices always ended up strung out along the course. The Keeper novices started behind the Channellers, but she was faster than most of them. It wouldn't be difficult to pull ahead mid-run, she thought, when they were deep in the forest, and come alongside Ionáin for a few moments.

But it was hopeless. Every time she tried to drift ahead, she only ever managed to pass one or two Channeller stragglers before Fiachna spotted her and snapped, 'Keeper Éadha. Fall back,' and as she slowed, Ailbhe and her friends would overtake her on either side, ramming her with their shoulders so she stumbled and went sprawling on the muddy track while they ran on.

As the only male Keeper, Fiachna made Gry start last to ensure he wouldn't overtake even the slowest Channeller. He'd often catch up with Éadha, as she picked herself up from the mud. Silently reaching down with one hand to help her back on her feet, then running alongside her for the rest of the circuit, matching her pace easily. Each time he did this, she quickly checked her thought-wall, all her senses alert to whether he was trying to probe it. She never felt anything; there was just the sound of his steady breathing as he ran beside her without a word. It threw her though, more than she liked to admit. She told herself it was because she was scared he suspected her after that first day in Matins. He was watching her maybe, to see if she made another slip; and that was part of it, but it wasn't all of it. It was him, too, his presence so close beside her. Something about him unbalanced her, like a pressure, like he took up all the space just by being there. And deep inside her, she could feel her silver power, twisting in response to him. As though it wanted to reach out, past her thought-wall towards the young man running alongside her, and she couldn't understand why.

She pushed it down, far behind her thought-wall, and ran on, never saying a word.

Afternoons were given over to demonstrations in the main arts of channelling – Building, Growth, Combat and Illusion. They saw towers of ivory and gold raised up around them by the Master Architect, only to be sent flowing back into the earth at the end of the demonstration as if they'd never existed. Watched as the Masters staged a battle in the air above them, using their yew staffs to send balls of white-hot fire shooting at each other, weaving golden nets of power as traps for the unwary.

In the second week, it was the turn of Cathal, the Master Grower, to demonstrate his art in a sun-dappled greenhouse at the southern end of First House. He was an older man, white-haired and slightly stooped, though Éadha could see how readily the power still flowed through him. The apprentices clustered around him, the Channellers in front and the Keepers behind. Ionáin was standing with Coll and Senan; Senan looked bored, as he always did when the lessons didn't relate to battles and killing things, while Coll's narrow face was intent as he watched the Master spread his fingers wide over a pot packed with earth. Beside him Ionáin was just as focused, his gaze never leaving the Master's hands. Éadha could imagine how much this meant to him, witnessing the very power that'd bring plenty back to Ailm's Keep.

Closing her eyes then, Éadha sensed the soft pulse as Cathal sent power snaking into the soil, the tickle of the seeds' answering start as they heeded the call to live, sending out their tiny shoots, drinking in the life Cathal was pouring into them so they shot upward, pushing aside the soil, their tendrils wavering in the air, blindly seeking Cathal's fingers, following them, up, up, twisting around his fingertips, as leaf after leaf fell open like a skirt falling to reveal the tiniest, roundest tomatoes shining on the stems.

'So, life begets life,' murmured Cathal as he lifted out the tomatoes and passed them around. As the tomato burst on Éadha's tongue it tasted of summer, of colour, of magic; inside, her buried gift twisted in longing, sharp like a needle pressed into her side. But she gave herself a mental shake. With everyone distracted, this was her chance. Moving soundlessly, she slipped closer to where Ionáin stood.

She'd almost reached him, too, when Fiachna's hand landed on her shoulder. 'Step back, Keeper.'

As she did, Ionáin glanced over his shoulder and, for the first time ever, she saw in his eyes a mix of irritation and worse, embarrassment. Beside her, Ailbhe and Muir sniggered while Coll nudged Ionáin. The back of his neck had gone bright red. Of course he didn't understand what she was trying to do. All he could see was her embarrassing him in front of his friends.

Standing there, Éadha boiled with frustration, but underneath there was a growing fear. Because she was beginning to realize that what she'd thought was the simplest thing – to stand beside her oldest friend in all the world – had become something almost impossible.

The demonstration ended and the Keepers stood in their usual line with their heads bowed, so the Channellers could leave the greenhouse first. Peering up from where she stood, Éadha saw that Ionáin was staring straight ahead as he passed her, his jaw still set in annoyance.

'It's this place, you know. It changes people.'

It was Gry. He'd dropped back to the end of the Keeper line to walk out with her.

Stung, Éadha retorted, 'Not Ionáin. You don't know him.'

Gry snorted. 'Especially Ionáin.' Éadha glanced across at him. 'That's what this place is for: to change people. Make them into good little Channellers. If they don't change, then Lambay is failing. And it never fails.'

In that moment Éadha wanted to scream at them all. At Fiachna for her manic vigilance; at Ionáin for being so focused on being the perfect Channeller apprentice he couldn't seem to look at her any more; at Gry for somehow always seeing more than he should. She needed to get away and so she didn't reply, hurrying on ahead instead to get changed for Vespers. As she pulled on her robe, she pushed down the gnawing fear. So the Code meant she couldn't get close to Ionáin in daytime. There was still the evening, the short window after Vespers and before lights-out when they were free. And Ionáin was a Channeller, not bound by the Code like her. He could come and go as he pleased, and from the very first, many of the Channellers had used that privilege to come visiting before lights-out.

Some, like Senan, were only interested in using their visits to flex their new status, turning up unannounced at bedtime for what he called 'inspections'. Éadha, Ailbhe and the other girls had to drag themselves back out of bed and stand to attention, their heads bowed, as Senan sauntered up and down the line, peering at each in turn while their legs shook with tiredness. Éadha's power, blocked away behind her thought-wall and unused since the day she'd arrived on Lambay, would begin to churn inside her as she stood at the end of the line. She had to fight to keep it down as Senan's flushed, excited face loomed over her.

'So, goatherd,' he'd say to her as she stared straight ahead, not meeting his eyes. 'You look tired this evening. Training not going well? Breeding will tell, you know. The lower orders just don't have the stamina, my father always says. What do you think, goatherd?'

'I don't know.'

'I don't know, *what*?' he'd say, satisfaction creeping into his voice at catching her out.

'I don't know, my lord,' she'd correct herself, keeping her voice toneless, though inside her power was raging, longing to strike out at him. 'I am sorry, my lord.'

Others were more discreet, calling to ask out particular girls and going walking with them in the dusk, as the evenings lengthened and spring eased towards summer. Gry hadn't been joking when he'd called First Island a Family mating zoo. Couples were quickly forming. It was all the girls in Éadha's dorm ever seemed to talk about. Who was seeing who, who'd broken up after hooking up, which were the most likely long-term pairings.

Ionáin, though, was one of the few Channeller apprentices who didn't come at all. Not once during Purification did he come to see her. For the first while, as she watched other apprentices appear night after night, she told herself he was exhausted. Or he was focused on his training, determined to wipe out his Family's shame. But he didn't look exhausted in lessons, or as he tumbled past her each day in the pack of Channellers brimful of excitement and entitlement, while she and the other Keepers stood aside for them, their heads dutifully bowed. He didn't look tired at all.

14

POWER. IN THOSE FIRST weeks on First Island that was all the apprentices could think about. Every day they were marinated in it, their mornings spent training for it, their afternoons watching it, and all the while prevented from touching it themselves. Éadha could feel the pressure building. Not just inside herself but in all of them. Pent-up, unused, her power churned and churned inside her until she felt it'd begun to curdle, that soon it'd burn its way out of her whether she willed it to or not.

It bled into her dreams, so where once she'd dreamed of dragons, now she dreamed of power. Of repairing the Keep to the cheers of Lord Aedan and Lady Úra, of growing whole fields of golden corn to feed everyone, of weaving beautiful illusions. She knew she shouldn't dream such dreams. Long ago and far away, someone had told her channelling Fodder was wrong, and she'd made them a promise. But in her dreams, just as on First Island, there were no Fodder, only the Masters' displays of wonders, and every morning the ache deepened as she dragged herself away from them back into the chilly reality of being nothing but a Keeper novice on a hard bench bowing to Channeller apprentices, and every day it got harder to remember why.

'Apprentices. I'm pleased to say your Purification is almost complete. Seven days from now, at the full of the moon, you'll begin your training proper.'

A thrill ran through the apprentices at Master Dathin's announcement on a fine, bright afternoon in early summer. They were standing in the Library, where the Master Librarian had been teaching them dragon anatomy. Standing at the back of the Keeper group, Éadha knew this was the moment she really should panic. But she felt only a kind of numb acceptance. It was as if the tendrils of molash smoke she breathed in every morning at Matins had built up inside her mind until they'd clouded it to everything but power. Ionáin, soft Ionáin with his tawny hair and his gentle smile, had faded away into the gloom, lost to her like a prince in a story hidden away in a glass tower guarded by spells and enchantments.

She'd failed, then. In seven days Ionáin would be asked to use his gift and he'd have nothing. Maybe it was for the best. After all, he was powerless. An empty vessel. Wasn't that what she'd been taught? That all that mattered was power. The shining hard certainty of it, the churning longing to finally release all that pent-up strength in one fiery blaze of immolation.

'Playtime's over,' muttered someone behind her as they walked out of the Library into the sunshine a few moments later, the Librarian dismissing them early after Master Dathin's announcement. She stumbled forward as Ailbhe and her friends pushed past her, an elbow catching her squarely between the shoulder blades. But while the four girls headed on across the bright courtyard on their way to the Keepers' quad, a familiar voice spoke behind her.

'Hey.'

It was Ionáin, standing there. Just himself, smiling at her with his old, familiar grin. It was, she realized, the first time she'd been on her own with him since they'd reached Lambay, the first time he'd spoken to her directly in weeks. Automatically, she began to straighten to attention, bowing her head to him as the Code demanded.

'Don't, Éadha, not to me, not when we're alone,' said Ionáin, a pained look coming into his eyes. 'I just thought since we've this bit of time before Vespers – d'you want to come see my rooms?'

A part of Éadha wanted to say no. To take this chance to push him away, the way he'd left her on her own in the Keepers' quad. Show him what it was like, to not be wanted. But her heart wouldn't let her give up this chance to go home, even just for a little bit, and so she nodded wordlessly, following him to his apartment at the western end of the Channellers' quad. As she waited for him to open the door, she wondered which Ionáin it was going to be. The one who'd kissed her by the light of the mountain campfire and told her she was his one thing, or the Channeller so controlled he could walk past her every day as if she wasn't even there.

His apartment was as luxurious and richly furnished as she remembered. As they came in, a cheery fire was burning even though it was hardly needed. Ionáin closed the door behind her, clicking the lock, and they sat down on the thick velvet cushions scattered in front of the fire. Settling beside her, Ionáin drew up his legs, clasping his hands around them and staring into the fire.

Seeing him up close for the first time in weeks, Éadha realized he'd changed; his face was leaner, his body stronger from the hard training and the rich, plentiful food, so much more nourishing than the thin fare they'd grown up with. It made him seem at once more handsome and more distant from the tousle-haired boy she'd grown up with. An ache went through her, to understand just how aware she was of every little change in him, from the stronger line of his cheekbones to the more defined muscles in his arms, taut against his Channeller tunic, and the new callouses on his fingers from handball practice. It was like some kind of cruel joke, she thought, to have triggered all this only to have him step away into his Channeller world as soon as they arrived on Lambay. A world that was right in front of her, but might as well have been a separate universe. A kind of grief shot through her, as the loss and loneliness of the last few weeks hit her. It'd been so new, she thought, this thing between them, and it'd felt so strong, and yet he seemed to be able to just... switch it off.

As she thought this, Ionáin glanced sideways at her, and some of that grief must've shown in her eyes, because he immediately said, 'Éadha, I'm sorry. I know it's much harder for you here. I wanted to come see you in your dorm, I just thought after that first day in handball with Ailbhe it'd . . .' He stopped himself and glanced around the room, with its silver decanters and cut glass, the thick rugs scattered across the polished floor. 'You know, I still can't believe I'm really here. I feel like a fraud most of the time,' he said.

She looked at him. 'You don't seem like a fraud. Whenever I see you, you look like you were born to be here.'

Ionáin frowned, turning to face her more directly. 'You know what's at stake here, don't you? My Family was so close to losing everything.'

'I know . . .'

He took a deep breath then looked across at her. 'Don't take this the wrong way, Éadha, but you need to try harder.'

That hurt, so much. She stared, stunned and fighting the urge to scream at him, *Have you any idea how hard I'm trying? Every day since we got here, I've been trying to get close enough to share my gift so you won't be found out as a fraud. But you're so obsessed with being the perfect apprentice, you're making it impossible for the one person you actually, truly need to get anywhere near you.*

She said nothing, however, biting it all back, though she couldn't stop her eyes from filling with sudden unbidden tears.

Ionáin scrambled up at once so he was crouching in front of her, reaching out his hand to push some loose curls out of her face, tucking them behind her ear, and the unexpected warmth of his hand brushing against that sensitive skin sent an involuntary shiver through her.

'Hey there, no, I'm sorry, I didn't mean . . .' He closed his eyes for a minute and then opened them again. 'All of this. The Code and the bowing, people pairing off, it's all just a game. None of it's real. But it's a game we have to play. That's all I meant. Fit in; don't draw attention to yourself. Maybe don't glare quite so hard at Senan when he does those daft inspections. Stop giving him a reason to complain so much about you, to want to put you down.'

As Éadha stared at him he sat beside her again, closer now. Reaching out a hand he gently cupped her jaw, turning her face so he was looking her straight in the eyes.

'Do you trust me?' he said intently. She closed her eyes against the blue of his, the way they seemed to look all the way into her, and nodded once, even as her conscience twisted at the thought she couldn't say those same words back. His very presence here in this apartment was based on her lie to him. 'I just want you to be safe. For them not to see you, to see us, do you understand?'

Dropping his hand, he turned to stare into the fire once more, the flames reflecting on his skin as he went on, 'The way Mother always explained it is you have to be a mirror. In a place like this with its rules and its games, you – we – have to mirror back to people like Ailbhe and Senan what they expect to see. Someone like them. So they don't see what's really there, and then they leave us alone. I have to be the loyal son, be friends with the right people, make the right ... alliances. And not let them see any points of weakness. Nothing they can hurt. But, Éadha, that's all it is: a game. A treasure hunt, where we've come to steal the treasure and bring it home safely, so no one can ever threaten the Keep again.'

He looked across at her, then with one hand reached out with his thumb to wipe away a tear still caught on her eyelashes before saying softly, 'We can do this. Another year, a few dragons and we'll be home again. It doesn't touch us, you and me. We're what's real. All this silliness, the robes and the bowing, it'll all be forgotten, nothing but funny stories to tell Béithe and everyone.'

Éadha let out a shuddering breath – at his touch, so soft and sure, and at his words, making sense of everything. As she did, Ionáin's eyes dropped to her mouth, his eyes darkening as they focused on her barely parted lips. There was a moment when everything seemed to stop between them, then he closed his eyes and drew in a deep breath, as if he was willing himself to refocus. But still she could feel it: the charge, rocketing up between them, the silver thread pulling taut. So that as he opened his eyes once more, it seemed like the air between them might start to vibrate with the sudden electric intensity of it. And she could see in his eyes how he was still fighting it, and she knew she wanted him to lose, to show her his need was stronger than his control. His thumb was still resting just below her eyelash, and now as she sat, utterly motionless, he stroked it softly down the skin of her cheek until it came to rest on her still-parted lower lip. She could feel the dry warmth of it, down to the tiny ridges in his thumb-tip, pressing against her.

'This,' he whispered. 'This, though, is exactly what we can't do.' Still though, his thumb didn't move away, pressing down instead a little harder, so that her lips parted further, his eyes never leaving them as he went on, 'We can't give them a reason to want to hurt you. I shouldn't have even asked you up here in case anyone saw, but I just missed you so much these last few weeks.' But even as he said it, his voice slowed, and deepened, as if the words were being pulled out of him. She stared at him, at the heat in his eyes, her entire being centred around his touch, and even though she understood what he was saying, that they should stop and she should leave, she needed this more. So instead she turned her face into his hand and kissed the inside of his palm softly, her eyes never leaving his.

As her lips pressed against that soft inner skin Ionáin groaned quietly and something seemed to give in him, because his whole hand twisted in one fast, fluid move to catch her under her chin and tilt her lips up towards his. His mouth, as it covered hers now, was hot and urgent against her already-parted lips, his tongue pushing in between them and claiming hers, all pretence at control gone. His other hand went to her cheek, pulling her in closer so he could kiss her more deeply. For Éadha it was like a balm, to finally feel it, that real, raw hunger suddenly unleashed. To know it was still there, underneath all that discipline and self-control. And the sensuality of his mouth driving into hers and, at the same time, the simple relief of it came together like a jolt, bringing her back to life, flooding heat all through her body and wiping out the loneliness of the last few weeks. Wiping away the days themselves, as if they'd moved into a parallel world where they hadn't stopped on the mountain, as if these were the only real moments, when his mouth was on hers and she was truly alive. Her hands came up, pushing into his tangled hair. She realized as she did just how much she'd wanted to do this ever since that day on the fell, burying her fingers in its soft thickness and dragging his head closer still, while her whole body arched up from the soft cushions towards his hard strength as he leaned over her.

The next moment Ionáin's door handle rattled as someone turned it, before realizing it was locked, and knocked instead. A voice sounded, polite and deferential.

'Sir, I'm sorry, sir, but Lord Senan is on his way over to walk with you to Vespers. I thought you'd want to know.'

Éadha and Ionáin stared at each other, their faces flushed in the firelight, both of them still breathing hard. Just for a moment Éadha closed her eyes, calming her breathing, then she straightened quickly, saying, 'Don't worry. I'm gone. I promise I'll be a better mirror too,' and even as she said that, something clicked into place in her mind and she saw at last how she'd be able to send her gift into Ionáin. She scrambled to her feet, her heart suddenly pounding, a grin spreading across her face.

'Do you know what? There's something I need to do before Vespers anyway,' she said, her grin broadening as Ionáin stared, baffled. 'It's going to make everything all right. You've made everything all right,' she added, crouching back down and hugging him with all her strength, before hurrying away, out of the servants' entrance Ionáin pointed her to, while he straightened his clothes and went to unlock his apartment door.

15

OUT THE SERVANTS' ENTRANCE Éadha ran, then back towards the Keepers' quad, taking the stairs to her dorm two at a time.

Ever since they'd arrived on Lambay, she'd been trying to get close to Ionáin to send power to him unseen. But his words about mirroring had changed everything. They'd spent weeks watching the Master Illusionist weave the most fantastical illusions: dragons, castles, battles. But what if she created something far simpler? Something that'd hide her power? A mirror. If she could hide her thread behind a mirror illusion, so a Channeller couldn't see its telltale silver, then she wouldn't need to be beside Ionáin at all. She could send it to him over any distance without anyone seeing.

An unfamiliar quiet hung over her dormitory, broken only by the hiss of a dying hearth-fire. The other girls must've already left for Vespers. She pulled Magret's book out from where she'd hidden it under her clothes. The pages glowed like a shout in the silent room with its dark wooden floorboards, its white walls and even whiter busts of bygone Keepers. She began turning the pages, searching for a half-remembered drawing of a Channeller weaving a mirror illusion to reflect the beautiful face of his lover.

She was concentrating so hard that the first she knew of someone else entering the room was when a hand, too quick for her to catch, snatched Magret's book from her grasp, swinging it above her head out of reach, a child's game played with deadly intent. She whipped round to see Ailbhe.

'Now, now. Think carefully, before you do anything rash.' Ailbhe's face was calm yet powerfully pleased.

'Please, give it back.'

Stepping back out of reach Ailbhe glanced down at the page. 'It looks quite like instructions on the use of power. How would someone like you come by something like this? Stolen, perhaps, on your special little visit to Ionáin's rooms?'

She smiled at Éadha, but her mouth was stretched, like a snarl. Éadha's stomach twisted with fear. How did Ailbhe know where she'd been? Was she watching her, the whole time?

'This needs to be reported to Fiachna.' Ailbhe turned on her heel, sauntering towards the door, tapping the book against her thigh.

'I drew them,' Éadha blurted out. 'The images. I dreamed them and painted them. I was thinking of bringing them to the Head Keeper myself. My gift, it's strong, I think, my lady.'

Ailbhe paused with her back to Éadha for a moment before turning and walking over to the fireplace. She propped the book on the mantel then picked up a poker and stoked the fire, tossing on a log as the flames stirred back to life. Crouching there, her shining hair a halo of reflected firelight, she turned to look up at Éadha.

'What would you know of gifts? Or strength? What are you, after all? Some wild child raised hundreds of miles from the nearest Channeller. What could you possibly know of our power, our legacy?' She stood and pointed to a marble bust behind Éadha's head. 'Do you know who that is?'

Bewildered by the abrupt change of direction, Éadha shook her head mutely, her eyes locked on Ailbhe's. Even in her terror she could feel the pent-up power radiating from Ailbhe. A question half formed in her mind – how could this girl only be a Keeper, with that much power inside her? But there was no time for such thoughts. Ailbhe was still talking.

'My great-grandmother. First-ranked Keeper of her year, a hundred years ago. And over there, by your bed, my great-aunt. Head Keeper on Second Island for twenty years. But you? What are you? A freak, a gamble no one is willing to take. A Fodder-wagon Keeper riding west to an early death in a dragon's breath.'

As the elegant girl with her elegant words like knives sliced away at her, in her deep heart's core, Éadha's own power, so long buried, uncoiled now, stung to angry life. Filling her so she had to rise up on the balls of her feet, flexing her fingers to hold it in.

Ailbhe turned back to the mantel. 'So, little freak. It's not enough for you to be allowed here on this sacred island. You think you can be the next Lady of Ailm's Keep? You know, I almost envy you your mediocrity. The freedom of it. Do you know how long I've been perfect? Since I knew there was a perfect to be, I've been perfect. The perfect hair, the perfect manners, the perfect smile.' And just for a second Ailbhe's voice wavered, before she checked herself and went on, her voice hardening again. 'Can you even begin to understand what it means? To have the bar set so high that now for all my life anything less than perfection will be accounted as failure?'

Reaching out a hand, she took Magret's little bound book down from where she'd propped it on the mantlepiece, tapped its cover once, twice, as if still thinking.

Then, turning to stare straight at Éadha, she tossed it on to the flames.

'No!' screamed Éadha in horror.

Ailbhe looked at her, her face expressionless. 'Consider it a warning. You do not get to take what is mine. Understand? Now do hurry or you'll be late for Vespers.'

In a moment she was gone. Éadha skidded over to the fire where the book's pages were melting and twisting as the flames climbed around them. From inside her, power flowed down into her hands, and she reached in and lifted out the charred remains. With a flick she killed the flames and the room filled with the acrid stink of smoke, melted ink and burnt paper. The front and back of the book had burned away, the pages inside eaten by the fire, so the once glowing colours were run and charred to brown and black, the pages buckled and jagged.

Cradling it in her hands, she huddled over the small, burnt thing, grief and rage fighting within her. Grief for the desecration of that perfect, joyous thing, for the loss of her one link to a world beyond this place that had no place for her. Rage at the girl who thought she could order her away from the person she loved most in all the world. It was no contest. Her anger, after all, had been building since the day she'd arrived on Lambay and they'd sent her to sit on a wooden bench. Stoked by all the petty humiliations, the nicknames, the bowing, the denial of herself. Her power, her gift, her dignity. Rage won, a blackness rising through her until it blinded her to everything but the pretty, dark-haired girl hurrying across the lawn to Vespers.

Rising to her feet, she ran to the open window, her power surging inside her as she did. Without breaking her stride she leaped out through it and landed lightly on the ground two storeys below. Ailbhe was just disappearing through the entrance to the cloisters at the far end of the Keepers' quad. Her own power wasn't enough to reach Ailbhe from here; she needed more. Without thinking she reached out as she'd seen the Masters reach out, day after day, the silver thread of her power snaking out instinctively to find and draw into her the life force of the Fodder hidden far beneath her feet. She'd show Ailbhe who was mediocre, who was nothing. Around her the world whited out as a tsunami of Fodder life force poured into her. This was more like it. She'd show them all. She took a deep breath, concentrating her power around her hands, feeling them begin to glow as she called up a fiery bolt the way she'd watched the Master Combat do. She only had seconds before Ailbhe disappeared into the temple, but that was all she needed.

She drew her arm back, ready to send her power bulleting through the air after the disappearing girl. But the next second she went crashing to the ground, as someone caught her round the waist and knocked her over. She went sprawling, the bolt scorching through the grass, spending itself harmlessly. Now she was pinned, whoever it was using their weight to hold her. Twisting her head she found herself glaring up at Gry, his face only inches away from her own, his eyes intent as he stared back at her. She could feel his strength in the way he held her, his body pressing the length of hers, trapping her. He was bracing, she realized, to see if she was going to fight him, blast him the way she'd been planning to hit Ailbhe. But the rage that'd driven her was already dying. She felt hollow, as if a chasm had opened up inside her and she was standing on its edge, staring down at what she'd almost unleashed.

She closed her eyes, then shook her head up at Gry from where she lay beneath him. 'It's all right,' she said.

Her stared at her for a moment more, those grey-green eyes so close she could see the gold flecks in them, then pushed off with his hands on either side of her and rose smoothly to his feet. The evening air swept over her as Gry's weight lifted off her and it seemed for a moment as if she could still feel the outline of his body across hers.

'Come on,' he said, reaching down with his hand to pull her upright. 'There's something I think you need to see.'

Éadha had started to shake uncontrollably, shuddering with the power she'd drawn and not fully used. Gry had already started to move away but glanced back when she didn't follow him, his eyes darkening as they took in her shaking body. With a shrug he pulled off his Vespers cloak, wrapping it round her. Overcome with shame at what she'd done, she had to resist the urge to bury her head in his chest, as if it'd let her somehow hide away from her own guilt. Gry said nothing, keeping his arms tightly squeezed across her shoulders until the shuddering finally subsided. She didn't resist when he took her by the hand and led her through the archway that faced out to sea.

The evening was still light, with only the faintest hint of summer's dusk around the edges. There was no one around; everyone else was in temple. They passed the stone jetty on the shore directly in front of the House, where visitors from Second Island docked, climbing the hill to the right of the handball alley and ducking in under the treeline. Here the trees grew right up to the water's edge, a dense undergrowth crowded around their trunks. Éadha had never come this way before. Gry pushed ahead, bending the branches so she could pass. After a little while the land ended, the ground dropping away beneath them into a narrow ledge of shingle, the stones clacking as the sea rolled over them, like a gambler rolling dice in his hands.

'Stand here,' he said quietly, gesturing to her to go in front of him, right to the edge of the treeline, both of them hidden by the undergrowth. 'Now look, over there,' he added, his voice by her ear.

Her body could still feel the weight of his from when he'd pushed her to the ground, and, without needing to look, she could sense now how close he was standing behind her, the way his body was shielding her from the breeze that'd started up behind them. It was different from the awareness she felt with Ionáin; it was more connected to her silver power, the way it always seemed to respond to his closeness, a reaction she couldn't consciously control. She forced herself to turn her head to where he pointed, looking across a narrow inlet at a shallow cove beneath a headland. A ship was moored just offshore, its rowboat pulled up, half out of the water, directly in front of the cove. Armed guardsmen were helping those on board to climb out. They moved awkwardly, half falling. After a moment Éadha realized it was because their hands and feet were chained; as she watched, one woman stumbled and fell on her knees in the water – in climbing over the gunwale, she'd tried to stretch her chained leg too far and toppled over. A guard jerked her back to her feet. There were about ten or twelve of these chained people, all dressed in worn, shabby clothes, their hair lank round their faces. They moved slowly, as if exhausted. A woman dressed in a Keeper's robe appeared from inside the cove and a guard handed over a rolled-up sheet of paper. Moments later the people had disappeared into the back of the cove, the guards were rowing back out to the ship and the beach was empty.

Gry whispered to Éadha, 'My aunt Hera was a Keeper novice here thirty years ago. She told me about this place. There's a whole network of underground passageways, caves and shafts beneath the island so Fodder can be brought in by boat and held underneath the House to be used for power without ever being seen. The Masters have been doing this a long time. They've engineered the system to make it nigh on impossible to see what's really happening unless they want you to.'

Éadha said nothing, but her eyes filled with tears of shame. She'd done it again, what she'd sworn to Magret she'd never do. She felt sick, the stolen power heavy like a stone inside her.

'We should get back.' Gry was whispering. 'It isn't a good idea to be caught near here.' They made for a small beech coppice in front of First House. Heads ducking under the branches, they slipped in and sat on a fallen tree trunk. Through the leaves they could see the lights twinkling out on Second Island as night began to roll in.

Beside her, Gry drew up his long legs, his hands resting loosely on his knees, saying nothing. Éadha had the sense he was giving her time.

'I made a promise,' she said after a little, staring straight ahead. 'Not to channel people again. But all it took was one Family girl sneering at me, and I broke it. Drawing power without even thinking about what I was doing to those people beneath me.'

Gry was silent for a few moments before replying. 'These first few months here, all the training, the pampering for the Channeller apprentices, the speeches about them being an elite. It's all a bit of a conjuring trick. You know that bit where the conjuror keeps you busy, looking at his right hand waving, while the left hand is busy popping the flowers into the hat? The apprentices don't need all this preparation to be able to use power. They just use it, channel the Fodder.'

Éadha bowed her head at the truth of that, remembering how easily she'd done it at home in the Keep.

'But do you think if, on our first day here on Lambay, they lined up people in front of the Channeller apprentices and said "Off you go, channel the life force out of them," they'd do it? Oh, some would, like Senan. There'll always be the ones who enjoy hurting other people. But most, no. They have to be seduced, brought along step by careful step from the moment they pass their Reckoning. You're unique. You're gifted, part of an elite, with everyone from Keeper down bowing to you at every turn.'

Only then did Gry turn to look at her, and it was like she was seeing his true self for the first time. A self hidden from the Masters and the apprentices behind a laconic detachment and a grand name. The absolute, passionate clarity and rage on his face as he went on, his voice hardening. 'And, oh, look, see the wonders of channelling, what it can do – the golden crops, the majestic buildings. And, oh yes, this is how it must be, because before channelling, men lived in hovels and starved, because otherwise the dragons will come and burn us all in our beds. Surrounding them in a web of imperatives, and all the while the one irrefutable truth about channelling, the people being drained for all this wealth and power, are hidden away out of sight, underground.'

Gry paused, his face flushing before he went on, biting out the words. 'What they're doing here, they call it Purification, but it isn't. It's seduction. Seducing decent people into believing they're so special it's their right to drain Fodder. They deserve to drain other people's life force because they spent a few weeks going on early-morning runs and learning how to grow tomatoes.

'And us Keepers with our bare dorms and our plain wooden benches, the desperation of those girls to marry the strongest

Channeller? Half our purpose here is to make them feel just how very special they are, a handy on-site reminder of their status as the elite. And as they get more and more used to being fought over by pretty girls, to their special apartments and their servants, their cushioned seats and being first in line for everything, they'll cling for dear life to the one thing that buys them entry to that world, the only thing that separates them from us – their ability to channel.'

He looked directly at Éadha and shrugged. 'So, don't be too hard on yourself. This place has been seducing gifted kids for four hundred years. Did you think you'd be immune?'

'How did you know? About me?'

'I sensed it, that first day at Matins. Your thought-wall broke, didn't it?'

Éadha nodded.

'Nothing since then though; you've hidden it well. You'd know, anyway; the Masters would be down on you in a heartbeat if they knew you were hiding a Channeller gift.'

'Is that why you've been . . . friendly to me, since we got here?' she said. 'Because you knew what I was?'

Gry looked sideways at her, the hint of a smile crossing his face. 'Are you fishing, Ailm?'

Éadha flushed, suddenly mortified and all too aware of the long length of him in the dusk beside her. 'No, no,' she said. 'I didn't mean . . .' She paused, trying to work out for herself what she'd meant. 'Nothing in this place is what it seems. I suppose I just wanted – some truth, that's all. To understand why someone like you would bother.'

Gry went very still beside her as her voice trailed away. Almost all the light had gone from where they sat in the coppice, with night falling outside. She could only just see his outline. It looked stark, almost harsh – the tightness of his hair, the planes of his cheekbones – and from nowhere a part of her wanted to reach out to him, to the pain she could feel holding him together. The pain, she realized, she'd been sensing from their very first day, without understanding what it was.

He shook his head. 'I wrote to my aunt Hera about you, the day after we met. She told me you grew up with Ionáin and his Family, and you barely met a Channeller your whole life until you got here. Maybe that explains it.'

'Explains what?' said Éadha.

'How you don't seem to understand just how extraordinary you are. Someone with your kind of power, choosing not to use it, even though it could make you the most valued, the most cherished apprentice on these islands. Someone with no name, no Family, giving up a guarantee of power and wealth and fame.'

Éadha stared at him, glad now of the darkness so he couldn't see the flush racing across her cheeks as he went on. 'Why wouldn't I want to do everything I could to help you? In this place that worships only power and taking and cruelty? It's like asking me why I wouldn't choose hope.'

Éadha felt her throat close over as she stared at Gry's outline in the shadows. Her whole life, she'd always been the protector. Ever since she'd been a little girl, Ionáin's shadow. Even now she was protecting Ionáin's secret with her own gift. She'd never thought, even for a second, that someone might want to look after her. She wanted to put out her hand towards his arm, so close to her own, almost as if she needed to touch him, to see if it was real. Her hand began to lift, almost of its own accord, but then she stilled it.

She didn't deserve this: to have this beautiful man talking to her about honour and protection. Not when she was a liar. When she was lying not just to Ionáin but to Gry now too, by not telling him why she was really here. To carry out her lie, right under everyone's noses.

She hesitated. Should she tell him? But, she realized, she couldn't do it. Even as he sat there breaking the Masters' spells. It wasn't, after all, her secret to tell, not if she was to protect Ionáin. So she said nothing and Gry went on after a moment.

'But, Éadha, this is only the beginning. When channelling proper starts next week, the stakes are going to get much higher. The choices we make, they get starker. And the walls you build, they need to be a lot higher.'

He let his words hang for a moment then smiled suddenly, ruefully. 'I sound more like my old nana every day. Soon I'll be walking the halls ringing a bell shouting, "Here be dragons." But, Éadha, you've been lucky twice now. Today was your second escape. I doubt you'll get another.'

16

THAT NIGHT, HER BACK still smarting from Fiachna's lashes for missing Vespers, Éadha waited until Ailbhe and the other girls had fallen asleep then slipped out of her dorm, through the Keepers' quad and on up into the forest behind First House. Tucked inside her tunic were the remains of Magret's book. Though the outer pages were badly burnt, she could still make out the drawing she'd been looking for when Ailbhe caught her.

In it, the Channeller had used their power to create a mirror that hung in the air, reflecting their lover's face back to them. Her plan was to use the same mirror illusion to hide her supply of power to Ionáin along the silver thread between them. She made her way to the ruins of a summer pavilion at the western end of the island. The whole forest was dotted with ruins like it, fantastical buildings summoned from the earth by long-ago apprentices practising their art, then left to crumble back into the forest. After setting a couple of were-lights on the ground, she stepped into the centre of the cracked floor, bowed her head and summoned up a silver thread of power. Reaching out her hand she sent the thread into a marble pillar that lay covered in ivy on the ground. Long and slender the thread stretched, no wider than her little finger, but clearly visible to anyone with eyes for power.

Then, with her other hand she began to weave a mirror round the thread, copying the gestures in Magret's book. As the mirror covered the thread like an invisible sheath, it gradually disappeared from view. Now if someone with eyes for power came into the pavilion, all they'd see was the glow of the were-lights, reflecting on the narrow mirror sheath that completely covered the line of her power, coursing along the silver thread. She offered up a silent prayer of thanks to the drawing's author, whoever they were. The mirror sheath itself might just be visible to a close observer, but Éadha was counting on the fact that the Masters and Head Keeper would expect to simply see any use of power by an apprentice, and wouldn't be looking closely for something hidden.

She'd six nights left to be ready to share her gift invisibly with Ionáin. Each one of those nights she slipped into the forest, staying out until dawn practising, until she was sure she could do it perfectly, the sheath hiding her power from the moment it sprang from her hand and arrowed towards its target. And as she pulled her power from belly to heart and out, she found that all the training and meditation had made her stronger, faster. That the tiny were-light she'd first made sitting under the oak tree after Ionáin's Reckoning had been growing all the while inside her, into a steady fire that'd warm her if she let it.

There was a deep joy for her, coming into her own powers, and even though her focus was on perfecting the mirror sheath, she also couldn't resist seeing what else she could do, summoning were-lights and small fireballs deep in the forest at night. Once more she could fly. Drawing only on her own heart's strength, she'd never be able to fly as fast or as high as someone channelling strength out of many Fodder — it would drain her too much — but it was enough. To be able to rise unseen among the trees, weave between the branches, feel the whisper of pine needles against her face as she flew through the canopy reborn.

Up all night practising, each morning she'd pull her hood over her head and half doze through meditation. She struggled badly, though, in training, her arms and legs trembling with tiredness. Ailbhe and her cronies were quick to spot this, gleefully taking the chance to deliver so many 'accidental' blows to the head in handball that Irial sent her to the Library for a few days to catalogue accounts of dragon patrols instead. Yet despite this, Éadha was still happier than she'd been since she'd arrived on First Island. In returning to her powers, she'd remembered herself; she'd taken back from Ailbhe, Senan and the Masters the right to have the last word in who she was.

With channelling proper about to start, the apprentices had a little more freedom, and in those quiet hours she'd slip away to the coppice in front of First House to practise or sleep or just sit staring out to sea. On the last evening before channelling began, as she sat with her back against a tree trunk, she heard feet moving softly behind her. It was Ionáin. He sat down, nudging her over to make room.

She didn't say anything, but inside she felt almost annoyed at his sudden appearance. After those brief moments together in his room, he'd gone straight back to ignoring her in public, stalking past her with the other Channeller apprentices without so much as a glance. She'd worked hard to make her peace with that, telling herself this was how it had to be on Lambay. But now here he was, unbalancing her all over again with his nearness. The way it reminded her of the last time he'd sat in beside her like this, that day on the rocky fell above Ailm's Keep, when everything changed between them. And just like that, her body shivered into awareness, remembering every touch, every caress since that day, like they were written on her body and only needed his touch to flare into life once more. It would've been better, she thought, if he hadn't come.

After a moment he said, 'I can't believe we're actually starting. I don't feel any different. Senan and the twins talk about being able to see threads when they inhale the molash at Matins, but all I can see is a sort of shimmer in the air.'

'I wouldn't worry; half of what Senan says is bravado,' Éadha replied, her mind automatically going to her gift, reassuring herself it was there, ready to be given.

More quietly, he went on, 'Linn told me Ailbhe's been bragging about putting manners on you. I wish you'd told me.'

Éadha's mouth turned down as she fought to keep her voice steady, trying not to picture Ailbhe's face as she threw Magret's book on the fire. 'It's fine. I'm fine. Ailbhe doesn't scare me.'

'What did she do?'

'She . . . she sent me a warning.' She glanced across at Ionáin, and though she tried, she couldn't keep the question out of her voice as she went on, 'She seems to think she has a claim on you.'

Ionáin shook his head. 'It's our Families – all the Families – they get a bit crazy about this stuff, and Ailbhe thinks . . .' He stopped himself before going on: 'But, Éadha, listen: it's only them. It's not me.'

'She seemed very sure, though. That she's going to get what she wants. In the end.'

'Stop it, Éadha. That isn't fair. Not when we both know who we are to each other. How could I even see someone else that way?'

Ionáin's face was a mix of hurt and frustration as he turned to face her. But the weeks of isolation, of frustration, had cut too deep. She needed more than this if she was to hold on, and so she said,

'No, Ionáin, I don't know, not any more. You say these things when we're together. But when you're with the other apprentices you're like someone else. Someone I don't know.'

'But, Éadha, I told you, it's a game.'

Éadha wanted to scream. How could he keep talking about games when these were their lives?

'Well maybe you're getting a little too good at playing it,' she bit out, climbing to her feet. 'Look, I've to go get changed for Vespers. Some of us get whipped if we're late.' Ionáin was staring up at her, a look of shock on his face at the anger visible on hers. 'I never asked for this. I know I don't have a name but I never asked to be your dirty secret.

Someone you can only talk to behind locked doors or hidden in the trees.'

Éadha's chest hurt as the words tore out of her. She'd never fought with Ionáin before, not ever, and it felt as though she was ripping her world in two as she said, 'I will wait for you. You know that. But I'm not so sure I know who I'm waiting for any more.' She turned to push her way out under the branches. But she didn't get past the first tree before her arm was caught from behind, and she was pulled back into the narrow coppice and round to face Ionáin, his eyes blazing.

'Don't do this, Éadha. You have to know. My whole life . . .' He paused. 'The shape of love in my heart is you. So how could I ever . . .?'

His eyes flashed all over her face, as if he was picturing losing her, and in the same moment Éadha was overwhelmed too by the thought of what it'd mean to lose him. Moving together, the two of them slammed into each other, Ionáin's hand going behind her head and angling her up towards him, his mouth driving into hers. In the same instant Éadha twisted her hands into his hair, forcing him towards her. Her lips parted and his tongue pushed in, sliding hard against hers. The force of his kiss pushed her backwards until she was against the trunk of the tree behind her, her back digging into its ridged edges.

And there was almost a fury between them, driving each one to possess the other, mixed with a shared terror at what they'd almost done. Ionáin's other hand had braced against the tree trunk as he pushed her back against it, trapping her there. Now though, both his hands came around to hold her face, cupping her cheeks so intently, as if his entire existence was focused on kissing her, laying claim to her lips, her mouth. She kissed him back just as fiercely, with a hunger as deep and as strong as his. He was so close now she could feel the heat of his body radiating through his tunic and the answering heat rising inside of her. Sweeping the length of her as he braced one leg against hers, so that for the first time she felt the whole lean, hard length of him, lining up along her body, like two pieces of a whole.

Now his mouth left hers, but only to kiss the sensitive skin around her mouth with soft, trailing kisses, as if he was intent on claiming every part of her and she wanted to cry aloud at the sheer, teasing pleasure of it. Her eyes flashed open to see his own just inches away, looking straight at her, never shifting his gaze as her breath shortened, to see the look in his eyes. The beauty of it: of him.

As if from nowhere, tears started in Éadha's eyes, even as Ionáin kissed her once more. One overflowed and ran down over his fingers. And she couldn't have said why she was crying, only that in this moment, for the first time, she truly understood the impossibility of this, of the two of them. She was tied to Ionáin because he needed her power, but the Masters, the Families – she knew now they were never going to let her have him. It didn't matter that it was real. His world didn't care; it'd just enjoy breaking them all the more. Ionáin might think they could play them at their games and outwit them. But since Ailbhe's attack, she'd seen this world's true face.

'Hey,' Ionáin said, as he felt her tears on his fingers. He pulled back, his eyes searching her face. 'Éadha, what is it?'

In the distance the temple bells began to peal, summoning them to Vespers.

Éadha rubbed the tears off her cheek with the palm of her hand. 'It's nothing. Don't mind me. All this –' she gestured behind her, towards First House – 'it's just harder than I thought. But you're right. We'll hold on. We have to. I'd better go; I really don't want to be whipped again.'

A moment later she was gone, ducking out under the branches and sprinting back to the Keepers' quad to get changed.

That night after Vespers, Éadha stayed out practising the whole night, only returning to her dorm just before the bells for Matins sounded. Though she hadn't slept, she was keyed up, her power surging inside her, ready to flash across to Ionáin. But as she walked into the temple and looked across to Ionáin's usual spot she saw he was pale and upset. Around him, the Channellers were whispering among themselves, only stopping when Master Dathin rose to speak.

'In keeping with tradition, the first trial of the Channeller apprentices took place before dawn this morning. I'm pleased to say all bar two of this year's students passed. I've posted the rankings outside the temple. These will be posted weekly until the autumn trials. Keepers, your assessment will take place before Matins tomorrow morning.'

After Matins the apprentices crowded around the rankings, looking for their names. Senan's name was at the top, followed by Linn's.

Ionáin's was one of the two listed at the foot of the page as unranked.

As Éadha stared at the ranking sheet, she heard Senan mutter, 'So much for the great flare of power at his Reckoning. I always knew it was too good to be true. That Ailm bloodline is tapped out. It's embarrassing, really, how they're trying to cling on to the Keep. I wonder if he'll be sent home.'

Beside her, Ailbhe's normally composed face looked stricken as she took in Ionáin's failure, while her friends hovered, and Éadha overheard Muir whisper to Síofra, 'He left straight after temple, didn't speak to anyone.'

The other apprentices soon dispersed to their quarters, and Éadha was left standing alone by the board, filled with a mix of fury with herself and a rising sense of panic. When Master Dathin announced the testing of the apprentices she'd assumed it'd be in class, not in some predawn visit to their rooms. Now all her planning and training had come to nothing. Ionáin had failed his test.

She needed to find him, find out what'd happen next. Was he going to be sent home? Could he ask the Masters to retest him? Even as the thought gripped her, she was moving, turning in the direction she'd seen him take. She was so preoccupied she didn't notice the tall figure standing in the shadow of the cloister until he called after her.

'He's not your responsibility, you know.' It was Gry, leaning against the east wall of the cloister, opposite the archway leading towards the Channellers' quad.

'You don't understand,' Éadha blurted out, not breaking her stride as she headed for the arch.

'I have eyes,' Gry responded dryly. 'He doesn't know you're gifted, does he?' At this Éadha pulled up, looking around her to make sure there wasn't anyone else there.

'This isn't any of your business,' she hissed angrily.

'We've already established you are my business,' said Gry, unperturbed, 'and you can't afford – this.' He gestured towards her. 'You heard Master Dathin earlier: they're testing us before tomorrow's Matins. Your thought-wall needs to be as strong as you can make it. Not stained with worry about a Family boy who clearly isn't worrying about you.'

He pushed himself away from the wall, stepping out from the shadows. It was going to be a hot day, the summer sun shining from a cloudless sky into the unshaded centre of the cloister. Now he was in front of her, the sun reflecting on the sharp planes of his cheekbones, picking up the gold flecks in his eyes. There was a challenge in them too, one she hadn't seen before. She had to stop herself from taking a step backwards, and deep inside, her silver fish started into life, churning in its lockspace behind her thought-wall. Stepping in close, Gry bent down towards her ear, his lips so close she felt his breath whisper down her neck as he murmured, 'Love isn't just waiting or sacrifice, you know. You deserve better than that,' before swinging away, on towards the Keepers' quad.

Éadha stood there for a long moment in the bright light of the courtyard. Eventually she gave herself a mental shake and set off for the Channellers' quad. But as she got there, she saw Coll talking to a manservant at Ionáin's door.

The servant was shaking his head. 'No, sir. I'm sorry. Master Ionáin hasn't been here since before Matins.'

Skipping breakfast, she used the time before class began to scour First House, even climbing up on to the roof, sure she'd sense his silver thread if she came close to him. But no one could hide like Ionáin when he didn't want to be found. He didn't appear in class all day, and after Vespers, when she went looking in the forest, she found no trace of him. It was almost dark when she finally returned to her dorm. As she climbed the stairs she felt desolate, just about convinced the Masters must've already shipped him off the island.

As she came into the room, Ailbhe and two of the other girls were talking. Ailbhe looked as distraught as Éadha, and she felt an unfamiliar twinge of fellow feeling, each of them in their own way tied up in Ionáin's destiny.

Síofra was sitting beside Ailbhe on the bed saying, 'It really is awfully bad luck, for you to have a second one fail their Channeller test. At least Gry has some power.'

'Go easy, Síofra,' interrupted Cara. 'You know it isn't definite yet. He'll be retested before they make a final decision.'

'When?' Éadha blurted out. The three girls stared at her. Éadha never spoke directly to them, or they to her. Éadha reddened under their surprised gazes but repeated her question.

'When will they retest him?'

Síofra answered with a roll of her eyes. 'Not tonight. They're testing us just before dawn, so there isn't time to do a ceremony for him too. But tomorrow night or soon after. They won't wait long to find out for sure.'

'Thank you,' said Éadha, though the girls were already turning away from her. She made for her bed, trying not to let on that she was barely able to stand on legs suddenly shaky with relief and remembered exhaustion.

That night she slept in her bed for the first time in days. When Fiachna shook her awake in the predawn darkness, a candle lantern in her hand, she easily identified the silver Fodder threads running from behind a screen at the back of the dorm. After Matins her name stood at the head of the Keeper rankings, followed by Ailbhe's, as the novice with the fastest, most accurate thread identification.

Let the Keeper girls try to twist that, she thought with some satisfaction, though when she turned round she thought she detected a warning look in Gry's eyes. She didn't say anything, slipping away to sleep in a nook in the Library, knowing there were sleepless nights ahead.

It took two nights before the Masters tested Ionáin again, two nights Éadha spent hidden on the cross-walk closest to Ionáin's bedroom window. She was so exhausted she kept slipping in and out of sleep, jolting herself awake, terrified she'd missed the examiners. Her vigil was finally rewarded when she saw a line of lanterns emerge from the other end of the walkway, passing close by her hiding place and entering Ionáin's quarters.

Éadha concentrated, seeing Ionáin's thread colour change and deepen as he awoke. With the skill born of those nights in the forest, she pulled her power from within herself, from belly to heart and out, and sent it flying invisibly through the air to pulse imperceptibly into Ionáin. As it did, she felt an answering start. With her gift flowing through him she knew he'd be able to see the silver Fodder threads the Masters wanted him to see.

Not long after, the swaying line of lanterns passed her once more. She pulled away, knowing as she did she'd left enough power with him that he'd feel its pull for the rest of the day.

Later, at Matins, she watched blearily as his familiar tawny head appeared, proud and erect in its usual place in the Channeller rows. The news had got around, and she saw the quick pats on the back from Coll and Linn, the nod from Master Irial as they rose to chant. In the classroom a new ranking sheet had been posted, with Ionáin's name now in fourth place.

They headed away out to handball practice. Still suspended, Éadha had to report to the Library, where the Master Librarian set her cataloguing old dragon reports. Eager as she was to hear how Ionáin got on, the day dragged, and when she was finally released she hurried to the beech copse, hoping he'd come again to find her. She sat, she paced, she climbed into the trees and practised her flying hidden among the branches, but he didn't come. She stayed so long that in the end she was almost late for Vespers, forced to use her last dregs of power to quickly fix the familiar mess Ailbhe had made of her bed in the dorm, before racing across a walkway and discreetly hurdling down on to the lawn in front of the temple doors, slipping inside just as they closed.

That night Ionáin was all Ailbhe and the others could talk about. He'd been so full of energy he'd beaten all comers at handball. Master Irial himself had challenged him to a game, and he'd almost bested the Master before he ran out of steam. Lying on her bed listening to the chatter, Éadha felt a flash of annoyance at her life force being spent so cheaply on games and impressing Keeper girls. But then she closed her eyes and thought of his thread shining in the night with relieved joy, and went to sleep well content with her day's work.

17

'I STILL REMEMBER MY first lesson in channelling almost twenty years ago. I know you too will remember today for the rest of your lives, as the day you truly came into your power. Let the channelling begin!'

The assembled Channeller apprentices cheered loudly as Master Irial finished with a broad smile. Fiachna, meanwhile, was as dry and as stern as ever.

'Keepers, today some of you will be paired with individual Channellers to keep for them. When I call the name of your assigned Channeller, take up position behind them.'

'Keeper Gry; Lord Coll of the Family Manon.'

'Keeper Éadha; Lord Senan of the Family De Lane.'

'Keeper Ailbhe; Lord Ionáin of the Family Ailm.'

Standing at the back of the group, Éadha saw the quick pats on the back from Ailbhe's friends. Ailbhe said nothing, but her eyes shone as she stood up. Éadha remembered the night in the Blackstairs when she sat by the campfire with Ionáin and he'd talked about her becoming his Keeper. How she'd assumed the Masters would actually want to put two such old friends together. How stupid she'd been.

At least, she thought, as she watched Ailbhe take up her position, she'd worked out how to send Ionáin power without needing to be next to him. But Ionáin being paired with Ailbhe had thwarted her original plan to fully supply him with her own life force, so he wouldn't be drawing on Fodder. With Ailbhe as his Keeper, she needed Ionáin to draw at least some Fodder strength through her; otherwise Ailbhe might start to wonder what was going on.

Éadha tried to push down her unease. It'd be all right, she told herself. She'd still give him most of the life force he needed; he'd only draw a little through Ailbhe. And after all, what choice did she have? The alternative, exposing Ionáin as ungifted, was no real alternative at all. It hadn't been since they'd arrived on Lambay.

The unease, though, didn't go away.

Fiachna was signalling to the Keepers to begin.

'Paired Keepers. Identify and hold a thread for your Channeller from those available. When you feel the pull of your Channeller's call, allow the thread's strength to flow through you to your Channeller.'

Éadha easily found a thread and held it loosely in her mind. Most of her, though, was focused on Ionáin.

She'd sent him her power as they stood in line outside Matins earlier, feeling a quick rush of relief as her mirror-sheath held and her gift flowed invisibly into him. But now was the first real test of whether he'd be able to use it. Standing a little distance away, Ionáin's face was tense as he listened to Master Irial's instructions.

'We begin today with the summoning of were-lights.

Using the power you've taken from your Keeper, bend your focus towards the palm of your right hand. There you picture the creation of a small light, about the size of an apple; the more clearly you can . . .'

He was interrupted by a small scream from Ailbhe and shouts of laughter from the Channeller apprentices near Ionáin. A fireball the size of a large pumpkin had popped into existence in his arms. Even from where she stood behind Senan, Éadha could feel its scorching heat. Ailbhe, Coll and Linn, who'd all been standing beside him, backed away quickly, Coll convulsing with laughter at the expression on Ionáin's face over the top of the rotating fireball while it sent out sparks in every direction.

'Ionáin. While I commend your progress, might I suggest we leave the conjuring of larger fireballs until we're outside and less likely to set First House on fire, hmm?' said Irial, before flicking open a window and sending the fireball bulleting on to the training ground outside. It exploded harmlessly in a hail of fiery sparks to the cheers of the entire class.

Éadha ducked her head to hide her grin and made a mental note to send Ionáin a little less power tomorrow.

So, at last, channelling proper began.

At first, Irial concentrated on the lighter uses of power – summoning were-lights, powering up fiery arrows for battle. The new Channellers gloried in their powers, setting the tiny were-lights dancing in excited patterns about the classroom and sending them crashing into each other to create miniature explosions.

Soon they were learning to fly. Even the most disdainful

apprentices, like Senan, couldn't help but whoop the first time they lifted themselves up off the ground and into the sky above Master Irial's head, wobbling unsteadily before taking off in flying circuits of the training ground, the more daring shooting on out over the sea with Irial shouting after them to come back for fear they'd run out of power and go tumbling into the water.

Games like handball took on a whole other dimension now they could fly up after the ball, somersaulting through the air and pushing off the alley walls. Out on the sea they powered small boats called coracles in furious races around the bay, weaving in and out between the marker-buoys, doing their best to tip each other into the waves.

While the Channeller apprentices flew above their heads, though, Éadha and the other Keeper novices remained firmly earthbound, standing on the edges of playing fields or on windswept shores as Fiachna drilled them relentlessly in the mechanics of keeping.

It was a bright summer morning, not long after they'd started channelling. The Channeller apprentices were shooting fireballs through narrow rings Irial had set in the air above the foreshore, target practice for their later lessons in dragon combat. Éadha and the other Keepers stood on the sandy beach near the water's edge, working on their thread control as they kept for their Channellers. They wore simple, fitted training tunics, having shed their cloaks so their hands would be more free to work the threads. Watching the apprentices beside her, their fingers shaping awkwardly round even a single thread, Éadha remembered seeing Huath's Keeper Treasa in action in

Ailm's Keep, her fingers flashing through multiple threads, so sure and so fast.

'Watch it!' Fiachna shouted at Síofra. 'You've let that thread get too weak. You should've switched away minutes ago.' Síofra flushed, her fingers shaking as she fumbled the switch away from one worn, pale thread to another stronger one.

'Too slow,' said Fiachna, marching over and gripping her hand. 'Every second you leave your Channeller on a fading thread they're in danger, especially when they're in mid-air.' Turning to the rest of the group, she raised her voice.

'All of you, it's imperative you assess the quality of each thread, anticipate when it's likely to weaken and switch *before* they fade to the point that there's a risk of them snapping.'

'Yes, Head Keeper,' the group responded. It was, Éadha realized, the closest they'd come yet to the reality of Fodder, at least for the Keepers. Though she noticed how careful Fiachna was only to talk about the threads themselves. Never the people they led to, who were still hidden away out of sight. How she always used abstract terms like 'quality' and 'strengths', making it easier to hold away the reality at the other end.

She wondered how much all the other Keepers understood by now about where the threads came from. But it wasn't something any of them ever talked about, at least not in front of her, and she already knew they weren't going to. So much of the Masters' world was this, she thought. Gradually coming to understand the unspoken things, and realizing in the same moment you couldn't ever talk openly about them.

Above them, meanwhile, Senan shot past with Eoghan, a Channeller apprentice from south Domhain and one of Senan's main allies. They were pelting fireballs at the target. Pulling up in the air directly overhead, Senan fired a few more at the ground by Gry's feet, where they sparked wildly in all directions until he'd kicked enough sand over them to put them out. Watching Senan shoot away, hooting with laughter, Éadha thought the contrast couldn't be more complete between the Channellers carelessly soaring far above them and the Keepers stuck on the ground below. Worrying about the threads keeping the Channellers in the air, making sure to keep up their power supply.

'For what it's worth, I do think it's deliberate.'

It was Gry, sitting beside her on a rock just above the tide-line later the same day.

They were perched a little distance away from the other Keepers during the all-too-short break Fiachna allowed for food. Shielding her eyes against the sun, Éadha looked at him questioningly.

'Your face, earlier,' said Gry, 'when Senan was being a moron. I think it's deliberate, the way they use us Keepers as a buffer between the Channellers and the Fodder.' In the afternoon light, Gry's face looked drawn, with dark circles under his eyes. From the first, Senan's mockery of him had been relentless, and now he'd come into his full powers as a Channeller, it was escalating all the time.

'Another Stage?' said Éadha.

'Yeah. That's what my aunt Hera says. They're less bothered about Keepers; they know we're completely dependent on them for what little status we get. But the Channellers are more precious – and more risky because they've real power, so they get the kid-glove treatment. Start them out with the good stuff – flying, racing, fireballs. Get them properly hooked on the magic, until they can't imagine life without it. All the while keeping that pesky Fodder reality at a distance, a kind of glorified administrative job for their Keepers to look after.'

Éadha remembered how entranced she'd been drawing on the silver threads for those first few days in Ailm's Keep, when she hadn't known where – who – they led to. The Masters weren't wrong, she thought. It was addictive, that feeling of being superhuman. Especially if you thought there was no price. She frowned.

'I know why Ionáin doesn't know about the reality of Fodder – there were no Channellers in Ailm's Keep. But surely these other Family apprentices do?'

Gry grimaced. 'I mean, yes, some Families like Senan's are known for being rough on Fodder, so he's probably known for years. But you'd be surprised how far some Families go to hide the reality from their kids.'

'How d'you mean?' said Éadha.

'My guess is when they're little they're told Daddy's rich and powerful because of his great gift. But at the same time, they never actually talk about where that power comes from – and kids pick that up. That there are things you don't ask questions about.'

Éadha thought about Ionáin's Family, the way they'd taught Ionáin everything about the Channellers' history. Everything except that one crucial thing.

'So do the Channellers go the whole way through Lambay never facing the Fodder?' asked Éadha.

'Second Island,' said Gry. 'Hera says that's when we can all see the Fodder – if you want to. They think they're hooked enough at that stage. You'll see though – some Channellers will instinctively avoid ever confronting reality. They leave all the thread-keeping to their Keepers, so they never have to face up to it. Then there are others who do realize, then try to draw as little strength as they can get away with once they understand the reality. That's really risky – the Masters come down hard on anyone they think sympathizes with the Fodder.' He looked across at Éadha. 'You already know this. It's the only way you can fight in a system like ours. Invisibly. Never letting on you're resisting at all, because if they see, then they'll destroy you.' Éadha remembered Ionáin and his talk about hiding who you truly were behind a mirror self, carefully reflecting back to people what they wanted to see.

'And then there are the ones,' Gry finished, glancing across at Senan, 'who think the cruelty is the point.'

So their training in channelling got under way.

Every day, as they stood outside Matins, Éadha bent her head and sent her power into Ionáin, giving him the strength to do all the Masters demanded of him. Learning, in a kind of shadow lesson to Fiachna's, how much power she needed to give him each day. In those first days, when she still had reserves of energy, and training was relatively light, she thought her daily gift to Ionáin was something she could absorb. But as the summer wore on, and their training grew more and more demanding, she learned how wrong she'd been.

If it'd just been Ionáin, she could've managed it. It was having to keep for Senan at the same time that made it almost unsurvivable. Not naturally skilful, he made up for it with an enormous, bullish physical strength and a sadistic determination to draw every last drop of strength he could get out of the Fodder threads she held for him. It took all of her skill in shielding to hold away his brutal power from draining her own life force in the process, and she quickly realized Fiachna had assigned her to Senan to protect the Family girls from his clawing, vicious draws. At the same time, it broke her heart to see those silver Fodder threads weaken and fade as Senan drew on them day after day. And so, as her skill in keeping grew, she began quietly shielding them too. Substituting her own strength for theirs when she judged Senan was draining them too far.

It took everything from her, everything she had, to keep Ionáin supplied with power, while also trying to shield the Fodder from the worst of Senan's draws. Week after week, she spent every spare moment either snatching sleep or eating, trying to find the energy to keep going from somewhere. Even so, she lost weight, her cheeks growing hollow and her skin dull. Her own performance as a Keeper suffered with everything else. Where she'd started out at the top of the rankings, by the end of the summer she was permanently ranked last.

Gry and Ailbhe, meanwhile, were easily the strongest of the Keepers, both adept at judging threads and maintaining their flow. Watching Gry calmly sustain the thread for Coll, one of the weaker Channeller apprentices, while he floundered in the air above him, a question started to form in Éadha's mind. But this and any other thoughts were quickly blotted out again by exhaustion. Bone-deep, heavy-headed, scratchy-eyed weariness that stalked her from the moment she woke until she collapsed on to her narrow bed each night.

Standing beside her every day on the sidelines as they kept for their Channellers, Gry was clearly baffled by Éadha's exhaustion.

More than once he tried to talk to her, whispering over his shoulder, 'Éadha, what's going on? Is it your thought-wall? Is that what's wearing you out? Because I know some tips . . .'

But she'd just stare back at him blearily, as if from a great distance, locked deep inside the misery of having to keep going when her entire body was ready to collapse.

It was a hot afternoon in early autumn. The Channeller apprentices had just started training in aerial combat out over the sea north of Lambay, in preparation for their eventual Westport postings. While the Channellers flew over the water, their Keepers had to follow them in their coracles, small one-person rowboats, so as to stay within reach of their draw and send it on to the Fodder, still hidden out of sight on First Island itself.

Éadha had sent power into Ionáin that morning as usual, then rowed out to where Senan was already waiting for her, high in the sky above. The sky was cloudless but there was a stiff breeze from the west, meaning she had to keep sculling with her oars just to hold her boat in position underneath Senan and stop her drifting further from First Island. Along with Linn and Coll, he was learning to create nets of power in the air, each apprentice taking a point and weaving a net between them with golden lines of power. They were meant to trap dragons in battle. Irial, though, had easily ripped apart their first two nets, and Senan was in a foul humour, shouting down at her, 'Hold steady, you idiot! You're slowing my draw.'

Over and over, he drew power through her, and as the afternoon wore on she grew steadily more tired, her arms aching with the effort of holding the boat steady, while the sun beating down on her exposed head left it pounding. Even after Linn and Coll had called it a day, Senan stayed flying above her, still practising drawing lines of power in the sky while she sat half slumped over her oars in a daze of tiredness. Without realizing it, she'd fallen into a doze, and as she did the thought-wall she'd built so carefully that morning loosened, letting slip the small reserves of energy she'd shielded behind it. Moments later, she was gripped by a savage, scouring sensation. It was Senan. She stared up at him, furious. Channellers drawing directly on the life force of Keepers was frowned on, other than in emergencies.

But Senan only smirked down at her. 'If you will be so pathetically slow, you leave me no choice. I need it for the flight back. You wouldn't want your Channeller in danger, now would you?' And with that he flew off towards the shore.

As he disappeared into the distance Éadha let out a shout of rage and frustration, but there was no one and nothing to hear her apart from a passing seagull. Slowly twisting in a half-circle on her seat, it dawned on her she was truly alone out on the water. All the other Keeper boats must've headed back to the jetty a while ago; she'd just been too tired to notice. All the Channellers had flown back to the island too. She was also, she realized, much further out from land than she'd ever been before. At the same time, it was sinking in just how much energy Senan had drained from her with that vicious draw; she could barely lift her oars. Meanwhile, the wind, which had been blowing steadily all afternoon, was beginning to strengthen. Even in the few minutes since Senan had gone, she'd drifted further from First Island. Fighting down a rising sense of panic, she forced herself to grip the oars but her strokes were shallow and ineffectual, her arms shaking as she tried to lift the paddles clear of the water.

What a stupid way to die, she thought, the wind simply pushing her out to sea faster than she could row back. Her throat was dry and her skin raw from sitting under the hot sun all afternoon. Her stomach heaved with the effort of forcing the oars into the water, but the wind was too strong and she was still going the wrong way. Her boat began to rock alarmingly as the waves around her grew stronger, water starting to slop over the gunwales, soaking her. She'd drifted fully out of the shelter of First Island now, out into open water, where she was exposed to the full force of the wind. Her hair was whipping so hard around her face she could hardly see, her hands slipping and struggling to grip the suddenly slick oars. She reached down inside herself for her power, but it barely flickered. She was too weak – Senan had drained the last of her strength.

'Éadha!' The voice came from behind her. She twisted in her seat. It was Gry. He was in his Keeper boat, rowing towards her. With the wind behind him, he caught her quickly, reaching out to catch her gunwale so the two boats knocked against each other. His face was creased with worry. 'Éadha, what happened? Senan passed me on my way back to shore, and when there was no sign of your boat I got worried.'

'Senan happened,' she managed. Gry's face darkened; she realized she'd never seen him truly angry before, a muscle jumping in his tight jaw as he stared at her exhausted face. 'Then the wind . . .' Her voice petered out.

'At home we call it the Dragon's Dance,' said Gry, making a visible effort to speak calmly. 'That hot, hard wind from the west you get in early autumn. The dragons love to ride it, but we humans need to be a bit more careful.'

He stood up in his own boat, balancing easily as it began rocking from side to side. The sun was beginning to slip down behind Lambay, colouring the sky a flaming red. All Éadha could think was how solid Gry looked, the only real, solid thing in a landscape that wouldn't stop moving around her, the waves heaving and the wind buffeting her while he stood with his legs braced, outlined against the darkening sky. There was a darkness creeping in from the edge of her vision and she was starting to sway in her seat, no longer able to keep herself upright.

'Hey, hey,' she heard Gry say, 'stay with me.' He swung first one leg, then the other over into her coracle. Now he was standing in front of her; his hand was under her chin, those bright eyes staring down at her as his own boat was quickly swept away by the wind and the waves. And she was surprised by how soft his touch was.

'Whaddya doin'?' she said, dimly puzzled that he seemed to be in her boat now for some reason. It was too small, surely, for two of them.

'Getting you back to land.'

''S my boat.'

'Yes, Ailm, it's a lovely boat. How about, though, before the wind tips us both into the Fiadh sea, you stand up for me.' He caught her under her arms and lifted her up. She half slumped against his chest, her legs unable to take her weight. She was, she realized, going to pass out from being drained, from dehydration and the heat exhaustion. She felt vaguely ashamed; she wasn't someone who keeled over like this. Her head was pressed against his chest. He smelled, she thought fuzzily, of salt and sweat and, underneath that, the smoky tang of molash and incense. He was so *warm* too, the heat radiating through his thin training tunic; and she realized she was starting to shiver with delayed shock, as if somehow she had permission to let go now because he had her. Someone had her. She had someone. Her eyes closed over from exhaustion, and without thinking she reached out towards him with her senses instead, as if to reassure herself he was still there. And there, in front of her, like the dragon all those months ago, there he was, shining before her. His light fierce, a core of bright iron running through him, and she felt her own power stir inside her in response: a singing rising inside her, something she could no more stop than the wind or the tide around her. A recognition; a finding.

'Ohhh,' she mumbled, her eyes still closed. 'I *see* you now. You're so bright. How are you so bright? How do you hold it in?'

'You're rambling, Ailm,' Gry said, though she felt through his chest how his heart thudded as he said it before he lifted her gently away from him. 'Now, we're going to shuffle round very stylishly and sit you down here, like so.' And he rotated her carefully in the narrow space then slid her down so she came to rest on the bottom of the boat, between his legs, while he took her place in the rower's seat. Moving smoothly, he bent forward to take up the oars and began to row against the wind in the direction of Lambay, now little more than a dark shadow against the fading light. As he did so, he looked down at her. 'Put your head between your knees and close your eyes. You've been drained but your energy will regenerate in a little while. You just need to rest.'

Éadha sat with her back slumped against the base of his seat, her head level with his thighs, blessedly out of the wind, sheltered from it by his body. From nowhere a laugh bubbled up inside her. Above her Gry said nothing, his lean torso bending forward over her head and stretching back in smooth strokes, cutting through the water. After a little, lulled by the rhythm of his strokes and the slap of the waves against the boat, she drifted off to sleep.

When she woke it was dark. For a moment she'd no idea where she was, then she realized her head was resting against Gry's thigh, and there was a small stain on his pants where she'd drooled in her sleep. She was instantly mortified; her eyes flashed upward to meet Gry's. He was sitting still, the oars in his hands, looking down at her, an expression she hadn't seen before in his eyes.

'I'm so sorry,' she said.

'Nope,' said Gry. 'No apologizing – you did nothing wrong.'

'I meant for drooling on you,' she said, nodding towards his thigh.

'Oh, well, yes, that you can apologize for. Though you were very cute.'

'I doubt it,' said Éadha, flushing despite herself at the thought of Gry seeing her asleep (and drooling). 'How long was I out?'

'As long as you needed to be.' Éadha drew in her legs, suddenly intensely aware of the fact she was sitting between his legs, of the warmth of his thigh where her head had rested until moments before and the heat radiating from the rest of his body, shielding her from the night-time chill beyond her small cocoon. But as she moved the boat began to rock alarmingly, reminding her they were still out on the water.

Gry looked down at her, his voice amused. 'I'm not sure where you're planning to go, unless you want to sit on me?'

Éadha subsided. He was right: there was nowhere else to go in the tiny boat. It'd been designed for one person and could barely hold the two of them. Gry bent forward, sliding the oars back into the water. 'Don't worry, it's not far. I just wanted to let you sleep it out before we docked.'

'Thank you,' she said awkwardly. 'For coming to find me.'

'What I don't understand,' said Gry, as he settled into a steady stroke, not looking down at her, 'is why you were so worn out in the first place. With your gift you should be able to keep for Senan in your sleep, even if he is a vicious brute. But you've been exhausted for weeks. So come on, spill it. What's going on?'

A lump rose in Éadha's throat as the weariness of the last few weeks came rushing back. She couldn't lie to him she thought, not after what he'd just done, but she couldn't tell him the truth either. Instead, she stared out ahead of her at the moon rising over the sea before saying, 'I made a promise, a long time ago. One of those promises you can't break. Keeping it is taking more out of me than I thought.'

'Another promise? Besides promising not to channel Fodder? You don't think you're maybe making too many promises?'

'You're one to talk,' said Éadha, rousing herself as the memory of those last moments before she passed out came back to her. The shining power she'd sensed in him. There was no way, she realized, that was only a Keeper's gift. She pushed away the thought of how her own power had responded to it. 'Earlier – I *saw* you. You let me see you, and it looks a lot like maybe you've been making hard promises too?'

They'd almost reached the small jetty in front of First House that was used for docking the Keeper boats. As they floated the last few metres, Gry said, 'For your sake – and for my Family's sake – I'm not sure that's a question I should answer. Once you're told something it's hard to unknow it if you're ever asked by people of power, and I'm not in the habit of putting people in danger. I'll answer a different question, though. Over the last two years I've watched my Channeller cousin change from a decent guy into a swaggering, entitled, selfish thug. I've walked the streets of Erisen at night when all the nice Family boys and girls are tucked up in bed, and I've seen the dregs of Lambay's channelling, cast off and left to rot on its streets. And I've thought a lot about choice. That there's an element of choice in what we let the Masters see and what we let them make of us. I choose to do less harm. If that answers your question.'

As he finished, Éadha realized she wasn't even surprised by what he'd just told her, even without saying it out loud: that he was hiding a Channeller gift too. Nothing else made sense after the extraordinary power she'd sensed in him earlier.

Gry glanced at Éadha with a challenging look in his eyes. 'So, back to you, Éadha of the many promises. Are you going to tell me what it is, this other promise you've made?'

Éadha was silent for a moment. 'In the spirit of not answering what we're asked, I've a question for you instead,' she said. 'Do you ever find it hard, giving it all up? Knowing you've a gift that'd make you the best of them all, and instead thugs like Senan get to abuse us?'

Gry leaned back in the boat and laughed up at the sky. 'Senan's the biggest moron on this island. Do you think for one second I'd let that idiot have any say in my life by basing my life choices on impressing him? Are you kidding me?'

Éadha stared at him for a moment before an answering grin spread across her face, his words loosening something knotted and painful in her chest.

He looked back down at her. 'I'm not saying it's easy, especially not for you. You're not protected by a Family name like me. But look, it's a bunch of old men in a house on an island, desperate to validate their own lives by indoctrinating another generation of youngsters to make the same choices they made. Why would I ever want their approval? It's a gateway to wealth and power, but you have to sell your soul to get it.'

They'd reached the dock. With a flick, Gry tossed the mooring rope round the landing post. It was time to climb ashore, back on to the island. Gry stood up behind her to catch the rope and secure it, and as the heat of his body pulled away from her, Éadha felt suddenly bereft, as if something she hadn't even realized was holding her up had been taken away. To her left loomed the bulk of First Island, the lights of First House visible a short distance away, up the hill from the jetty. A wave of dread hit her, as hard as the waves that'd slapped over her boat and almost drowned her earlier, at the thought of going back there, to the lies, the humiliations and the overwhelming cost of it all.

'We could just keep going, you know; row on to Erisen, go into hiding, try to find other people like us,' she said abruptly.

Gry stared at her, his expression still, before leaning

forward and lashing the rope round the stern. He paused for a moment, his hands still on the rope, his back to her as he replied quietly, 'Don't get me wrong. You're worth running away for. But I don't think you mean it. Not yet.'

Without looking at her, he stepped across on to the dock, then turned and reached out a hand to pull her up after him. Her legs were still shaky, but at least they could take her weight now, she thought, as she stepped on to dry land. Gry still had a hold of her hand, and with a small tug he pulled her forward so she half stumbled against his chest. His arms came round her, enfolding her and she had to fight a sudden urge to wrap her arms round him in return. Resting his chin on her head, he said, 'This place, it forces terrible choices on us all. Fight the Masters and get sent for Fodder – or become one of them. Use or be used.' An edge of bitterness crept into his voice as he went on. 'Look at me, a nice Family boy who happens to know how bad this system is. But I'm still not prepared to be destitute, or on the run from the Masters, or end up as Fodder. I might not be prepared to drain people's life force, but I'm still staying in the system, keeping my Family name.'

The pain in Gry's voice as he said this broke Éadha's heart. She knew what he wasn't saying, that for him to openly defy the Masters would destroy not just him but his Family too. It was, after all, the same awful compromise she'd made. Making the choices that protected the people he loved while trying not to lose too much of himself. Without thinking she leaned back a little in his arms and lifted a hand to touch his cheek gently; and she'd time to think how different he felt from

Ionáin, the power she could feel underneath that warm skin. Gry closed his eyes and breathed in at her touch.

'Don't do this to yourself,' she whispered. 'This is what love is. Making the hard choices, not the cleanest ones.'

They stood there for a moment, not saying anything, then Gry took a deep breath, dropped his arms and stepped back, clearing his throat. 'Speaking of hard choices,' he said, his normal dry humour coming back into his voice.

His arm across her shoulder, the two of them climbed together back up the hill towards the Keepers' quad.

18

THE LEAVES ON THE chestnut trees that ringed the training grounds were beginning to turn; in the mornings now, the pitch was stiff and white with frost when they first came out to training.

In that chilly first hour, before the late autumn sun had time to burn off the frost, the Channellers practised their flying. They had leave to channel power to keep off the cold, surrounding themselves with their own personal pockets of warm air while the Keeper novices stood underneath them shivering.

Already drained from supplying Ionáin that morning, Éadha stood at the edge of the playing field, her feet numb in her thin boots. A little distance away from her stood Ailbhe, warmly wrapped in a wool coat, her face prettily flushed with the cold, shining hair peeping out from beneath her soft cap. As well as being paired with her as his Keeper, Ionáin was spending more and more time with her outside training, joining her in the ref each morning for hot drinks to stave off the autumn chill, or sitting beside her in the evenings when the Master Illusionist wove his tales above their heads.

Éadha told herself it didn't matter, to trust Ionáin. That it was all just a game. But it was hard to remember as she watched them laughing together as Ionáin flew above her head, tossing a shining chestnut down from the top of the tree for Ailbhe to catch. At what point did a game stop being a game and become its own reality?

She sensed the change before she heard anything, a thrill running through the icy air. Master Irial felt it too, turning to stare up the hill above First House. Black-clad riders had appeared at the forest's edge. Sending an apprentice to fetch Master Dathin, Irial flew up to meet them as they emerged from the trees, pulling a large wagon made all of metal and reinforced with inner and outer rows of bars. A dark shape lay on the wagon floor. As the riders neared the bottom of the hill Masters began to appear from First House, pulling on their robes, clutching their yew staffs. Éadha recognized the white-blonde hair of Lord Huath at the head of the riders at the same moment that Ionáin, still flying above them, cried out in a voice filled with fear and wonder, 'Dragon!'

Their training cancelled, the apprentices gathered in the ref. Ionáin, though, managed to wheedle his way into the Receiving Room to see his uncle. He appeared in the ref a little later, climbing on to a table to report the news as everyone clustered around him.

'It's a young dragon. My uncle caught it four days ago. It's one of the spawn of the she-dragon we saw in the Blackstairs in spring. He's been hunting them on and off ever since. He killed two, one escaped west he thinks, but this one, the smallest, he managed to capture alive. Master Combat is beside himself with excitement. It's the first time Lambay has ever had a live dragon. It's too young to be a danger; it can't breathe fire yet and it's only the length of a man. My uncle says even one of us could put it down.'

Later that day the apprentices were taken to see the captured dragon. It lay in its iron cage a little distance away from the main House. Little was known about the stages of growth of young dragons. They were fiercely protected by the she-dragons, hidden away on the western isles or on the most impenetrable northern peaks until they were old enough to fly and breathe fire. Éadha knew the Masters were intensely wary of their captive. A full-grown dragon could best even the most seasoned Channeller; the flame alone would kill anyone in its silent burning path, and the Masters had no way of knowing how far the young dragon was from coming into its power.

Master Irial and the Master Combat called them to a halt some way away from the cage, where Huath and several of his guards already stood, watching the creature. The dragon lay inert on the floor, curled like a cat, its haunches pulled into its belly and wings folded flat along its ridged back. Only the eyes gave any sign it was anything other than a creature channelled from stone. They were great and golden, unblinkingly regarding the apprentices as they craned to see, straining against the barriers set in a wide circle round the cage. Éadha's heart began to thump unbidden in her chest, her silver fish flickering into joyous life. She closed her eyes, sending out her senses and there it was in front of her, shining, a piece of the sun fallen to earth, blinding in its purity. She gasped and stepped back, looking about her. Couldn't everyone see it, what they had lying there before them?

The Master Combat, apparently oblivious, had started explaining the dragon scales. How, once fully grown, they'd cover the body in iridescent mail, hard as silver, flexible as skin, undulating sinuously when the dragon moved. They were impervious to normal weapons, shattering arrows and swords unless they were powered by a Channeller. Even then, he told them, it took the power of twenty threads just to pierce the underbelly where the scales were thinner.

In front of them the dragon lifted its head as though it scented something. Lord Huath immediately stepped forward, raising his staff and sending a short burst of fire directly into its face. The young dragon reared back, opening its mouth though nothing came out. Huath's eyes gleamed with vicious delight, as he followed up by ramming his iron-shod staff through the bars. It retreated further, until it was pressed against the bars behind it. Éadha's power twisted in sudden, savage fury at Huath's cruelty, while behind her Ionáin placed a hand on her shoulder.

'You're burning up,' he said quietly. The touch of that familiar hand pulled her back. Huath, meanwhile, returned to stand with the two Masters. Éadha leaned briefly, almost imperceptibly into Ionáin's touch then pulled away before it was seen by Ailbhe or any of her spies. Ionáin moved too, standing next to the twins, who were still staring, fascinated, at the dragon in its cage.

That night she couldn't sleep. With no training that day, for once she had power to spare coursing restlessly through her.

With a grin and no one to see her, she spun a pocket of heat around her and flew down from the Keeper dorm through the quad tunnels and out into the night, with its vertiginous carpet of stars flung from one horizon to the other, the sea below her pacing like a caged beast to the shore's edge and back. Lifting one hand above her, she began to spin, faster and faster until she was nothing but a blur of energy, then shot up into the sky, up, up, whirling until the stars became streaks of light she was outrunning. Below her she saw the dragon, felt it quivering with longing in its iron cage. Down she dived to land in front of the golden eyes, hands cupping a single werelight. They regarded each other, the girl and the dragon.

'*Mahera*,' hissed the dragon, drawing its lips back, teeth already the size of Éadha's hand glinting in the light.

Closing her eyes, she pulsed her remaining power into the emptiness before her. She felt the dragon's hunger, felt a savage longing in that moment to let everything go, to disappear. The dragon, though, nudged the side of the cage closest to her, bringing her back to herself, breaking the link between them.

Training remained erratic for the next few days and Éadha was able to get away to the Library, sneaking down each night after lights-out. She flew up to the shelves beneath the dome, to the books forbidden to apprentices. '*Mahera*,' the she-dragon had said to her in the stony mountains and her child had repeated it here underneath the eastern stars. If she could understand, if she could speak to it, then perhaps she could understand the intense connection she felt. But the only stories she found were the ones she'd heard as a child. The story of Kaanesien, the eldest dragon, how it burned Erisen's keep to the ground and his Keeper, Bríd, died saving him. She could make no link, though, between these stories of monsters and the beauty, the purity she'd seen in the young dragon. The sense of connection she felt when she went near it. At night she dreamed of the touch of dragon scales, of flying on dragon's wings through soft flakes of tumbling snow. She dreamed she stood on the training ground, keeping for Ionáin when he flew back to earth and bowed before her. She looked down to see she'd been covered in a dragon's iridescent skin; over her shoulders she felt the wingspan, light, tremendous, as she spread them wide and sprang into the darkening sky. When she woke the next morning, she finally understood what *Mahera* meant.

They were brought to study the dragon again later that day. Huath had left Lambay, and the dragon was growing fast, its head almost touching the roof of the cage. Below the open space where they stood, a full-masted ship had put in at the east dock. It was a rare sight, the ship almost too large for the jetty. The white sails strained in winds blowing straight off the sea, drawing every eye. Seeing their gaze, the Master Combat explained.

'This will transport the beast to Second Island in seven days' time. It needs to be put down before it poses a serious risk. The kill will form the basis of the upcoming graduation trials on Second Island.'

Éadha felt the words as a punch to her stomach. All the time the young dragon had been on the island she'd been tethered to it, walking around First House on an invisible leash that ran from her to the impossible creature chained to an iron floor at the island's heart. In a daze she returned to her dormitory to change. The room was empty, a rare moment of solitude. From underneath her bed she pulled Magret's burnt book, looking for something on the fire-eaten pages to make sense of what she felt. At its charred heart was the picture she was looking for, of a man and a dragon entwined. The man was holding his staff above his head, the dragon's wings raised about him; the colours of each had run into the other in the fire's heat. She'd always assumed it was a representation of a battle between man and beast, but now she had eyes to see, she finally understood.

She slipped away in the early dark, back down to where the creature lay still. It watched her intently. She called up a were-light in her hand. The dragon looked at it pleadingly.

'I know,' she said. 'I understand. You want to do that too. Let me show you. *Mahera*. Sister.' The dragon placed its head against the bars.

'*Mahera*,' it hissed in reply. And so, quietly, patiently, Éadha set about teaching the chained dragon to channel power from within itself. Night after night she slipped out, pulling power up from inside her, showing the dragon how she created the were-light from the life force within. And slowly, surely, the dragon began to respond. It was very young still, ramming its head in frustration against the bars when it failed to produce flame. The cage was too confined for it to extend its wings fully, but it flexed them as far as it could, bending its long neck down to the girl like some creature caught and frozen in mid-wingbeat, holding perfectly still as it bent all its attention to the hand cupped in front of it. At last it caught the trick, of pulling the thread of power from belly to heart to throat to produce a soft whoosh of flame, drawing its lips back in dragon laughter as she was forced to leap out of the way or be singed by a fiery bolt. But it didn't have the strength yet to burn its way out of the cage and escape, while Éadha, drained from supplying Ionáin each day, hadn't enough power to be sure she could do it either.

On the day before the Masters were due to move the dragon off the island, Éadha reported to the infirmary, pleading illness. It wasn't difficult: exhaustion had stalked her for weeks. While darkness fell and the Masters and apprentices gathered for Vespers once more, she lay in a narrow white bed in the infirmary. The room about her faded as she focused everything on the thread running to the cage, now on the dock.

The dragon crouched, ready. And slowly, like someone unpicking a weave, she began to pour every atom of her being into the golden heart of the dragon. On and on it pulsed, each heartbeat sending more and more of herself, until she felt she must disintegrate and reassemble once more in the belly of the beast until finally, ah, the silent dragon roared. Roared until the trees shook and the sleeping crows roused crying from their roosts. Threw back its head and roared its pain and loneliness and thanks in a great, fiery breath, melting the bars holding it down so at last it stretched its wings to greet the sea winds and sprang soaring into the stormy sky.

And oh, how she wanted to stay with it, within it there in the sky, riding the night wind. Above the turret where she lay like one dead, the dragon circled once before opening its wings to be carried home on the east winds of the approaching winter. And in her white bed Éadha lay, unravelled and alone.

19

IN THE CLAMOUR AND the panic that followed the dragon's escape Éadha's collapse went almost unnoticed. It was several days before she regained consciousness. When she finally woke, she just lay still, staring at the ceiling, floating on a soft cloud of exhaustion. Just to have it stop, even for a little while, the wheel she'd bound herself to that day so long ago when she stepped in to help her friend.

A small sound to her right made her realize she wasn't alone. With an effort she managed to turn her head and saw Ionáin, asleep in an armchair by her bed. His hair was growing out, she thought. It was starting to look more like his old tangled mop, and his face in sleep was soft and relaxed. So different, she thought, from the aloof, distant figure who strode about the halls of First House with the other apprentices. More like the Ionáin she'd grown up with in Ailm's Keep. Her heart twisted inside her with regret, and longing. How much she'd give to be there with him now. To go back to their old life far, far away from the Masters. As she watched, he stirred, his eyes coming open then widening as he saw she was awake.

'Hey,' he said softly, rising from his chair and coming to crouch down beside her bed, covering her hand with his. 'Welcome back. You gave us all a fright. How d'you feel?'

She tried to answer, but her voice was still almost gone; it took several goes for her to manage a hoarse 'I'm all right.'

Ionáin's face darkened as he watched her struggle to speak, his brows drawing together and his eyes hardening into anger.

'They've gone too far this time,' he said, rising to his feet, pacing across the small space. 'I can't let her keep treating you like this.'

Éadha tried to shush him, tell him it wasn't Ailbhe's bullying this time, but the effort it was taking her to say anything only upset him more.

'This is insanity, you being hurt because of me. Senan's told me stories about how far Keeper girls will go to eliminate someone if they think they're a rival, but . . .' He shook his head from side to side, slowly. 'This place. I thought I knew what we were coming into. The status games, the coupling – I thought I knew.' He looked across at her then, and there was a new expression in his eyes, one she hadn't seen before, almost one of grief. 'But it's more than that too. There's a darkness . . .'

Éadha's heart went cold. What had he learned? But before Ionáin could say anything else, a nurse came bustling in and saw him standing there. Immediately she stepped in.

'My lord, please. The Master Healer was very clear, the patient needs to sleep. It's only a couple of days until she's to keep for Lord Senan in the autumn trials.'

Her tone was polite but unyielding and after a moment Ionáin nodded once, briefly. He leaned down to Éadha and gave her hand one last quick squeeze, his eyes suddenly blazing with determination as he murmured,

'I will fix this.'

A moment later he was gone. The nurse fussed about for a few minutes, straightening her sheets and checking for fever before leaving Éadha alone once more.

The next morning, when she woke she felt more like herself. With an effort she pushed herself upright, then shakily swung her legs off the bed and on to the floor. From beyond the closed door, she could hear someone moving about. Levering herself upright, she shuffled to the door. She was dressed in a thin white infirmary gown that reached down to her knees, the cotton brushing against her legs as she moved. Leaning against the door frame, she peered out, expecting to see the nurse again. Instead, a familiar dark-haired figure stood with his back to her in an alcove opposite her room. Inside the alcove was a wooden counter, currently strewn with bunches of dried herbs. From where she stood she caught the tang of fennel and the bite of poppyseed. Gry was stripped to his training vest and bent over, absorbed in grinding seeds into a paste with a pestle and mortar, the muscles in his arm jumping as he rhythmically ground the fine shells. She stared at him without saying anything, knowing she didn't need to for him to sense her standing there. Sure enough, after a moment he laid down the pestle and without turning round said, 'Not dead then?'

'Not dead,' she replied, her voice still hoarse but at least audible now. He turned to face her, leaning back against the counter as he folded his arms and looked her up and down. She was suddenly intensely conscious of just how thin her gown was, as his eyes came to rest on hers. 'How are you here?' she said abruptly.

Gry looked at her, the ghost of a laugh in his eyes as he said, 'Can't a chap take an interest in herbs without people reading things into it?'

'So, not keeping an eye on me?' she said, her mouth twitching.

'Fishing again, Ailm?' Gry said. 'This secret promise of yours you insist on keeping. It's proving expensive, hmm?'

'It wasn't that,' said Éadha, slowly shaking her head. 'Not this time.'

'Well, whatever it was, it almost killed you, Éadha,' said Gry, frustration creeping into his voice as he looked at her. 'Just . . . can you stop spending yourself so lightly?'

'Some things are worth spending yourself for,' said Éadha quietly, and in her mind's eye she pictured again the moment when the young dragon burned its way out of the cage and sprang into the night sky. With a growl, Gry pushed himself away from the counter and came to stand in front of her.

'Not to the point of almost dying, they're not. When I heard the healers couldn't wake you, I almost . . .' And he turned away, one hand raised, as if he wanted to take hold of her but knew he couldn't, that she was still too fragile. 'I need you here. I need you to not be dead. Do you hear me?'

'Gry –'

'No. If you're going to almost die, you can't expect me to stand here and say nothing. I know he got there first. I know that. If I could, I'd go back in time to be the one you met first.'

'You'd have to go back pretty far,' said Éadha faintly, a traitorous heat beginning to rise through her body at the ferocity in those gold-flecked eyes, the way he was standing over her, as if only a superhuman effort was stopping him from catching her up in his arms.

'Close your eyes,' he said abruptly. 'Will you do that for me?'

And Éadha knew she should say no, that she should step back into her room and close the door before this, whatever it was, went too far. Before she did something she knew she shouldn't. But even as she whispered, 'No,' her eyelids flickered closed, as if she couldn't help herself, couldn't stop herself from responding to the question in his voice, because it was a question she also needed to know the answer to.

'Now *feel*,' came the quiet command, and it was like he'd set a match to her soul. With her eyes closed her power took over, reaching out without conscious thought to the young man standing facing her. As she did, she felt him step in closer. There was a sensation of something falling away and then it shone out, there, so white and blinding in front of her, the molten core of Gry's power as he released his thought-wall and stood before her, his whole self. Whole and completely vulnerable. Her breathing grew shallow as she took in the glory of it and felt her own power respond instinctively, massively, from deep inside, her silver strength beginning to pound at her own thought-wall, as if it wanted to smash it all down and reach across it. To finally touch him, the power of him. Any minute now, she thought, she was going to lose control; her power was going to take over and she *wanted* it to. To lose herself in this feeling that was rising up inside her like a force wave. To be taken over.

As if from a great distance, a voice sounded, faint but insistent. It was her nurse, speaking to someone else at the foot of the stairs leading up to the sick bays. The next moment there was the sound of her feet on the stone stairs, echoing up into the first-floor hall where the two of them stood, lost in each other. Éadha's eyes flew open at the same time as Gry's and his power snapped out, smothered in an instant. Like someone being released from a spell, Éadha swayed a little where she stood, as her body became her own once more, no longer the slave of her power. With one last glance Gry turned away, back to the counter again. Éadha stepped back into her room and closed the door just as the nurse reached the top of the stairs.

20

THE GUESTS HAD BEEN arriving all morning, some on horseback across the land-bridge, others on sailing ships moored offshore, channelling in to alight on the dock. It was raining heavily, but the Masters had raised a power dome above the combat field the night before. Parents and apprentices stood about inside the dome in small groups, and the air was filled with the hubbub of greeting.

Éadha sat a little way away from the combat field, on the edge of the handball alley, her back against the wall. Behind her the diverted rain spattered noisily into the stone alley. Only her face was visible, the rest of her wrapped and hooded against the chill in her Keeper's cloak as she watched the steadily growing throng. The elegantly ageless mothers, the proud, confident fathers, all impervious and certain to the core. And why not? This was their world, built by and for their breed, and it fitted them like a second skin. The power that radiated from these Families was as insidious and implacable as any Master's Inquisition. Every large gesture, every loud laugh, every immaculate outfit said: *We're better than you. You who are different, know that your worth is less than ours. Look at us and feel shame. Feel less than us, and when you're on the floor, bow down to us.*

Éadha could feel it, the force field of dominance that flowed out from the crowd in front of her, as surely as she could see the power that shone from Master Irial's staff to hold off the rain. It was the power she felt every day: in her dorm, in class, in the ref. Everywhere, like a pressure on the back of her head, pressing her down on to her knees.

But something had changed since she'd returned from the infirmary. A dragon had called her sister, there, on that field under a dome of stars. She'd filled it with her heart's gift and it'd burned the Masters' cage into a twisted heap of metal. As she sat there on the damp ground in her thin wool cloak, it felt as strong as a dragon's mailed skin, impervious.

'Keeper, on your feet.'

Master Irial's sharp tone broke through her thoughts.

'Lord Aedan has asked to greet you; go at once.'

Over at the viewing platform, Éadha's heart gave a lurch to see the familiar faces of Lord Aedan and Lady Úra, Ionáin beside them, beaming. She walked over, and to her surprise Lord Aedan held out his arms towards her and enveloped her in a warm hug. As he did, all the memories of her beloved Keep she'd so carefully hidden away came rushing back in a wave that raced all the way from the North Tower over the forests and mountains, across city and sea to crash against her heart.

'You're recovered, I hope? Master Healer told us you'd been unwell.'

'Yes, my lord,' she replied.

'He fairly scolded Ionáin earlier. Seemingly he insisted on staying by your side all those nights you were unconscious. The Master's convinced that's why Ionáin's power stuttered for a few days.'

Éadha looked across at Ionáin, who'd flushed bright red as his father spoke. He was dressed in combat gear, banded across his chest and down his arms. He was now taller than his father, than her, she realized, finally fully grown, while the months of training had turned his naturally slender build into something lean and finely honed. Even his face looked different – stronger, more defined, his jawline set with determination. Her heart lifted suddenly and, before he could say anything, she turned back to Lord Aedan.

'Master Healer is as bad as Béithe when it comes to fussing, my lord,' she said. 'Ionáin will do you proud today, I've no doubt.'

'Well said,' replied Lady Úra. 'Now come, Ionáin, we're sitting with Lady De Paor and I want you to come say hello.' As the three of them walked away, Éadha heard Úra continue. 'Though all anyone can talk about is this dragon escaping. I don't know what your uncle was thinking of, bringing it to First Island like that. We're lucky it didn't try to kill all of you.'

'Huath's hunting it again, isn't he?' she heard Aedan reply, before they went out of earshot. Éadha offered up a small prayer for the young dragon as she headed for her spot on the sidelines. From there, she saw Ionáin and his parents join an immaculately dressed, silver-haired version of Ailbhe. Moments later Ailbhe herself appeared beside them. She was as beautifully turned out as ever, dressed specially for the match in a tailored combat bodice and skirt showing her trim figure, though Éadha saw how her mother reached out to straighten her bodice and tuck her hair behind her ears. Éadha was suddenly conscious of how she was still in her plain training tunic. The Ailms and the De Paors, meanwhile, all embraced each other, laughing and chatting until Master Irial called for the contestants to take the field.

In combat the apprentice Channellers were divided into two teams. An apprentice was knocked out if they were pushed outside the playing field boundaries or if they were knocked off their feet on the ground for a count of five. The winners were the team with the most members left standing at the end of the match. Ionáin was the captain of one team with Linn. Senan was captain of the other team with another apprentice, Cormac, as vice-captain.

Linn was heavily padded, with two Masters stationed on the sidelines to protect her. As the strongest of the Keeper novices, Gry had been assigned as her Keeper as usual. Taking up position beside Éadha he said quietly, with a nod towards Senan, 'Be careful today. He'll do anything to win.'

Éadha nodded, her mind going towards her thought-wall, making sure her gift was hidden carefully behind it, along with some reserves of energy.

Master Irial went to stand in the centre of the playing field and addressed the parents.

'Welcome all to the annual autumn trials. I'm proud to say this is one of the strongest apprentice years I've had the privilege of training. Their skill, commitment and loyalty is outstanding and I'm confident the future of the Families is in safe hands. My lords, lady – a clean fight, please. You may begin.'

The teams quickly took up their positions. The possibilities were endless, and the captains would've spent days assessing the strengths and weaknesses of the different apprentices – who'd take on who, who needed shielding, who could fight best in the air and who on the ground. The aim was to keep as many apprentices in play for as long as possible; if one side got a significant numerical advantage early on, it'd all be over quickly. Even the strongest Channeller apprentice wouldn't be able to withstand the combined strength of seven or more apprentices on the other team ganging up on him.

Éadha knew Ionáin's instinct would always be to lose as few men as possible. That was his weakness when facing a ruthless fighter like Senan. He'd spread himself too thin trying to save everyone while Senan would abandon the weakest players on his team or line them up as frontline fodder early on to protect the stronger players and save their strength.

True to form, she saw Ionáin and Linn take up positions at the far ends of the playing space: typical protector stances. On the other side, Senan and Cormac withdrew three layers behind their players, forming a tight clump in the centre. Then the time for thinking was over as she felt the wave of Senan's onrushing channel hit her, harsh and demanding. For the trials the apprentice Channellers were permitted to use up to three threads, so the skill of their chosen Keeper came into play, ensuring they switched between threads at the right moments and maintained a steady flow. As each thread was slightly different, there was always a moment of adjustment when a Channeller moved between them. A good Keeper would judge not only the strength of the thread but also the best moment to switch.

The teams had been picked to give the spectators an even contest, and so it proved. Ionáin and Linn were everywhere, protecting their team, diving in with their staffs to head off bolts. Senan, meanwhile, sat back, husbanding his strength for occasional thunderbolts, watching as his team pulled the two opposing captains the length and breadth of the pitch. Slowly Ionáin and Linn began to whittle away his buffer of apprentices, as first one, then another was knocked out of the field of play, blasted by bolts of pure power they couldn't deflect with their staffs. The playing field was ringed by Masters ready to catch apprentices before they could sustain serious injury, though Senan hit one student so hard he was catapulted out over the sea, and it took Irial and Dathin's combined effort to create a safety net and stop him crashing into the choppy waters.

They were entering the final quarter when the last line in front of Senan and Cormac was cleared away. They'd paid a high price in numbers for their strategy — only two apprentices apart from the captains were left on the field. But they were fresher; Éadha could feel Senan's ready power humming through her. By contrast Ionáin and Linn were battered and weary. Ionáin had only two lines of power left, one having dropped off, while Linn had just one. On Linn's signal their remaining four apprentices pulled in close as they advanced on Senan and Cormac.

Six to four – though tired, the odds were in Ionáin and Linn's favour. Now it was about running down the clock and holding on. Senan, who'd stayed on the ground throughout, flew up into the air, holding his staff in combat stance.

'Hope you enjoyed the warm-up. I suppose it's time we gave the visitors a real game, hmm?' Bowing his head he sent an almighty blast sweeping in a half-circle in front of him. It was so powerful it sent two apprentices tumbling at once. Ionáin dived to try to catch one, and Senan immediately took his chance, sending a fiery blast hurtling straight at Ionáin's exposed chest. The crowd, filled with experienced Channellers, gasped. Éadha's instincts took over. Closing her eyes, she sent her power rocketing into Ionáin. Senan's blast still sent him flying backwards. He hit the ground with a sickening thud, but Éadha's power cushioned the worst of the impact. Linn was there in a heartbeat, Ionáin's hand shooting up as hers came down and she lifted him into the air before he could be counted out. The crowd whooped in relief and delight. Ionáin retreated, dazed, shaking his head, two apprentices pulling in front of him protectively.

Linn whirled about to face Senan, eyes blazing. 'See how far you get trying that on me.'

Senan knew as well as anyone there that a direct blow like that to Linn would get him sent off. He fell into a defensive stance as she flew at him. His line of power faded, the Fodder now completely exhausted by his almighty draw moments before. As his Keeper, Éadha needed to switch away to a fresh line. But she was drained herself from the surge she'd just sent to Ionáin and, instead of a smooth pick-up, she faltered, dropping the spent Fodder line but fumbling the switch to the fresher line. In that moment Linn swept in, crashing with her shoulder into Senan, knocking his staff out of his hands before shooting a ball of power from her palm into his chest. Unable to draw power from the Fodder, Senan tried to channel power from Éadha instead, but her thought-wall was too strong, blocking his draw so his channel came back empty and leaving him without any power to absorb the impact. Linn's blow sent him flying, sprawling in an ungainly heap just outside the play line. He was out of the match.

While Ionáin and Linn's team turned to face Cormac and the one other remaining apprentice, Senan scrambled to his feet, livid. He raced over to where Éadha stood and grabbed her by the shoulders, screaming into her face.

'You cheat! You dropped that Fodder line then shielded yourself on purpose. You sabotaged me to help Ionáin – you'll be sent as Fodder for this.'

His eyes were blazing, his face bright red with effort and rage as he spat the words at her. Already shaken by the effort of saving Ionáin and the realization she'd messed up with the Fodder line, Éadha's heart shocked into overdrive at his face so close to hers, filled with what looked like hatred. With an effort though she forced herself not to react. Beside her, Gry said, 'Hey, Senan, she's just keeping for you. She can't magically make you any good. Stop being such a sore loser.'

Senan's face darkened further and he raised his fist as if to blast Gry. Gry didn't move a muscle though, only stared back at him, his face expressionless. At the same moment, Master Irial stepped in between them.

'Senan. If Éadha has deliberately failed you, she'll be severely punished. Might I remind you, however, of our audience.'

Senan's eyes darted up to where his father and the other Lords Channeller sat in the gallery. He clamped his jaws shut, turned on his heel and stalked over to where the rest of his team were watching the last few seconds of the match.

Meanwhile, the Master Librarian, who'd been acting as a touchline umpire, gripped Éadha by the shoulder and pointed her towards First House. As she began the long trudge up the hill, she heard the gallery behind her cheering. Ionáin and Linn's team had won.

Moments later came Master Dathin's voice. 'Lord Ionáin, Lady Linn, as our victorious captains I present you with these yew staffs, made from the wood of the temple trees. When you leave Lambay, may you wield them always to the greater glory of the Ailm and Manon Families.'

21

'APPRENTICE KEEPER ÉADHA. YOU'VE been accused of knowingly withholding power from your assigned Channeller. You understand how serious this allegation is. The first rule of keeping is to obey your Channeller. Without question. While we discourage them from drawing directly on their Keepers other than in an emergency, it's their choice to make. Master Irial, what's your view? Did she deliberately withhold?'

Master Dathin was standing by the lectern in the Library, Master Irial and the Master Librarian sitting behind him, their expressions stern. Éadha stood, head bowed, in front of them.

'The reasons this Keeper is assigned to Lord Senan are well understood,' said Irial. 'While she's had a recent health issue, the arrangement has broadly worked. However, we've also all noted her efforts to remain close to Lord Ionáin. In my view, therefore, it's likely Senan wasn't able to draw on her as she's still weak from her recent illness, and, in the moment, she was also distracted by what appeared to be a serious injury for Ionáin.'

'Master Librarian?'

Barely glancing at Éadha, the Librarian responded dismissively.

'She's too close to Ionáin, given her lack of breeding and the availability of other more suitable partners. This morning's incident simply proves the inadvisability of excessive closeness.'

Standing in front of the Masters with her head bowed, Éadha was angry. Angry because she'd moved faster than any of the Masters to shield Ionáin and they couldn't even see it. Angry because these old men were talking about her like she was no more than a piece of meat.

She knew if she looked up now the anger would show in her eyes. Some sense of self-preservation kept her staring at the floor while Master Dathin came to stand in front of her, placing his hands on either side of her head for an Inquisition. His was an implacable force, filling her head, dominating every thought as he sifted through her mind. She was exhausted from sending her strength into Ionáin and still shaken by Senan's screaming fit, but her rage sustained her, and in her rage she welcomed the intruder. He might be immensely strong, but he wouldn't break through her thought-wall if she didn't will it. She'd defeat him on his own ground and he wouldn't even know he'd been beaten.

After a few moments he dropped his hands and nodded to the other two Masters.

'I see exhaustion and distraction but nothing intentional.' Addressing Éadha directly, he went on, 'Apprentice Keeper, you're barred from attending the end-of-term trials celebration tonight. When you arrive at Second Island you'll also attend remedial Keeper training in the Fodder Holds. Perhaps that'll teach you the advisability of staying focused on your own Channeller's needs. Now, gentlemen, let's return to our guests.'

That night Éadha lay alone in her empty dorm, listening to the distant music from the party. It was their last night on First Island. The next day, they'd sail to Second Island, where the Channeller–Keeper pairings became more formalized. It meant that for the girls in her dorm, tonight was important, a last chance to convince the Masters of this or that pairing. Sure enough, when Muir, Síofra, Cara and Ailbhe burst into the moonlit room in the early hours full of chatter, this was all they talked about – Cara excitedly congratulating Síofra for finally pairing with Cormac after he'd taken the whole term to choose between her and Sibéal, Muir breathlessly telling Ailbhe what a stunning couple she and Ionáin had made when they stepped out on the dance floor for the first time, he so fair and she so dark.

They finally fell asleep just before dawn and Éadha could uncurl from where she'd been lying, wide awake and facing the wall, desperate not to let them see how much they were hurting her. Slipping past their sleeping forms, she headed out of the Keepers' quad and down to the dock. Her chest hurt with the same pain that'd been lodged there like a stone ever since the day Ailbhe had burned her book and she'd understood just how implacable they were – Ailbhe, the Families, the Masters. How much they thought they owned the world. Owned her, and Ionáin.

She passed the spot where the dragon had been caged, but all traces of the melted and twisted metal had been cleared away. Sitting on the jetty, legs dangling over the edge as the seawater slapped at the struts beneath her, she stared up at the lightening sky and thought of the young dragon, finally able to stretch its wings wide on the wind. She knew it most likely had flown into the west, away from Channeller strongholds. Yet she still felt connected to it, to the power she'd given it that lay now in the dragon's fiery heart. There was a comfort in that, she thought, despite everything. To know there was a world beyond this closed universe of Channellers and Families, that the dragon was flying far above them all on the world's winds, with a power beyond the Masters' understanding. Beyond their control.

To her left she could just make out a scorch line, almost overgrown now, as though the dragon had burned a line in the ground as it broke free. Curious, she climbed to her feet and followed the line to a copse of new birch trees. The dragon must've burned down the trees here, all the way back to the walls of First House. While the Master Grower had clearly been at work, it was still possible to see where the new growth began, at a heavy oak door set in the wall.

As she peered towards the door, she heard Gry's voice and turned in time to see him step out from beneath the trees. He was talking to a tall woman with a weathered face and bright eyes, and he was still dressed in his formal clothes from the party earlier, a dark-blue tunic open at the throat, and slim-fitting black pants. Seeing Éadha, his eyes widened, and he moved swiftly towards her.

'You got through it then?' he said as he reached her. 'Dathin's Inquisition?'

It was the first time she'd been close to him since that day in the infirmary; deep inside she felt her power kick in recognition. She wondered if it always would now, whenever she came close to him. In response to his question, though, she nodded with a half-smile. 'Our great Masters concluded I was far too silly to have done anything on purpose. Generalized feebleness and emotionality was the verdict.'

'Well done,' said the woman beside him. 'Dathin is a powerful Inquisitor. Your wall must've been very strong.' Her eyes were keen as she looked at Éadha, and Éadha found herself thinking she wouldn't ever want to be on her wrong side.

'This is my aunt, Lady Hera,' Gry said, and Éadha saw the pride in his eyes as he said it.

'It's good to finally meet you. Gry has told me of your brave decision. Your courage does you credit,' said Hera, at the same time reaching out a hand to help Éadha off the mound of soil she was standing on, adding, 'You might, though, want to come down from there.'

Éadha looked at her in confusion, then glanced down and realized with a start of horror she was standing on a freshly dug grave. She recoiled, stumbling off the mound, while Hera said, 'Yes, most unfortunate. Master Dathin told me last night that they spared no effort in hunting that young dragon. When emotions run high, the cost in lives mounts quickly. I'd say four Fodder at least were just buried here.'

Éadha stared, appalled, as Gry put his hand on her shoulder. 'You weren't to know.'

'Is this where they bring them out?'

'Yes, normally the door and the burial ground are well hidden by trees, but the dragon's fire burned away the cover. I wanted to show Aunt while she was here. These graves – and the ones over there.' Gry gestured towards where older burial mounds shouldered out of the ground. These weren't the graves of Masters, Éadha thought – those were entombed in marble in the crypt beneath the temple. The farthest grave was set on a rise against the wall of First House. Once it would've looked east to Second Island, before the trees grew up, before it was hidden from view. Unlike the others it was marked by a headstone, clearly ancient, its edges worn and pock-marked, with lichen growing up its front.

SISTER was the one word pressed into its granite, etched too deep to ever be worn away, even by centuries of weathering.

'So much we must forget in order to make our choices bearable,' said Hera, who'd come to stand beside Éadha. Gry stood on her other side, and Hera reached out one hand to grip her nephew's arm, her voice filling with emotion. 'In my time here, there were rumours her grave existed, but I could never find it. I am glad to have seen it, this once.' Turning to Éadha, she continued. 'Leah. Sister to the Three Brothers, eldest and most gifted of them all. She lived out her days alone over there, on the furthermost east island of Domhain, in a fortress raised by her brothers just to hold her. Too far from land to use her power to escape.'

She gestured across the sea towards Second House, black on the paling skyline, her expression bleak. Éadha stared at her, stunned. All summer long she'd watched the Masters weave illusions from the Annals, the founding tales of how channelling first came into the world. She'd been hearing stories of the Three Brothers her whole life. Finally she found her voice to stutter out,

'But the Annals – they don't mention a sister?'

Hera grimaced as she turned away from the graves. 'Come. I'll be late for the land-bridge if I don't go now.' She made her way back to the stable yard, the two apprentices alongside her. The land-bridge was being raised for departing guests and her horse was already saddled and waiting.

'No one outside our Family speaks of Leah any more,' she said to Éadha, as she reached her mount and swung herself up. 'Our ancestor Shem was the only one of the brothers to leave First Island, horrified at what his brothers had done to his sister, moving out west to found our House. He passed on some memory of his older sister to his descendants, but you'll find no word of her here on Lambay.'

Gry turned towards Éadha. 'That was the part of the story that always frightened me most when I was little. Not the battles, but how it's possible to make someone disappear so completely. As if they never existed, even a member of the Founding Family.'

'Her power didn't fit with the world her brothers were building. The world we live in now, of Fodder and Holds and Families,' said his aunt. 'As long as there've been Channellers, it's always been their way. To snuff out a challenge before it even knows itself to be a threat, Sister save us.'

A memory stirred in Éadha, of Béithe comforting the maidservant in the kitchen of Ailm's Keep with those same quiet words. 'Sister save us.'

'She must've scared them very much,' said her nephew.

Lady Hera looked down at the two young people. 'But the dragons remember. Let us hold to that.' And, raising her hand behind her in farewell, she rode away, leaving the two of them standing in the stable yard in the pale light of morning.

PART III

Second Island

22

BOAT TIMBERS CREAKED AND white sails snapped. Beneath the sails, the Keeper apprentices drew their capes tight against an east wind sharp with the threat of winter, while Fiachna steered them expertly into the shadow of the granite cliffs of Second Island. Ahead, the last of the Channeller coracles bumped each other as they edged into the sea cave that was the only entrance to Second House.

Salt-blasted and wind-chilled, the Keepers arrived at last into the still waters of the cave. A Master stood waiting as they docked, holding a silver lantern. Master Joen, the Apprentice Master on Second Island. He was as tall as Master Irial but with a heavier, barrel-chested build and dark colouring.

Facing him, Fiachna recited the formal words of transition. 'Master Joen, I commend these apprentices to your care, to be trained and held on this island until they're deemed Risen.'

With his large frame, black hair, thick eyebrows and weather-beaten skin, Master Joen made a daunting first impression as he glanced over the shivering Keepers sitting behind her. His first words were mild enough, though, as he nodded and said, 'My thanks to you, Head Keeper

Fiachna, journey safe,' before gesturing to the apprentices to follow him.

A cylinder of light had been hollowed out of the cliff, steep stairs winding about it to the top. While the Channeller apprentices had already flown straight up the light well to the surface, the Keepers had no choice but to pick their way like ants up the rock face, holding on tight to the thin stair-railing, the only barrier between them and a long fall to the cave floor. At last they emerged, breathless, into a courtyard deep within the walls of Second House.

'Let's go,' said Master Joen, giving them no time to even catch their breath before setting off.

The cliff where Second House had been channelled was little more than a blasted rock at the end of things, the only green the hardy cordylines and sawgrass clinging to the stony ground. Faced with less space, the Master Architects had raised their creation as high as they dared, a defiant fist against the winter storms that came roaring in from the icy tundra of the north. Channeller walkways criss-crossed the space above them, rising level after level. The buildings looked inwards, windows facing each other across the courtyards. Nestled within those mighty walls, yews flourished on smooth lawns and freshwater fountains drawn from deep within the rock played serenely.

As they walked through the cloisters, Master Joen began to tell them a little of the history of Second House. 'As you know, the first channelled buildings were raised by the Three Brothers on First Island and on the mainland, in what is now Erisen. However, in the early days of their power, they also came here, to Second Island and channelled a building on the spot where we now stand. To mark this . . .'

But as she listened, all Éadha could think of was what Master Joen wasn't saying. Of what Hera had told her, how that first building had been a jail for their sister, Leah. Of the raising of this place to contain whatever terrible wrongness in her the Brothers had so feared.

And she realized that now she didn't know what to believe from these stories she'd been hearing all her life. The Master Illusionist's tales, the Annals, the rows of scrolls in the Library – none of it was about truth or the recording of facts. What it was about, what it was truly about, was the creation of a story to make now – the Channellers' world of Fodder and lords – an inevitability, the only possible world. And a truth like Leah's truth, whatever it was, didn't, couldn't, exist if it had no place within that one true story of now. She thought then of her own hidden power. How it too seemingly didn't exist in the Masters' world. A shiver went through her as she tightened her thought-wall round it.

They'd reached the end of their short tour, arriving into a courtyard at the heart of Second House, where Master Joen went to stand in the centre with the Channeller apprentices. The Keepers lined up behind their new Head Keeper on Second Island, Maebh.

'Apprentices. No doubt you're tired from your journey, so I'll leave the formal welcomes to the ball this evening. As most of you know, this evening's ceremony marks the start of the graduation season for this year's graduates. In the coming weeks you'll join them in their celebrations, until they depart after midwinter for their Westport postings. For now though, there's the small matter of quarters and allocations.'

A murmur went through the group as Joen said this, and with it a palpable increase in tension on the Keeper side.

'First things first. Captains Ionáin and Linn. As our trial victors, to you goes the choice of quarters.'

Just as on First Island, each Channeller apprentice was entitled to an opulent suite, with Ionáin and Linn both opting for airy quarters high in the main towers. For the Keepers, though, it was going to be all change. Pulling a tightly rolled scroll from her sleeve, Head Keeper Maebh stepped forward once the suites had been allocated.

'Keepers, when I call your pairing, take up your position behind your assigned Channeller. When I'm done, accompany them to their apartments, and move your things into your Keeper's cubby.'

Where on First Island they'd lived in dorms, on Second Island they'd be living in their assigned Channeller's apartment as their personal Keeper, serving them alongside the ever-present, ever-wordless manservants. Only the few Keepers not directly assigned to a Channeller would live in a dorm.

All around Éadha, the other Keepers stood with their heads bowed, rigid with tension. So much turned on this one allocation for so many of them – their hopes of a life of status and ease as the wife of a Family lord, even of avoiding a Westport posting altogether. For all their coldness on First

Island, Éadha still had some sympathy for the pale, anxious faces around her now; life as a Keeper wasn't easy, and their assignment in the next few minutes would likely shape the rest of their lives. As Maebh started to read out the list, the first few couples followed the expected lines. Then came the first big change.

'Lord Coll of the Manon Family: Keeper Síle.' Beside Éadha there was a muffled gasp from Muir, her hand going to her mouth. She'd been dating Coll from the start of First Island. Éadha could see the Masters' logic: Coll was one of the weaker Channeller apprentices, while Síle was a very strong Keeper and the Masters probably thought they made a stronger pairing overall. It was hard not to feel sorry for Muir as she turned away, trying to hide her tears, and Éadha could see the sudden awkwardness in Síofra and Cara standing next to her, neither knowing what to say, even as they waited to hear their own fates.

Meanwhile, Maebh had moved on to the next pairing.

'Lady Linn of the Manon Family: Keeper Gry.' Of course that made sense too, Éadha told herself as the names were read out. Pair the one Channeller girl with the only male Keeper. Linn was easily the most decent of the Channeller apprentices, and Éadha knew she should feel relieved for Gry. Why then did it feel so painful to see him greeting Linn with a friendly eye-roll, and realize the days of him living in the dorm next door were really over? There was no time, though, for Éadha to think about what this meant, as the allocations continued.

'Lord Cormac of the Reilly Family: Keeper Cara.'

'Lord Ionáin of the Ailm Family: Keeper Ailbhe.'

And even though it wasn't, couldn't, be a surprise, Éadha's heart still twisted when she heard the two names called out together, at the sense of finality it carried. Knowing they'd be living together now in Ionáin's apartment for the next term. Like Leah, it seemed, she was being cleared out of the way, written out so the true story of a love match between Houses Ailm and De Paor could be told.

Senan's name was the last of the Channeller names read out; Maebh paused for a moment before saying,

'Lord Senan of the De Lane Family: Keeper Éadha.'

So there it was. For the next term she'd be living with as well as keeping for, Senan. The most sadistic Channeller of them all. This was no attempt at a marriage pairing. Most likely it was because Joen and Maebh had been warned about Senan's brutality, and like on First Island, they wanted to protect the Family girls from him. And maybe, too, it was part of her punishment for messing up at the autumn trials. Senan, after all, had seemed very keen that she be disciplined. Either way, as the two names were read out, Éadha realized all the apprentices around her had gone quiet. There was none of the usual sniggering from the other girls, or the laddish nudges between the Channeller apprentices. Instead, there was a sense, even if they'd never say it out loud, of a game maybe having gone too far. Senan, though, gestured to her imperiously with one finger. Fighting down a rising sense of nausea, she obeyed. In that moment there was nothing else she could do.

'Everyone, proceed to your quarters and get settled in; I'll see you at the Welcome Ball,' finished the Master.

Senan had chosen an apartment directly below Ionáin's, in a tower looking out west towards First Island and Erisen. A long, richly carpeted hall led from the entrance to the main suite, a cluster of bright, beautifully appointed rooms leading off a central sitting room. Éadha was in the Keeper's cubby, a plain, whitewashed room just inside the main door with one narrow west-facing window set deep in the walls. The first thing she did was check there was a working lock on the door, then, breathing in deeply, she focused on her thought-wall, making sure it was as strong as possible, with her gift buried far behind it. Being quartered so close to Senan, she couldn't afford a single slip. She knew what he was like from First Island: the way he'd revelled in needling and humiliating her and the other Keeper girls. She couldn't let him get to her, she thought, not when she'd so much to hide. From beyond the door she heard Senan's drawl echoing down the hall.

'Of course you're staying the full night at the ball. It's the first night when they finally stop treating us like children and let us get our hands on the Fodder, all guaranteed young, all volunteers. You wouldn't want to miss that, would you? You're not going to be a prude, now are you?'

'No, of course not,' came Ionáin's voice. 'I'm just not a big one for parties, that's all.'

'Leave it to me. I'll show you how to enjoy yourself in true Channeller style. Keeper, come here.'

At this last, Senan raised his voice. Reluctantly Éadha made her way down to the central chamber. Senan and Ionáin stood outside on a stone balcony jutting over the sea. Waves could just be heard crashing at the base of the cliff far below. White curtains billowed as the two stepped back inside. Senan sat down at a desk inlaid with ivory and gold leaf, leaning back in his chair to stare at Éadha. Her skin crawled at the expression in his eyes, and even though she'd buried it as deep as she could, still she felt her power stir.

Ionáin moved away, pouring himself a drink from a beaten silver jug standing on a sideboard.

'Pour me one too,' said Senan. 'I'm gasping still from that race earlier – who'd have thought Coll was such a neat sailor?'

Éadha forced herself to stand silently in the centre of the room until Senan turned back towards her.

'Keeper, you'll have to lay out my clothes for the ball. My manservant is ill, but I told Master Joen you can fill in until a replacement arrives from Erisen. That's right, isn't it? You were a servant or goatherd or some such in Ailm's Keep?'

At this Éadha flushed red but held her tongue. Ionáin handed Senan a full cup.

It was the first time she'd been near Ionáin since the trials. Seeing him up close, her heart gave the leap it always did. He, though, didn't look at her and went to stand again on the balcony.

'Now, Ionáin, don't sulk,' Senan called after him. In a conspiratorial whisper he said to Éadha, 'Your little stunt quite took the gloss off his win at the trials. Everyone thinks you helped him by deliberately blocking my channel and I should've won.'

'But that's not true,' she blurted.

Senan continued as if she hadn't spoken. 'I volunteered to help Master Joen ensure you never forget your place again, and now here you stand, assigned to me. I hope you're looking forward to it as much as I am.' Though she'd already guessed as much, a part of her felt a fresh unease to hear Senan saying it out loud: she was someone he had permission to hurt.

Mostly though, she was focused on Ionáin, hurrying over to the steps leading up to the balcony. 'Ionáin, I didn't block Senan on purpose; it was an accident.'

'Uh-uh-uh, naughty,' came Senan's voice as Ionáin finally turned from staring out over the sea, no look upon his face that she could recognize.

Instead, for the first time in her life she saw a resemblance to his uncle Huath, some hardening about the eyes and the mouth. Staring into space, not meeting her eyes, he spoke distantly, formally. 'Keeper Éadha. I appreciate in the past I've permitted familiarity of address because you're a member of my father's staff. I must, however, remind you that here on Second Island all Channellers should be addressed by their proper titles, both in public and in private.'

Éadha drew her head back as she stared up at him, half smiling as if to acknowledge the bad joke that this was, *had* to be. He'd never held a grudge in his life, couldn't bear to stay mad with anyone. She was the harsh one, the one who had to be coaxed out of a sulk.

'Ionáin?' she said.

Ionáin said nothing. Took a long drink and came down the steps past her to join Senan by the desk. She swivelled as he passed, staring at him in disbelief.

She knew his face so well – so much better than her own. All she needed was the slightest widening of his eyes, a sideways sliding glance as he passed her, and she'd know this wasn't really happening. But his features were frozen into a fine, tanned mask as he settled himself on a divan, flicking some imaginary dust off his pants.

'Lord Ionáin?' she said, still staring, mutely pleading until at last he raised his eyes towards her. Eyes that were just that, nothing more, shuttered and dark as he looked at her.

'I trust you'll give good service to Lord De Lane during your time as his Keeper,' he said before taking another drink.

'Attaboy.' Senan chuckled delightedly. 'Now, Keeper, run along. I'll call you when I need you.'

Éadha swung about on her heel and left, willing the tears back, tipping her head up so they couldn't overflow down her face as she walked unsteadily down the corridor that was suddenly a hundred miles long. In her room, her bag lay open on the bed. Her eyes were caught by the soft gleam of amber, just visible beneath her spare tunic. She pulled it out. It was the little tower Ionáin had given her for her birthday, more than half a year and over a lifetime ago, when he'd bowed to her, his face shining with laughter, and called her 'my lady'. Holding it loosely in her hand, she sat in the bare space of her room and stared at the wall as she heard the outer door open and close. Ionáin was gone.

Buried beneath her thought-wall, her power churned in response to her hurt and her fear. Ionáin had abandoned her, and now she was trapped in this apartment with Senan, having to bury every scrap of her power and her rage so as not to give him any excuse to hurt her, or report her for further punishment. In that moment, as her power roiled inside her, she wasn't sure how she was going to do it. Without thinking, she let some of it flow into the hand holding the little tower, the heat so intense the amber base started to melt.

That was how she was, she thought, staring down at it expressionlessly. She and Magret's little book both, scarred by their time on Lambay. Maybe it was right the tower should be the same. Another marker of the damage this place was doing.

Senan shouted from down the hall, 'Keeper – here!'

Killing the heat with a thought, she tucked the half-melted tower out of sight beneath her mattress before making her way to Senan's bedroom, forcing herself to keep her eyes down as she entered. He pointed to clothes laid out on his bed; she was to dress him. A part of her wanted to recoil but she pushed it down. She would get through this. His outfit was elaborate, layers of fine cloth overlaid with an embellished tunic, heavy trews and calf-leather boots. With her aunt's eye she could see the hours of skilled craftsmanship in every panel of the tunic. He shrugged it on carelessly, tugging petulantly where it caught slightly round his waist.

Éadha thought of Ionáin. He'd always been as light as a feather when they were smaller. She'd been able to lift him for years, until it became too much of an indignity for him to be given a boost up a tree or on to the cottage's curved roof. She loved the lightness, the spareness of him, the slender fingers, the elegant length. Her chest hurt at the memory, as she loosened the ties on Senan's tunic until he was satisfied. She was desperate for him to go. She knew her thought-wall was more vulnerable when she was upset like this. But as he was leaving, he turned at the door and said,

'Make sure this place is immaculate; I expect I'll have people back later. Oh, and before I drink too much to remember, you're to report to the Fodder Hold tomorrow morning for your remedial training. Now, hold still.'

In the next instant Éadha sagged as though from a blow to the stomach. Swift as thought, Senan had channelled her, draining her energy so she sank to her knees in the sudden weakness. She stared up at him, saw the pleasure in his eyes as he watched her fall to the floor, and she understood. Yes, he'd chosen her as his Keeper because he knew he could hurt her, but no, it didn't matter how good her self-control was, or how carefully she avoided provoking him. Because in the end someone like him didn't need a reason, just the knowledge he could. Because she was no one.

'Just needed a little extra for the party,' he said as he strolled on out of the door, leaving Éadha sick and shaken on the ground. For a few moments, as she lay there, she thought she might be losing her mind. If she'd known, when she first thought of coming to Lambay to cover for Ionáin, that this was the price, would she even have left Ailm's Keep? She lay still, staring at the pile of Senan's discarded clothes on the floor, waiting for her strength to return. As she did, though, she found herself remembering Gry's words in the Keeper boat weeks ago, when he'd laughed up at the sky at the idea of letting Senan determine the choices Gry made. *He was right*, she thought. She might be trapped as Senan's Keeper for now. But she would *not* let Senan be the reason she failed at what she'd come here to do. That power he did not have. And so, slowly, painfully, she pulled herself to her feet. She would go on.

23

TENDRILS OF MUSIC AND laughter snaked down the corridor to wind themselves about Éadha, pulling her aching legs towards the Banqueting Hall. It was her first time going to a formal ball and she didn't have a suitable outfit, so she was still in her normal Keeper tunic and pants, tucked into her old leather boots. She'd left her hair loose; she hadn't cut it since she'd arrived on Lambay, and now it hung down her back in long, dark curls. Enormous doors stood wide open, revealing an antechamber that opened into the space beyond. Storey after storey it rose, reaching the full height of the tower. All the way up there were balconies and cross-walks, and in between cushioned eyries. The walls were hung with tapestries, while heavy red curtains framed the deep-set windows that led on to stone terraces built over the sea. As Éadha stepped into the antechamber, the setting sun shot its last golden flares through the western windows as it sank behind Erisen. Were-lights sprang into life all through the hall as the daylight faded, a relay of torchbearers catching and carrying the sun's light on into the darkening night.

Fires were lit at intervals all round the walls with alcoves in between, some filled with tables of laughing apprentices, others discreetly curtained. Just like on First Island, there were tables creaking with food: freshly channelled nectarines, plums and strawberries from the greenhouses all piled high, luscious sweetmeats and cakes of every description. But this time there were also decanters of wine from the vineyards and barrels of beer brewed from force-grown hops standing all around the room, ladles and rows of goblets beside them.

On the balconies above, musicians played, fiddles and flutes swirling. Powerful bass drums, normally used to set the beat of a house raising, throbbed all the way down to the roots of Second House far below their feet. As Éadha arrived, Eoghan flew up in the air to where the fiddlers stood, shouting, 'Come on, put a bit of life into it – it's a party, not a funeral!' before grabbing a violin and playing a whirling frenzy of a tune, channelling power into his fingertips until they blurred, moving across the strings with impossible speed, flying all the while higher and higher until he was playing from just underneath the tower dome. Beneath him the apprentices gathered, cheering and clapping.

In front of Éadha, a red velvet rope barred her entrance to the main hall. A senior Keeper gestured her towards a bench against the wall of the antechamber.

'Apprentice Keepers may only enter at the grace and favour of a Channeller.'

Gry and some other Keeper students were already sitting there, and she settled down beside him. He was dressed in a midnight-blue tunic with white wings embroidered on his collar, the signet of the Flemin Family. His long legs were stretched out in front of him, one crossed over the other.

'Better get used to this,' was all he said to her, before tipping his head back and closing his eyes.

The hall was packed, not just with Éadha's year but with the previous Second Island class – the Risen. They'd just passed their final tests, and at midwinter they'd ride away to their Westport posting. But until then, they'd share Second Island with Éadha's class, the two groups overlapping.

Used to her smaller class on First Island, this throng of eighty or so apprentices laughing and chattering in the Banqueting Hall seemed enormous to Éadha. The skills of the Risen were also far beyond Éadha's group. They'd spent their term on Second Island learning the crafts of illusion and dragon combat, and this was their chance to show off. All through the hall illusions swirled: starbursts of colour showering down from the dome, scenes from famous battles racing across the tapestries and out into the night to disappear with the snap of a finger.

Remembering Senan's gloating about finally getting his hands on what he'd called the volunteer Fodder, Éadha looked about but she couldn't see any. Ionáin meanwhile had arrived shortly after Éadha, sweeping past in a phalanx of Family apprentices, Ailbhe at its head, regal in a silver column of a dress. He didn't even glance her way as he passed her bench. He was dressed in an embroidered tunic Éadha's aunt had sewn for him not long before he left Ailm's Keep. She remembered how he'd grumbled about the fittings when they'd sat together on the fell just before his Reckoning. 'It's nonsense – all I need is one warm coat and a pair of good boots. D'you think if I pass my Reckoning I'm going to waste my time on stupid parties when I could be flying?'

The disconnect between then and now left her dizzy. When she closed her eyes and focused, she could sense a thread between them, silvery and true, snapping taut wherever Ionáin went in the Banqueting Hall. Yet when she opened them again, there he was, downing glass after glass of wine – a thing she'd never seen him do before – and laughing loudly at Coll's jokes with the same, new hardness in his eyes she'd seen earlier. Not once acknowledging his oldest friend in all the world perched on a hard bench beyond a red rope.

'Talk to me,' said Gry abruptly. Éadha looked sideways, surprised; she'd thought he hadn't been paying any attention. He pulled himself a little further upright, so his eyes were level with hers. 'Stop making it so easy for him.'

Éadha drew back a little, even as she felt her silver fish stir into life inside her at the look in his eyes. 'What d'you mean?'

'Stop making it so bloody obvious you'll come running as soon as he clicks his fingers, no matter how much he ignores you when it suits him.'

Éadha flushed and said hotly, 'It's not like that.'

'Isn't it?'

'I don't play games like your kind.'

'Ouch,' said Gry, sitting forward, his eyes on the group in front of them. 'We do talk sometimes, you know, you and me. That's not playing a game. It just happens to also remind him other people see you too. You're not his secret.'

'He's doing what he has to,' said Éadha, more quietly now, as if her heart couldn't summon up the energy to lay those words down like the marker they should be. The memory of the look in Ionáin's eyes in Senan's apartment was still too raw.

'Maybe,' said Gry. 'But he's also being very stupid. Leaving you alone with me like this.' He waggled his eyebrows dramatically. Éadha laughed out loud at his expression, though deep inside she felt her power surge in restless response. Gry's face softened before he went on. 'It's like you think you don't exist for anyone except him. That you're just lucky if he even notices you.' He paused, then said, 'But have you seen you?'

Éadha stared at Gry – the way the candlelight picked out his cheekbones and hooded his eyes, so they seemed darker, more intense. As if he was reaching out to her beyond words to ask a question that couldn't be said out loud. She closed her eyes and just for a second reached out with her power towards him, feeling again, as she had in the infirmary, the sense of a power just as caged and ferocious as hers, her body responding without any volition on her part at the thought of what it'd be like to touch – to *really* touch – a power like that. The fire that'd unleash. How it might burn her up. She swallowed and turned her face away, back towards the party. It was the molash in the air, she told herself, heightening everything, making her body turn traitor. It wasn't real.

She wasn't ready for the thought that mightn't be so true any more.

Beside her she heard Gry let out a long, slow breath before saying, 'Good talk.'

She said nothing, willing her heartbeat to settle down.

'But just to give fair warning. After this –' and he nodded over to where Ionáin was standing, still ignoring her – 'I'm done playing fair.'

'Don't I get any say?' said Éadha, turning back towards him and raising her eyebrows.

'That's the point,' said Gry. 'I don't think you realize you do.'

They were interrupted by a loud shout from Senan. He'd turned red-faced and irritated as his group began to disintegrate, the Keeper girls leaving him to go and watch the Risen Channellers weaving their beautiful tales. Éadha saw Ionáin shuffle across the centre of the hall to join Ailbhe, followed closely by Coll. She'd never seen him drunk before, his face flushed and hectic, his hair in disarray. She watched, baffled, as he clutched a wine goblet to his chest before calling a servant over to refill it, swaying slightly on his feet until Coll dragged him to a seat where he slumped, propping his head up with his hand.

At the same moment, Linn passed by the velvet rope. Seeing Éadha and Gry there, backs and legs numb from their long vigil, she waved them in with an expansive hand.

'Come in, come in, how silly, come in,' she cried, before wandering off unsteadily. In the centre of the room Senan called loudly to the Risen Channellers.

'It's all very well for you to play with pretty pictures, but is that really all you can do? Surely it's about time we used some real power?' He flew up and out on to the highest west-facing terrace, followed by some of the Risen.

'Very well then, cousin,' a blonde-haired boy called back, laying his yew staff down. 'Ever heard of were-diving?'

'That sounds more like it.'

'The rules are simple. One person sends a were-light diving to the sea as fast as they can; the other has to dive and catch it before it hits the water or take a dunking.'

'All right. Ready? Go!' Senan called up a shining were-light and sent it streaking down towards the waves far below.

His cousin raced to the balcony and in one fluid movement dived over the wall and powered down after the tiny light, arms straight out in front of him, legs kicking as he sent power pulsing through them, flashing past cliff walls slick with water. Although the light had a good head start, he gained quickly on it and caught it well above the spray thrown up by the waves crashing below, swooping around gracefully and back up to land on the terrace without a drop on him. Everyone had gone to a window to watch the race by then, some of the Channellers flying out into the night sky for a better view.

Senan's cousin turned to him, laughing. 'Your turn!'

Lacking his cousin's experience, Senan's start was slower, but he accelerated hard and caught the little light just above the waves, wetting only the backs of his hands as he scooped it up and away. The game was on, as Channeller after Channeller flew out into the night, plummeting towards the sea. The Risen showed them other games: obstacle races around the turrets, in and out of the windows, through tunnels. Others flew out with their Keeper partners, who shrieked and clutched them about the neck when they saw the sheer drop below. The night was filled with the sound of laughter and screams, lights winking in and out of existence.

But as the sky lightened towards the east, one by one tired Channellers began to filter back into the hall. Éadha had put a shield in place after Senan's raid on her earlier. She was glad of it, as from all around the room she sensed Channeller threads snaking out, seeking power to replace what they'd drained by their antics. Senan wandered over to where she stood. She felt his power brush against her wall and come away, her strength too well hidden now for him to be able to find it. After a moment's puzzlement he shrugged and thrust his goblet at her.

'Fetch me a refill. I'll be over yonder,' he said, gesturing towards an alcove where the curtains had stayed drawn all evening. She filled Senan's cup and went to the alcove, pushing aside the curtains to hand it to him. As she did, her eyes met a row of slumped forms, some fallen to the floor, others sitting, heads on the table. At first, she mistook them for drunk students. But as her silver fish gave a sudden leap of recognition, she realized that all about her were Fodder. Her eyes widened in shock as her senses registered the scale of the life force sleeting past her from the alcove, out and up into the Banqueting Hall. Inside, her silver fish twisted as though it longed to join the streams of power flowing soundlessly by. So, this was how they did it. They were here in the hall, just as Senan had said, but kept discreetly behind a curtain. That way the more squeamish Channellers wouldn't have to face the reality of what they were doing while the more brutal, like Senan, were free to come in and drain them directly.

In front of her Senan sat, holding the hand of a thin, dark-haired girl lying almost unconscious beside him. As Éadha watched in horror, the girl moaned and tried to pull her hand away; it was almost entirely encased by Senan's large hands as he gripped her tightly.

'Sit,' he commanded. 'This'll be part of your remedial training anyway.' He held up the limp hand. 'Now this one's almost useless. If I take much more she'll go past the point of recovery; she won't have enough energy left to eat and restore herself. A good Keeper would've switched me away a while ago. My father always says the trick is to keep them at the point where they're too exhausted to waste any energy talking or moving, but not so spent the thread is compromised and they tip over into an irreversible spiral.'

He dropped the girl's hand, losing interest, and she slid limply to the floor. At Senan's nod a manservant dragged her to the back of the alcove, where he opened a narrow hatch and loaded her into it. Closing the hatch, he rapped once sharply on the side. The sound of distant machinery could be heard, echoing faintly up a shaft from far below. At Éadha's questioning look, Senan smiled.

'Fodder hatch. Sends the used ones back to the hold. We should get some fresh ones in a minute.' He sat back, staring at Éadha over his wine glass. 'Best cure for a hangover, a good drain. Young ones are the best; my father says their energy is the most cleansing. Second Island is known for the quality of its Fodder; only the best for us Channeller boys. You'd make good Fodder, you know – all that fresh country air in Ailm's Keep, hearty walks with young Ionáin. For your sake you'd better hope your remedial training goes well. There's only one way off this island – as a Risen. Fall at this hurdle and you'll spend the rest of your regrettably short life as a hangover cure for us Channeller boys down in the hold.'

He pushed back the bench. 'Come and tell me when the new Fodder arrives, there's a good Keeper.' He'd left the curtain ajar as he went back out, and through the gap Éadha could see the Banqueting Hall, grey now in the first light of morning. Half-emptied goblets stood on every surface, half-eaten food still piled on plates or ground into the carpets. Here and there students slept on velvet seats or slumped against walls, the occasional couple wandering past, holding each other up as their heads formed the apex of an unsteady triangle.

Senan wandered through the centre of the room, pausing to kick an insensible form. It was Ionáin, passed out still clutching his goblet, clothes stained and drenched from his failed were-dive earlier. Éadha drew the curtain and sat staring ahead of her, fighting with everything she had to hold herself still, not to scream her horror and her rage, while she did the only thing she could. Sending her strength silently, invisibly into the people around her. The only sounds in the alcove were their shallows gasps as they struggled to hold on to enough energy to keep breathing, while the Channellers in the hall beyond drained them again and again to stave off their hangovers.

In. Out.

In. Out.

In.

24

FOR THE RISING CHANNELLERS, Éadha thought, the days that followed on Second Island must've felt like a dream of perpetual twilight. Of mornings spent sleeping off the hangover from the night before, rising in bedrooms with the curtains closed against the afternoon sunshine, bathing and eating in a haze before dressing in some fine outfit, channelling fresh energy and going in search of that night's party. Second House was hung with lanterns that came alive in the early winter dusk, drawing the apprentices on and out into the night. Every night after that first Welcome Ball there was another party hosted by the Risen somewhere on the island: in apartments, in courtyards, out on the battlements, down by the lake at the heart of the island.

It was a tradition as old as Second House itself and the Risen's first duty as fully fledged Channellers, this hazing of Ionáin and his classmates. It was also the Risen's last hurrah before they left on a year of dragon patrols, a life of sleeping on bare ground, living off rations and knowing not all of them would return. Taken together it made for a wild ride, as the Risen lost themselves under the winter sky and dragged Ionáin's class into the night with them.

Each Risen Channeller took it in turns as ringmaster for the night, competing to outdo each other – the wine and beer, the exotic foods, the wildness of the music, the dancing. Smoking braziers burned molash. Inhaling it heightened the rush of power, so the threads around them were more visible, shining in the smoke. The apprentices would lift glowing coals from the brazier with tongs and place them in a silver bowl, cover their heads with a hood and lean over, breathing in the smoke while the coal burned. Then lying back, they'd drain power, the drug heightening the senses so the life force flowed into them with an almost ecstatic surge of pleasure.

And slowly, night by night, the Fodder were more in evidence. Always discreetly hidden behind a curtain or a screen, but accessible now, to the curious. Some, Éadha saw, stayed away. Avoided the curtained alcoves, changed the subject when it came up. Others, though, pressed eagerly in, gawking at these creatures – the 'volunteers' – finally revealed. They were almost always young – not much older than the Risen Channellers, young men and women dressed in plain grey shifts. They weren't chained like the people Éadha had seen in Ailm's Keep, but sat docile, heads bowed, never speaking, even when the Channeller students sat beside them, heads spinning on molash, seizing their hands to drain their life force more directly.

Of them all, Senan took the most sadistic pleasure in the effect of his channelling. Each evening as she dressed him, Éadha was forced to listen to him speculating about who they'd get, griping petulantly about used goods when the same faces appeared. 'That boy last night was far too weak;

I only got one were-dive out of him. If he's there again this evening I'll have something to say,' or 'If she's there tonight, that'll be three days in a row. I'll finish her tonight for at least a week though, see if I don't.'

Her self-control held despite this; she never reacted no matter how much he sickened her. And every night she made her way to the Banqueting Hall after tidying his quarters. Attendance was compulsory even though she, Gry and the other less popular Keepers spent most of their time on the benches at the entrance.

'It can't be an exclusive party unless someone is excluded,' noted Gry dryly on yet another evening spent trying to get comfortable on those hard seats.

Senan, the twins and Ionáin still formed the same core group as they had on First Island, but were joined now by Ailbhe, Cara and their hangers-on. Ailbhe never left Ionáin's side, keeping him supplied with wine, hanging on his words. From what Éadha could see, he hadn't been sober since their first night on Second Island, a wine goblet never leaving his hands. He shrugged off Senan and Coll's teasing when he was too drunk to compete in whatever contest the Channellers had dreamed up for that night: riding his horse into a ditch at the start of a race around the island, or tumbling head first into the water before any were-diving contests.

Éadha, meanwhile, had simply faded out of his world. Ionáin didn't speak to her, didn't look at her, seemed to move in a reality where she didn't exist. As she and Gry sat together on yet another night when his group strolled in past them without a glance, Gry nudged her.

'The Masters should really be making more of our powers.'

She was hunched on the bench, hands clasped round her knees, but this startled her into turning her head. 'Shh!' she muttered. 'Someone might hear you.'

'But these powers of invisibility we seem to have developed. Surely they could find some use for them?'

She sagged back, closing her eyes with a 'humpf' of a half-laugh.

In front of them, the band had started playing a round of traditional airs – laments about Channellers losing their Keeper loves to a dragon's fiery breath. All around the hall, couples were coming together to dance in slow, intimate circles. She saw Ailbhe stare up at Ionáin under her lashes, her expression meaningful. He was just finishing a large goblet of wine, but then he set it down and reached his hand out to her. The two of them wrapped their arms round each other, Ionáin closing his eyes as Ailbhe rested her head on his shoulder, swaying in time to the music.

'Come on,' said Gry. 'How about we don't give them the satisfaction of sitting here like sad little rejects? After all, there's no rule that says we can't have our own party.' He stood up, stretching out a hand to pull her up as well. She didn't resist, too full of the pain of fighting down her reaction to seeing Ionáin in Ailbhe's arms. Without a word Gry led her out of the hall into the corridor beyond, where they could still hear the music but they were alone, together.

'My lady,' said Gry, bowing in the silence of that cool, high space, his eyes holding hers as he reached out his hand. She stared at it for a moment before lifting her own and taking it. And it was like being brought back into the world, a reminder that, after all, she existed. He stepped in closer, his strong arms encircling her, his hands resting on the small of her back as the tendrils of music slipped out into the hall and wound about them both.

A part of her knew she shouldn't be doing this. Going in so close to him, after the way her body had reacted to his power in the infirmary. But another part of her was too hurt and angry at what Ionáin was doing, at how far he was going, to care any more. If this let her forget, even for a short while, it was worth it. For a few minutes the two of them swayed together, almost awkwardly, their bodies still finding the rhythm of the music, learning how to move against each other. And as they did, Éadha felt a deeper beat begin to stir inside her. Gry's chin came down to rest on the top of her head; he breathed in deeply, so she felt his chest rise and fall against her. Without realizing it, as they'd found each other's rhythm they'd moved together, closer, and closer still so that now she could feel the lean, hard strength of him down the whole length of her body. Her breath grew shallow as she felt her own body start to respond to the feel of him. *This is all wrong*, she told herself, though the thought felt slow and fuzzy-edged, as if she couldn't hold on to it through the heat that was beginning to rise through her, while his hips swayed against hers to the distant beat that seemed to come at the same time from inside them both, commanding them, subjugating them to its slow, insistent rhythm.

'Show me the real you,' Gry whispered, his lips brushing her ear and lingering there. She closed her eyes at his words, at the way they called to her power, yearning as it had for months now towards his, and she couldn't – she couldn't fight it any more. He was too close, the sense of that latent power, caged in his body, too strong as he leaned into the sway of the music. And so, with a thought she let it fall, her thought-wall, the one she'd kept in place since the day she'd first set foot on Lambay. She let it go, her power, her silver strength shining out in all its beauty and its vulnerability, and she heard Gry give a small in-drawn gasp above her, as he reached out with his senses.

'Éadha,' he said, in a voice filled with awe and wonder, 'I've never . . .'

He didn't finish, only lowered his head to rest against the side of her head, and she felt rather than saw how in that moment he let his own wall fall, so his power shone out too: the bright molten core of him. And she knew they were taking a terrible risk, there in a draughty corridor outside Lambay's Banqueting Hall, but she could no more stop her power responding than she could hold back the tide or still the wind. Her hands clenched into his fine shirt as she felt it, the galvanic *kick* of her power rising up to meet his. And they were two people clinging to each other as the powers within them roared up. Helpless in the wave of desire that crashed over them both as their powers churned, and churned, begging to come together: to set fire to the world. Éadha gasped, realizing how desperately close she was to losing every shred of control she had over herself, her body nothing more than a vessel for the sudden raging desire that threatened to overwhelm her.

'Gry,' she begged, her voice ragged. His head came up, and in his eyes she saw mirrored the same blinding desire, and only his arms holding her up stopped her knees from buckling underneath her.

'Gry,' she said again, a sob rising in her voice, 'I can't do this.'

'Éadha,' Gry groaned, his voice hoarse. With the last vestiges of her self-control, she loosened her arms from where they'd crept round his neck, letting them fall back to his chest, though she still couldn't summon the strength to push him away. Dropping her head, she pressed her forehead into his chest, and her voice, when she spoke, was muffled, 'This . . . this isn't real. It's our power. Not us.'

'Define real,' said Gry, his voice tight, and she could sense the immensity of the effort it took, for him to bring his power back under enough control to be able to say even that. 'Because it feels pretty real to me.'

'I want you, Gry,' she said, and it felt as if every word had to be torn from a place that didn't want to let her speak, only to feel, only to yield. 'You have that power over me. I'm asking you not to use it. Please. Don't make me betray who I am, not any more than I already have.'

'Why should I help you stay loyal to someone who doesn't even deserve you?' he said, his voice so low it was almost guttural.

'Because it isn't about him. It's about me, who I am. He trusts me. Don't make me hate myself by betraying that. Please, Gry,' she whispered.

With a great, shuddering breath, Gry dropped his hands from round her waist and stepped back. Tears stood in her eyes as she stared at him and felt the wave of desire begin to subside, as they both slowly, painfully rebuilt their thought-walls, locking away their power and becoming again the half-persons they'd chosen to be in this cursed place.

'Just don't say this isn't real,' said Gry, as he turned to go back into the hall. 'Only that it isn't what you choose. I deserve that at least. To be real to you.' And he was gone, leaving her alone in the stone corridor, to her lonely, unsated love.

25

THOSE FIRST DAYS ON Second Island may have been a twilight time for the other apprentices, but for Éadha it was a time of two worlds. A world above and a world below, linked only by the slender shafts sunk into the cliffs beneath Second House. Master Dathin had ordered her to go for remedial training as punishment for failing Senan at the autumn trials. So, starting on her first morning on Second Island, the day after the Welcome Ball, Éadha rose each day just after dawn and slipped through the morning halls to the heavy gate that barred the entrance to the Fodder Holds.

The first time she reported to the entrance she was met by Head Keeper Maebh. Where Fiachna was tall and almost gaunt, Maebh was of average height, with rounded curves that showed even under her Keeper robe. Her expression, though, was as severe as Fiachna's, her lips compressed as she looked Éadha up and down.

'So you're the troublemaker? Well. It's always good to learn early where troublemaking leads. Come,' she said, and led her into a windowless wooden box. With a jolt, Éadha felt herself falling.

'Don't worry,' said Maebh with the ghost of a smile as she saw Éadha's knuckles whiten, gripping tight to the handholds cut into the box sides. 'It's Channeller-operated, and we're not short of power down here.'

They passed several doorways cut into the rock as they descended. Following Éadha's gaze, Maebh said briefly, 'Those upper levels are my office and the infirmary; below are the holds. I'm just about to start my rounds, so you'll follow me.'

They landed with a soft thump on the sandy floor of the lowest level and stepped out into the main Fodder Hold. It was a cavernous space at sea level, a sequence of natural caves hollowed out further by the Channellers over generations. The walls were bare rock, fresh water running down them in places and collecting on the sand and stone floor into rivulets that led eventually to the sea outside. In front as far as she could see stretched row after row of bunk beds, some four and five beds high where the cave roof permitted, others only one or two where the ceiling sloped down to the floor. The light was dim: torches set into the walls, hissing and flickering in the damp air.

Maebh set off ahead of her, accompanied by a group of Keepers and guards. Éadha fell in behind. Many of the beds in the first section were occupied by sleeping forms and Maebh stopped at each one, carefully examining the occupant, taking their pulse, lifting their eyelids, measuring their waists and barking instructions. Most were left to sleep on; some were put on to trolleys and wheeled away to the lift. In one case the person didn't respond at all. Shaking her head in irritation, Maebh gestured to one of the guards, as Éadha realized with a jolt the person was dead. The guard wrapped the body in its bedsheet and hoisted it over his shoulder, carrying it away.

In the next cave people sat in a circle on stone seats hollowed out of the wall. Each seat had arms and a ledge in front, with each person chained to their seat, the chain just long enough to allow them to slump forward on to the ledge but no further. Above them rose a shaft, hollowed out in the cliff, so their life force could be more easily reached from the surface. Beneath the row of stone seats, a narrow trough had been dug into the floor. Sick with horror, Éadha watched as streams of urine trickled from some of the seated forms into the trough, which sloped down into the natural rivulets to be carried away. They were the Fodder currently in use, being channelled from far above by the Masters and apprentices going about their daily business on the sunny surface of the island. More even than the state of the people around her, it was the brutal efficiency that scared her most. The way the seats were designed to hold them up, the shaft allowing easy access to them from above, the culverts for the urine so they wouldn't have to be moved even to relieve themselves.

While Éadha fought down her nausea, Maebh examined each person in the circle, tipping up their chins to check the eyes, feeling some for signs of fever, reaching briefly into their minds, assessing their strength. She stopped at one fair-haired girl and turned to a young Keeper, clearly irritated.

'Why has this one not been kept for evening duty? We're short on presentables at the moment with the current attrition rate.'

'Yes, Head Keeper, I'm sorry. Master Joen specifically required a full complement today as they're completing the Library extension. I was planning to put her on a double shift, covering tonight as well.'

Maebh thought for a moment. 'Very well. It's not ideal as she'll be low by tonight and might expire depending on the games. Still, we've the fresh shipment arriving tomorrow, so we should have enough cover if she does. Keep her watered and if the extension is done early put her down for a sleep – even a couple of hours and we might not lose her.'

Her rounds done, Maebh returned to the lift, Éadha still in tow.

'Running repairs,' she commented as the doors closed. Éadha was glad she didn't seem to expect her to say anything. After what she'd just seen, she wasn't sure she could. 'It's the largest Fodder Hold on Domhain,' Maebh continued. 'It's a logistical nightmare, trying to keep so many inexperienced Channellers supplied with power every night, as well as providing the Masters' power for the day-to-day running of the House. We've to run several shifts day and night and the attrition rate is high. Your classmates are a rough group, and when we lose Fodder it's a long journey from Erisen to bring out more. We're having to manage on a skeleton supply at the moment until the next shipment arrives. And then we'll have all the Masters claiming they need the fresh Fodder more; they all love that first draw.'

The lift stopped at a door cut from the rock.

'I'm assigning you to Records. It's where we usually put apprentices sent for disciplining. Good for motivation.'

They'd entered the Head Keeper's offices on the higher levels. Here the rooms were bright, with windows tunnelled from the rock looking out to sea, furnished with sturdy wooden tables and chairs. Éadha was directed to another group of Keepers leafing through piles of paper.

These were the Records, details of the people sent by boat from Erisen to Second Island as Fodder. In each case they listed the age, the weight and the technical assessments of their reserves, as well as the reason for being sent. Some were 'volunteers' – skilled workers ordered by their Channeller to do a stint in order to make up numbers, or as a punishment for some minor transgression or simply because there wasn't enough regular work for them to do. Others were 'swept' – unemployed, unskilled people who could be taken at any stage by a Master or Channeller for use. Last were the renegades – those considered to be opposed to or critical of Channeller rule. Some caught on tracker patrol; others reported by Family members or Masters for holding problematic views.

After the first few confusing days, the allocations began to make sense to Éadha.

The renegades were the most dispensable, sent where particularly heavy drains were likely, meaning a real risk of losing their lives. The swept were next, slightly less likely to be assigned to fatal work, and finally the volunteers, those with the best chance of surviving their time on Second Island

and returning to Erisen; though whether they'd ever regain the strength to resume their former lives was a matter of luck.

They came in every shape, size and colour: young, old, men, women, craftspeople, musicians, skilled and unskilled, ugly, beautiful. The Channellers didn't care; they were simply a resource, vessels for the energy that sustained the Channeller way of life. Éadha was put writing out fresh arm tags for each of the Fodder, listing their basic details and strength levels. She sat with a group of junior Keepers, listening with a mix of revulsion and fear as they swapped tales of people's different ruses to conceal their strength. Some of the renegades, in particular, had rudimentary shielding skills, but an experienced Keeper could quickly break through to find whatever pathetic stores of energy they'd hidden away; anyone caught doing this was severely punished. Every time she heard the Keepers joke about breaking down Fodder defences, Éadha's senses went instinctively to her own thought-wall, praying this was one defence Maebh and her Keepers weren't able to detect.

As Maebh told everyone every day on her rounds, 'The best kind of Fodder is exhausted Fodder.'

This was her one overriding goal: efficiency. Keep the Fodder permanently drained to the point of near collapse, give them the minimum amount of time to rest and recover before being drained once more. That way they needed less supervision and had no strength to plot dissent, or try to escape.

'In the first few years of this hold,' she told Éadha on one of their lift rides down to the ground floor, 'you'd have a few every year who'd try to escape. Kill a Keeper, steal a boat. Some even got part of the way to the mainland before the Masters caught them. That's when the old Head Keepers realized just how precise we needed to be. Work out a man's reserves, down to the last breath,' she said with grim pride. 'Then make damn sure they haven't the energy left in them to think, or plot, let alone rebel. That'll do it. We have it so down now, we barely need guards in here any more.'

While most of the Fodder stayed below ground in the holds, a few were sent to the surface in the service lifts that connected the holds to the school at various points. The Masters mostly didn't need them close by to channel them. But it was easier for less experienced Channellers if they were nearby, and for some, like Senan, there was also a sadistic thrill in seeing the effect of their power. And so some Fodder, drugged to ensure their docility, were sent each night to the parties above ground. Always the youngest and most presentable ones, or as one Keeper said to Éadha one afternoon, 'Who wants to channel a woman who looks like your mother? Rather takes the fun out of it.'

'It's always the same,' remarked Maebh on her rounds one morning as midwinter approached. 'They arrive from First Island hardly using their powers, but by the time the Midwinter Ball comes around we're flat out down here as they channel from first thing in the morning to clear the cobwebs until last thing at night to shake off the day. By the time they leave here, they can't live without it.'

And Éadha understood this was the whole point of the endless parties and contests – the Masters' way of ensuring the Channellers got so hooked on power they couldn't imagine a life without it.

Every day Éadha was released in time to report to Senan's quarters and help him get ready for that evening's parties. Going from the dark, oppressive hold to his elegant suite filled with light and air, the sense of dislocation was absolute. The morning felt like a dream, a recurrent nightmare of slumped bodies and clipboard-carrying Keepers. It was only when she saw her handwritten tags on the wrists of the Fodder in the alcoves at the end of the night that the day came about full circle.

In Éadha's time underground, Maebh was never so crude as to say Éadha might end up there herself. There was no need; a week in Records was all she needed to see how easily a person might fall foul of the Masters or the Families and end up in a Fodder Hold, watching their life force trickle out of them, day by changeless day. Éadha understood. For those apprentices for whom the seduction of First Island didn't work, the Masters didn't hesitate to use fear. Showing them the choice, after all, was binary. Above or below, using or being used, living or dying, just as Gry had said that night on First Island.

Thankfully she hardly needed to send any power to Ionáin. He wasn't channelling at all now, getting so drunk at the nightly parties his friends had given up trying to persuade him to join their games. It was just as well because as her time in the hold wore on, Éadha's heart began to fail her. She'd draw the line from belly to heart, but there it stopped, too full with what she'd seen in the hold to want to release her gift on to Ionáin. He had to know he'd hardly any power now she was only sending him the bare minimum, but he didn't seem to care, pleading a cold when the drinking excuse didn't work, or draping his arm about Ailbhe with a meaningful wink at Senan. It meant, though, that she'd some spare strength inside her. And so one afternoon, as she draped an embroidered tunic over his shoulder, she asked Senan if she could keep for him when he drew power at the parties.

'I've learned so much from my remedial training and it'd really help my practice, my lord.'

Senan paused in pulling on his tunic and stared at her for a moment, standing there with her head bowed, the very picture of a proper Keeper even as, deep inside, her power churned with loathing. In the afternoon light his eyes were bloodshot and his face redder than ever, the endless partying taking its toll even on his bullish constitution. Then he gave a short chuckle, tickled by the idea. 'Why not? In fact you probably should've been keeping for me from the start, when you think about how much power I need. Yes. Why not.'

So, that evening, as Senan sat in the Fodder alcove, she sat beside him and when she felt his channel reach through her, she bowed her head and relayed it on to the young Fodder men and women beside her.

Senan was a brutal Channeller, adept at judging the power available and taking a vicious pleasure in pulling every last drop. But in Éadha he'd a Keeper who knew each one of those Fodder victims' faces, ages and just how far they could be drained and still left with enough strength to lie awake a half hour before sleep, whisper a word or two to the person on the bunk opposite, maybe even remember for a little while who they had once been.

Quietly, invisibly, but with iron determination, she blocked his grasping threads when she judged they'd had enough and instead drew her own strength from belly to heart and out, back into Senan, shielding those morsels of life with her own.

26

Éadha's seat in the Records room was near one of the windows hewn into the cliff face. Outside, cormorants wheeled and dived into the sea below while light-winged terns arrowed past, dropping from their nests built far above on rocky outcrops.

The Channellers were taught to glory in waste, to burn away the power as soon as it coursed into them, shooting up into the wind, pushing against it as a thing to be defeated. In her power, she was more kin to the birds than to them, Éadha thought. Kin to the young dragon who'd flown away on the world's winds all those months ago. Like them, her power was limited by her heart, by her strength, and so she flew within the wind, let it take her where it would, grateful for the impossible lightness of it, the brief absolution from the bonds that tied her to the earth.

As Éadha sat staring out of the window, Head Keeper Maebh marched through the Record room, snapping to the junior Keepers to follow her as she moved towards the lift. Éadha fell in at the back. These rounds were going to be particularly tense, as this was the day of the Midwinter

Ball, the last and greatest of the winter parties. Maebh was worried they might run low on power. Éadha was standing near a tower of bunks, listening to Maebh grumble over attrition rates when there was a soft thump. A girl hardly older than Éadha had slid from her bunk and lay unconscious on the floor beside her.

'What is it now?' snapped Maebh.

A Keeper bent to examine her. 'A volunteer presentable, Head Keeper. Seems to be dehydrated and spent.'

'Oh, for goodness' sake, that's all we need. Apprentice Keeper, bring her up to the infirmary, tell the nurses we need her in shape for tonight or I'll personally review their own files.'

Éadha half lifted, half dragged the girl over to the lift. She was heartbreakingly slight, her thin, triangular face slack as Éadha tried to avoid bumping her against the stony floor. Once inside the lift, Éadha laid her down gently on to a trolley and bent over to get her breath back. She knew the little face. She was one of the Fodder regularly sent up to the parties. Young and with a shadow of prettiness about her emaciated frame, she counted as a presentable. She was one of about ten girls of similar age most often sent up. They'd no names down in the hold, but Éadha had given them names of her own – this one she called Donn, brown, after her hair, which even matted and lank was still beautiful. She lifted her hand, thinking she'd send a pulse of energy into her when Donn's eyes snapped open.

'Don't.'

Éadha pulled her hand away in shock.

The girl sat up, swinging her legs down and swiftly loosening the trolley's wooden sidebar; she jammed it into the gap between the wall and the lift, so it juddered to a halt. 'That'll give us a few minutes.'

'What're you doing?' asked Éadha, now thoroughly bewildered.

The girl lay back on the trolley, spent. 'If you give me much energy now, then the infirmary will spot it and they might start asking questions.'

'You know?' asked Éadha.

'Of course I know.'

'Do you all know?'

'Not all of us, but some, we have eyes for power and can see the threads,' said Donn. She smiled grimly at Éadha's shocked face. 'Yes, it's almost funny. A whole island full of learned Masters, a hold crawling with Keepers measuring us down to the last breath and not one of you ever thinks to wonder what we can see. Don't worry, by the way, those of us who can see, we won't say anything about what you're doing. We'll take it to the grave.'

'I'm so sorry,' whispered Éadha.

'For what?' said the girl. 'You're one of the decent ones.'

'But how can you bear it, every day, being used up like that?'

Donn stared at her levelly. 'You have to break. That's what gets whispered to every person their first night in a Fodder wagon, or a hold, or some Family Fodder Wing. Accept this is how it is and let go of any ideas you had about yourself, any hopes you might've had. That way lies madness, trying to hold on to some rope made of dreams or love, hoping you can climb up it and out, back on to the surface, back into your life. You have to break, accept there's no way out, no way around. This is all there is for you now. Once you're broken you can learn how to just exist, that the only way is to go through it. And then, if you do come out the other side, what you have is a husk that still walks, still breathes, that maybe one day you can fill up again with things that are worth something. You'll never be the person you were; you had to give that person up to survive. But you might make a new person who's just as worthy.'

Éadha stood, frozen, staring at Donn.

'Here,' said Donn, scrabbling beneath her thin robe and pulling out a package. 'This is for you. A thank-you.'

'What do you mean?'

'There are those who hold back, quietly, gently. Trying to spare us within the limits of their ways. It's like a whispered conversation that only we can hear, every night up there in the halls, the touch of those who refrain.'

Éadha thought of Gry on First Island, telling her how there were always apprentices who tried, in their different ways, to minimize the harm they did while not being caught by the Masters.

'But you,' said Donn, 'you shine. That's what we call you: Grianán, the shining one. You've something none of us have seen before. We see your light, the way you block the fair one's spidery threads before they can suck us dry. It gives us hope that maybe it doesn't have to be like this, for always and forever.

'We know you've hidden yourself so they can't see what's inside you. But just for one night we can make you beautiful on the outside even if they can't see what lies within.'

Éadha stared at the little package, the size of her hand.

'The power you leave us with, we have to use it up or the Keepers will detect it. So, we cast about for something we could do. Some of us were seamstresses in our old lives, and I could steal bits and pieces from the students' rooms when I'm called for private sessions.'

Seeing Éadha's distressed face, she lifted up a tired hand and patted Éadha's arm. 'Please, take this as it's given: with joy, not sadness. Being able to do something for another is, after all, the essence of living rather than merely existing. It brought us back to ourselves, for a little while, to do this thing.'

There was a sharp snap as the wood broke and the lift juddered back into motion. Éadha hid the package beneath her tunic. 'What's your name?' she asked quietly, staring ahead as she waited for the door to open.

'Seoda,' she murmured, closing her eyes. 'Go, shine for us.'

27

ÉADHA DIDN'T TOUCH THE little package under her tunic but the thought of it carried her through a trying afternoon. Senan was at his most viperish, keyed up about the ball and taking it out on anyone unfortunate enough to be near him. By early evening his bed was piled with outfits he'd tried and discarded, years of craftsmanship and toil tossed aside like so many scraps of paper.

'How am I supposed to appear in public if you can't even lay out a proper outfit?' he raged. 'This is the Midwinter Ball on Lambay, not some goatherd's campfire. Some of us have a Family name to uphold.'

The ball was the final big celebration before the Risen left for their dragon postings and Éadha's class began their training. It was also Senan's last real chance to pair off with someone before the humdrum of Matins and classes took over once more. For all his power and his impeccable Family name, his vicious temperament frightened even the Family girls, schooled as they'd been since childhood in soothing the egos of vain and pampered Channellers. He'd set his sights early on Linn, confident she couldn't resist the logic of a match with the strongest male Channeller. He hadn't reckoned with her complete disinterest and that, as a Channeller female, she outranked him and couldn't be bullied, impressed or ordered by him to do anything. Confused and thwarted by this unfamiliar impotence, as the days dwindled towards midwinter he turned to the Keeper girls, only to find he'd missed the boat. The best-connected were already spoken for, or quickly paired off with Risen Channellers on Second Island. Senan was one of the few left without a partner. Only girls from minor Families and commoners like Éadha remained, and Senan was never going to accept a consolation prize.

His best hope now was to detach a Keeper girl from another Channeller – something the Masters only permitted if the Families and the girl herself agreed. So Senan, son and heir of the Family De Lane, found himself in the utterly unfamiliar position of supplicant. On his best behaviour, trying to win over girls he'd mocked and teased unmercifully all term on First Island. It did nothing for his mood in private as all his suppressed rage exploded in tantrums and punishments for Éadha and his luckless manservant.

Those hours before the Midwinter Ball saw Senan at his most petulant. Yet even though it would've made her life easier, Éadha couldn't help but be glad the Keeper girls were thwarting him. To see that maybe, after all, there was some limit to what thugs like Senan could demand. After storming his way through the afternoon, he shouted at her, 'Pick up every single thing or there'll be hell to pay later,' before sweeping out of the door, resplendent in a white tunic embroidered in gold thread.

She tidied up quickly, conscious that every apprentice was expected to arrive in time for Master Dathin's farewell speech to the Risen. It wasn't just the apprentices; the Masters and the Keepers emerged too from their studies, towers and holds to say goodbye to the Risen and mark the beginning of the new term. It was also the only night all winter when Keeper students had the right to enter without waiting on the grace and favour of Channellers.

The room immaculate once more, Éadha stepped out on to the terrace looking west to where the sun had just disappeared below Domhain's mainland, its last rays catching on the distant towers of Erisen. Carefully she opened Seoda's package and unfolded what lay within.

It was a bodice and skirt. The bodice had been pieced together from scraps of yellow and gold cloth of different hues, some embellished with sparkling stones, others plain and smooth. It was in the shape of a Channeller combat tunic – bare arms, crossed at the breasts to bind them steady, fitted at the waist. The skirt was a single piece of the softest cloth Éadha had ever felt, falling like water to the ground, so light it lifted at once in the sea-breeze, ready to fly on the winds, white as a dove's wing, as a wave top, as a summer cloud shining in the sunlight. Éadha slipped them on, looking at her reflection in the window. She'd no shoes apart from her Keeper boots, but this dress was light incarnate; she'd fly to the ball on bare feet that didn't need to touch the ground.

Fly she did, dropping soundlessly from Senan's terrace, the air rushing about her, caressing her legs through the softness of her skirt. She landed soundlessly on the furthermost balcony of the Banqueting Hall and stared down at the crowd below. Later they'd disperse, into the alcoves, out on to the terraces, but for now all were in the central rotunda for Master Dathin's farewell to the Risen.

After the solemn blessing glasses were raised and the music began, while the talk built from a subdued murmur to a steady roar. Éadha stood detached at first, looking down from her hiding place, feeling immune from them all, as if the dress was a kind of armour. But, she thought, she owed it to Seoda and her friends to show them their dress, the thing of beauty it was. She headed down the circular stairs and slipped into a Fodder alcove. Seoda was there with several of the usual presentables. Now she knew to look for it, she saw the quick dart of Seoda's eyes as she entered. She bowed, holding the skirt out so they could see how it fell, smooth and shining to the floor.

'Thank you,' she mouthed. 'It's so very beautiful.' With the briefest turn of her head, Seoda flashed her a quick smile.

Éadha was turning to go when she was knocked over by Senan, pushing through the curtains. 'I beg your pardon, my lady,' he began. 'Here, let me help you up.'

Taking her hand, Senan pulled her carefully to her feet. Only then did he meet her eyes, his own widening as he realized who it was, dropping her hand. He stepped back and looked her up and down.

'Keeper, where did you steal that dress? Are you so fond of the holds you want to spend more time down there?'

Éadha ducked her head, her mind racing. 'My aunt is a seamstress at Ailm's Keep,' she said quickly. 'She made it from leftover scraps Lady Úra gave her. I thought it right to wear it to mark the Risen's departure, my lord.'

It was the right thing to say. Senan was counting on the Risen leaving to improve his chances of winkling a Keeper girl free from her soldier love. He smirked and wagged a half-drunk finger. 'As long as it doesn't give you any notions. Silk purse from a sow's ear and all that. I'll be watching. Anything out of line and I'll confiscate it.' He sat on the bench beside Seoda, dismissing Éadha. 'I won't need you for this one, but be around later.'

Heart thumping, Éadha took a goblet of wine from the nearest table and hurried back up to the curtained balcony. Staring down at the revellers, she focused, trying to see how much power Senan was drawing from Seoda. He couldn't need much this early, but it was a bad sign if he was channelling this soon.

As she concentrated, she saw Ionáin enter the rotunda beneath her. He looked tired as he always did these days, his fair hair straggly and unkempt, his fine tunic marked by wine stains that wouldn't come out. Ailbhe was shadowing him, putting a hand on his arm when he reached for a drink. He ignored her, filling a beer tankard to the brim so it sloshed and spilled when he raised it to his mouth and drank deeply. He looked around the Banqueting Hall as he did so. For a moment, his eyes met Éadha's and she saw him take in her warrior's dress before he turned away. Leaning over to Ailbhe and her friends, he pointed them towards the Master

Illusionist, who was just beginning to weave a dragon battle. As soon as they'd turned away he ran lightly up the stairs, two at a time until he reached Éadha.

Éadha's heart lifted as it always did, as it always would, to see him so close after weeks of him passing her by each night, the familiar blue eyes for once staring straight at her with a look both intense and questioning.

'What are you doing?' he hissed.

'Nothing,' she replied defensively. 'Just watching the party.'

'I mean that dress.' That hurt. She expected no less from Senan but she'd thought more of him. He took her arm, his fingers hard, pulling her after him towards a long window behind them. It opened on to a stone balcony; Ionáin pushed through the curtains and on out into the cold night air. It was just starting to snow, white flakes tumbling down out of the darkness.

'Ionáin, what's going on?' said Éadha, confused.

But Ionáin said nothing, only stepping forward to encircle her waist with one hand, while with the other he sent power out of himself so they both lifted up into the air. They were already up high, the balcony looking straight down to where the winter sea crashed against the rocks at the foot of Second Island's granite cliffs.

Instinctively Éadha reached for her power, ready to give Ionáin more strength if he needed it, along the silver thread that still bound them despite everything. At the same time she felt her body respond to his nearness, without any volition on her part. The way he was pressing her close against the length of him as he flew them higher still, up past the long windows of the Banqueting Hall, their curtains closed against the night, up to the next level, just under the highest turret of Second House's East Tower. Built into the stone was a wide alcove, bigger than the nooks in the hall and furnished with a rosewood table and velvet sofa, while the side that looked out over the sea was made entirely of dragonglass. It lay in darkness as Ionáin flew up level with it, swung the glass open and landed them both inside, closing the glass behind him. From beyond, Éadha could still hear the distant crashing of the waves far below; inside that enclosed space there was only the sound of their breathing as they stared at each other, Éadha still bewildered and Ionáin's face grim as he dropped his hands and stepped away from her.

'What's going on?' Éadha demanded again, while Ionáin opened his palm and called up a were-light so it cast a golden light in the alcove, reflecting on the polished wood and the soft velvet of the wall hangings and the seating.

'I'm sorry,' said Ionáin, stepping away from her and running a hand through his hair, where a light dusting of snowflakes had landed in their flight upward. 'I just had to get you out of there, and this was the only place I could think of.'

'Why?' said Éadha. He stared at her, a frown appearing on his face.

'Why? Because of that dress. How you looked, standing there.'

'What?' said Éadha, now thoroughly bewildered.

'I thought you understood. We've been doing so well. But when I saw you there, looking like that, all I could think was now the others will *see* you, and that'll only make it so much harder for you, again.'

Éadha stepped back, and now it was her turn for her hands to go to her head, clutching at her temple in frustration as she turned away from him. 'I can't do this, Ionáin. I can't live like this any more, where looking marginally less bedraggled than usual is enough for me to be – what? Punished, by those psychopaths? And how can you say we've been doing well? Have you seen what this place has done to us? To you?'

Ionáin said nothing, his eyes pained as he watched her.

'All I've left of you any more is memories, Ionáin,' she said, her voice softening. 'Some days it feels like they're just a dream I had once. That this is the only reality and I'm a fool for thinking it could ever be anything different.'

She thought of Ionáin dancing with Ailbhe, his arms around her waist. Of her dance with Gry. 'It's too hard,' she said simply. 'There's too much in this place pulling us apart. Telling us we can't be. The power, the rules, the Families – all of it. Maybe . . . maybe we need to finally accept it. The impossibility of this. Of us.'

A yawning black chasm seemed to open up inside her as she said those words. Words she hadn't meant to say, but it was as if they were being dragged out of her. The bitter fruit of all those lessons, over all those months, in humiliation. In control and in power. Her voice trailed away as she stared at him, standing in the centre of the alcove in the were-light; and he looked so beautiful, with his tawny hair, his golden-brown skin, his eyes such an unbearable blue in the dimness that she loved him all over again. There was a stunned expression on his face as he said, 'How can you stand there, looking like that and think for one second I could ever, ever give you up?'

He made to move towards her and she stepped back a little. She knew if he touched her with those hands she wouldn't be able to think and she needed to think, to do the right thing. And if she loved him, she thought, if she truly loved him, wasn't the right thing to let him go? Hadn't it been the only real choice since the day they first set foot on Lambay? The choice she should've known all along she'd eventually have to make. Not just to sacrifice her power for him but to sacrifice herself, so he could have the life he was always meant to have.

'Ionáin, please, just think,' she said, her voice barely more than a whisper. The back of her legs brushed something soft; she'd retreated as far as the red velvet couch against the alcove wall. There was nowhere else for her to go. Behind Ionáin's shoulder, she could see them both reflected in the dragonglass, see the thick flakes of snow hitting the glass and sliding down, as outside the winter storm grew stronger, like a beast prowling beyond the glass, trying to break in. Ionáin's expression had a fierceness she'd never seen before as he took in how she retreated from him, her hands half lifted in entreaty as she went on, forcing the words out,

'I can't give you the life you should have. I never could. You deserve better than this, hiding and sneaking and lying all the time.'

For a long, stretched moment he stood there, like someone frozen in mid-step, as if her words were an invisible leash, binding him in place. Then something inside him seemed to snap and he was moving towards her so fast and so hard there was nothing she could do, as his left hand reached out and caught the nape of her neck while in the same moment his right hand came round her waist, flattening against her back, pulling her into him. He tunnelled his fingers into her hair, pulling her head back so her face was tilted upward as his mouth came down to meet hers. There was no finesse in his kiss, only bruised, hurt love, but as his lips covered hers Éadha felt her heart combust, at the love and the pain in his touch, meeting hers, healing hers as she kissed him back, her own hands going up to his face to pull him closer. Her lips parting on a breath as his tongue pushed in, sliding against her own, claiming her mouth, deeper, and deeper still as she rose up on the balls of her feet, tilting her head back further so he could kiss her more deeply, as all the pent-up longing of those long days on Lambay, of walking past each other like strangers, of their hunger so long denied, pushed down as it built and built in the two of them, exploding from them now, as they lost themselves in each other.

His hand still holding the back of her neck, he guided her down on to the couch, resting her head on a cushion as his body followed hers, as if now they'd come together they couldn't stop. They needed to feel the heat of each other's bodies, while all the while the thick snowflakes tumbled past the window a few feet away, hiding them from the world. Inside just a single were-light floated above their heads. Éadha stared up at Ionáin's face, the long, dark lashes, the way the light caught on the planes of his cheekbones, the fullness of his lips, the fierce possessiveness in those midnight-blue eyes.

All traces of the dissolute, heavy-drinking apprentice of the last few months had vanished, the only reminder the golden stubble shadowing his jaw. Instead, he studied her face with a clarity and an intensity that seemed to see all the way into the very heart of her. She drew in a breath at the lean beauty of his face, desire roaring up inside her once more; she needed his mouth on hers, the weight of him, the lean, muscled strength of his body pressing her into the yielding softness of the velvet cushions underneath her.

Ionáin lifted his head, his eyes roving over every inch of her face before dropping to the patchwork bodice, her breasts rising softly from the lightly boned corset. With the softest of movements, he traced the backs of his knuckles across the sensitive skin, letting out a quiet groan as her skin flushed in response. Éadha gasped a little, biting her lower lip to stop herself from moaning at his touch, but she couldn't stop herself from arching upward towards him, yearning to feel his hand on her once more.

Her white skirt was pooled around her legs, her bare feet visible; as his eyes swept down the length of her, Ionáin caught sight of them and he whispered, suddenly contrite, 'Oh, Éadha, I'm so sorry. I never saw you were barefoot, pulling you out into the snow like that; your feet must be frozen.'

And he reached down with one hand, gently bending up her leg until his warm hand could reach her toes, enclosing them. A shiver went through her at the heat of his touch against that sensitive skin, and she buried her head in his neck as his fingers gently kneaded one foot then the other until the numbness left them. With irresistible deliberation he began to trace his hand up her leg, sliding past her foot, up the long length of her shin until he reached the glimmering white silk of her skirt. She let out another gasp as he pushed his hand into its white softness, pushing it up, over her thigh. And now Éadha was completely lost in the slide of silk over her heated skin followed by the warm roughness of his hands, pushing, pushing, up towards the very centre of her, her skirt falling away as he spread his fingers wide on her inner thigh, just above her knee and began dragging his hand so softly, so surely upward.

Turning his head, he leaned over her once more and covered her mouth with his own; and now she thought she'd lose herself entirely, pulled apart between the hunger of his mouth and the path of fire his hand was tracing as it inched, so slowly yet so irresistibly, further and further up the oh-so soft skin of her inner thigh.

Without conscious thought she lifted her hands, tangling them in Ionáin's hair, gripping him fiercely as her tongue slid against his, their breaths mingling and growing slower and shallower as their kisses deepened and Ionáin's hand hardened on her thigh, as if he was marking her for all time. A new sensation began deep inside her, coiling and tightening as he slowly, surely increased the pressure from his fingertips until she almost couldn't bear it, reaching with both her hands and dragging his head down towards her. Her existence narrowed to a single point of time, of pressure, of love given, taken, lost and broken apart to only feel until, from far beyond their stone-and-velvet cave where the snow flurried and their kisses became whole lifetimes lived in an instant, a bell sounded. Tolling midnight.

Ionáin lifted his head.

Éadha loosened her hands in his hair, and inside a part of her heart broke in two as she saw the memory of Lambay, of where they were, of the world that lay beyond their tower room, return to Ionáin's eyes.

'Don't,' she whispered then. 'Come back to me.'

But Ionáin looked down at her, at the white purity of her skirt and the fierce outline of her bodice, her skin gilded honey-gold in the were-light and her dark hair pooled behind her on the velvet cushion.

Drawing a breath still filled with desire, he said, 'No.'

Bracing his hands on either side of her, he began to lift himself up and a chill swept over her body, like a kind of grief. 'Not here,' he said then. 'Not like this, in this place, hiding away like we're doing something wrong. You were right, what you said before. About us having nothing here but hiding and lying. I want to come to you in the sunlight, Éadha. I want to stand before you and swear my life to you. Because we're more than this. We're better than this place and I will not give them you. I will not give them us.'

Ionáin sat down on the edge of the couch, while Éadha pulled herself up so she was sitting. He turned to look at her and there was so much love in his eyes as he said, 'I don't want the memory of my first time with you to be tainted by being here, in this place.'

He reached out his hand to take hers and squeeze it. 'It isn't too much longer now until spring. In some ways I think it'll be easier when we go to Westport and people have to focus on fighting actual dragons.' He climbed to his feet.

Éadha pulled up her legs and clasped her hands round them as she looked at him and said, 'But there'll never be a good time for us. Some perfect day when we can just be together. Isn't that the whole point of everything we've learned here?'

Ionáin stared down at her, and the look in his eyes was one she'd take with her until the day she died, as he said simply, 'I have to believe there'll be something better than this place. Something worthy of you. I've waited all my life for you. I can wait for that.'

Éadha dropped her head then and climbed silently to her feet.

Moments later, they were flying back down through the still-tumbling snow, and Éadha's body ached all over again to feel the warmth of Ionáin's body so close to her own as he held her tight. As they flew, he buried his head in her shoulder and murmured, 'We'll get through this.'

But Éadha still couldn't shake the sense of grief she'd been feeling since the moment he'd lifted himself up and said 'no'. The sense the world wouldn't give them many chances like this. As they flew, she found herself concentrating on remembering the feel of his body, his hand against her back, how they fitted together; as if some instinct was telling her she needed to remember this, to store up these memories against what was to come.

They touched lightly on to the balcony once more and stepped apart to stare silently at one another, oblivious to the cold and the snow. A few moments later Ailbhe appeared through the curtains, her expression grim as she took in the two of them standing there. The world that'd stopped so briefly had begun to turn again, and Éadha knew she needed to go.

Murmuring an excuse, she slipped back into the hall, but she was reluctant to leave altogether. Even though her body still ached, her heart was full because, after all, she was loved. She went to stand in a quiet corner of the hall, watching as Ionáin left with Ailbhe and her friends. Around her, the party was getting progressively wilder.

A short while later, Gry arrived in through the main hall entrance. He was as striking as ever, in a white tunic with gold thread on the collar, stark against his dark skin. Somehow, she thought, he managed to look entirely detached from the increasingly drunken partying behind him. She saw how his eyes searched the room until he found her, and how he pushed through the crowd until he came to a stop in front of her, taking in her still-flushed cheeks and bright face with those grey-green eyes that always saw far too much.

He stared at her for a long moment before giving a single nod and turning away, to face out towards the party, no longer looking at her. Not, though, before she'd had time to see the pain in his eyes, and even in the roar of the crowd, she could feel the charged silence stretching between the two of them before she said at last, 'I'm sorry.'

'Nothing for you to be sorry for,' said Gry abruptly, still staring straight outwards. 'Just next time maybe warn me. Especially if you're going to look like that. It's hard on us mere mortals.'

'Ah, Gry,' said Éadha then, her heart aching. 'It's just me; it's just a dress. It was a present from a girl in the hold. I helped her a bit, gave Senan my energy to protect hers, and she was being kind back. I had to wear it, to say thank you.'

Immediately Gry's forehead creased, and now he swivelled round to face her directly.

'What d'you mean, "gave Senan your energy"? How is that even poss—' A stunned expression came over Gry's face, as if something was just dawning on him. A look almost of panic came into his eyes. 'Éadha, do you mean you . . .'

But before he could finish, a familiar voice shouted, 'Keeper, over here!'

It was Senan, beckoning to her impatiently.

'I have to go,' Éadha said then, resting her hand briefly against Gry's chest. 'He's meaner if I don't come quickly. I'll see you tomorrow.'

'Éadha, no,' said Gry urgently. 'We need to talk about this. I need to know . . .'

'Keeper!' shouted Senan, pointing towards a Fodder alcove.

'I have to go,' said Éadha again, stepping round Gry. She looked back over her shoulder. 'Tomorrow, all right?'

'About time,' said Senan as she came in. 'You do realize if you don't satisfy me, I'll get you sent for further remedial training, yes? Do you want that?'

'No, my lord,' said Éadha, keeping her head down, knowing her love would show in her eyes, and determined not to let Senan see it. 'I'm sorry.'

Senan grunted, then she felt his thread spring into life, barrelling through her and on to Seoda and the other presentables. With practised skill she funnelled the minimum from them, added some of her own strength instead and sent it back hard and fast into him. After a few moments he'd enough for his next were-dive, and he swept out of the alcove.

It was a long night. Ionáin and Ailbhe never returned, but the other apprentices were determined to make a night of it, running through all the old favourites one last time: diving, racing, illusions. Couples danced, flew, held each other with new intensity. Senan was in the middle of every race, every contest, drawing power almost continuously, running it down as fast. Éadha was shaking with the effort of managing the flows, substituting her power when she felt the Fodder could no longer take it, until she was so drained herself she felt like slumping in beside them, crawling into a service hatch to be carried back down to the holds and oblivion for a little while.

Shortly before dawn the hall began to empty out, couples slipping away on to balconies and up into eyries for a last embrace. Senan at the last found himself standing alone in the centre of the rotunda, candles guttering around the walls, the fires almost out and the were-lights long since departed with their creators. He picked up and drained a half-full goblet of wine.

'Keeper,' he called to Éadha once more as she sat on a bench by one of the fireplaces, cold in her thin dress in the predawn chill, trying to stir some last life from the embers. She came over to where he stood staring at her.

'A little bird tells me you were a naughty girl. What did I say about stepping out of line, hmm?'

'My lord, I'm sorry, I thought I'd kept well for you?'

'You were seen with Lord Ionáin at the start of the evening, sneaking out on to the balcony, no doubt giving him a twirl of your shiny dress.'

'My lord, I'm sorry, I . . .'

'Did I give you permission to speak? Did I?'

'No, my lord.'

'It's simple. You have one thing to do – stay away from Lord Ionáin. Master Dathin was very clear when he spoke to me after the trials. Ionáin has to be saved from himself. He's too soft; he has this ridiculous notion of loyalty to you. He was doing so well, all winter. I blame you, running around half-naked in a stolen dress, making eyes at him, doing lord knows what else to get your claws back into him.'

He seized Éadha's arm, half dragging her across the empty floor.

'Lord Senan, please, you're hurting me,' she cried out, as she stumbled after him.

He closed his hand even tighter round her arm. 'You think that's hurting you? You've no idea. I'll show you what real Channeller flying is, not the prissy floating Ionáin uses to seduce the ladies.'

Pulling her after him, he lifted her into the air, hanging awkwardly by the arm. Out through the window he flew and up, higher and higher. Up there it was frighteningly cold, and Éadha's shoulder ached badly, her arm twisted and raw where Senan's thick fingers dug into it.

'So, Keeper, how do you like it?' he shouted down at her. 'If I let go now, just think how long those few moments would be before you hit the water. Just long enough for you to shit yourself before you die.'

And he let go.

Éadha started to fall, faster and faster, her skirt tangling her arms and flapping around her face so she couldn't see, didn't know how far she was from the towers, from the cliffs underneath. Just as she started to gather her power to stop her fall, she felt herself caught by the arms once more, the jolt almost pulling them out of their sockets. It was Senan, laughing hysterically. He flew them both back into the almost empty hall, landing them in one of the Channeller eyries just beneath the domed ceiling.

As soon as he let her go, Éadha scrabbled backwards away from him in the enclosed space. The eyrie was a circular cushioned nook set high in the wall, accessible only by channelling. A velvet curtain could be drawn to give privacy. They were typically used as love seats, places for couples to hide away. Senan jerked the curtain across and turned to her.

In the dim light, she could see his eyes were bloodshot from the long night of drinking, and he was red-faced and panting from the cold and the exertion of dragging her through the air into the eyrie, where he seemed to fill the narrow space.

'So where did you really get that dress, hmm?' He reached across and fingered the soft material of the skirt. 'That's the finest Erisen silk; even the Family heads would think twice before making a whole dress of that material; it takes so much Fodder to grow the crops in this climate. So don't tell me Lady Úra gave her servant scraps, you little liar.'

Taking the delicate white sheath in both hands, he ripped it in two so that it slit all the way up to her thigh, to where Ionáin's fingers had caressed her skin just a few hours ago. Éadha let out an involuntary gasp of shock. He wasn't really doing this, was he? This wasn't really happening.

But he was still moving, gripping her thigh with one massive hand as she pressed as far back as she could into the cushions, trying desperately to stay out of his grasp. He caught her chin in his other hand, tipping her head back, examining her face coldly as if he had all the time in the world and she was no more than a piece of meat.

'Just what is it Ionáin sees in you? You're no more than passably attractive, your power is pitiful, you have no name. It must be something else. What is it you used to do for the good little lord on those cold northern nights? Maybe I should find out for myself.'

He leaned in, twisting her chin towards him with his hand.

'No, Senan, don't, you'll . . .' she cried, finding her voice at last. Immediately he lunged forward, clamping his other hand over her mouth.

'Don't?' he said, tilting his head almost questioningly, staring down at her. 'Don't? Do you think someone like you gets to tell me what I can or can't do?' and he leaned closer, digging his elbow into her shoulder, pinning her down.

'One word, Keeper, one word and I'll have you thrown in a Fodder Hold for the rest of your worthless life,' he grunted as she began trying once more to squirm away from him. He dropped his hand back to her thigh, tightening his grip so his fingers seemed to almost reach bone, forcing her leg aside so he could lean in closer. She wanted to scream at the pain of it.

And a part of Éadha was wholly terrified now as she shook her head frantically, trying to push him away, to break his grip on her chin, the hard fingers squeezing her jaw, forcing her mouth open as he bent over her. Knowing he would not stop. But another part was detached, watching herself struggle as if from outside her body, wondering, instant by crawling instant, could she do this, could she bear this, should she submit as she had in so many ways over all the long days and weeks as his Keeper. Was this another part of the price she had to pay: to pretend to be something he could break? Dampening down the power she could feel rising within her, all to hide her secret, to protect Ionáin, was it worth this?

And then the two parts of her collapsed into one, and the answer was no. This was not to be borne. She was light, she was power, and she didn't have to bear this; she wouldn't bear this. As it did all those months before in the face of Magret's Inquisition, her strength powered up through her in a boiling tsunami of rage, the force wave roaring up at Senan, hurling him back against the wall of the eyrie. In the same instant the curtain was rent aside and Gry appeared, his face a blaze of fury. He blasted Senan with a white bolt of furious power just as Éadha's own power flung him away from her. The two blasts at once knocked Senan unconscious and he toppled, limp, from the eyrie towards the floor of the hall far below. A fall from that height would kill him instantly. Gry dived after him, catching him just before his head hit a table and lowering him safely to the floor.

As Éadha looked on horror-struck, Channellers began to converge on Gry where he stood by Senan's unconscious body. Master Joen appeared, still pulling his robe about him, papers whirling up and empty glasses toppling over in the speed of his arrival. Gry looked up to where Éadha peered down from the eyrie and gave the tiniest shake of his head. Master Joen spoke to him once, too softly for her to hear. Gry nodded briefly, closing his eyes and rubbing his neck tiredly. In the next moment Master Joen had marched Gry to the door of the hall, where he was taken away by a group of guards. It was a long time before anyone noticed Éadha stranded in the eyrie where she sat, eyes wide and hands wrapped round her knees, holding her torn skirt about her, shivering in the cold air.

28

SEVERAL HOURS LATER, ÉADHA was sitting outside Master Joen's private study. She was still in the bodice and the skirt Senan had ripped, although someone had given her a Keeper cloak to partly cover it. She hadn't seen Gry since he'd been marched away, and Senan had been taken to his apartment. Her power twisted anxiously behind her thought-wall. She'd no way of knowing if he'd regained consciousness yet, if he'd registered her blast as well as Gry's. If she was about to be marched away too, her true power revealed. She had to fight down the urge to run. There was nowhere to run to on this island so far out on the Fiadh sea.

The study door opened, and Head Keeper Maebh beckoned her in. It was a sunny, book-lined room overlooking the central courtyard. Through the windows Éadha could see the yews shading the central fountain as it plashed quietly in miniature echo of the sea's ceaseless song beyond the thick walls. Maebh took a seat to one side of Master Joen, behind an enormous oak desk, and gestured to Éadha to sit on the other side.

'Keeper Éadha,' said Master Joen then, his face like stone.

'We've brought you here to verify what Lord Gry and Lord Senan have told us about last night's events.'

Éadha nodded, too tense to speak. So Senan was awake, but what had he said?

'We understand Lord Gry intervened because he believed Lord Senan may have been pressing you too strongly. In his concern for your well-being, his full gift, which he was not previously aware of, was triggered.' Master Joen paused. 'Is this true? Was Lord Senan pressing you?'

Éadha thought of those frozen moments in the eyrie, of Senan's hand on her chin, his wine-soaked breath on her face, and she nodded once, jerkily.

'Yes, Master Joen,' she said, almost inaudibly. She saw his eyes go down to the torn fabric of her skirt, taking in the bruising already visible on her thighs and jaw. Beside him, she could see Maebh doing the same. After a moment's silence, Master Joen said,

'Very well. However, you must not speak of this to anyone outside this room.'

Éadha bowed her head, filled with a sudden relief. So Senan hadn't registered her blast, only Gry's. Her secret was still safe, because of Gry.

Gry.

She lifted her head. 'Master Joen, Head Keeper Maebh, what'll become of Lord Gry?'

A look of irritation crossed Master Joen's face and he drew himself up as if to dismiss her, but the Head Keeper laid a hand on his arm and spoke kindly.

'Keeper, this is a matter for the Masters and not your

concern. Suffice to say the ways of power have always had some fluidity. This isn't the first time we've had to deal with an apprentice Keeper whose power developed further into a full Channeller gift. He'll undergo a process of reconditioning with me in the holds. If we're satisfied, he'll join next spring's intake on First Island as a Channeller apprentice. Whatever happens, though, he won't rejoin your class.' She paused before continuing. 'As for you. Take your things to the empty Keeper dorm and sleep there for now, while Lord Senan recovers. You may take it your remedial sessions in the holds are also at an end. I'll need you to focus on your Keeper duties for Lord Senan, especially as your class will now be one Keeper short. Do you understand?'

Éadha understood there was nothing she could say except, 'Of course, Head Keeper.'

'You may go now,' was the only reply.

Dismissed, Éadha made her way to her small room at the entrance to Senan's apartment to collect her clothes. As she slipped in, she heard voices echoing down the corridor, Senan's among them along with Coll's, Eoghan's and Cormac's. As she stuffed her few things into her satchel, she heard Cormac say, 'How's the head feeling now?'

'Nothing a good drink won't cure,' came Senan's reply, sounding as brash as ever. 'Pour me one, will you?' There was the clink of glasses and a brief pause before Eoghan said, 'When Master Joen talked to you, did he say anything about Gry?'

'Ha,' said Senan. 'If it was my decision I'd send him straight to Westport as Fodder for the dragon-slayers. If they don't it's only because of his name and the fact House Críoch is the main way-post on the way to Westport, so the Masters can't afford to alienate the Family. But I can't see him ever being released back into polite society. I mean does anyone seriously believe he "didn't know" he was a Channeller? How could anyone ever trust that lying little Fodder-lover again? Would you let him stand by you on a dragon patrol? He'll never be entrusted with Family lands now, no chance.'

'I heard his aunt Hera was visiting friends further down the coast, and her boat's due in tomorrow morning,' said Eoghan then.

'It's a waste of time coming to plead for him,' scoffed Senan. 'I reckon even if he isn't formally sent for Fodder, they'll still channel him a bit while he's down there. Just to make sure he gets the message: you don't embarrass the Masters.' Senan chuckled. 'That'd be fun, knowing I was channelling that snivelling Fodder-hugger in the name of his re-education.'

'What about you, Senan?' asked Cormac then. 'Time to make your move now Gry's out of the picture?'

'With Linn? She knows the Masters and her Family won't countenance a match with that Fodder-lover now,' came Senan's reply. 'She'll be outflanked and delivered to my tender care to breed lovely Channeller babies before the year is out.'

Unable to bear listening any more, Éadha slipped away, making for her new Keeper dorm. Maebh had told her to go to the empty dorm rather than the one where the unassigned Keepers lived; maybe because she didn't want them seeing

Senan's bruises. It was now late morning, and she'd been awake for almost a day and a half. She could feel the shock and the exhaustion waiting to overtake her, but she couldn't let them. Walking over to the white-plastered dorm wall, ignoring the ache from her bruises, she rested her hand against the stone and began trying, with everything she had, to find a thread down through the rock to where Gry was being kept, far below. She needed to find him.

As she stood there, her eyes closed, her mind went back unbidden to the moment in the alcove with Senan when Gry appeared, ripping aside the curtain and blasting Senan away from her. She thought of Gry's face, how it'd blazed with courage and fury. He'd been watching the whole time, she realized, staying all night somewhere in the Banqueting Hall after Senan called her away, because he knew she was still there, and he was protecting her.

Éadha dropped her forehead against the unyielding stone as the realizations multiplied. Gry knew she'd chosen Ionáin and he *still* chose to stay up all night and into the morning, watching over her. He'd been her bodyguard, and she didn't deserve it.

Because of her, he'd outed the Channeller gift he'd worked so hard to hide. Now for the sake of that one moment, he was going to have to be a Channeller for the rest of his life. He'd have to spend almost another year on Lambay, and if Senan was right, he might even be channelled as Fodder. It was too much. He'd given up too much for her.

Clenching her fists she tried again, sending every scrap of her awareness further than she'd ever sent it before. Surely she'd be able to find Gry's thread, to see if Senan's boasts were true, if he was being channelled down in the hold. But she could find no trace of him through the obdurate stone. He was too far away, too well shielded. She could find nothing to hold on to. Still she didn't give up, moving to sit cross-legged on her bed and trying once more, not caring whether anyone might come in and see her. All the rest of that day she sat, and on into the night, trying with everything she had to reach him. And she failed.

She finally passed out from exhaustion shortly before the sun rose. As she slept, she dreamed Senan was gripping her arm, forcing her to keep for him, while he drained Gry's life force until he collapsed unconscious. She woke with a muffled scream of horror, her arms and legs flailing, and only then registered she was still in the bodice and skirt she'd worn for the ball. The skirt Senan had ripped when he'd attacked her. Shuddering with revulsion she pulled them both off her and flung them into the corner of the dorm, then caught sight of the bruises on her thighs and her arms, the marks in the shape of Senan's thick fingers where he'd gripped and dragged her. She hadn't eaten anything since before the Midwinter Ball and her stomach was empty, but at the sight of those livid purple marks she still couldn't stop the wave of nausea, forcing her over the side of the bed and on to the floor, to retch again and again, though nothing came up. There was nothing left in her.

Classes were due to begin again that morning, and she'd woken just in time for Matins. But though she managed to dress herself in her Keeper uniform and shamble through the service and the introductory lessons, it was all done in a numb haze, without conscious thought on her part. As if her mind was shielding her from the full horror of everything that'd happened.

Leaving the class that afternoon, she saw Ionáin pushing his way towards her through the other apprentices, looking worried. She couldn't face him, couldn't face what talking to him would force her to face. The realization that Senan's attack had poisoned everything. That now if she ever tried to think of those moments in the East Tower with Ionáin, she'd remember instead how Senan had forced open the mouth Ionáin had kissed, ripped the skirt Ionáin had held, gripped the thigh Ionáin had caressed, so the marks she carried were Senan's, not Ionáin's, and she didn't know how she'd ever be able to get through this. So instead she put her head down and hurried out of the classroom before Ionáin could reach her.

She did, though, have one hope she was holding on to like a lifeline: the fact Eoghan had said Lady Hera would arrive the next day. And so later that evening, after Vespers, she made her way unseen through the central quads and dropped down the light well that led to the sea-cave entrance. Settling herself in for a damp night, she wrapped her cloak about her, pushing herself into a cleft in the rocks where she'd be less visible. She woke at dawn to the echo of voices in the cave. A ship was heaving to at the stone jetty, an armed guard leaping ashore to make the ship fast. There was no sign of Master Joen or any other welcoming party.

Éadha watched until she saw Lady Hera appear on deck. She wore a heavy embroidered cloak with a rich velvet gown underneath, while a gold torc encircled her neck. Her face was as keen as ever, but there was no disguising the strain visible in her drawn expression, the set line of her mouth as she waved a guard's hand away impatiently and came on down the gangplank. Stepping on to the dock, four guards lined up behind her. Everything about her, thought Éadha, seemed designed to project her Family's wealth and strength. As they strode along the dock it was a daunting sight, and she had to work up the courage to step out of her hiding place, a bedraggled sight in her soggy cloak, hair damp and matted with sand.

'Lady Hera. Could we talk?'

The guards moved to shield the older lady, but she gestured to them to halt.

'Éadha.' Hera gazed at her for a moment then said, 'Of course; come here, child.' She embraced Éadha briefly, her thin arms holding her tight for a moment before releasing her to move towards the stairs.

'We'll have to climb and talk. If I can reach the surface before that thug Joen realizes I've arrived early, I might be able to speak to Maebh alone for a moment about how they're treating my nephew.'

They began the steep ascent up the rock face, Lady Hera setting the pace, Éadha behind her, and her guards to the rear.

'Now, speak. I must save my breath for climbing.'

'Gry. Some of the Rising Channellers have said he may be used as Fodder as part of his punishment. That we might be channelling him during lessons.' She paused, unable to keep the horror out of her voice.

Lady Hera looked back at her briefly as they climbed. 'Spiteful gossip, nothing more. They're braggish ghouls, gloating over the misfortune of someone whose boots they're not fit to clean. Gry won't be drained as Fodder. They wouldn't use a First Family heir so. They know it'd alienate our Family for all time, even risk another Channeller war.'

For the first time since Senan's attack, Éadha felt she could breathe all the way in, as the overriding fear that'd choked her throat eased slightly.

'Thank you,' she said. They climbed for another little while, then Éadha went on.

'Could you give Gry a message for me?'

'Of course.'

'Could you thank him, for what he did? And tell him I'm sorry?'

Lady Hera paused a moment on the stairs to catch her breath, holding hard to the thin rail and gazing up briefly to the top, still far above them. She swung about then to stare down at Éadha standing several steps below. 'The thanks I will relay. But the sorry?'

Éadha looked away from that direct, assessing gaze. 'It's my fault Gry is in the holds, that he'll never be able to go home.'

'How do you conclude that?'

'I wore a dress . . .'

'It must've been quite a dress.'

'We talked once, long ago, Gry and I, about how hard it is to hold back. That to be invisible, to endure the contempt and not rise to it, is the right thing to do. To play the long game. But I was given a gift of the most beautiful dress. I wanted to wear it so I'd be noticed, just once. Because I was missing someone and I wanted them to see me, just that once. But then it all went wrong. I was noticed, and Lord Senan, he wanted to hurt me for having shown myself in a dress.'

Her voice wavered as she forced down the memories those words brought rushing back. She went on. 'And when he attacked me, I hesitated. I tried to endure in the very moment when I should've said *enough*. Gry, he knew. He knew better than I did there has to be a line. He stepped in to save me, even though he knew I could save myself. Now he's locked away in there somewhere and I can't feel him anywhere, can't tell him I'm sorry.'

Hera paused for a moment, then sighed. 'Éadha. Take it from an old woman who's worn many pretty dresses and turned many Channeller heads in her time. Never, never apologize for being young and lovely and wearing a dress so the boy you like sees you for the beauty you are.'

She continued on up the stairs then paused once more, out of breath. 'Gry will be fine. Don't be misled by his doddery aunt who can hardly climb some stairs. He's the heir of one of the Founding Families. The Masters wouldn't cross us lightly, and we look after our own. Your concern does you credit. But it's a dangerous indulgence. When you are, oh, twenty-five years old and far from here, sit down some sunny afternoon and have a good cry. But in this moment, you must focus. The Masters will be scrutinizing every Keeper now to see if they missed anyone else. You cannot afford a single misstep. You don't have a powerful Family name behind you, and the Masters would very quickly write you out of existence rather than endure another embarrassment so soon after my nephew. It's what they do best, after all.'

They were still some way from the top, and Éadha could see Lady Hera was tiring badly from the effort of talking and climbing.

'My lady, please, you don't want to be exhausted for your meetings. Let me help you.'

Her power kicking quietly to life, Éadha lifted Lady Hera from the ground. The two of them floated up the remaining section, their feet only inches above the steps. Lady Hera turned to her as they rose, a look of puzzlement on her face.

'I can't sense where you're channelling from.'

Éadha was focused on keeping their feet low as they approached the surface, and without thinking she replied, 'Myself.'

Lady Hera's expression changed to one of purest shock. She opened her mouth to speak, but before she could say anything, Master Joen's face appeared over the rim of the light well. Éadha dropped them both instantly so they were back to climbing the steps. Lady Hera closed her eyes, rearranged her expression and turned to look up at the Master, who flew down, making a show of lifting Lady Hera the rest of the way. In the hubbub, Éadha left, unnoticed by anyone but Lady Hera, who watched her go before turning back to Master Joen.

Éadha didn't see Lady Hera again on Second Island, as she was closeted away with the Masters. But the next day, when

Lady Hera was due to sail, there was a knock at the dorm room door. It was one of her personal guard. He bowed and handed Éadha a small, tightly rolled scroll.

'Her Ladyship asked me to give you this. She thought it might help you endure what must be endured. Sister save you, my lady,' he said then, bowing once more before leaving.

Éadha unrolled the scroll. It was short, the ink still fresh.

'*All right, Ailm. Don't. Stop tearing yourself up over what happened,*' it began.

Éadha's skin prickled at the words; she could so easily see Gry saying them. The bright look in his eyes, the way his lips would turn up at the corners.

'*I told you that day on First Island, you're worth protecting. I meant it and I'm glad I did it. But, Éadha, I need you to read Leah's story now, because it turns out it's your story too. You need to understand you're more precious than you know, and you absolutely mustn't let the Masters discover your true abilities. Please. I still need you not dead.*'

Those first few lines were separated from the rest of the scroll's text by the heading 'The Sister', and as she read on Éadha could see at once it was a far older story, told in the formal style of the Channeller histories they'd studied on First Island.

The Sister

There was once a family of one girl and three boys. The girl, Leah, was the firstborn. As she grew towards womanhood, there awoke in her a gift newly born in this world. To take the strong young life within her and with it reach down into the ground and coax seeds into life, to call the stones to bind together and rise from the earth, to turn life into light or fire or flight.

She shared her power with her baby brothers, sang them to sleep with were-lights dancing above their heads, wove beautiful stories in the air, channelled playhouses for them from the earth. As they grew, they yearned to be like her, but they did not have her gift. They became envious of their sister, for she was beloved among the people of their land for the wonders she could create.

Then one day the oldest of the boys, Erisen, found he, too, could fly, fight, create were-lights, do all his sister could, by taking Leah's life force and drawing it into himself. He gathered his brothers then and they, too, learned the way of it.

At first Leah was happy to let them channel from her, for she loved and trusted them, and the power they drew, she gave willingly. But they grew greedy, draining her more and more. She became gaunt and weary. Soon her power was not enough for them. They began to draw the life force from all those around them. So channelling, as it is now known, as it is taught by the Masters and used by the Great Families, came to be.

The brothers became powerful and wealthy, using their power to drain and subjugate people in the lands all around them. Their sister wanted no part in this, and at first they let her be. But as people came to Leah for help, her brothers began to fear that her gift, where she gave of herself to help others rather than take from them, made them vulnerable. There was no place for her gift in the world they were building, where channelling was a path to dominion over others, not service.

So they stole her away one night, fired up with the life force of the very people who had come to her for help. She had no chance against their might, no heart to fight the brothers she loved and the power she had helped unleash. On Second Island they imprisoned her, in an island fortress raised just to hold her. Too far from land to use her power to escape, leaving her to live out her days broken and alone.

29

THE ART OF ILLUSION was the initial subject of lessons in the early days of their new term on Second Island. After that, the focus would shift to dragon combat training, as preparations for their Westport posting began in earnest.

Creating illusions required relatively little power but significantly more skill and control than the crafts studied on First Island. It was a difficult art to convey as so much of it was internal; an act of imagination and focus, to conjure the images in the mind and channel them out to take shape in the air. Some who'd been strong students on First Island, like Senan and Cormac, struggled now, unable to catch the trick of it, forcing it so it fled from them through their reaching fingers. Others, though, were like amphibians taking happily to their second element, moving effortlessly from water up and out into air. Ionáin seemed to be one such, an artist born. In class it seemed he'd always known how to create the illusions; he just needed to be reminded of that fact. Before long he'd moved far beyond the rest of them. Ruadh, the senior Master Illusionist, let him work on alone, simply pointing him towards paths he might explore, from which he returned with creations of such crystalline beauty it broke the heart to watch them shimmer into unbeing at the end of each lesson.

Once the theory lessons ended and the apprentices began channelling in class once more, Éadha increased her supply of power to Ionáin, making sure to gift him so much he'd hardly need to channel anything from the Fodder he touched. She was helped by him specializing in Illusion, as it was the art involving the least use of power. Thrilled to have an apprentice so gifted in the art he loved, the Master Illusionist even managed to have Ionáin excused from some other lessons to concentrate on it.

For the most part, in class, Éadha was silent. Gry had been her one ally in lessons, and with him gone she'd no one left to talk to anyway. Sometimes whole days went by when she didn't speak to anyone. She missed him every day, only understanding now he was gone just how much she'd depended on him to always be there with a quip or a wry joke, puncturing the madness of the Masters. During lessons, she did the bare minimum to avoid getting into trouble. In their initial classes on the theory of illusions she was able to avoid Senan entirely. But, on the morning their practical lessons began, Maebh gestured her towards her normal Keeper spot behind Senan. Fighting down a wave of nausea, Éadha took up position wordlessly, trying not to see the smirk on Senan's face as she did, at this confirmation there were to be no consequences for him for what he'd done.

Underneath her carapace of silence, though, something new was growing inside Éadha. Born in the crucible of the eyrie with Senan on midwinter night, it was fanned to life by the scroll from Gry and Lady Hera. Day by day it grew, taking on a life of its own, feeding itself on the plentiful scraps of humiliation, cruelty and fear that littered her days. She hunched over it at night, held it close to keep her warm, though it was a while before she gave it its true name.

And that name was *rage*.

She read and reread Leah's scroll until she had it by heart, each time stoking her fury. The Channellers, the Families, the Masters – they all lied. They'd had a choice at the beginning of things, and they chose dominion. They chose power over others, and exploitation, and they hid the fact there was ever even a choice, building their temple of lies here, on the very spot where the choice had died. They'd lied and they'd lied until they'd built a whole world on a lie. A lie that created monsters like Senan and Huath.

For all their ceremonies, their histories and their Annals, she was more the heir of the First Channeller Leah than they were. Her drawing of her own life force to create and to give was descended from the first sister more than their twisted corruption of power into dominance and control could ever be.

She understood, too, finally, the danger she was in. Had been in all along. That while she'd been worried about the Masters discovering the truth about Ionáin, now she understood it was her gift the Masters hated above all else. Because it revealed the lie at the heart of their entire world. That power could be had only by taking it from others.

Ionáin meanwhile was still trying to catch her alone,

waiting for her before and after class, outside Matins and Vespers. She knew she should want to go to him, but even though a part of her missed him desperately, she couldn't do it. Too much had broken since their night together in the East Tower.

Her body hadn't been the same since those moments in the eyrie. At night she'd dream of the sound of Senan's breathing, his fingers digging into her face. She pushed her bed up against the door, lying there for hours, listening for any movement in the hall outside. After class, she spent as much time as she dared pounding the running tracks along the cliffs, getting fitter and stronger, returning to the lean hardness of her years in the Keep. But no matter how fit she got, or how exhausted she was falling into bed, still the nightmares came. The knowledge that her body had made Senan want to hurt her had destroyed something, robbed her of any ease in her own skin. And she didn't know how she could face Ionáin, face the thought of his arms holding her, when she could no longer face herself.

On a deeper level, too, there was the realization of how far she'd almost let Senan go, when she'd had the power to strike him down all along. All just to hide her secret and ultimately Ionáin's. How little value she'd placed on herself. What that'd almost cost her.

This was the other, more tangled reason why she couldn't face Ionáin. The sense of there being too much she couldn't talk to him about. And she knew, she *knew* it wasn't Ionáin's fault. It was because of the secrets she'd been keeping from him, ever since the day she'd stepped in and given him her power at his Reckoning, without ever telling him. Or further back even, when Magret told her of her gift, and she didn't go to him in the Keep. It wasn't his fault he knew none of this, and she'd no right to blame him for not knowing all the sacrifices she'd made. Yet a part of her did.

And then there was Gry. How was she to tell Ionáin about Gry, when she wasn't even sure herself what this grief she was feeling for him meant?

So the days after midwinter passed, in a haze of sorrow and silence, anger and avoidance.

It was a chilly morning in the Hall of Illusions, almost two weeks after the Midwinter Ball. Outside, a late winter storm howled against the windows, and all the apprentices were keeping their cloaks on for the warmth. Inside, the air shimmered with illusions, the Master Illusionist having given them a free hand that morning. Senan had tried to recreate a famous early dragon battle, deliberately making his Kaanesien into a grotesque, misshapen monster.

Ionáin, meanwhile, had created a replica of the East Tower, complete with the glass alcove they'd taken refuge in during the snowstorm on midwinter night. Staring at it numbly, Éadha could see how he'd remembered every detail from that night, down to the tumbling snowflakes, the velvet sofa they'd lain on, the single were-light that'd hung over his head as he kissed her. The only thing missing was the two of them, lost in each other.

He was still trying to reach her, she thought. Trying to find other ways to tell her not to let go, and as she stared at his illusion she felt a twinge. Like something from a long time ago that she couldn't quite grasp any more, but she knew it'd been bright, and light, and filled with love. A lump formed in her throat. Had she ever really been that happy? It was the first time she'd felt anything other than fear, guilt or anger since that night. She pushed it down though. She wasn't someone who got to be happy. She knew now where such feelings led. The terrible price for her and anyone she cared for.

At the end of the class Ionáin's illusion shimmered into unbeing. That was the truth of it. It'd only ever been a mirage. But as she followed the other Keepers out of the hall, a hand caught her from behind. It was Ionáin, taking advantage of the fact Master Ruadh had already left.

'Éadha, please,' he said in a low voice. 'What's happened? Why won't you talk to me?'

Éadha stayed facing away from him, but Ionáin came round to her side. She could feel his gaze on her, hear the mix of confusion and concern in his voice.

'People are saying you were mixed up with whatever happened between Gry and Senan at the ball, but I can't get a straight answer out of anyone. Please, whatever it is, I can help but you have to talk to me.'

She couldn't look at him. If she did, he'd see everything in her eyes. She couldn't talk to him, because if she did, she wouldn't be able to stop. She pulled her arm out of his grip. 'My lord, I'm not your Keeper. If you need something, you should go to her.'

Out of the side of her eyes, she saw Ionáin step back with a look of disbelief. 'What're you talking about? I want to help you.'

'You're mistaken, my lord. We were never able to help each other.' She fought to keep the tremor out of her voice. 'We were always better off alone.' And she walked on out of the room.

After that she shut down completely, unable to handle the contradictions that were fissuring within her until she felt she'd break apart. And when they encountered each other in class or in the refectory or the temple, each time she stared through him, eyes blank. As if he were a passing stranger, while she went on alone.

30

THE TERM CONTINUED AND Éadha endured. As winter kept its tight grip, she woke each morning believing she couldn't get up, couldn't go through the old exhausting routine. But there was no choice. So she pulled herself one foot at a time from her bed and shambled down to Matins.

Still assigned to keep for Senan even though she'd moved to the dorm, each day she stood along the wall of the Hall of Illusions, funnelling his draw as he created his misshapen illusions. Of all the consequences of that night, this was the most bitter. Knowing he thought he'd got away with his assault. That he could attack her, violate her, leave her bruised and battered, and still she had to keep for him. Secure in the knowledge that almost no matter what he did, he'd always be more valuable to the Masters than her. But to know that, right under his nose, she was blocking his draw, stopping him from draining the Fodder to the point of collapse – that was her way back to herself. Proof that after all he hadn't broken her. That in her own quiet way, she was still fighting, and now she understood what she was fighting for.

After those first few weeks of illusions, the morning came for the apprentices to begin dragon combat training, the last of the Lambay arts. The class was in the ref, filling up on warming food, when Ailbhe came in looking drawn and pale, hurrying over to where her closest allies sat. They huddled together and murmurs began to spread from the little group outwards.

Moments later silence fell. Ionáin and Linn had come in holding hands, hair tousled and bleary-eyed, heading straight for food, piling each other's plates high with fruit and sweetbread, giggling and murmuring back and forth before heading over to a corner table where they sat, backs pointedly to the watching room. Ionáin reached over and took Linn's hand again, working his fingers in between hers, and she leaned into him, tucking her head under his chin.

Shock waves reverberated through the class all that day. But that same evening, Senan headed for Ailbhe's room dressed in his finest clothes. The next morning when he and Ailbhe swept through the doors of the classroom holding hands, the Channeller world, having momentarily wobbled on its axis, righted itself once more.

Determined to convince the world their pairing wasn't a consolation prize, the two proud, ambitious creatures quickly installed themselves as undisputed king and queen of the class. Senan redoubled his efforts to take first place in their year, while Ailbhe had a ship sent from Erisen with the most exquisite wardrobe, offhandedly sharing it with friends and allies. They threw parties for the select few in Senan's rooms, ingratiating themselves with the Masters for Fodder and molash supply so their evenings became the talk of the island.

Éadha watched it all through her numb haze. Told herself it was for the best, that Ionáin, after all, was only doing what she'd asked, what she'd been telling him for months: accepting the impossibility of them ever being together. And Linn, after all, was far better for him than Ailbhe: kind, talented and powerful.

That was it, Éadha realized. The solution she should've seen all along. With her Channeller gift, Linn could be the one to cover for Ionáin now. Be the Keep's Channeller, save his Family. Save the day. All that remained for her now was to get Ionáin through the rest of his training and that'd be it. Job done. And she'd be free. Free from the Masters, from the Head Keepers, from Senan, from Ailbhe, from all of them. Alone, but free. It was the best she could hope for, after all the harm she'd done – to her aunt and uncle, to Magret, to Gry. A way, perhaps, to ensure people like Senan didn't want to hurt her any more, because she wouldn't be there. She'd stopped playing and walked away. Let them win, if that was what it took.

The Masters meanwhile were progressing to the next stage of dragon combat training. It was also the most difficult, for the Masters and the apprentices. As far as was possible by their craft and power the Masters tried to recreate a true dragon battle. The Master Illusionist created the illusion of a life-size dragon, complete in every detail (though privately Éadha thought he deliberately made his vision more nightmarish, with none of the beauty of the real thing). Master Joen, as

Master Combat on Second Island, channelled enormous bolts of real flame that roared from the mouth of the illusion-dragon as it wheeled in the sky. The Rising Channellers then had to face this fiery nightmare with a Fodder wagon as their sole power source shared between them, just as they would on their dragon patrols in a few months.

Defeating a dragon was more a matter of skill and tactics than brute force; a full-grown dragon could easily outfly or overcome a single Channeller unless they'd massive Fodder resources at their disposal. During the simulations, the apprentices were expected to study the dragon and identify its characteristics and whether there were any patterns to its flight that might make it possible to predict where it would go in response to the first blow. The favoured tactic was a series of quick successive blows from multiple Channellers positioned along its likely flight path that tore its wings and sent it plummeting to the ground. The danger the apprentices faced as they fought the fiery illusion was real. They were dependent on their Keepers for a steady resupply of power from the wagon as they poured it out of themselves, into their yew staffs and out as firebolts that flew at the target.

Linn and Senan, as two of the strongest apprentices, were expected to take the lead in these combats, which demanded a carefully choreographed response. But beneath their superficial cooperation there was a real, enduring niggle between them, with Senan still smarting from the humiliation of Linn choosing Ionáin rather than him, and a determination on all sides not to be beaten by the other.

The combat ground was well outside the main House on a large rocky outcrop that jutted out to sea. As they prepared for a full combat session one afternoon, Senan strolled over to Éadha.

'Well, Keeper, it seems this is to be our last outing together. My dear Lady Ailbhe has asked to be formally paired with me as my Keeper for these last few weeks.'

Keeping her head down so Senan wouldn't see the relief in her eyes, Éadha replied, 'Yes, my lord.'

Senan turned towards the combat ground before glancing back. 'You know, I feel I really do owe you something, some little recognition of all the trouble you caused me, between your sabotage at the autumn trials and then your melodrama over nothing at the Midwinter Ball. Let's make this a session to remember. Reinforce all the lessons you've learned during our time together, shall we?'

He lifted into the air, arrowing his thread through her and on towards the Fodder wagon parked at the edge of the combat ground. Éadha picked up the threads, counting and assessing the strengths available, dropping some as they weren't needed yet. That day's illusion wasn't finished. Ionáin stood by the Master Illusionist, helping him create and hold the dragon illusion.

There was always a polite scramble at the start of the session as each of the Keepers tried to get the best, strongest threads for their Channeller from the limited supply in the Fodder wagon. The rule was that a Keeper had to release a thread to another if their Channeller was in active combat, but some Keepers were inclined to hoard threads at the outset to reduce the risk of running low. Éadha was unconcerned by this jostling, confident in her ability to supplement the threads with her own power if needed.

Finally, the dragon illusion was ready. Supported by the Master and Ionáin, it rose into the air, flapping its enormous wings, the length of a battleship. It seemed to be truly flying rather than being lifted by the power flowing from the two yew staffs pointing towards it. Throwing back its head, it roared, then shot up into the sky. Senan, Linn and Coll rose after it. Watching the direction of the dragon's flight, Linn shouted instructions to those behind her, using established Channeller combat codes. The Channellers lifting up behind her flew into position, forming the points of a net. At Linn's word they shot energy towards each other's staffs, between them weaving a golden net of power across the dragon's path. It wouldn't hold it but would slow it down, allowing Senan, who'd taken up position behind the dragon, to fly in and hit it from behind. He'd aim for the weakest point on its back, the join where the wing sprouted from the back and there was a sliver of unmailed skin.

Something had been nagging at Éadha since picking up the threads from the Fodder wagon, some familiar sensation. As Senan flew into position above her, she bent again towards the threads, held loosely in her mind until they were needed. She fingered through them like beads on a string, holding and testing them, seeing if she could catch at that sensation again. At the last thread, the weakest of those she'd chosen, she felt it again. Bending all her concentration towards that weak signal, it came to her. It was Seoda, there in the

Fodder wagon. Her thread was almost unrecognizable but unmistakeably hers. Éadha's heart caught. She hadn't thought Seoda, as a presentable, would be sent out in a Fodder wagon. She immediately blocked her thread so Senan couldn't draw hard on it, substituting as much of her own power as she could instead.

Above them Master Joen sent a gout of flame roaring from the dragon illusion. It plummeted towards the waiting Channellers. On Linn's signal the net of power sprang into life, shining dimly in the winter sunlight. The dragon flew into the net, its wings becoming briefly entangled, its progress slowed. It roared and flamed all around it, so the Channellers had to break away or be burned. Several strings snapped as they flew, enough so the dragon could gather speed once more. Senan came flying in from behind, staff raised, pulling a huge surge of strength from the threads held by Éadha for a concentrated bolt of deadly power, but the dragon was pulling away too quickly, and his bolt shot harmlessly through where the illusion had been seconds before, to land with a splash in the waters beyond the combat ground. Master Joen was normally kinder than that, letting the apprentices score hits on his illusion if the shot was good, but clearly Ionáin wasn't inclined to let his classmates, and especially Senan, win any easy victories over his dragon.

The hunt was on then, the apprentices galvanized by the challenge, quickly realizing Ionáin was taking them on. Senan hurled himself into the fray, drawing gulps of power through Éadha. He was drawing so ferociously she was hard-pressed to manage the flows between the remaining threads, all of which quickly came under strain. All the while she was watching Seoda's thread, seeing it weaken further. Her block on Senan's channel was sparing her the worst of it, but she was still fading further and further, her line hardly visible in the sunlight glittering on the waves in front of them.

She squinted up at where Senan was holding position, waiting for the dragon to come back round. The Fodder wagon as a whole was dangerously low in strength. Ordinarily he'd be the first to call for a pause to bring out fresh Fodder, always greedy for as much power as possible. As she shaded her eyes, she saw him look down at her, a focused expression in his eyes. The next moment her knees buckled as he pulled power savagely out of her and the Fodder. And she knew that this vicious draining of the Fodder was all entirely deliberate – his parting gift to her.

She panicked then, reaching down within her to try to find more reserves of power. But her own strength was running down too fast now, trying to cover Seoda and the other threads from Senan's clawing, relentless demands. Her legs began to tremble and dark smudges appeared in front of her eyes. Shaking her head, she tried to force herself to concentrate harder, to keep shielding Seoda, but she was weakening dangerously with each vicious draw from Senan.

Head Keeper Maebh saw nothing, preoccupied by her own work keeping Master Joen supplied with power for his illusion, caught up in the excitement and beauty of the pretend combat that was playing out in a fiery dance above them as the apprentices traded bolt for flame and the illusion-dragon wove in and out between the massed Channellers, its wings torn but still aloft and coming back to fight on.

Meanwhile the real, invisible battle between Éadha and Senan for the life of a Fodder girl stretched and stretched like a rope pulled ever more taut. Éadha grew more and more dizzy, struggling to focus on the lines she was defending with her very life. No longer able to stay on her feet, she fell to her knees on the ground, her hands thudding down, her head hanging, the world darkening around her. Every scrap, every hidden pulse in every nerve she sent up that silver line. Still Senan hauled, savagely, mercilessly, until at last Éadha had nothing left. She toppled over, darkness rising to greet her. As she faded out, she felt something snap, a tight-drawn hawser cut loose and whipping, for a moment flying free as if filled with life, before falling limp. And she knew Seoda was dead.

Éadha lay almost unconscious on the ground, like a swimmer under water, able to dimly hear the sounds in the air above her. She wanted to stay like this but she felt her silver fish nudging, pushing her back to the surface. Stiffly, reluctantly, she swam back up to unwelcome consciousness. At Éadha's fall, Senan's thread had broken too. Seeing this, Maebh had stepped in to keep for Senan so he could land safely. Above them the dragon winked out of existence, the only trace it'd ever existed the fireballs that raced on through the empty air, the hissing as they splashed into the waves suddenly loud in the silence.

All of them had sensed the fragile thread snapping out of existence. It was the first Fodder killing for the class. The

Channellers flew back to the ground, the Keepers barely remembering to hold the threads that let them descend. Ionáin and Linn ran over to the group gathered beside Éadha. Her heart had resumed its normal work pumping life around her body, but she couldn't move yet.

Senan came down last, talking loudly as he landed. 'I don't know what's wrong with her; I didn't touch her, just the Fodder. Really bad-quality stuff we had today too – that last one had hardly anything in it.'

'Thank you, Lord Senan, that's enough,' said Master Joen, guiding the group away from the wagon and back towards the House.

'All of you, in the light of this interruption, we'll continue back in the combat room. Be prepared to answer questions on the flight path and dragon characteristics when we resume.'

Turning to Éadha, still prone on the ground, Master Joen continued, 'Keeper Éadha, you know that in the event of a Fodder wagon expiration, it is the responsible Keeper's duty to dispose of the remains and look to the remaining Fodder. You will observe this duty. It will be good preparation for your Westport posting. The soil here is too shallow for a grave, but there's a boat on the shore. Row out an appropriate distance, and use stones to weigh down the body.'

As the class began to move away, Éadha levered herself up to a sitting position. 'Why'd you do it?' she whispered, her voice hoarse.

'What?' asked Master Joen.

'Why'd you do it?' she asked again, louder. Senan was walking straight ahead, not looking back, already some way away from the killing field. She pulled herself to her feet and screamed after his retreating back, 'Why'd you do it?'

Senan looked back then, but only to roll his eyes at Maebh. 'Control her before she gets into real trouble.'

Maebh took her arm then. 'Keeper Éadha, you don't speak to a Channeller like that. Get to the wagon; see to the disposal. That is all.'

31

AFTER EVERYONE BUT THOSE locked in the Fodder wagon had left, Éadha sat for what felt like a long while on the short grass of the combat ground. A huddle of daisies by her feet nodded their white heads in the sea-breeze. She stared at them sightlessly. She knew Seoda was dead, knew it from the hollow place in her chest where the thread binding them together had snapped. But to do as Maebh had ordered, to open the wagon and see Seoda's lifeless body, touch it, lift it, bury her in the restless sea. How was she to do that?

So she sat there unmoving on the grass until an image came into her mind of the other people still chained in the wagon, trapped beside the body, and the horror of that finally drove her to her feet.

Moving stiffly, every muscle protesting, she opened the wagon doors. She was met by the smell of sweat, urine and fear so familiar from the holds, its wrongness stark as it seeped out into the sea air. As she did, every face in the wagon turned to look at her – all except one. Seoda's small white face was leaning against the door jamb as if she were only sleeping a while.

She'd probably only been a few years older than Éadha, but she looked far older, her emaciated body aged by the months of relentless channelling. In death none of her beauty remained except for her hair, still the same beautiful chocolate brown. Her hands lay limp, and trailing out from under her sleeve was a small strip of white silk, the same silk she'd used to make Éadha's skirt. It was tied round her wrist, with one end still coiled in the palm of her hand as if she'd been gripping on to it like a talisman while Senan had been draining every scrap of life out of her, over and over again until he'd taken everything and she'd died.

A sob rose inside Éadha then, her face crumpling as she said, 'I'm so sorry.'

With hands that shook, she unlocked the chains that bound the Fodder. But when she moved to lift Seoda out, a grey-haired woman sitting beside her said quietly, 'Grianán. This one time, while we can, let us say goodbye.'

Éadha stepped back wordlessly. As she did, one by one they began to reach across the narrow space to brush Seoda's cheek or squeeze her hand, whispering their goodbyes to her, because in the holds you could never speak out loud. Éadha turned away. She had no right to be part of this grief. They had a right, these people who'd suffered alongside Seoda. But she had no right, not when she'd failed her and, in failing her, let her die.

Behind her, the men and women began climbing out of the wagon. They were clearly exhausted, but there was, too, an unyielding determination to honour their friend, as four of them carefully lifted out the little body, wrapped her in a white sheet taken from beneath the wagon and carried her down to the shore. There they placed her in the boat then helped Éadha push it out into the waves.

When she reached deep water, Éadha shipped her oars, but she couldn't just tip Seoda over into the sea as Master Joen had ordered. Instead, holding the body in her arms, she dived down with her. As she swam, she could feel her strength beginning to return, her silver fish flickering into life, and it felt like treachery. On the seabed, she arranged a grave of stones to hold down the white sheet, uncovering Seoda's head so that her hair floated free, waving in the current, and she could see the sunlight dancing on the water above her.

With her power returning she could hold her breath for a long time without needing to return to the surface. As she worked, she thought of what Seoda had said when she'd stopped the lift to give her the dress, and Éadha asked how she could bear it, and she'd replied, *You have to break, accept there's no way out, no way around. This is all there is for you now. Once you're broken you can learn how to just exist, that the only way is to go through it. And then if you do come out the other side, what you have is a husk that still walks, still breathes, that maybe one day you can fill up again with things that are worth something.*

It'd been such a small hope. To lose everything, just not to die. But Senan couldn't even leave her that.

An unspeakable sense of futility rose inside Éadha then as she looked at her hands, cut from prying up stones to weigh down the body. What was the point of her power if it'd never be enough to stop someone like Senan?

She understood now why she dreamed of dragons. It was a dream of finally being able to stand against them, these evil men. Tilting her head back, as she stared up at the water's surface and the empty sky beyond, from the deepest part of her she sent out a great wordless cry, '*Mahera!*', from deep underwater. Just for one instant she thought she felt a response, an answering tremor along some impossibly long, invisible thread. Afterwards she still held herself down there beside Seoda, unwilling to let the water carry her back up to the surface because then it'd truly be over, and she'd have to face what came next. Almost idly she wondered how long it'd be before her power ran out once more and she drowned. Would she just fade out there on the seabed beside her friend? But in the same moment an obdurate refusal rose inside her. The Masters had brought too much death to this island already. Leah had died here. Seoda had died here. Countless Fodder had died here. All those deaths, so easily erased.

She wouldn't give them another.

So, eventually, she swam back to the surface and rowed ashore as the sun began to set. The people from the Fodder wagon were there, watching her.

Still dripping wet, Éadha told them, 'I won't bring the wagon back until Maebh sends someone out to look for us. When they come I'll say the burial went awry and I was waiting until daybreak rather than waking everyone bringing back a wagon in the middle of the night. So do what you wish; just try to stay out of sight of the House. But for now, I'm spent. Wake me whenever they send out the guards.'

So saying, she sagged down to the ground and was asleep almost before her eyes had closed. She slept on as the sun set and the moon rose over the eastern shore, as the stars appeared, first one, then many, and spun across the sky. She didn't see the people wolfing down the bread stored below the wagon. She didn't see as they built a fire beside her from driftwood, though the sweet smell of applewood as it burned might have eased her dreams. She didn't see two of them row out and with old skill catch fish unused to being hunted in this Channeller domain of force-grown food. She did surface briefly as an old woman held her and gently tipped a warm fish broth into her mouth before drifting off once more, warm now at last, within and without. The people sat long around the fire that night, murmuring quietly back and forth, before climbing back into the Fodder wagon at the first sign of the sky lightening over the sea. The first Éadha knew was a gentle but insistent shaking. She opened her eyes to the old woman's face staring intently into her own, in the early light of a hazy morning.

'Grianán, you must wake. The fair one, he comes, and you must be ready.'

Éadha wiped away the drool from her mouth and stared at the woman, still befuddled by the heaviness of her sleep. The woman climbed into the Fodder wagon, closing the door after her.

Éadha climbed to her feet and saw a figure on horseback approaching, someone from the holds no doubt come to check where their Fodder wagon was. She breathed in deeply, at once grateful and surprised that she felt almost fully restored to her power, her silver fish giving a welcoming flick as she bent her mind a moment to it before looking towards the rider once more. There was a light sea mist that stretched its tendrils across the combat ground, and it was hard to make out features. But something in the turn of the head, the impatient kick they gave their mount as it scrambled up on to the level ground meant she knew it was Senan.

Automatically she began building her thought-wall, but as she did Seoda's pale face flashed into her mind and she stopped. The façade of mundane thoughts fell apart. Unguarded and empty-handed she raised her head to face him as he cantered up out of the mist.

'I thought I'd find you here, when you weren't at Matins,' he said, reining in his horse and looking down at her.

'What is it you want, Lord Senan?' she asked, staring levelly at him.

'You asked me a question yesterday. Ask me again.'

Between jaws suddenly clenched so hard they hurt, Éadha said, 'I asked why you killed that girl.'

'Because I can. Because you needed to know that. Because I can see it in your eyes, even though you try to hide it. You haven't learned yet.'

Her voice still steady, Éadha asked, 'What, precisely, haven't I learned, Lord Senan?'

'Watch your tone. It's simple. If you don't want to spend the rest of your life shackled to a Fodder seat in the holds, you need to get it into your head that I control you. I own you. And I can end you anytime I want, just as I did that girl yesterday.'

'So why didn't you? If you'd a problem with me, why not take it out on me? Why kill her, when she was nothing to you?'

'I did take it out on you. I didn't care whether that girl lived or died, but you obviously did, and yet you helped me kill her. You kept for me and held the thread open until it snapped and she died. So, if you want to blame anyone for her death, blame yourself.' He smirked down at her. 'Now run along back to the holds with the wagon before you get into more trouble, there's a good girl. And every time you feel guilty about your dead Fodder friend, do remember me.'

Senan had wheeled his horse about when Éadha spoke once more, loud enough for her voice to carry clearly on the rising wind. 'Her name was Seoda, and she was beautiful and strong, so much stronger than you or I will ever be.' He stared back at her as she continued, standing erect as her hair was whipped about her by a sea-breeze come to blow the fog off the headland. 'She survived down in the holds, where they peel away every shred of human dignity and joy, and she endured. Here on this island of lords and Masters, she was one of the only people I met with strength enough to show kindness. This girl, who was starved and drained, denied her humanity in every way possible, was kind to me, gave me hope. So yes, I did care that she died. You broke my heart yesterday when I couldn't save her.'

Senan climbed down from his horse, the familiar flush of irritation suffusing his face. He stopped directly in front of her and jabbed his finger in her face. 'How dare you speak to me like that, you stupid bitch? Maybe yesterday wasn't enough of a lesson for you. Maybe you need a lesson a little closer to home right now. Have you ever been really drained by a Channeller? Would you like to know what it's like, to be our Fodder, drained of every shred of your strength, over and over again? Would you like to find out, you stupid, worthless thing?'

And he seized her hair, in the same moment reaching out along the thread between them, the now-familiar pull, but more savage now, ready to scour her insides out with his clawing power. Éadha stood unmoving and stared straight back at him. Inside with a flick she threw up a translucent, shimmering wall so his power rebounded straight back up the channel and into him, hitting him squarely in the midriff. She followed it with a single blast of her own that sent him flying backwards on to the sand.

All the rage, all the grief, all the pain and all the guilt over Seoda, Gry, her aunt and uncle, Ionáin and the nameless, numberless others she'd failed roared up within her until she must disintegrate if she couldn't get it out of her. With barely a flicker of power she rose in the air and flew to where he lay on the sand, shaking his head to try to clear it. Looking down at his sprawled body she said, 'You ask me how I dare? This is how I dare.'

She hit him again and again as he tried to rise, so that he sprawled on his back, arms and legs outstretched. He tried to reach out to the Fodder in the wagon, to draw power from them to retaliate, but she blocked his threads with ease.

'Uh-uh, fair's fair. I'm not drawing power, so neither can you. Let's see how that goes, shall we?'

He'd cut his lip as he fell, arms flailing, and as he wiped away the blood she came and stood over him. She could feel him trying now to draw directly from her, but for the first time there was a look of real fear in his eyes, as it began to dawn on him that he couldn't.

'Look at you. You fool yourself that you're powerful. You're an empty shell. A husk of vanity and ego needing to be filled with other people's lives, their energy, their passion, to have any substance at all. See how I block you? See how easy it is to make you powerless? See how empty you feel, all of a sudden, without all your little people to drain and make you feel the big man?'

Senan scrabbled backwards until he fetched up against a large rock jutting out from the sand, a mix of incomprehension and terror on his face. She followed him, her hand still outstretched.

'Look around, my lord. Here, now, you are alone. For the first time in your misbegotten, warped life, Senan, Lord of the Family De Lane, you stand alone and you are empty. You've spent your whole life filling yourself, puffing yourself up with other people's life force, living off other people's lives and, foolish boy, you never once looked inside yourself to see there's nothing there. You and your precious Masters. They take you and spoilt children like you and hollow you out so there is no heart, no soul, nothing left but an empty vessel good only for filling with power, endlessly using other people's lives to feel even half alive yourself. And look where it's got you, here on this beach, with me, empty and useless.'

'You fucking bitch, you're insane! What the fuck do you think you are doing?' he screamed then, struggling still as she flattened him once more with ease as he tried in vain to draw power from somewhere, anywhere, but there was no one he could reach, only seagulls that circled above them and the Fodder shielded in the wagon. Éadha stared at him expressionlessly as he put a shaking hand on the rock behind and tried to lever himself up.

'It's as you said, my lord. As this is our last session together, we should reinforce what we've learned from each other. The lesson you can take from me is that everything you think you know is a lie. You thought you'd power over me only because I let you think it. Because not in this world or any other world would I ever care what scum like you thought of me.

'I walked straight into your citadel, into the heart of your power and none of you even knew me for what I am. With your stupid incantations and ceremonies, your pathetic need to feel important and in control, and all the time we exist separate from you, uncontrolled by you, laughing at you.'

And though she knew she was signing her own death warrant, she didn't hesitate. With one final blast of power, she knocked him back to the ground, instantly unconscious.

32

TAKING SOME CHAINS FROM underneath the Fodder wagon, she bound Senan before rolling him over to lie hidden behind some rocks. Then she opened the Fodder wagon. The old woman who'd warned her was sitting by the door.

'Do you want to try to run?' Éadha asked.

The woman shook her head. 'There's nowhere we can get to.'

None of the other Fodder said anything, and after a moment Éadha nodded. 'I'll bring you back to the Fodder Wing. You shouldn't be blamed for this. Then I have to run, before he wakes.' She nodded in the direction of Senan's unconscious body, his feet just visible behind the rock.

The woman's eyes widened in shock before she said, 'Grianán, they'll kill you for this. Take the boat. If you use your power, you might be able to make it to the mainland before they can catch you.'

Now it was Éadha's turn to shake her head. 'There's someone I need to find first.'

So, with hands that trembled, Éadha drove the Fodder Wagon back to the hold's entrance shaft, slipping away before any Keepers saw her. Stopping off only to grab her satchel from her dorm and sling it across her chest with Magret's book, the amber tower and Seoda's dress inside, she hurried through the still silent cloisters. Ahead of her the Hall of Illusions was lit from within by a rainbow of circling lights. Ionáin was inside, practising in the early hours as he always did before classes began. As she came through the doors, the lights started to fade. Ionáin shook his wrists in frustration, not understanding why his power was faltering. Éadha hadn't gifted him anything since the morning before, and he was almost out.

He looked up and saw her in the doorway. The remaining lights above his head snapped out and the room slowly filled with sunlight, as a look of relief came over his face. 'Éadha.'

Éadha stared at Ionáin from where she stood in the doorway of the hall. He looked so different, she thought, from the underfed seventeen-year-old he'd been when they first arrived on Lambay last spring. He'd always been beautiful, but back then he was still underweight from the years of austerity in Ailm's Keep. Now, though, after the months of training and plentiful food on Lambay, he looked like a warrior prince. He was in his training gear – short-sleeved combat tunic and slim-fitting black pants – his bare arms taut and muscular, his body far stronger looking. His face was leaner now too, the high cheekbones and strong jaw more defined, though his eyes were still the same endless midnight blue they'd always been. Eyes that stared at her now as a question overrode his initial relief.

'Éadha, what is it?' he said, taking a step towards her as she still didn't move.

A lump came into Éadha's throat then as she thought of Senan, bound on the stony shore but not for long. Soon he'd come round and raise the alarm. She'd no time; she had to run.

But how could she give this up, this beautiful boy she'd loved her whole life? How had she denied herself this? And then she was moving, without conscious thought, or rather with only one thought, that she needed Ionáin to know how much she still loved him.

With only a few steps she crossed the short distance between them and her arms were round his neck, pulling him down towards her. As his lips met hers she kissed him fiercely, desperately, and all the pain, the loss, and the loneliness of those last dark weeks was in her kiss. Ionáin met her with a ferocity and a need of his own, his lips covering hers, claiming hers as if his life depended on it. As if he understood too, without needing to be told, how much she needed this. That with every touch, she wasn't just loving him but healing herself, erasing Senan's violation from her skin, from her bones. Bringing herself back to life, and to love.

Deeper and deeper they kissed, standing there in the centre of the Hall of Illusions, lost in each other, and it was as if time ceased to exist for them, for a little while. But time can't be denied forever, and so at last they both pulled back, Ionáin resting his forehead against Éadha's and dropping his hands to take hold of hers.

'Hi,' he said softly. 'I missed you.'

'Hi,' she said back, just as softly. 'I missed you too.'

'What happened, Éadha, after the ball?'

Taking a deep breath, Éadha began. 'You were right.

About my dress making people want to hurt me. Senan, he dragged me to an alcove, and he . . . , he hurt me.'

At her words Ionáin's body went rigid, though he didn't say a thing as Éadha continued. 'He didn't get far, but it was like he broke something in me. I couldn't trust my body any more because it made him want to hurt me. It's why I couldn't . . . these last few weeks . . .'

'I'll kill him,' said Ionáin, his voice low and savage. He dropped her hands and straightened up to his full height, a look of pure fury on his face.

'It's all right; at least, it is now,' said Éadha hurriedly. 'I don't need you to fight him. I've dealt with him, trust me. But, Ionáin, I need – I need to tell you everything now. There've been too many secrets between us and it's killing us.'

With an effort, Ionáin brought himself back under control. He was too angry to speak, but he nodded once, abruptly, for her to go on.

Éadha said, 'Gry was there when Senan attacked me, and he helped me to stop him. But he's paid a terrible price for showing his true gift and is locked away down in the Fodder Hold. It's my fault he's lost his future, and it's another part of the reason why I couldn't come to you. Because I don't deserve to be happy when he's suffering like that because of me.'

Now there was only pain in Ionáin's blue eyes, and a dawning loss as he took in what she was saying and the unconscious ache in her voice as she said it. 'Do you love him?' he said. 'Is that what you're telling me?'

'I chose you,' she said simply. 'But you've made it so hard, Ionáin. Ignoring me, insulting me in front of Senan, dancing with Ailbhe. I know you've always said you're playing a game, but at some point it got too real. It hurt too much.'

Ionáin stared at her for a long moment, then said at last, 'I'm sorry, Éadha. I hurt you and I'm so sorry.' He paused. 'This is on me. But, Éadha – you're the strongest, bravest person I know. You know that, don't you? All our lives, you've been the strong one. The one I looked up to and wished I was more like, ever since I was eight years old and you came into my room the first night and made everything all right. Why do you think I love you so much? Your courage, your strength – I've loved you for that my whole life. It doesn't make it right, what I did. But please, Éadha. Tell me I haven't lost you, because I was too in love with you to remember you're human too.'

Éadha took a shaky breath, overcome by the simple need in his voice, in those blue eyes, but there was one more thing she needed to say: one question she needed an answer to. 'You told me in the Blackstairs that you knew you had to give your life to saving your Family. And I understand that. But I need to know how far you'd go. If you'd sacrifice us, for that.'

Ionáin stepped back, his hand going to his hair as he shook his head and turned away from her slightly before turning back, a look in his eyes more intense than any she'd ever seen, as he said, 'Every single choice I've made on these islands has been about protecting you. Not my Family. You. I've spent the last year doing things I hate, pretending to like people I despise to protect you.

'It's easy for someone like Gry to be all cool and laconic, openly looking down on the whole thing like it's beneath him. His Family are literally the oldest, the most powerful and the furthest away in all of Domhain. He can afford to insult Senan and those other idiots. I don't have that luxury. The Masters *hate* a failed Family more than they hate Fodder, and they're just waiting for me to fail so they can write us out of existence – send you, me, my father, everyone we know for Fodder.

'I despise Senan, I always have, a lot of the other guys too. Ailbhe's just trying to survive her own shit hand, but she knows I never cared for her. I was just a means to her end. It's why me and Linn pretended to get together these last few weeks. Ailbhe wanted us married as soon as we graduated so she wouldn't have to go on dragon patrol. She even organized a posting behind the front lines with her uncle for me, as a bribe. The only way I could get out of it was to go with Linn, because she's higher status. She's like us – there's a girl at home she's been in love with forever, and Senan was pushing her really hard. We realized we could solve each other's problems. Pretend to pair, let the other two's egos do the rest, then split up after we graduate. But it's all for you, Éadha – so I could be free to choose you.'

And even though she'd told herself he'd been playing the game, Éadha still felt relief, even joy, to hear Ionáin's words, as he caught up her hand and said, 'Please, Éadha, don't give up on us. We just have to hold on. Don't do anything stupid, don't give them any cause, then it really won't be long until we can go home to the Keep.' He turned to look at her. 'I just hope you won't mind that I won't be much of a Channeller.'

She froze.

'I couldn't live with myself to be a Channeller like Senan or Uncle Huath, now I've seen what it does to the Fodder,' he continued. Seeing her shocked face, mistaking it for dismay, he hurried to reassure. 'Oh, don't worry, I'll still be lord. But I've become quite good at avoiding drawing on Fodder. Like getting roaring drunk at all those parties so Senan and the others would give up on trying to get me to play those mindless games and I could avoid all that awful, wasteful channelling. I spent weeks in here before lessons started, learning illusions so they'd think I was some prodigy and let me steer away from Fodder-heavy stuff like combat. I know I've a gift but there are ways . . .'

'But you haven't,' whispered Éadha, as the fragile tower of hope that Ionáin's words had built for a few shining moments came crashing down, swept away like a grain of sand on the shore where Senan lay, bruised and bound by her rage.

'What do you mean?' asked Ionáin. 'Of course I have to channel, so we can hold on to the Keep.'

'I mean, you haven't a gift. Or not one that's flowered yet.'

Ionáin stared at her.

Éadha stared down at her hands, unable to look at him as she continued in a low monotone. 'It was me. At your Reckoning. You were about to fail. Master Dathin was about to drop his hands. I thought it'd break your heart to fail so publicly like that, so I sent my power into you. That's what Master Dathin saw, when he raised your hand and called you gifted. My power, my gift. Not yours.'

Ionáin had dropped his hand and was staring at Éadha in shock. 'What?'

Éadha held out her hand towards him and called up a small were-light in her outstretched palm, looking across it at Ionáin's face as he took it in. The incontrovertible proof of her gift. He stood up and took a step back, his eyes going from the little flame to her face and back again, and she watched as his world collapsed around him.

'I thought it was what you wanted.' Tears stood in her eyes. 'It'd been your dream ever since you were little, to be a Channeller and save the Keep. After I'd done it once, I had to keep on doing it so you wouldn't be found out. I pretended to be a Keeper so I could come here with you and keep sending my power into you.'

Ionáin had started to back away from her as she spoke, over to the other end of the enormous Hall of Illusions, as far away as he could get from Éadha.

She called after him as an unspeakable fear began to squeeze at her heart, trying to pull him back to her with her words. 'I thought I was helping you, helping your Family to stay in the Keep.'

Staring at her down the length of the hall, Ionáin said, 'What have you done?'

'I thought it was what you wanted,' she stammered again.

Ionáin stared at the ground and spoke in a low voice. 'You had no right. None. I am not your puppet, your avatar for you to manipulate.'

Éadha was shaking her head, the tears streaming down her face now. 'No, Ionáin, no. It wasn't like that. I know it's hard to hear you've no gift, but I thought . . .'

'*You thought*. Always what *you thought*. Just once would you actually listen to me, let me actually tell you what I'm thinking? It seems you've been projecting all these thoughts on to me, assuming you know my every thought, but you really, really don't. All they are, are echoes, projections of your own hopes, your own fears. If you wanted to know what I thought about failure back then before my Reckoning, why didn't you ask me? I would've told you. I would've always told you anything you asked.'

He looked up at her, tears in his eyes too.

'Don't you see what you've done to me? You've made a lie of my entire existence. I'm here in this hellhole draining innocent people day after day because of you, and I didn't even know it. Because you didn't think to tell me, because it didn't occur to you that I deserved to make my own decisions over my own life.'

He turned away again. 'How could you do this? I thought you loved me.'

Éadha cried wildly, 'I do love you, I do.'

He sat on the edge of the stage, his head in his hands, rubbing his temples as if he could rub away the hurt if he just did it hard enough. Still not looking at her he said slowly, tiredly, 'No, you don't. You don't love me. You think you own me. That you can make decisions for me, that you know my every thought better than I do, that you can fool me into believing I'm something I'm not. Did you enjoy it? Did you laugh as your proxy Channeller struggled to hold on to some shred of humanity in this place? Oh, get out. Just get out. I don't want to even look at you.'

Éadha started to walk over to where Ionáin stood, thinking if she could just touch him, hold him again, she could make him understand. And all the time her head hammered with the urgency to be gone as she thought of Senan lying unconscious on the stony shore. He'd come to soon enough. There was no time for this, and yet it was the crisis of her life and nothing would ever be more important than getting this boy in this room to look at her the way he had just a few minutes before.

'Ionáin, we can't do this, here, now – it's what I came to tell you. Something has happened and you have to . . .'

He turned to look at her then, his eyes stone cold as he spoke carefully, levelly. 'Stop. Do not come one step closer. Hear this. I do not "have to" do anything you tell me. You will never make a decision for me again. You will respect the decisions I make for my life. And right now, I want you gone. So, if you love me . . . get out now.'

Éadha stopped then, as if he'd raised a wall of power in front of her, unable to take another step. She felt sick to the heart. It'd all gone so wrong, the thread between them, always so straight and true, grown so badly knotted and tangled she could no longer find the way along it to reach him.

But before she could say another word, she was lifted from behind and thrown against the wall so hard her head rebounded off the stone, and she crumpled in a heap to the ground.

33

IT WAS HARD TO think with the pain; or, rather, all she could think about was the pain and how to make it stop. There were other things on her mind, she knew, but she couldn't hear them over the ringing of the pain. Slowly, very slowly, she picked herself up from the floor of the Hall of Illusions. She had time to see the streaks of blood on the polished wooden floor and think how strangely sticky blood was, before Master Dathin struck once more.

This time his power just flattened her against the wall, halfway up towards the dome. A fall from this height would break most of the bones in her body. She was pinned and helpless, unable to move a finger. The pain from the first slamming hit of body against stone began to subside a little, enough that she wasn't fighting to stay conscious and could focus on the familiar figure in front of her. He'd always been bear-like. Now, power coursing through him, he seemed twice the size of a normal man, his black cloak and shining yew staff barely containing the might within.

He spoke calmly, the deep voice carrying easily in the silvery acoustics of the Hall of Illusions. 'I'm intrigued. Just what were you planning to do? There's no way for you off this island. Even if you stole a boat there's no way you could outrun us or reach the mainland with your pathetic little candle of power, held oh-so piously to your chest. Virtue may keep you warm at night, but it won't protect you against a real Channeller. You might've ambushed Lord Senan alone on a bare rock but here, standing above the greatest Fodder pool in all of Domhain, do you really think you have any chance?'

Éadha hung there, legs dangling, arms stretched out cruciform. Her tongue was thick, and she tasted blood as she forced out the words. 'Ionáin, he knew nothing.'

'I don't doubt it. I sent him to wait for me outside. I came in at the end of your little heart-to-heart. You seem to have quite let him down. He was your only friend since Lord Gry was sent to the holds, so you are rather alone now, aren't you?'

'What'll happen to me?'

'Same as happens to all your kind. You'll be locked away, tested, and when we're done, channelled as Fodder.'

Éadha looked at him.

'You didn't think you were the first, now did you?' said the Master.

'I know Leah was the first true Channeller, before your kind warped her gift into your perversion.'

'Oho, strong words for someone who can't move a muscle. Yes, a few of your kind are born every generation. Most never know the power they have. Either they're sent to be Fodder, or they're told at their Reckoning they're nothing but Keepers. Those few like you who stumble on your true gift we can easily deal with. That's the useful thing about being in power for several hundred years. Very little happens that hasn't happened before. You and your kind are an evolutionary dead end, entirely pointless and easily defeated. Not that I need to tell you, given your current situation.'

'If I'm such a dead end, why don't you just let me go? You're right – I can't defeat you, I'm not a threat,' she panted, breath constricting as he steadily tightened the power that enveloped her and pressed her into the wall.

'Really, that's all you've got? "Please let me go and I'll be good"?' Dathin mocked. 'I'm disappointed. You don't rule an entire culture for generations by taking anything for granted. The First Brothers were right when they brought Leah here to end her days. She might've been unable to beat them, but they understood her very existence could cause unnecessary disquiet.

'The people of Domhain accept the Channeller system because they believe this is how it has to be. They accept lives of quiet hell being drained as Fodder because they believe this is the only way.

'But your gift, where you draw on yourself to give to others – that's the very essence of weakness. It'd turn us into their servants, not Masters.'

He tightened his grip even further, watching with detached interest as she began to gasp, unable to speak, barely able to breathe. 'Power, as you can see in your own case, is control. So no, we won't be letting you go. You will quietly, invisibly disappear, and when you die, your secret will die as it has been born: unspoken and unknown again and again every century since the First Sister came out here to end her days.

But I didn't come here to chat to a Fodder-loving ingrate. No doubt you've been gathering your strength, hoping to make a break for freedom. So this ends now.'

He raised his yew staff to send a bolt of power towards her, enough to knock her senseless.

But he was right – she had been reaching down into herself. As she felt his bolt leave the staff, she lifted her shield, shimmering and silver, so the shot reflected back towards him. His grip that had her pinioned shifted as he instinctively moved his staff to block the power rocketing back at him. In that instant, she was free. She shot up into the air directly above him. Master Dathin fell into a fighting stance and began firing rapid bolts of power at her. It was a classic move for a ground-based Channeller, and she'd spent months watching the Channeller apprentices learn the sequence. She avoided the shots with ease, diving and rising like a swimmer through the patterns. She wasn't a large target like the dragons these tactics had been devised for and she could avoid him all day, though he'd sense enough to stay near the door so she couldn't escape. After some minutes he realized he wasn't going to catch her and began weaving a net of power. Without other Channellers it took time to set the points, but he was in no hurry. She could see what he was doing; once the net was in place, he could pull it tight round her and then she really would be trapped until other Masters arrived and took her down.

She began to shoot her own bolts down at him – not as powerful as his, but precise, burning hot. He was less mobile than she, his large frame slow to move out of the way, and she hit him square in the chest so he staggered back. On one swoop she came in too close and with ferocious speed he whipped his staff round and hit her with a fiery bolt right on the shoulder. It sent her crashing to the ground, and he was almost upon her before she recovered enough to fly up again.

Across the room, she saw a slight movement. It was Ionáin, standing quietly by the entrance, behind Master Dathin. He gestured to her to fly down behind the viewing gallery at the centre of the hall, along the west wall. It would give her some shelter from Master Dathin, though he could quickly blast it aside. She dived down, avoiding two bolts as she flew and landed with a rolling tumble behind the wooden seats. Coming up, nursing her shoulder, she saw herself staring back at her.

For an instant she thought there was a mirror behind the stands. But then she realized it was an illusion. From the last dregs of the power still in him Ionáin had created a replica of her. More beautiful than she'd ever be in real life, a dream image of her he carried in his head, but recognizably her.

As Éadha stared, the illusion sprinted out from behind the stands and flew up into the air. Master Dathin immediately sent bolts after it.

This was her chance. Staying low behind the stands and then racing across the open space, she made it to the door where Ionáin grabbed her hand and pulled her out.

The cloisters outside were as peaceful and as sunny as they'd been when she'd come to find Ionáin. The fountain played in the centre, and it was so quiet she could hear birdsong as she panted, trying to catch her breath and examining her shoulder to see how badly burnt it was.

She looked up at Ionáin standing watch by the doorway. 'You saved me,' she said between breaths.

He turned to face her. 'There's no time – you have to go. He'll destroy the illusion any moment now.'

'Come with me; we can go together.'

He took her face is his hands, looked straight at her with those blue eyes that could see all the way to the very heart of her, and she'd never seen such sadness, such a sense of ending. 'Éadha, I just found out that everything I thought about myself, who I am, who you are, is a lie. You have to see I can't go with you.'

Sorrow roared up inside her then until she thought she must choke with it. This couldn't be happening. She couldn't be losing him. But he was leaving her even as he stood there, holding her. He was leaving, and she was alone. For the first time in her life, she was truly alone.

'Ionáin, no . . .'

His head lifted as they both heard the roar from the Hall of Illusions. The windows were lit by flashes of power from within.

'Run,' Ionáin said, taking her by the shoulders and turning her towards the colonnades.

'Ionáin, I . . .'

'Éadha, *RUN*!'

34

SHE RAN, LEGS FLEET and effortless. But her breath still came in gasps like someone who'd been running for miles, the air fighting to get through the choking lump in her throat. It was hard, rigid with tears still to be cried. As she ran, the temple bell began to toll, calling all to class. Soon these empty halls would be thronged with apprentices and Masters. A plan half forming in her head, she stopped at the doors of the Banqueting Hall. There was no one there to bar her entrance this time. In the Fodder alcove she wrenched open the service hatch. The lift rested at the bottom of the long shaft, but she didn't need it, pulling the doors shut after her and flying down in near-perfect darkness, enveloped by the immense weight of the granite cliffs, the only light a faint rectangular glimmer round the edges of the lift far below.

Burning through the lift she stepped out into the holds. This early in the morning the night Keepers would just be finishing their shift. Her face would be known down here. If she had a convincing enough air of a girl with an errand and her luck held, she might just win through to the iron door leading out to the sea-cave entrance. Ailbhe's sailboat hadn't returned yet to Erisen and was moored in the dock. But as she hurried through the hold, nodding to the occasional Keeper passing with a lantern, she noticed a door not far from the sea cave that'd never previously stood open. Inside it was brightly lit, with carpets and furniture visible through the doorway. It had to be Gry's quarters. She veered swiftly and peered in. His long frame was visible on a single bed set into an alcove in the far wall.

She'd assumed he was asleep, but as soon as her head came round the door his face lit up. 'Éadha, how are you here?' he hissed.

'Shhh. I can't stay. Are you all right?'

'I'm fine.' Éadha saw then his ankle was shackled to a long chain that allowed him to shuffle around his quarters but no more.

He saw her look and shrugged his shoulders.

'Are they channelling you?' she asked, looking over her shoulder back into the main hold as she spoke. No one was paying them any attention.

'No. Judicious exposure to the suffering out there, implicit warning this is what happens to bad boys, no channelling. They're not looking to start a second Channeller war.' His look changed quickly to one of concern. 'But what happened? Who's after you?'

'Dathin, everyone else too, I suppose.'

'I'm so sorry. I half guessed it that night at the Midwinter Ball, when you talked about shielding that girl, then Hera told me she saw you use your power on the stairs. I thought you were only a Channeller, like me. If I'd realized you were a Leah that day in the boat off First Island, when you said we should just keep going – I'd have rowed you all the way to House Críoch myself, instead of telling you to just hide your power. If you make it out of here, go to Hera. Our Family will do everything we can to help you.'

They both heard it then – the sound of the lift clanking in its shaft. Gry's face darkened.

'Unlikely to be the morning delivery of pastries. If you have a plan, I'd put it into action now.'

She was halfway to the sea-cave entrance when the lift doors opened. Out came Master Dathin, Master Joen, Master Ruadh and the Second Island Librarian, their Keepers close behind. Quickly they fanned out and began searching for her. Éadha dived into the nearest empty bunk and with all her shielding skill shut herself down into a lifeless bundle of drained Fodder slumped unconscious after a night's channelling. Every scrap of power, of energy, she hid behind a thought-wall made of her exhaustion and pain. She heard the Masters approach, talking quietly to each other as they surveyed the enormous space, trying to work out where she might've gone to ground. She waited until the line of searchers had passed her bunk and then she quietly began the short walk to the cave entrance.

She'd have made it, too, if a junior Keeper from her time in Records hadn't seen her and called out cheerily, 'Éadha, what brings you back down here?'

All four Masters turned at once, raising their yew staffs as the young Keeper screamed and darted out of the way. Éadha immediately lifted her shield, and in the same instant Master

Joen began shooting at her, followed by the other three. One, two, ten shots at once, all pulsing into her shimmering wall and rebounding to the shooters. After Ruadh and the Librarian took hits from the rebounds, they changed up. Aligning their staffs so they all shot at the same point, one after the other, creating a continuous stream of power that overwhelmed her shield, burning through to hit Éadha on the legs, the arms, the side of her head before she could fly up into the air. There was a burning smell, of singed cloth and skin. She flew upward, feeling dazed from the blow to the head, which had burned away part of her hair. Ruadh followed her while the others remained on the ground. She was surrounded.

It was the fight of her life. Without a staff like the Masters', she sent her power flowing through her hands, using them alternately to shield and to shoot. The shots came from everywhere at once, from men schooled in warfare all their lives. But she was a warrior born, and she knew their formations almost as well as they did, from her long days on the sidelines of the combat grounds.

With a sure grace she danced through the hail of bolts, sending some back twofold, deflecting others, avoiding still more. When Ruadh and Joen both drew their staffs back at the same moment to send massive fiery bolts in her direction, she arrowed straight up in the air so they shot at each other instead. She dived down behind the Librarian, who was heavier and slower than the others, using him as a shield so he took a blow meant for her, direct to the chest, staggering backwards and falling to the ground with a heavy thud.

Their Keepers meanwhile ringed the edges of the fight, concentrating intensely as they connected their Masters to the Fodder nearest them, their fingers flashing, like weavers working the strings of a loom. Switching between threads, dropping them as they weakened and snatching others instead from the people lying prone in the bunk beds further inside the cave.

Éadha didn't have the Masters' reserves of Fodder power to draw on, but she was drawing only from her heart, not dragging strength from reluctant prisoners, and so her shots came faster, more easily. The four men struggled to adjust to the speed of her, slow to move out of the way as she answered their long lines of power with short bursts of white fire. Where she could, she blocked their threads reaching towards the Fodder so the Masters' power fell away, and she could dive through the gaps created by their faltering. Out of the corner of her eye, she saw their Keepers' bewilderment as she cut off the threads they were holding, stopping them from reaching the Masters. At first the Masters blamed their Keepers for not being fast enough with the threads. There were shouts of fury echoing against the cavern walls, turning to confusion as they realized then what Éadha was capable of, stopping the very threads that were the heart of their power.

She meanwhile was trying to fight her way to the cave mouth, thinking she'd have a better chance against them out in the open. But each time they blocked her escape, and in the end she knew it was all a beautiful dance of death to which there could only be one ending. Trapped in a narrow space with only her own heart, her own strength to draw on, surrounded by

Masters fuelled and furious, there was to be no mercy shown her, no chance taken. All they needed was time: time to wear her out, to exhaust her power and close in for the kill.

She dropped to the ground, too tired now for the energy needed to stay in the air. The circle of Masters began to tighten around her, Ruadh still in a pattern above her head, the others on the ground, as the Librarian got back on to his feet, cutting off any possible escape route. Her shots became more sporadic, weaker. All her strength now was focused on her shielding, preventing them from landing the knockout blow that'd finally deliver her to them. Panting and helpless, she retreated against the wall of the holds, feeling the familiar cold slickness behind her.

Seeing her trapped, they began edging closer to her, yard by yard, hunters with a wild beast at bay. Master Dathin, who'd held back a little until now, stepped forward. He pushed up his sleeves and raised his staff for the devastating shot that'd finish her off. As she backed and backed, she'd ended up close to Gry's quarters. From the corner of her eye she saw him give a slight nod and, summoning the last of her strength, she caught the nearest Master, Joen, by surprise, leaping straight over his head and landing with a diving roll at Gry's door.

As she landed, he said, quietly enough not to be overheard, 'Take me hostage.'

There was no time to think. Master Dathin would turn and hit her in seconds. Rising to her feet, she caught Gry round the neck with one hand while holding the palm of her other hand inches away from his head.

'Stop or he dies,' she panted, as the Masters turned to face them. She could see the calculations running across their faces – could they hit her before she could kill Gry? – and the realization she was faster than them.

'You wouldn't dare,' snarled Joen.

'Try me,' she said, and in the same moment dragged Gry backwards into his quarters, and kicked his door closed.

Inside, she immediately dropped her hands, releasing Gry. He turned and jammed his chair under the door handle before looking at her.

'A minute, maybe two, before they blow this.'

Badly winded from her fight, Éadha bent over, her hands on her thighs, trying to catch her breath while ignoring the pain from the various wounds on her head and her shoulder.

'Éadha,' Gry said then. She looked up at him. 'Just outside my door to the left, there's a metal flap. The chute for dead Fodder. It leads straight to the sea. Channel power from me now, and it should be enough to let you fight your way to the chute and get a good distance from here.'

'I can't,' she panted. 'Then I'll be as bad as them.'

Still standing by the doorway, Gry shook his head. 'No. It's not the same. It's a gift from me to you, not something taken. Don't you see? This is about more than you and me. It's about hope for all of us. You have to get off this island and this is the only way.'

Éadha straightened, looking him in the eyes as she said, 'No. I've hurt too many people and you've already given up too much. It isn't fair.'

With a growl of frustration, Gry crossed the narrow space in two quick strides and before she could even react, he'd caught her up in his arms and he was kissing her. And it was like an explosion in her mind, whiting out as his lips met hers, and they were so hard and so strong, driving into her until she almost didn't exist. There was a fire roaring up inside her to meet his, to burn the world down. In the same instant, she felt him drop every guard so that his power, his entire life force shone out in front of her. Without needing to think, without letting herself think, she reached out then, along the wild thread between them, and she took him into her, the entire strength of him. He was giving himself to her, every part of him, and it was like standing in the heart of a silver gale, silent and blinding and utterly overwhelming.

On and on his strength pulsed into her, and now he wasn't holding her any more, as the life force poured out of him and his body began to weaken. His head slipped down, so it was resting against hers, and she tried to stop, she did, but he whispered, 'Don't stop; let me do this,' and so she didn't stop, even as his legs buckled, and she had to lay him down, unconscious now, on the sandy floor. As she did there was an explosion behind her, and the cave door catapulted across the room, ripped from its hinges and crashing into the far wall.

Master Dathin stood in the entrance, the other Masters just behind him. Swinging his staff up, he pointed it at her, and she felt him pause as his Keeper drained the Fodder all around him for a killing blow. She stood then, flexing her fingers, standing up on the balls of her feet before sending a blast of almighty power rocketing straight into his unguarded chest. As he fell back, she ran through the gap, and her run became a dive so that she was already flying by the time she hit the Fodder hatch and burst through it. She flew down the long, pitch-black slide, hearing the slap of water at the end and the next moment she was engulfed by the freezing, inky-black sea.

35

SHE HUNG A MOMENT in the water, trying not to think of the countless bodies of the Fodder that must be lying below her. Still, when her arm brushed something, she couldn't prevent her shuddering recoil, thrashing away desperately from the imagined clutch of some half-rotted corpse there in the darkness. Slowly she calmed herself, treading water. She could hold her breath a long time with the power within her but not indefinitely; she needed to come to the surface. Cautiously she sent out small bursts of power, creating a faint light that struggled to pierce the murky water, travelling up until they hit rock. She was beneath the island, millions of tonnes of sea and rock above her. She tried not to panic.

Her silver fish was churning inside her, filled with the power Gry had given her. She forced herself to relax and heed it. As she did, it grew within her, filling her until she was all sleek power, suddenly sure and in her element. Without needing to think she stretched out then, hands forming a delicate inverted-V shape, her body undulating in a sinuous wave of power that left a trail behind her as she moved smoothly away, headed unerringly towards the surface and the light.

She swam until Gry's gift gave out, and there was a joy in it, even in the midst of her heartbreak, to be weightless, the water's caress like a mother's hand smoothing away her pain, absolving her of all she'd done. But when the power ran out she was forced to rise, aware of being cold and wet only now as her head came up out of the water. She'd almost reached First Island. The swell around the island's wooded shoreline was heavy, and at first she struggled to reach the shore, her power almost gone, before finally managing to make it on to a narrow shelf of shingle, half swept up on an inrushing wave. Here, the trees grew right to the water's edge, their roots visible where the sea had washed away the thin soil. She pulled herself up the shallow bank by holding on to the roots and collapsed on to the ground just inside the treeline.

She knew the Masters had to be on their way. They'd know First Island was the only place she could swim to. She needed to hide. Her power was too drained to survive another direct fight. Through the treeline she glimpsed the outline of a fallen-in building a short distance away, one of the many dotted around First Island, raised by some long-ago Channeller apprentice and now a ruin, stone and tree bone merged into one. Giant roots snaked out through doorways, branches curved through crumbling windows, while the roof had long since collapsed.

With the last of her strength, she dragged herself over to the half-arch that'd once marked its doorway, and crept in. In the corner, there was a nook formed by two collapsed walls and some enormous roots. They lifted off the ground slightly, leaving a gap not visible from above. She slipped in underneath them. She was still shivering and sodden from her swim, but her exhaustion was so great that even so, after a few moments she slipped into unconsciousness on the stone floor.

Outside, day darkened into night as she slept, and lightened back to day again. Above her, the first fingers of dawn were stretching across the horizon when a shadow passed overhead, circling the ruin once.

She was woken by the sound of a voice shouting, 'Bring Lord Huath! I've found her!'

It was a young guard, crouching on the stone floor and peering in at her, his eyes wide and terrified. There were answering shouts for him to, 'Come away, before the traitor blows your head off!'

She heard the familiar sound of a Fodder wagon labouring up the hill from First House, bringing the power for Huath to use to kill her. A sudden defiance rose up inside her. He might have caught her, but he wouldn't find her huddled and terrified.

Slinging her satchel across her chest once more, she climbed back out over tangled tree roots, hard like bone, stretching up over the shattered walls. And all she could think was that she'd fight her way back to the sea and let the waters take her before she'd let Huath touch her. Do anything to shake his impregnable certainty that the world and all that was in it was his to control.

Lord Huath's fair hair appeared through the trees on the other side of the building, and he looked down at where she stood, nursing her scant store of power. 'Well,' he said, 'haven't you given us the runaround?'

The Fodder wagon creaked to a halt behind him.

'To think you were there all that time, creeping around Ailm's Keep, poisoning my nephew, and none of us knew. I should've ended you years ago. This is the gratitude I get. Half the Masters on Second Island wounded, two sons of noble families needing to be reconditioned and I'm going to be late for a party I'd almost been looking forward to, because, it seems, if I want you ended I'm going to have to do it myself. The Masters want me to keep you alive, let them study you. But they're not here yet, and I'm not really in a studying mood.'

And he swivelled his yew staff around almost casually before sending a shot of such blinding ferocity that it burned away her clothes where it hit her in the stomach, opening a wide gash across her belly. The choking smell of burnt skin filled the air as Éadha toppled backwards off the tree root and on to the shattered stone. She stared stupidly down at her stomach, half expecting to see her silver fish evaporate into the air through the gash as blood began to pump out.

But it wasn't gone. Fighting the urge to scream in agony at the sudden, blinding pain of it, she pushed the edges of the gash together with shaking hands. It was clean where Huath's fire had seared through flesh and skin. Bending over, she wove a filigree of silver threads across the opening, a mat of power that'd staunch the bleeding and hold the wound together for now. As she did, she used her feet to push herself back underneath the tree roots, out of sight. There was the sound of feet approaching.

'I'm still sensing power; she's not dead yet,' came Huath's voice. 'I don't want my head taken off by a bolt, so let's do this.'

As he spoke, the wall to her right began to shake, stones that'd been sealed together for centuries protesting as they were pulled apart, until with a slide and a shudder the remains of the wall collapsed. There was no way out; she was trapped. Huath could kill her any number of ways. Bring down the other wall on top of her, or drag her out and finish her off himself, there on the shattered remnants of the ancient building.

Her body, already exhausted from the earlier battles and the long swim, was weakening rapidly from the gash in her stomach, even though she'd stopped the bleeding. There was no way she could fight Huath off in this state, and all she could think now was that she wished she'd drowned instead. Huath was the Channeller she'd always feared and hated the most, ever since that day he'd terrorized Ionáin as a small boy. It was a bitter thing to realize he was going to be the one to finish her. Rage filled her then. She would not die cowering in a hole. She would make him look her in the eye as he killed her.

She reached for a thick tree root to lever herself up. But to her shock, her hand passed straight through it; it was an illusion. What her hand landed on wasn't the smoothness of roots, or the cold hardness of stone. It was something altogether greater, altogether more powerful than wood or stone. Something warm and alive. The next moment, a jolt flowed up her arm and in her head a star exploded as a voice spoke, smooth and hissing like metal sliding on stone.

'*Mahera*,' it said, and the world went white.

Her head snapped back on her neck as the young dragon sent power flooding into every cell of her being. It was like and unlike anything she'd ever felt before. Unquestionably hers, the power she'd given it all those months before, but grown so strong, so mighty from being held in a dragon's heart; so beyond anything she could've imagined.

Dimly she heard the sounds of Huath and his men shifting the fallen stone, searching for a body. With a flick she healed the wounds on her belly and her shoulder. The power within her overflowed and when she looked behind her she saw it'd taken the shape of great golden wings, hazy and transparent. And she understood that for her, fear was ended.

Climbing up between the roots with easy steps, she stood above Huath, and she was rage, she was fury, she was vengeance. Her voice when she spoke echoed with the voices of the silenced.

'We endure and we will outlast you.' She shot up into the air, up and up, spreading her wings so they blazed in the morning light.

Huath came after her, roaring to the men below as he powered up their arrows. She stopped them easily with a thought, and they fell lifeless to the ground.

He flew on, levelling his yew staff at her once more. 'Bitch, you are one; I am many. You might have pretty wings, but I've killed many with wings as pretty, and you don't frighten me.'

Holding herself steady in the air, she stared at him. 'I should. I am the end of your world and all of your kind. You should be frightened to death.'

With a gesture she blocked the threads from the Fodder wagon, so that he only had the power already drained to draw on. Still he flew on, too overcome with rage for caution, higher and higher so they could see the outline of First Island below them, Second Island in the distance and the sun on the towers of Erisen. She flew easily, feeling the air rush past, the surge as her wings lifted her high on the morning wind.

He whirled his staff and, with all his years of dragon combat, lay down fire in her path, to catch and tear at her wings, but they were illusions impervious to fire, and she flew through them unharmed, wheeling about as she felt his power begin to fade, spent in firebolts that fizzled into nothing. He hung there in the air, only understanding then that he'd no power to draw on. He reached out, as he'd reached out all his life to those around him, those he'd taken and taken from in a neverending stream of lives defiled.

But she blocked them all, all the spidery, grasping threads, and watched as the realization hit him then that a man, alone, cannot fly. Still she watched as he began to fall, unmoved and unmoving as he tumbled down the morning sky, over and over the flash of his white-blonde hair, falling faster and faster towards the trees below until at last he disappeared without a sound beneath the canopy.

'*Mahera*,' she said softly.

The young dragon uncurled from where it'd hidden itself inside an illusion of stone and tree bone.

Éadha bowed her head, returning the power it'd given her along the golden thread stretched between them.

The dragon spread its wings above the trees and sprang like

a cat into the air of morning. It flew up to greet her; girl and dragon, heads bowed towards each other, almost touching as the sun cleared the sea. A watcher would've seen their wings blaze gold in the sunlight, until the girl extinguished hers with a thought and the dragon rushed up beneath her. She caught one of the huge thorny spikes with one hand and sat astride the enormous mailed back between the wings.

The dragon swung its head towards her and seemed to smile.

Together they flew, the girl's power flowing into the dragon as it wheeled once above First House. The dragon threw back its head and sent a bolt of flame shooting towards the wall with the small oak door facing east, incinerating the new-grown trees in an instant. Below, she could make out Masters and Fodder wagons, fiery arrows being readied, yew staffs cocked. There would be a day, she thought, for that fight, but it was not today.

And so the dragon flew away north and west on the world's winds, its impossible flight powered by one girl's heart, beating steadily in time with the dragon's wings as they left the Channellers far behind them.

Acknowledgements

I started writing what became *Her Hidden Fire* as a way to try to create some joy after a run of personal heartbreak. I wrote it on the stairs during baby naps, in the car during lockdowns, and in coffee shops where they let me hide away in the corner with my battered laptop (with a thank you to the good souls in Strandfield, Forgefield, Rocksalt and especially Panem, where they tell me about lemon blossom in Sicily and always ask how the writing is going).

I wrote it to try to make sense of years of working all the jobs – fruit picker, singer, cleaner, bar tender, factory worker, boat hand, waitress – seeing the extraction economy for what it is and trying to work out how you hold on to your humanity in the middle of it. I do, though, have to apologize for my shameless thieving from Irish geography to create Domhain. I grew up in the shadow of the real Blackstairs, so I was always going to drag them north with me for this story.

Ever since I started writing, I've found myself blurting out, often to complete strangers, '*I'm writing a book*' – like I need to say it to prove to myself it's true. And everyone I've said it to has only ever been generous about it. Which has taught me that we still, despite everything, love stories, and are kind. But because acknowledgements should try not to be longer than the book, I can only say thank you to some of the kindest here. To Philip Womack, the first person to tell me I'd written a real book, for his unstinting support. John Whelan and Alison Quinn, for their wise counsel. Harvey, Jennifer, Chris and Helen, who told me it was OK to keep going. Teasie Fleming, Deirdre Phelan, Genevieve Mohan, Mick Brennan, Tony Hanway, Deirdre McMahon and Sorcha Nic Mhurchu for being truly decent.

To Niamh Mulvey, not only a brilliant agent, but the person I want to be when I (finally) grow up, and Ivan and Sallyanne at Mulcahy Sweeney. To the ridiculously talented and hard-working teams at Penguin Random House, including Beth Fennell, Alice Grigg, Sophie McDonnell and Jess Mackay. A special thank you to Professor David Stifter for his help with Ogham and Old Irish.

And to my editors Linas Alsenas, Emma Wood and Jenny Bak. Years ago, I heard a writer say their editor's name should also be on the cover: that's how I feel about *Her Hidden Fire*. I guarantee pretty much anything half-decent in this story is down to their insight, vision, tenacity and an awe-inspiring (if occasionally terrifying) commitment to excellence. (I do, however, bags any mistakes as mine. Those I keep.)

Last, thank you to my family, Maya-Rose, Éanna, Aodhán and most of all Conor. Is tusa mo chroí. The writer Oliver Burkeman says sometimes you have to decide what to neglect, in order to choose to do what matters most. I choose love and I choose stories, and I'm the luckiest person in the world that my family gives me both.

Photo © Conor Brennan

Clíodhna O'Sullivan is a writer based in Co. Louth, Ireland. She works as a legal counsel and plays in a band, Molasha (you can find them on Spotify!). She's married with three children, as well as far too many cats and a dog.

PENGUIN BOOKS

HER RISING FLAME

Éadha's epic story continues in *Her Rising Flame*, the next book in the series. But it isn't just Éadha's story any more – other characters share their perspectives too. Read on for a sneak preview . . .

I

Lambay, Second Island

'ÉADHA, RUN!'

For a frozen instant, Éadha stared at Ionáin, her eyes wide with shock and pain. Then she turned and sprinted away from where Ionáin was standing, by the fountain in front of the Hall of Illusions.

Within seconds she'd crossed the courtyard and disappeared through the stone arch into the cloister beyond, though Ionáin could still hear the sound of her feet on the flagstones. He could even picture her as she ran: sprinting in that determined way of hers, head down and completely focused. Her hair had come loose in the fight with Master Dathin and it'd be flying out behind her now – the long, dark curls so much like when she was younger and wouldn't cut her hair all winter because she said it kept her warm out herding. How many times had he raced her like that when they were little, the two of them at full tilt across the dips and hollows in the forest behind Ailm's Keep? The difference now, though, was in how impossibly fast her footsteps sounded. Proof, if he still needed it, of her power. The gift she'd been hiding from him all along.

Then even that sound disappeared. All that remained was the quiet plashing of the fountain. Deep inside Ionáin there was a sense of something winking out – a link between the two of them breaking. A link he'd always thought was love, but turned out to have been power.

Hers.

Directly in front of him stood the massive iron-bound doors of the Hall of Illusions. Master Dathin was still inside. After a single, furious roar when he realized he'd been fighting an illusion of Éadha instead of the real thing, he'd gone silent. No doubt he was drawing fresh power. He'd burst through those doors any second now.

Ionáin's mind was working furiously, trying to make sense of all that'd happened in the last few moments. The brutal fight between Éadha and Dathin; the Master's absolute determination to destroy her, leaving her no choice but to run. As the echoes of Éadha's footsteps died, instinctively Ionáin focused his senses to follow her thread, willing her to get as far away as possible before Dathin appeared. But when he did, he felt nothing. It was as if someone had dropped a hood over his head. He knew the touch of Éadha's thread as well as he knew his own hands; there hadn't been a day this last year on Lambay when he hadn't reached out for its silvery reassurance. Now, though, there was nothing: not Éadha's thread, not the shimmer of the other apprentices' threads as they hurried to class in the cloisters beyond the courtyard. Not even the massive presence of Master Dathin behind the hall doors, or the threads surely stretching from the Master right now as he drew power. Ionáin knew these threads were all around him, a translucent network of life and power, but he couldn't feel them any more. He was cut off. Senseless. Blind.

With growing horror, Ionáin reached inside himself. Just for an instant he felt a flicker of the power he'd drawn yesterday for a dragon illusion, but he'd used the last of it to create the illusion that let Éadha escape. Now all he had left was a guttering candle burned down almost to nothing. As he reached for it, it blinked out of existence. Éadha's words from a few minutes ago played over in his mind.

My power. My gift. Not yours.

And as Ionáin registered the absolute emptiness inside him, he understood what she meant: not just that she was gifted, but that he really wasn't. His body went cold as the realizations began to multiply. He should've failed his Reckoning last spring. He did fail it, but Éadha had somehow covered it up. All the joy and relief he'd felt this last year that he was finally safe and could protect his Family and Ailm's Keep, had all been based on a lie. And now Master Dathin knew.

He started to turn automatically, ready to run. He needed to get out of there before Master Dathin appeared. But in the same second he thought, *My parents.*

If he ran now, what would happen to them? Ionáin forced himself to think it through, even though every muscle in his body was tensed and screaming at him to flee. He was powerless. He'd been prepared for that possibility back before his Reckoning – even though he'd spent this last year thinking that danger had passed. Éadha had begged him to run just before his Reckoning, he remembered. Had she known then he wasn't gifted? When had her lies started? *Think*, he told himself again. Don't get distracted.

Before his Reckoning, he'd told Éadha he couldn't run from the risk of failure. He had a Family, people who needed him to stay within the system or they'd be punished. As he thought this, from within the Hall of Illusions, Ionáin heard movement and he straightened, breathing in hard and forcing his features into a calm, controlled expression. After all, he'd done nothing wrong. He'd get through this and protect his Family. He still wasn't someone who got to run.

The hall doors slammed open. Master Dathin appeared. He was almost unrecognizable: his face distorted by fury, his body swollen with fresh power. Realizing Éadha was gone, he let out a furious bellow before he caught sight of Ionáin.

'You,' he snarled, all his thwarted rage focusing on the young man standing in front of him.

Immediately Ionáin stepped forward, his hands raised and his mouth open to explain, but it was too late. Had always been too late, because Master Dathin was already lifting his staff and firing a bolt of pure energy at Ionáin. As the Master's shot hurtled towards him, Ionáin instinctively shaped his hands to create a shield and deflect it, just as he'd been trained. Because it seemed he still hadn't accepted, not really, not in his bones, that there was nothing there any more. There wasn't one drop of power left inside him, so the space between his hands stayed empty and Dathin's shot scorched straight through, smashing into his undefended forehead. The blow knocked Ionáin backwards, sending his head slamming against the marble lip of the fountain behind him. The last thing he felt was icy water submerging him, as he slumped into the basin and out of consciousness.

There were sounds. Garbled, meaningless sounds. Ionáin could only just hear them, as if they were coming from far away, and he couldn't make sense of them. He started to fade out again but the sounds wouldn't stop. Instead, they got louder and began to form into words.

'Ionáin? Ionáin.' That was him. He was Ionáin. 'Can you hear me?'

It sounded like Linn's voice, though oddly muffled. This was, he realized, because he was still partly submerged in the water pooled in the fountain's marble basin, his body lying where he'd fallen after Dathin's blast. Only the shallowness of the water had saved him from drowning.

He could tell by the the light slanting into the courtyard that it was some hours later, maybe late afternoon. He pushed himself upright, the movement detonating multiple explosions in his head. His forehead ached where Master Dathin's blast had seared into him, and there was a vicious pain across the back of his head where he'd smacked it on the marble.

'Ionáin, what the hell happened to you?' It was Linn, bending down to look at him with a worried expression. Behind her stood Coll. There was no sign of Master Dathin. 'We heard there was a fight this morning, between the Masters and Éadha of all people. And no one's seen Senan all day. Did Éadha do this to you?'

Ionáin started to shake his head, grimacing as this sent more pain lancing through his temple. He lifted a hand to the back of his head. It came away covered in blood. Out of the water, the gash had reopened. It was bleeding freely now.

'No,' Ionáin began. 'Éadha didn't do this. She isn't . . .' He stopped himself.

How could he say any more what Éadha was or wasn't, when it was obvious he didn't know? Had never known. He'd seen the end of her fight with Dathin this morning; how she'd flown up into the air, blocking the Master's mighty shots and shooting back with a clean, white fire he'd never seen before. How extraordinary she'd looked under the high ceiling, haloed in the dawn light as it seeped through the arched windows. She'd fought off Lambay's most powerful Master like someone born to battle, not a girl Senan had treated like a glorified slave for months. And there hadn't even been any thread: no link to Fodder. Nothing. Just her. Impossibly her.

Linn, meanwhile, was staring down at the blood on Ionáin's hand. 'Shit, that looks bad,' she said, reaching out to grip his shoulder and guide him towards a stone seat. 'Sit and don't move. You'll only make it worse. Coll, go get the Master Healer.'

Lowering himself gingerly on to the seat, Ionáin wondered where Éadha was now. He guessed Dathin had gone hunting after her. A chill went through him as he remembered how swollen with power and hatred the Master had been.

Ionáin's thoughts were interrupted by Coll, returning with the Master Healer and two Keepers. The Healer was one of the younger Masters on Second Island, with auburn hair and a beard he kept neatly trimmed. He was normally brisk and good-tempered, well used to dealing with apprentices' training injuries with minimum fuss. His face now, though, was grim. He and the Keepers were all stripped down to their tunics, their sleeves rolled up, as if Coll had disturbed them in the middle of something.

'Stand back,' he called to Linn as he hurried over. The two Keepers went to stand on either side of Ionáin, while the Master turned to Linn and Coll with a ferocious look in his blue eyes. 'Go. Say nothing of this. If you do, I'll know it was one of you and I'll have you both sent to the holds for reconditioning.'

Visibly shocked, the twins nodded immediately and left without another word. Only after they were well gone did the Healer turn to look at Ionáin.

'You can walk,' he said.

'I think so,' replied Ionáin, standing up again, one hand still over the cut on the back of his head to stem the bleeding. His sodden clothes dripped noisily on to the flagstones.

'It wasn't a question. You will follow me and you won't speak again until I tell you.'

The Healer led Ionáin out of the courtyard, still flanked by the two Keepers. They were there, Ionáin realized, not to help him, but to make sure he didn't try to run.

They walked along the stone colonnade to the east of the central cloister, but instead of making for the South Tower, which housed the bright, airy rooms of the infirmary, the Master headed instead for a vertical cylinder hollowed out of granite at the heart of Second Island. It was the stone shaft that led deep underground, into the Fodder Holds.

Ionáin's steps slowed as he realized where they were headed. Dread gripped him at the thought of going so far down into the darkness, and at what was hidden down there. But as he faltered, the Keepers caught him by an arm each and bundled him along without breaking their stride. His heart rate had sped up, but his thoughts still felt slow and confused. He was being marched down into Lambay's deepest caves, to the place where the Masters drained people for power, and he couldn't think. Unbidden, he remembered Master Joen's words from a few days ago, during a combat lesson in the armoury.

There'll come a time in your Westport posting when you suffer a sudden loss. Your Keeper flamed in battle, say, or your Fodder wagon burned. In that moment, you'll be in shock. That's when your mind becomes your greatest enemy. Its every instinct will be to shut down. To survive you must learn to fight this, because the ability to stay clear-headed in the depths of horror is the only difference between those who survive and those who die in a dragon's breath.

The Keepers were still bundling him along, every bump and jerk sending a fresh jag of pain through his injured head. Closing his eyes, Ionáin forced himself to focus on it. He could use this pain, the urgent sharpness of it, to cut through his numbness.

His power was gone; he'd never had any. It'd been Éadha's all along and now she was gone too. For the first time in his life, there was a chasm in his chest, as deep and wide as the shaft sunk through the heart of the island, where her betrayal waited for him. And yet: he couldn't let the shock bludgeon him stupid now. He had to think and he had to choose – who and how to be, and what to say that might just keep him alive.

Stepping out into the open air of the shaft, the Master Healer flew down into the hollow. From behind, one of the Keepers pushed Ionáin on to the narrow stairs that clung to its sides. He'd never used them before, having simply flown with the other Channeller apprentices. Now he had to inch his way down the steps, achingly conscious of his hands, still wet and slippery, gripping the narrow guard-rail that was the only thing between him and a fall of hundreds of feet. About halfway down, the Keepers stopped at a door cut into the rock face. It led into a long tunnel lit by torches, where they marched him past a series of metal doors. As he stumbled along, Ionáin wondered if they'd caught Éadha; if she was behind one of these doors, battered and bloodied from her fight with Dathin. He forced the thought away as the Keepers turned in at the last door.

Inside, it was unexpectedly bright, though freezing cold, and the room was lit by an enormous circular window cut into the island's western cliff face. There was no sign of Éadha, but near the window stood the Master Healer, and with him Master Joen, the senior Master on Second Island.

For the first time since he'd stood with Éadha in the Hall of Illusions, Ionáin felt a flicker of hope. Master Joen was one of his uncle Huath's oldest friends. They'd battled dragons together for years in Westport. Surely he wouldn't want him harmed. Neither Master, though, took any notice of him. Their heads were bent together, Joen gesturing angrily towards First Island visible in the far distance through the wide window. Ionáin realized Joen's cloak was torn in places and his wrist appeared singed, the skin blackened.

Did Éadha do this? Ionáin wondered, with a start. Had she beaten Master Joen too? Had she – impossibly – escaped?

He felt a surge of relief at the thought, followed by a small, unexpected dart of pride. But that was wiped away in the next moment as the two Masters moved towards him, revealing what was behind them: a Stone Chair, waiting to take him.

The granite chair that rose in front of the window was small, relative to the size of the room, yet it seemed to take up the entire space. It would've taken immense power to create, even for a Master Architect. Channelling heat into the surrounding granite until it dissolved into a liquid magma that flowed out and down into the waiting sea, all while holding the image of the chair steady in his mind, its shape emerging as the stone around it melted: this chair was the room's reason for being.

Topped by a semicircular stone headrest, the chair's sides were shaped into two hinged, L-shaped funnels to lock a person's arms in place, while similar funnels forced the legs apart so an Inquisitor could step in more closely, for easier access to the head.

As he stared at its granite implacability, Ionáin felt his mind go numb again. It was too much. Only a few hours ago he'd been one of his year's best Channeller apprentices. Liked by the other apprentices, respected by the Masters for his abilities and set for a golden future as Lord of one of the great Families. Now he stood bruised and bleeding, held captive by Keepers and about to be tortured in a Stone Chair. He closed his eyes and forced himself to breathe in hard. He needed to stop this before it all went too far. To remember who, after all, he was. On the out-breath he shook off the Keepers' restraining hands and stepped forward.

'Master Joen,' he said, standing straight, his eyes fierce as he attempted to summon all the arrogance of ten generations of Ailm lords before him. 'We need to talk.'

He might as well have cried out to the sea winds beyond the glass. Neither Master gave even the slightest indication they'd heard him. The two Keepers just grabbed him again, harder now, their fingers digging into his arms, and a deeper fear caught at him. Weren't they even going to give him a chance to explain?

'Master Joen,' he said again, and this time he couldn't entirely keep a note of pleading out of his voice. As he spoke, there was a knock at the door and another younger Keeper appeared, flushed and panicky in a bloodstained apron.

'Master Healer,' he stammered. 'The infirmary, they say you need to come . . .'

'Go,' said Master Joen. 'I'll deal with this.'

The Healer nodded. Moving towards the door, he glanced briefly at Ionáin before saying over his shoulder to Joen, 'Given the recent head trauma and blood loss, doing it now may kill him.'

For the first time since they'd brought him in, Master Joen looked at Ionáin and his eyes were like stone as he replied, 'Indeed. But not until I've taken everything I need from him.' He nodded and the two Keepers dragged Ionáin over to the chair, locking him in place with his arms and legs trapped inside its granite channels. The cold stone of the headrest smarted against the open cut on the back of Ionáin's head. Master Joen stepped in between his outspread legs, raised his hands, placed them on Ionáin's temples and began.

Inquisitions were one of the last things Channeller apprentices studied on Second Island. It was a very different skill to channelling, with no Fodder power drawn. Instead, using the silver threads that linked them to everyone else, the Channeller sent a part of their awareness along a thread directly into their subject's mind. Ionáin's class had only just begun their training under Master Lugh, and the first thing he'd taught them was the need for control. To enter another's mind was a violation, a ripping down of the fundamental wall between their thoughts and the outside world. Any emotions the Inquisitor brought with them would blaze into their subject's mind like someone setting an uncontrolled fire.

But as Joen forced himself into Ionáin's thoughts, he was clearly beyond caring. His fury at how Éadha had completely fooled him came flaming down the thread into Ionáin, detonating inside his mind so that he screamed in sudden agony. The Master wasn't even trying to examine him. He just wanted to hurt him, there, in his deepest thoughts. It was like being stripped naked in front of a watching crowd and whipped to the point of unconsciousness, yet Ionáin couldn't pass out because Joen's presence in his mind wouldn't let him. He was pinned there, forced to feel every blow.

Only when his initial fury was spent did the Master finally pull back and start his Inquisition, ripping into Ionáin's most recent thoughts and memories – those nearest the surface of his mind. When Joen reached the encounter with Éadha in the Hall of Illusions just a few hours ago, the words 'Show me' sounded inside Ionáin's head as an irrefusable command, forcing him to relive his last conversation with Éadha from the moment she appeared in the doorway, her heart-shaped face set with determination and her bag slung across her chest, ready to run.

You don't have a gift . . .

As Éadha's quiet words played in his head, Ionáin felt once again the same sick shock he'd felt in the moment she held out the were-light towards him. He could sense Joen's disbelief, too, as the Master forced him to play and replay the moment she told him it'd been her power all along. And each time Ionáin felt the same pain but now also the nausea of knowing what was coming and not being able to stop it, only to relive it at Joen's command, forced to see how complete her betrayal had been. The one person in the world Ionáin thought loved him for himself, lying to him all along.

Finally, after four, or five replays, Joen pulled out of his mind, dropped his hands and stared into Ionáin's eyes for a moment.

'You pampered, oblivious idiot.' He turned to one of the Keepers, who stood waiting with a writing pad. 'To the Masters of Lambay. Inquisition of Ionáin of the Ailm Family confirms the traitor Éadha gave him power so he appeared to be a Channeller. He was unaware.'

Nauseous and only half-conscious, Ionáin still felt relieved. At least now they knew he hadn't deliberately tricked them. But Joen was already moving back to stand between his legs.

No . . . No. No more, thought Ionáin, not realizing he'd spoken out loud until Joen nodded to a Keeper who stepped forward and stuffed a rag into his mouth. Again the Master came, fast and hard, into his mind. This time he went ripping deeper into Ionáin's memories, tossing them aside like bits of paper as he went, back through every encounter with Éadha since they arrived on Lambay.

Every touch, every smile between them was laid bare to the Master's pitiless gaze. The midwinter night just weeks ago in the East Tower when she'd lain beneath him, her soft body arching up towards his in the were-light. Their fierce, angry kisses in the beech coppice on First Island, then all the way back to the day they'd sat on velvet cushions by the fire in Ionáin's apartment and he'd sworn to her it was all only a game; that only the two of them mattered.

'You were quite the liar, weren't you? Making promises to Lady Ailbhe you had no intention of keeping,' said Joen. 'Not as good a liar as the traitor though. She had you wrapped around her little finger. Ready to betray everything your Family ever stood for, and all the time you didn't have the first clue what she really was.'

Now the Master was pushing even further back, all the way to Ailm's Keep. When he realized, Ionáin's mind rose up again. *Please, not home*, he begged wordlessly. The Master brushed his refusal aside as if it wasn't there, drilling back without remorse until he reached Ionáin's Reckoning day almost a year ago. With another *show me*, he forced Ionáin to relive it.

Only at the end did Joen pause on the moment when Ionáin, overwhelmed by relief and joy, caught Éadha in his arms in the centre of the Great Hall, burying his face in her cloud of dark hair and whispering in her ear as his lips brushed her skin, 'Will you wait for me?'

And Ionáin saw it now, in the memory Joen was forcing him to play: the look of horror in Éadha's eyes as he stepped back from her. She'd known even then his joy was all based on her lie. It turned out the truth had been there in front of him all along. He'd just been too stupid, too caught up in his dream of saving his Family, too in love to see what was written on her face.

Master Joen resumed his dictation. 'The traitor gave him power at his Reckoning, then posed as a Keeper. There's no way a servant girl could devise such a monstrous conspiracy. Most likely she was the instrument of Lord Aedan, turning to the Prohibited Acts in his desperation not to lose Ailm's Keep. Dispatch two Masters to the Keep, with an armed guard.'

At this Ionáin began writhing in the granite chair, straining at the locks and trying desperately to spit out the rag. He pictured his mother, Úra, and his father, Aedan: the terror they'd feel when they saw Channellers riding up to the Keep with soldiers. This was insanity. Joen, and the other Masters, so possessed by rage at Éadha for fooling them they'd lost their minds to it. Joen, his face expressionless, watched Ionáin strain for a moment, then gestured to a Keeper to remove the rag.

'My parents.' Ionáin gasped, his mouth red and raw. 'They knew nothing, I'm sure of it. You don't need . . .'

But Joen was already turning away. 'I'm done with this Fodder. Take him down to the hold and give him to Head Keeper Maebh with my compliments. She always needs fresh supply. Tell her I expect him to be dead within days.'